DEATH IS EASY

SECOND CHANCES
BOOK 1

LETTY FRAME

FOXY KNIGHTS PUBLISHING

Editing: Melissa Smith
Cover Design: EC Editorial

DEATH IS EASY

"It's nothing against you, Nova," my fated mate says, *"but you're not good enough."*

I was a werewolf who was rejected by her fated mate. It's an act that's usually saved for the worst kinds of people—criminals, abusers, murderers.

Not eighteen-year-old girls celebrating their birthday with their family.

I was betrayed by those closest to me. My family were mortified that I had embarrassed them, and my Alpha and Luna were angry their son had been matched to me in the first place.

In a brutal move, I was banished from our pack with nothing but the clothes on my back and a grieving wolf...

Until six years later, when my billionaire boss, and the most powerful Alpha lion shifter, Atticus Phoenix, walks into my life. He calls me his, but I don't believe it. I can't trust it.

Especially not when every man in his inner circle adds to the claim.

They're strong and powerful, and I'm... *not good enough.*

But when the man who broke me comes to Atticus for help, mated to my sister, of all people, and these powerful men offer me revenge... can I accept it, even if I can't accept them?

CONTENT DISCLOSURE

Death is Easy is the first book in a paranormal reverse harem series. This means that not only will the female main character (Nora) end up with multiple mates at the end, but this book *will* end in a cliffhanger because there are going to be another two after it.

Now, I'd like to start this book off with a content disclosure, and it's directed especially to those who suffer from mental health issues and need the foresight to make healthy decisions for themselves.

This book has the capabilities of triggering someone who suffers from anxiety, PTSD, or depression. That's not an exhaustive list, but it should warn you of the type of struggles Nora goes through during this book. There will be more than brief mentions to depression, low moods, and the dark thoughts that go along with it, and you need to keep yourself safe first and foremost.

Please, don't read this book if it could hurt you. As someone who battles her own mind daily, this book was written to help me during a time where I needed an outlet and Nora came to life to provide that for me. I felt Nora's story was powerful enough to share, and it's taken until now where I'm mentally ready to actually deliver it.

Because I wrote this so that when I was feeling this low, I had something to keep my mind quiet, a lot of this is based on *my life* and *my reactions*. This means that this book is not an accurate representation of all people in the same circumstances, just some. Some parts might resonate with you, and some might piss you off. Everyone reacts differently, so please keep that in mind when reading.

Words are powerful tools—don't be the asshole who uses them to put another person down, and yes, contrary to some belief, authors are human beings.

I truly hope this book shows anyone struggling that they're not alone in their struggles, that they're not unlovable because they're not perfectly happy all of the time, that your mind is a fucking liar.

If this book happens to help someone understand what a loved one might be going through, because they've never been in that situation themselves, then I've done what I wanted.

Don't suffer in silence. Help is always available.

I repeat, your mind is a liar.

Love always,

Letty!

This book is dedicated to you, my readers, for picking up this book. Hopefully if enough people buy it, I'll be able to afford to get myself some real therapy instead of needing to trauma dump it into this book.

Okay, time for the real dedication.

This book is dedicated to the greatest therapist I've ever had. If it weren't for her, I wouldn't be here today. It's a scary thought to think about now that I'm watching my little girl yell mama at her toy pig, but back then when the darkness was all I knew, it was my reality.

She saved me in more ways than one, and I can't ever thank her enough for that.

Mental health can be a lifelong struggle, but you're not alone, no matter how much you think you are.

You are worthy. You are loved. Your mind is a liar.

You'd never know the battle she fights everyday just by looking at her.

— ALI D JENSEN (2022)

PROLOGUE
NORA

"*H*appy birthday to you. Happy birthday to you. Happy birthday, dear Nora. Happy birthday to you."

I look into the faces of my closest family members, at the way they're all hovering around me, and pure elatement fills me. Neve's hand is on my shoulder, her false nails digging in ever so slightly as she stands as close to me as she can, but she's got a grin on her face when I look up at her. David is sitting in the seat next to me, a cheeky grin on his face.

My mum is sitting directly opposite me and she blinks away tears that I know are only there because her mama wolf instincts are so strong today, and my dad winks at me when I meet his light brown eyes.

He's holding the cake out in front of me, the candle in the middle a sparkler, and is standing on my other side. I'm surrounded by them, and it makes me feel so loved.

My parents and siblings are all grinning, each of us sharing happy smiles, as they end their song, and then my mum starts the cheers.

"Hip hip, hooray!" she calls, and everyone bar Neve truly

gets into it. Over and over, I sit here giggling as my mum counts up to eighteen with David and my dad cheering her on, and when she reaches the final *hooray,* I lean forward to blow out my candles.

"Keep blowing," my mum says when nothing happens.

It takes a minute for my brain to register why. They bought trick candles—my favourite. It takes me about eight blows before they're finally out, and I don't think I dropped the smile once. My dad takes the cake over to the side to cut it up for us.

Today is important, more so than any other birthday I've had. Not only am I now a legal adult in the eyes of the human *and* wolf government, but in wolf society, there are extra perks. Perks I can't wait to take advantage of.

You know, as long as fate is working with me.

My wolf has finally matured, and now we're able to find our soulmate.

A soulmate is the other half—or other piece—of your soul, and they're the person or people you're destined to be with for the rest of your life. A mate who has been matched with you by fate.

This is one of the most sacred moments of being a wolf, and I'm finally at the age where I get my chance.

It's a simple process, albeit a long one. To find your mate, your wolf is hunting for a specific scent. There's something about the person that appeals to you, and the moment you scent it, the bond hits you both.

But no matter how easy—*and romantic*—the process is, there's no guarantee how long it will take. Your mate isn't necessarily the same age as you, although it's rare that there's more than a few years between mates. Your mate might not be from your pack, either.

But that's not going to diminish my hope. We've got a lot

of unmated males in our pack, and I'm hoping that my wolf will find her destined in at least one of them.

It's the moment I've dreamed of since I've been a young girl, and I'd hate to be like the pack members who have been searching for ten, fifteen years and have still yet to find theirs. I want my happy ending—my fairytale romance.

My parents found each other on my mum's eighteenth birthday, and they've got the perfect mating. I need to be as happy as they are.

Over the years, I've used every single bit of my good luck to wish for my mate. Every birthday candle blowout, every stray eyelash, every 11:11, and that's not all I've sacrificed.

"You're lost in the clouds. I bet I can guess why," my mum says, nudging me with a teasing grin on her face. I shrug, her movements causing her jasmine scented perfume to tickle my nostrils as she laughs. Her smile transforms her face to breathtakingly beautiful, and it's hard to not fall for her charms.

Her dark brown hair is the same shade as mine, but it's shorter, only reaching her shoulders. She always wears the same cream headband, and leaves it down. Her eyelashes are naturally thin, but she never leaves the house without fake eyelashes on, so you'd never know.

Like me, she's on the shorter side, but whereas I embrace it, she dons heels to try and hide it.

There's a clatter over at the counter, and we both turn to look at each other before turning around to where my dad is standing, still cutting up the birthday cake.

My dad always hoped to be an enforcer for the pack, but he never managed to achieve his dream. I'm not saying his frame has anything to do with why, but it wouldn't surprise me if it were. He's lanky, very lanky.

My dad is slim, with very little muscle mass, and he has

3

the cardio levels of a wolf ten years his senior. He's got a receding hairline, his dark brown hair having started to thin out and even grey—even if he refuses to admit it.

His eyes are a light shade of brown, ones my sister inherited from him, and they're currently narrowed as he focuses on the cake in front of him.

My mum sighs, shaking her head in bemusement. "Brandon, they don't need to be perfect. We're going to eat them all the same."

"Yeah, yeah," he says, sticking his tongue out as he concentrates. He still takes another few minutes before he starts handing out slices, ignoring the giggling from David and I. Neve's more interested in her phone, her hair hiding her face so I can't even see if she's grinning with us, but at least she's present this time. "The biggest piece goes to the—"

He pauses, and as his eyes glow a bright amber, I know that he's connecting with someone through the mind link.

The mind link is a telepathic connection that we can access. There's a familial bond that we share with family members. There's a pack bond that is controlled by the Alpha of a pack, and it enables you to talk with anyone who is initiated into the pack. And, finally, there's a mate bond that's shared between mates. It's different from the other mental bonds, which is just another thing I'm excited to share with my mate.

I'm not sure who my dad is communicating with, but the conversation only lasts for maybe fifteen seconds before it's over. He rubs the back of his neck and shoots my mum a look I don't understand.

"What's wrong?" Neve asks, a tenseness I've never seen from her settling in her body. Her shoulders are rigid, and she gently places her phone atop the table after locking it.

4

Another thing that surprises me. *What's going on with her?* "Dad? Who was that?"

"Alpha Newitt has called an urgent pack meeting," my dad replies.

"I thought it was tomorrow," my mum says with a small frown, and he sighs and gives her a one handed shrug. "Okay then. Let's not keep him waiting."

"But what about cake?" my brother, David, whines. His full bottom lip pouts as he flutters his eyes. His eyelashes are something I'm super jealous of—they're dark, long, and thick, and with our darker complexion they're even prettier.

"We can have cake when we're back." My mum ignores the pout from her youngest son, suddenly all business. It doesn't stop David from becoming even huffier though. He crosses his arms in front of his chest, and it's amusing to watch the prepubescent pre-teen think he's going to win.

"What's the meeting for, Mum?" Neve asks.

I don't know why she thinks my mum has an inner ear to the Alpha, but it makes me laugh. It's not like we're one of the high-ranking families, so we're not included in the Alpha's inner circle. We'll find out what is going on once we get there.

"We'll see," my mum replies, tucking her hair behind her ears. She seems nervous, but also... excited? *Does* she know something?

Well, I'm also excited for the meeting, but I doubt it's for the same reason as my mum. Every wolf in the entire pack needs to attend the pack meetings, unless specified by the Alpha, so that means if my wolf is going to find her mate within the pack, today is her first chance to do so.

As my parents lock things up and get David ready, I rush upstairs, much to my parent's chagrin, and change my top before joining them.

5

You only get the chance to make a first impression once, and I'm not going to meet my mate wearing the birthday girl shirt.

"Let's go find out what's going on," my dad says, patting Neve's shoulder as he opens the front door. "I think you'll be happy about it."

When we get to the meeting area, we're surprisingly seated near the front. It's not where we usually sit, and it's annoying because it means that instead of being near the doors for people—potential mates—coming in, I'm as far away as can be.

I'm half turned in my seat, my legs shaking as I examine every single face to enter. It's so busy though, that I'm not sure it'll prove successful.

"Settle down," my mum says, but I ignore her. I'm far too excited. I look around the room, occasionally meeting people's eyes as I try to get my wolf to work with me. She's bored, uninterested, and it's slightly disappointing.

The scents in the room are blending together, and it's hard to differentiate them between different members of the same family. I genuinely thought I'd be one of the lucky people who would spot their mate instantly and we'd have our happily ever after.

I just don't think I was very realistic in my goal.

I keep watch as everyone comes through the door, and the sniffing I'm doing is getting on my mum's nerves, but I don't care. I'm more focused on the fact that not a single person appeals to my picky wolf.

Not a single person.

Dejected, I turn back around and get comfortable as we wait for the Alpha party to show. It's not unusual for our Alpha to call a meeting and then arrive half an hour later, even if it is frustrating.

6

"Don't look so upset, Sis," Neve murmurs, and I sigh. "You'll find him."

"Yeah."

I can only hope. The doors open once more, and a delicious scent overtakes my senses. A strong smell of clementine assaults my senses, with hidden undertones of spice. I freeze in my seat as my wolf begins to whine in my head, alerting me to the fact that our mate just entered the building.

I repeat... *our mate just entered the building.*

As the Alpha, Luna, and the future Alpha, Kennedy, walk onto the stage, my eyes don't stray from the younger man. His shoulders are rigid, and I know he can sense it, too. The moment he's facing the crowd, his eyes meet mine.

What are usually bright green eyes are pure amber because his wolf is to the surface, and tingles appear across my skin as a feral growl leaves his throat. There's a commotion with his parents, but I don't pay attention.

My wolf has chosen. We've found our mate.

With his reddish-brown curly hair, that he pays special attention to maintaining, and bright green eyes, he's pretty handsome—as long as you have no desire to be in the sun for long periods of time. His pale skin becomes littered with freckles come summer, and it only adds to his charm.

He's one of the fittest members of the pack, constantly working out, and it shows in his muscular frame. I lick my lips, imagining that my tongue is running across his abs...

Down, Nora, down girl.

He's got a charm about him, one that comes from both his wolf's stature and his exuberant personality. He's cheeky, charming, and so fucking attractive I want to combust.

My mate is every woman's dream, and somehow, Fate deemed me worthy enough to land him.

Me. A nobody within the pack. It's practically unheard of.

Kennedy Newitt. Future Alpha. Twenty years old. The most eligible bachelor within our pack. He's been searching for me with no hope for the last two years, and by his reaction, I know he's as happy as I am about this.

"Mate," I mouth, and he attempts to storm forward but is stopped by his dad. I can't decipher the expression on my Alpha's face, but he seems mad. *Does he understand what's happening?*

My wolf is torn between cowering from our unsettled Alpha, and leaping for joy because we've found our mate. She doesn't do anything except freeze under the indecision.

"Thank you all for coming. I'm sorry to cut this meeting off before it begins," our Alpha says. "We can reconvene another time. Thank you for coming on such short notice."

Alpha Newitt is not very happy, a tightness in his facial features as he holds onto a fake persona of calm in front of the pack. His large frame is wrapped around his son, refusing to let him move. But the tension isn't just affecting Kennedy. Kennedy's tense body language is doing little to calm my wolf. She wants to go to him, to help comfort him, but she's scared. *I'm* scared.

Our Luna comes over to where I'm sitting, frozen in my seat, and motions for my family to stay behind as our pack clears out. My mum nods, and reaches over my lap to take Neve's hand.

Our Luna stays next to us, her eyes raking over the pack, narrowing occasionally as she takes stock of the current situation. She's got long blonde hair, the type you can only achieve by spending a couple hundred at the hairdressers each month, and the kind of tan that's not possible in the UK without sunbeds.

She's wearing her usual pearls with a navy dress that looks really pretty on her. Her boots are impractical, but stylish, and I'm kind of nervous about mating into a family of perfection.

Until I look back at my mate, and the nerves fade away as my wolf howls in my mind.

My mate is the future of Alpha of our pack. *I am so fucking lucky.*

My dreams of a perfect life, and a perfect mate, never took into account his pack rank. Instead, I focused on the aspects I care about—a man who loves me, who puts me and our family first.

But this? This is the ultimate jackpot. I'm going to be Luna one day, and I'll get to be the mother to not only my kids... but the entire pack. Fate has been kind to me.

Once the room clears and the door slams shut with an echo through the hall, the Alpha lets Kennedy loose, and he storms over to me. My mum edges away slightly, dropping Neve's hand as she does, because my mate's dominance is unsettling her.

I dart to my feet, and his hands cup my cheeks, and he smiles at me. His two front teeth are kind of crooked, and it's absolutely adorable. Everything in me lights up at the attention, and I can't stop the giant grin that covers my face.

"Hi," he murmurs.

"Hi."

I giggle, unable to stop the butterflies raging in my tummy. I'm so elated at the news. My mate is the future Alpha. I'm going to be the Luna of our pack. I just can't stop repeating it!

"We need to talk," Alpha Newitt says, but the tone of his voice is anything but happy. What do we need to talk about?

9

This is cause for a celebration, especially since Kennedy's waited all this time for me. "Ken, take a seat."

Kennedy nods, dropping his hands from my cheeks, and as he steps away from me, my heart sinks. Every single step he takes that's further from me takes even more warmth from me. I'm left standing on shaking legs that are barely able to hold me up, hating the effect him sitting a couple feet away has on me.

His dad mumbles something, causing Kennedy's face to drop. They're tense as they switch to the mind link to argue, and after a moment, Kennedy looks resigned. I'm clearly missing something here.

"Sit down," the Alpha says, and although he's not looking at me, I know it's directed at me. I immediately sink into my seat, not able to look away from Kennedy but powerless to my Alpha's command.

"The pack meeting today was to discuss mating opportunities for Kennedy," the Alpha says, looking at my dad with a firm nod. My dad seems sheepish when I look at him. *What's going on there?* "As you all know, Kennedy is twenty now, and he's had two years to find a mate. His wolf hadn't picked yet, and we're now out of time."

"But—" Kennedy starts.

"But now he's found his mate in your youngest daughter," the Alpha says, frowning so badly that his eyebrows look like one, with a crease between. I don't like where this is going.

I *really* don't like where this is going.

My Alpha turns to me, and the hatred in his eyes makes me flinch. "Nora, you're not a suitable candidate to run this pack with my son."

"But—" I attempt to protest, despite the sudden rush of anxiety. We're told as kids to never argue with our Alpha, it's one of the first rules we're ever taught, and I've just broken it.

And I don't regret it.

My mate might not seem willing to fight for me, but I'm going to fight for him. For us.

"Shut up, Nora" my dad hisses, and I can hear him grinding his teeth. *Shit.* Neve reaches for my hand, squeezing it gently, trying to offer comfort. *It's not her reassurance that I want.*

"Dad," Kennedy says, and my wolf yips in my mind at the sound of his voice. It's a smooth baritone with a strong Northern accent. "I understand what you're saying." Wait... what? I'm sure my betrayed, pained look is affecting his wolf, but the man doesn't seem to notice. *Or care.* "But if not Nora, then who? We can't have a pack without a Luna—she needs replacing."

Only moments ago, I was elated. He was touching me, bonding with me, and choosing me. My blood turns cold, or at least that's how it feels, and tears spring to my eyes.

How can he willingly throw me away?

"If I can't have my fated mate, then I get to pick my replacement mate," he decides. He sounds like a brat, like his favourite toy has been snatched away and he's got to make do with second best.

But am I just imagining that?

"It's nothing against you, Nora, but you're weak," Kennedy tells me. A minute ago, he was so excited... *what changed?* "I need a strong Luna who can handle the job. You're too fucking nice, and the pack don't respect you. They'll never be able to respect you. This"—he motions between us both—"won't ever work."

"He's right, honey," my mum says softly as she tucks my hair behind my ears, and uses the most patronising tone I've ever heard. "You can find a new mate, and you'll have the full support of your parents. Do this one thing for your pack, give up your mate, and we'll help you achieve your goal."

"No," I whisper, biting my inner cheek so hard I draw blood.

This is a joke, right? They can't seriously be telling me to give up my mate. I glance around the room, and other than my brother, who is far too immature to be present for this conversation, they're all eager and expectant.

What kind of sick person would suggest leaving my fated mate and be this happy about the idea of it?

"Lunas are there to help the Alpha, and that includes making the tough decisions," Luna Newitt says softly. Like my mum, she's using a patronising tone, treating me like I'm stupid. "There's no time for compassion because you need to be objective."

"You cried when I killed a spider earlier," my dad reminds me, and tears spring to my eyes as I remember the way he stomped on the eight-legged arachnid *for fun*. "You're not cut out to be Luna, Nora. Don't fool yourself into thinking otherwise."

The gleam in his usually dull brown eyes shows me how proud he is of me. But I'd be a fool to think it's because I've mated above my current social standing. No, he's proud because he thinks I'm going to do this one thing for my pack. He's proud because he thinks I'm going to willingly give up half of my soul.

I've always been the selfless daughter, but this time, they're asking for something I can't give.

They're asking me for something nobody could give up.

"Fate thought I could handle it," I say, crossing my arms and sitting up straight. Nobody is on my side. David's too young to care, but even Neve, my sister who was holding my hand, doesn't believe that I can do this.

How have things gone wrong this fast?

Their lips continue moving, but the words don't register in my mind. I physically can't grasp that they're doing this to me. My parents, who are meant to love me, to support my dreams, to want the best for me. My Alpha and Luna who are meant to be the ones to support their pack members, to make sure that their pack is thriving, to be the example that we all need.

My mate, the man who is meant to cherish me, to love me, to be the other half of my soul.

These people are meant to want the best for me, yet all they want to do is destroy my life. They're hurting me, and they don't even care.

A stinging sensation hits my cheeks, and I look into the furious face of my mother. Her amber eyes are glaring at me, and as a ringing sound echoes in my ears, sound returns. My cries fill the room, an action I didn't even realise I was doing, and anger is the only emotion I can smell.

They're all furious at me.

"I, Kennedy James Newitt the third, the future Alpha to Riverstone, reject my mate, Nora Nouvel Hart. I willingly sever all ties to you and your animal, and I understand that this will permanently renounce you as my mate." The clinical tone, the disinterest in his gaze, and the smell of disgust from the man that is meant to be my mate causes my sobs to increase in volume.

Searing pain shoots through me, a burning sensation in my chest. I fall to my knees, my head banging on the seat in front of me, as my wolf loses it within me, and when Alpha Newitt howls, it washes over me.

His wolf's command completely bounces off me.

I don't recognise him as my Alpha anymore.

"She's no longer a wolf," Alpha Newitt scoffs, turning his back on me quite literally. *She's no longer a wolf.*

The words echo through my brain as my wolf cries and whines get quieter but no less intense.

To her, her mate is dead. Kennedy severed our bond, and she can't wrap her mind around the rejection—around the loss. He doesn't want us, but she doesn't understand that. There's a hole inside that should be filled with our connection to our mate, and that's all she can focus on.

My family and the leaders of my pack decided I was weak and useless because I have compassion. Me being a good person, a nice person, has cost me my entire life.

To her, her mate is dead.

To me, he was never alive to begin with.

1

NORA

Six Years Later

"Good morning," I say as I lead my client down to my office. His longer strides are causing me to anxiously walk even faster, and I'm desperately trying to control my breathing so he can't hear how unfit I am.

I open the door, gesturing for him to go in first. My office isn't new to him, he's a regular around here, as shown by the way he's already helped himself to coffee from the break-room.

My office is just like all the others on this floor, big enough for a desk, a couple bookshelves, a filing cabinet, and two two-seater sofas with a coffee table in the middle of them. I've got a navy rug under the coffee table, and a few pillows on the sofas.

The thing I love most about my office is the greenery. I've got a few different plants that I'm very good at keeping alive, but their smell is what prompts me to keep them.

They're crisp, fresh, and they appeal to me in a way nothing other than the outdoors does.

I take a seat on the sofa opposite him, crossing my legs at my ankles, since he's chosen to sit over here rather than at the desk. That lets me know this visit is more personal than business.

"How are you doing?" I ask.

"Morning, Nora," he says, smiling at me. His perfectly white, straight teeth glisten at me. They're only as white and straight as they are because he's paid to have them done this way. "I really appreciate you taking the time to meet with me again. I know how terribly busy you are."

A Southern man who moved up North years before I was born, it still surprises me that he has the dialect and accent belonging to that region. He never goes back down south, but if he did, I bet they'd hear the subtle differences in his tone.

His dark hair is specifically dyed to hide the greying, and the suits are perfectly tailored to his body to accentuate it. He's a rich man and cares a lot for appearances.

He's sweet, though, and truly cares for people, which is why I like him.

"I'm never too busy for you, Fred."

He nods, and it's only a few more minutes of small talk before he starts explaining the reason for his visit—his daughter.

Solving other people's problems is one of my primary responsibilities, and it's the part I love the most. I'm a senior paralegal at Legal Pride, a law firm within my small town of Callent.

With the firm being a branch of a giant corporation, we're pretty much left alone to do what we need to make sure our clients in this town are kept happy. It's a great balance between the small-town life I need and the chance to do some good.

Being a paralegal, the majority of my time is spent helping clients with their day to day problems, the ones that aren't big enough to warrant them taking time away from our busier lawyers. I manage my floor of paralegals, and we work closely with the solicitors to ensure that the people in our town have all of their legal needs met.

My job changes on the daily, but still fits into its little box of safe, which is something I love. Variety is the spice of life—or so they say. I live alone, and so I spend as much of my time at the office as possible. It's therapeutic in a way, to focus on other people's problems instead of my own.

If you keep moving, you're never able to feel alone.

Six years ago he ruined my life, but that only made me come out of a challenging situation and make a different life for myself—a *better* life. *Although, I'm not sure I believe the last part.*

I owe everything to my firm, though, because they put me through law school and have given me a reason to continue living.

I spend the morning organising a plan with Fred for his daughter, making sure we loop in her therapist so that everyone involved in her care is on the same page. Nobody said life was easy, but this girl is suffering tremendously, and it's truly not fair.

She won't truly understand how much her father cares for her until she's out of her situation, but for their sake, I hope it's soon. He's a good man, and she could do a lot worse... believe me.

Some parents disown their children and make them leave the city and struggle alone at the tender age of eighteen years and zero days old. Imagine being ripped from the only life you have ever known, and on your birthday at that. Can't imagine it? Don't worry. My life story shows you how it actually works, and it's not a fairytale, no matter how many wishes I wasted asking for one.

My name is Nora Hart, and this is my story of second chances. The question is... will I learn that I'm able to be loved, or will I give up and lose myself to the voice in my head?

The past six years have shown this toss-up changes on a daily basis. My mind is my enemy, and the goal... *my* goal is to survive. My therapist used to tell me the goal was happiness, and I just need to work for it. *But how can I be happy when I spend all my energy trying to survive?*

The key to that is something I've still not found.

Once Fred leaves, thankfully, a lot calmer than when he first arrived, I continue with my planned day. I've got two appointments with clients, and then one with Rob, one of the junior solicitors to go over my caseload.

It's a standard day for me, one that I can just throw myself into, and not have the chance to breathe. *Or panic.*

I volunteer to help Lacey set up for the mock trial happening tomorrow. Her brother is a trainee solicitor here, and he's nervous about the process. It's nice catching up with her as we work.

When it hits five, I send my staff home and finish doing the set-up myself. It's something that has made my staff appreciative of me, this willingness to be hands-on, but it's something I do for myself. It's selfish, and so whenever I'm thanked or praised for helping, I can do little more than give a smile. I don't deserve their gratitude.

My house is somewhere I go to sleep—if I manage to drive myself to exhaustion on that particular day. It's not a home. It's not even a safe place. It doesn't bring me comfort to be there. It's this thing that my bed is contained in.

The day that ripped my life apart was also the day I became an adult. That meant my parents—*and pack*—could buy me a tiny little house in a tiny little town and leave me there without any repercussions. Legally, they did their job. They promised to check in on me and see how I was doing, but that was the last time I saw them. Six years. It's been six whole years.

The first few months are hazy, and all I can remember is being in pain. Pain so profound that I don't know whether I ate, whether I slept, or any single thing outside of the battle I was having with my own mind.

The first year after that haze was hard. The hardest thing I have ever had to suffer through, and I'm now a law school graduate and a senior paralegal at a prestigious law firm. Law school was difficult, but I'd do it all over again if it would mean I never needed to repeat that first year.

This company gave my life a purpose. I might not have a pack anymore, I might not have a family anymore, and I might not even have a wolf anymore... but I do have a purpose. You can't kill yourself when you have things to do tomorrow.

My purpose is to continue being the one thing that my pack and family decided was bad. I get to be compassionate towards my clients and do my best to make their lives better.

It's a simple life, but it's mine. One I clawed my way up to after hitting rock bottom.

Well done me.

2

NORA

"Nora," Kim calls, and I plant a smile on my face before turning to greet her. Kim's a senior partner here, and at forty, the amount of success she has in her career is something I aspire to have. That, and her extroverted personality.

She's wearing a bright pink suit, the neon so bright for this early on a Tuesday morning, but she pulls it off. The make-up she's wearing is as bright and eye-catching as the suit. She's got a black shirt underneath the pink blazer, and her heels are double the height of mine—and mine are at the required length, meaning she does it for her own enjoyment.

Kim is already a good few inches taller than me, maybe 5'8" or 5'9", and with the heels she's over 6 foot. It means I've got to look up at her, and the power imbalance makes me a little nervous.

But I do appreciate the way she carries herself. I wish I had that level of confidence.

"Hey. How are you doing?" I ask, giving her the best smile I can muster.

I wasn't prepared to fake happiness just yet. I thought I had another ten minutes of zombie girl time.

She starts telling me about her date last night as we head up to our floor, and it's easy to nod in all the right places. Kim doesn't need a second person to converse with her. Her infectious personality and bubbly attitude are enough to keep it going.

It's not until we're outside my office, one that's a detour for her since she's two floors up and my office is not near the lift, that she taps her forehead with the palm of her hand and groans.

"Silly me. Okay, so I originally sought you out to give you a warning, and got a little distracted. You're such a good friend that way," she says, twirling her blonde hair around her fingers. It's long, about the same length of mine, just reaching her lower back. Unlike me, though, who prefers the standard pony, she will often have hers in lots of different styles. Today is the tamest I've seen it in a while—most of it down freely, with an elaborate braid down the middle of her hair.

She blinks, and her luscious lashes distract me from the pink contacts she has in. I return the smile, waiting for her to get back on track. "One of the big bosses is going to be here today, he's visiting from another branch. He shouldn't be coming down here, but I just wanted to give you the heads up so you know."

"Okay, thank you," I murmur, ducking my head to avoid eye contact. I know I'll be blushing, but I don't want her to see the shame flash across my face.

"He's doing a meeting with the senior partners—boring stuff, you know how it is. He's lovely, though, and isn't going to be interested in what you're doing down here." Slightly rude. "But I know you get nervous around new people, and if for whatever reason you bumped into him, I didn't want you to be blindsided."

I do not get nervous with new people, for the record. I get nervous around *shifters*. That's a very big difference; one humans should understand since they struggle to be around shifters themselves.

But this warning is coming from a duty of care because a while back, my struggles decided being a home thing wasn't enough. I had a panic attack—this is what my psychiatrist called it, even if I disagree—because a jaguar outed himself to me. It was my first time around one ever. He was also my very first shifter since leaving the pack and losing my wolf, so I was terrified.

I no longer have my wolf senses, which means I can no longer sense danger, and a jaguar means nothing but danger. Of course, I was scared.

But how do you explain that to your *human* boss without sounding crazy? You can't. So, instead, I had to open up to her about my anxiety disorder—the one my therapist claims I have, but I disagree.

I'm not depressed or anxious, I'm just a shell of a woman who lost the very thing that made her special.

Now, I'm just a woman trying to do as much good as possible before the darkness wins and I never need to open my eyes again.

"I really do appreciate you looking out for me," I say instead. She nods and heads off. That's her good deed done for the day.

The morning passes by really quickly with no sign of this mysterious boss, which is exactly how I like it. It's been quiet and easy, allowing me to catch up on paperwork.

Which is exactly how I don't *like it.*

It's given me too much time with my thoughts.

But as soon as I leave my office to grab lunch... I know that my quiet morning is going to change. A little girl is sitting in the waiting room alone, crying. She can't be older than five, based on her size, but her gorgeous ginger hair is covering her face.

She's got a long, green coat that screams middle or upper class, and added in with the polished shoes and expensive chain around her neck, I'm only confident in my guess. She's got nothing to keep her occupied either, no toys or a tablet, which is surprising.

I hesitantly head over there, crouching in front of her. "Hi, sweetheart." She looks up, and her green eyes are so wide, so fearful. She's hyperventilating, and I could kill whoever left her out here alone. "What are you doing out here?"

"My daddy is with the rude lady," she says, her tears drying up but the panic not leaving her tense body as her eyes rake over me with an assessing look. The look that if it came from an adult, I'd be the one hyperventilating. "They told me to wait here but that was ages ago and I'm scared."

"I see," I say, keeping my smile in place despite the anger that races through me. "So, your daddy is with a rude lady, is he?"

I move to sit on the chair with her and pull out my phone, much to her pleasure. She hops up on her knees, leaning into me as she tries to see what I'm doing. I go to the company's website so that I can narrow down who her dad is with and why she's been left here to cry alone.

"Have you ever played *Where's Wally*?"

She laughs, and nods. "I'm so good at it."

"I bet you are. Well, this is even easier because there's nothing to hide them. Want to see if you can spot the mean lady for me?" I ask, feigning excitement so that she sees this as a game. Pulling up my photo, since I'm at the top of the list, I show it to her. "Is it... this lady?"

"No," she says, giggling and shaking her head. Her ringlet curls bounce around her face, and she seems to have lost the anxiety she was carrying. It makes me happy because that look never should've been on her face. "That's you."

"It is," I reply, tucking my dark hair behind my ear. "Okay, then what about this lady?"

She shakes her head, and we go back and forth until we figure it out.

"Ah, okay, I know this lady," I say reassuringly, and she looks at me in... shock? Awe? "If you come with me, I'll show you one of my friends, and I'll go find your daddy for you, okay?"

"A nice friend?" she asks quietly.

"The nicest of friends," I promise. She thrusts out her pinky, and I laugh before wrapping my own around it. "Pinky promise. See, now I can't break it."

I take her hand, catching an unfamiliar man standing, watching us. I can't see much about his face, but it's clear that he not only heard what is happening with the little girl, but he's not ashamed about snooping.

His dirty blonde hair is longer on the top, with a natural waviness to it. He's very tall, and has broad shoulders. He's wearing a suit, but his jacket is done up so I can't see much more about his body. That's a shame.

Wait... why do I want to see his body?

I shake my head, blinking, as I try to rid myself of thoughts that are unfamiliar to me, and go back to analysing the man—this time from a *professional* gaze instead of a personal one. He's not one of my clients, so I make a mental note to see who he is when I'm done with the little girl. I can only handle one drama at a time.

I round the corner, and head over to our reception desk where Doris is sitting. Doris is one of the nicest women I've ever met, and one of the most efficient. She's been at Legal Pride longer than I've been alive, and she truly loves her job.

She's now a widow, and her children don't live close by, so she gets her social interaction here.

"Doris, could you keep an eye on..." I trail off, and crouch down next to the little girl. "Sorry, sweetheart, I never asked you for your name."

"Lily Wilkins. I'm 5 years old, and my birthday is on the twenty-second of June, 2017. I live at number 47, Willow Drive."

"Wow," I say, dropping my jaw in exaggerated surprise. "You are so smart."

"I know."

And modest.

"Well, that's a gorgeous name," I say, standing back up and turning to Doris with a smile. "Could you watch Lily? Her dad is with Morgan, and I'm going to see what's going on since they've been a little while."

"Of course." Doris immediately draws Lily into her orbit, offering her candy from her jar.

With that settled, I head over to Morgan's office, unsurprised when it's locked. I knock loudly, fully aware of what's happening in there, but desperately hoping I'm wrong.

"Morgan, it's Nora. Can you open up, please?"

"Shit." That was a very masculine voice, and unless Morgan's practising using a deeper tone of voice, it's clear that this is Lily's dad and not my employee. *Great.*

As things rustle inside and drawers are slammed shut, it

doesn't take a genius to figure out they weren't sitting at the desk talking. Typical.

I don't move, patiently waiting.

"What?" Morgan snaps, yanking the door open to glare at me. Her pupils are blown, the tiny ring of green surrounding them, as she struggles to catch her breath. There's a shine of sweat across her forehead, and I can't tell if it was because of what she was doing in there or panic at being caught.

Her pink blouse is untucked, the buttons mismatched as if she's hastily gotten redressed. Her trousers are wrinkled around the knees, and she's put her heels back on but she's missing one of the invisible socks.

"Do your shirt up correctly, and make sure that your client finds his daughter with Doris," I tell her softly. Her nostrils flare as she quickly turns to look behind her when there's a sound from her... client. "Then meet me in my office. You have fifteen minutes."

She pales and nods, turning back to look at me before closing her door. I hear them arguing quietly, but that's not a conversation I want to listen to. It'll only make things worse for her.

As I exit the corridor, that same man is still watching me, his head tilted to the side. I step closer, and see his ocean blue eyes following me. His nose is concaved, with a straightness some people would be jealous of. His cheekbones are high, and his chin is protruding, with a strong jawline.

He's got some thin, neatly shaved facial hair that covers his jaw, goes down underneath towards his neck and rises to the middle of his cheeks. It's a darker blonde than his hair, but matches his upward eyebrows.

He's model worthy, his face a work of art. But his good

looks are not what drew my attention. *Well, at least not at first.*

It's his aura of intrigue and confusion that caught my attention. He's out of place here, but he's desperately trying to fit in, trying to dim the power and allure that he has.

It unsettles me in a way that I don't appreciate.

"Can I help you?" I ask, taking a couple of steps in his direction. His eyes widen, his nostrils flaring as he inhales, but with no anxiety building within me, I feel confident enough to stop in front of him. "Are you waiting for a meeting with one of our paralegals?"

"No."

"Oh," I murmur, my brows furrowing as his short snap doesn't help me. "Are you wanting to book a meeting with one of them? This floor is used for meetings, but if there's somewhere else I can direct you to, I'm more than willing to help."

"What are you going to do with Morgan?" he asks, with a crisp tone of voice. The demand to his words doesn't go amiss, either.

"Excuse me?"

"The woman having an affair with a client." He says the words so simply, like it's something that happens every day.

"I'm sorry, but I have no idea what you're talking about," I reply, cursing her inwardly.

Fuck. This is just what we need—a client knowing about Morgan's mistake. It's bad enough that small town gossip can ruin lives... but when there's an air of truth to it, it's devastating.

He raises one eyebrow, a smug smirk on his face. I lied earlier, he's not attractive at all.

And here I go again, lying to myself. If he's not attractive, Nora, why do you have butterflies?

"I'd love to be able to help you, but if you're not after help, I'm going to have to get security to show you out," I say, shrugging my shoulders as I pretend this isn't the most nerve-wracking conversation of my life. "This isn't a public building, and with the nature of our work, it needs to be a confidential and safe space for staff and clients."

He nods, seeming slightly amused. "I've got a meeting with Mr Davis in ten minutes. He asked me to wait here, so no need to call the security team."

"Ah, wonderful." Fucking hell, Nora. *Wonderful?* Let's hope he doesn't share any of this with Tim Davis. Today is not my day. "I'm sorry about the twenty questions, but I do need to protect the space."

"Don't be," his smooth voice answers as he edges a little closer. I look up at him, the height difference startling. Even with my four inch heels, I don't reach his shoulders. An amused smile radiates over his handsome face, and I note even his teeth are perfect. "You were really nice to the little girl."

"Shouldn't I have been?" I ask, my breathy tone giving away desires I don't even understand myself.

He shrugs and sits down on the chair I was at not even ten minutes ago, now putting a balance between us. I can look in his eyes without needing to snap my neck.

"So, back to Morgan," he says, spreading his legs in the way men do when they're getting comfortable.

"I'm sorry, sir, but that's not something I'm going to talk about with a client," I say, smiling. Albeit a little tensely. "It was lovely meeting you, though."

Lies.

He might not make me anxious, but the feelings he's ignited within me have.

To my complete dismay, Morgan and her client choose

that moment to round the corner, and it's hard to hold my groan in. Timing is everything, and today, it's not working on my side.

Morgan shoots me a panicked look when she spots the client, the *real* client, unlike the one shuffling behind her. Her client seems unconcerned with what is happening, a cool air around him, which only makes me hate him more.

Morgan, on the other hand, is visibly rocking back on the balls of her feet, and if I still had my shifter senses, I know the scent of her anxiety would be filling the air. Her hair is clearly unbrushed, and she's trying to smooth out her pants without drawing attention to it.

"Nora, hi. Could you grab the child for Mr Lewis please?" Morgan asks, her voice breaking on the word child.

Oh, wow, I don't even want to know.

"Lily," I supply, and the man nods as he checks his cheap, tattered watch. My eyes track the movement, not matching that item to the way Lily is dressed. He doesn't seem concerned about Morgan or even his daughter. What is wrong with people?

I head around the corner, hoping nobody speaks in my absence. Morgan's mess is not one I want to clean up with a client of all people.

"Lily, sweetheart, I found your daddy," I say gently. She smiles and thanks Doris for the snack.

"What's going on?" Doris asks, and I shake my head instead of replying. This isn't the kind of thing I can gossip about, not that I would even if it were permitted.

Morgan is in a lot of trouble for breaching not only ethical policies, but the company ones, too. She's going to need her union rep because unfortunately for her—and me —her actions have led to me needing to suspend her.

"Let's go, Lily," Mr Lewis snaps, tugging on his

daughter's hand a little too roughly for my liking. I let out a slow breath, not wanting to snap, and the only thing that calms me is the smile on the little girl. She's unfazed and waves bye on their way out.

"Nora... I, um," Morgan says, stuttering over her words as she looks at the client in front of us with horror in her eyes.

"Let's talk in my office," I say, and she nods.

"Mr—" she starts, but I cut her off. I do not need her talking to another client with the situation as it is. In about 15 minutes, she's going to lose her right to do so on company property, so I'm just getting a head start.

"Let's go," I say firmly, and she sighs and follows behind me. Once we're sitting in my office, I grab one of the dictaphones, and she bursts into tears. I reach over and offer her a tissue, even if they are just crocodile tears.

"I... I'm sorry," she cries, clutching at her strawberry blonde hair. "It was one time. It was a mistake."

And that was her first and second lie. This has been going on for a while, it seems, nobody can have a technique down that well for a first time, and she definitely doesn't regret it.

I don't understand how a woman in her position can throw her life away for sex. It would've been so easy for her to pass the case to someone else, and pursue this relationship ethically outside of the office.

"Do you want your union rep here?" I offer in a pause between sobs. "I'm sorry, Morgan, I really am, but even just once, this is a very serious matter. It's not something we can let go, it breaks so many rules."

She nods through her tears, and I call HR to get a union rep sent down. I hate that she's in this position, even if it's her own fault, but I hate even more that it's me who needs to handle it.

I've not faced many disciplinary problems during my time as Senior Paralegal, and this is one of the worst that's happened. Once her rep arrives, we go over the details of the affair, and despite her repeatedly insisting it was a one time thing, I still suspend her.

Her rep and I discuss the infraction a little more, and I'm just pleased that now that the initial meeting is over, I can pass it off to someone higher. This is way above my pay grade.

It's now time for lunch—albeit delayed by an hour—so I can cry this out, too. Unlike Morgan, mine will be real.

The client from earlier is still sitting there when I leave, and I frown. "Did Mr Davis not come down for you? I can—"

"He did," the client says, cutting me off with a cheerful smile on his face. He stands, and luckily with the distance between us, I don't need to put any additional strain on my neck. "Can we talk?"

"I'll need to check with Mr Davis, but if he's okay with it, sure," I reply, biting my lip as I try my best to remain calm.

But my thoughts are racing as I try to come up with any reason why he'd want to meet with me that doesn't include talking about Morgan. His relaxed demeanour isn't helping either because it reminds me that I really don't hold the power here.

I have no idea about his billables, but he's still a paying client.

"I'm not a client, Ms Hart." *Huh, maybe he's not.*

Wait... what? My jaw drops, but I quickly close my mouth and narrow my eyes as I take in his still relaxed demeanour. "No?"

I hope my tone is cool and collected, maybe an air of breeziness like this doesn't faze me.

31

I don't think that's true, though. I think he heard the panic.

"I'm a manager with this firm," he says gently. He pulls out his wallet and shows me his office ID, sadly using his thumb to cover his name. Damn it. *I wanted that for purely* professional *reasons, of course.*

Fuck me. Great.

What happened to Kim's reassurances that he wouldn't bother coming down to my floor? What a day for him to visit.

"Oh. Then I do apologise, especially since things have been a little weird between you and I," I murmur, ducking my head to hide my blush. I've just made it sound like we're in a relationship, or there's something to that level going on here. *What is wrong with me?*

"So, can we take this to your office?"

"Sure," I whisper, turning back around and letting him follow me. Sometimes, things just don't go my way. By sometimes, I mean all the damn time.

"Would you like some tea or coffee?" I offer, but he shakes his head as he sits in one of the chairs across from my desk. I wasn't offering to be polite, but for a minute alone to calm down, so his refusal only makes my heart sink further.

He looks around my office, lingering on the desk with a small frown. I'm not sure what is offending him, but something has. He takes in the bare walls, and his frown only deepens.

"So, I'd like to discuss Morgan," he says.

My clammy hands are fingering the bottom of my skirt, and I sit down behind the desk when his gaze drops to the movement. I don't want him learning my nervous tells. "I'm aware you're several ranks higher than I am, but I can't tell you anything about the investigation. I can give you the details for the manager who will be taking it over if you'd like?"

He purses his lips, leaning forward in his chair. This man is confident and dominant, and I highly doubt the word no is something he hears, so I genuinely fear for what's going to come out of his mouth.

That is until he grins at me. "I thought as much."

"Is that all?" I ask before taking a deep breath when he shakes his head.

"Don't look so scared," he says. "I wanted to talk to you about a proposition I have." *A proposition?* "I work at the main branch, in Oxley, and I'd like to offer you a job."

"Excuse me?"

"There's an opening within our Oxley branch, and after talking to Mr Davis, I think you'd be the perfect fit for it."

He's deadly serious. So serious, in fact, that he's not even smiling. I don't get it. Why is he wanting to offer me a new job? Did I mess up?

"No need to panic," he says, smiling once again. I don't like that he can sense my emotional shifts and acts on instinct to reassure me. Well, more accurately, I don't like that it's working. There's an air about this man, something I can't pinpoint, but it makes me feel... safe. "It'll be a promotion, Nora. You'll be doing the same thing you're doing here, but on a bigger playing field."

"There are only seventeen people that work here," I tell him. "I completed law school eighteen months ago, and started here only a week later. I was shocked when I was very quickly promoted to being a senior paralegal, but now, you're telling me you're offering me another promotion? I don't understand how that works. I'm a paralegal. I've got a few years experience in this job. It doesn't make sense."

I worked here part-time during my studies, and then during every holiday and summer break, so I do have more experience than you'd have thought, but not enough to warrant a promotion.

"You impressed me today, and I have the means to offer you a job I think you're more capable of doing, and it's an increase in salary. I don't understand why your immediate answer wasn't yes."

"Oxley is a large city; we're currently in a small town. Oxley has a population of close to eight million people; my small town has less than five thousand. It would require moving to a new house, learning the ropes of a new kind of city, and will be an increase in responsibilities." With a wry smile I add, "It's not like you disclosed the salary bump either."

"So, there's no boyfriend to consider?" he asks, sitting back in the chair, appearing completely relaxed. This man doesn't seem to do anything by halves, and winks at me.

"I don't think that's any of your business."

A smirk appears on his face as he goes, "I think it's something your boss would want to know." I want to argue with him, but I don't because it does things to me. *Like igniting a fire in me, one I've not felt before.* I take a deep breath, and his nostrils flare. He's amused, clearly.

Bastard.

Is this all a joke to him?

"Look, get me an offer in writing, and I'll consider it. Until then, I've got actual work to do." I will not be considering it, but I want him out of my office.

He bursts out laughing. "You're something else, Nora."

That's a very overused line by men, and one I truly hate. Am I meant to be flattered?

"I think you're a very smart woman, and I think we could

34

really get along," he says, cocking his eyebrow and even adjusting his tone. The ability to sense when I'm getting unsettled is something that only unnerves me further. "Don't you?"

"Considering I really don't know you... no, I don't think so."

"I'll leave your offer with HR," he says, standing with a pout on his face. Seems the alpha male doesn't like sass because as soon as I argue, he quits. "But if you wanted to get to know me... we could do dinner. Are you free tonight?" *Never mind.* Clearly, he took it as an invitation for something more.

"I'm working."

"And as your boss, I'm more than willing to give you the night off," he offers, and I avert my gaze. This will only end badly, and I've already had my fated mate reject me.

Humans don't have the bond wolves or other shifters do, so there is literally no guarantee we'd work. One heartbreak per lifetime is enough for me.

I look up and shake my head, causing him to give me a sad smile. Why does his sad smile make me feel guilty?

"I didn't think so," he says, his shoulders stooped as he places a card on the table. "I really hope you decide to take the job offer, Ms Hart. That branch could really use your expertise, and I think you could be really happy there if you gave it a chance."

"Thank you," I say, grateful when he leaves.

As he leaves, I swear his footsteps were heavier than they were on his entrance. I count to ten, giving him plenty of time to get away from my office before going to lock my door. It's time for my break, which means nobody will come looking for me for about 45 minutes. I slide down it and rest my head on top of my knees before silently bursting into tears.

Today has been challenging. My emotions are so messed up inside me that I don't know whether I'm crying because of what happened with Morgan or because of a blonde-haired man I know will wreck me.

I don't think I can come back from rock bottom twice.

I take a few minutes—ten according to the clock on my wall, but who is counting?—to pull myself together before finally heading out for lunch. The temptation to skip it is strong because my anxiety makes it hard to eat, but I need the time out of the office. When I enter the lift, unsurprisingly, he's there.

Thanks, universe. I really needed this gift from you.

"I'm sorry," he whispers, and when the door closes, he pulls out a handkerchief. I hesitantly take it, but I have no need for it since I refuse to cry again. "I'm really sorry, Nora. I shouldn't have added on to an already stressful day."

"You didn't, sir. I'm fine."

He steps closer, pressing the alarm to stop the lift, and gently cups the side of my jaw, his fingertips reaching the middle of my cheek. I can't fight the pull I have to him... and strangely, I don't want to.

With a tiny tilt of my head, I press into his hand a little more, desperate for the contact between us. He gently wipes away my tear marks from before and pulls me into a hug.

My brain is frozen, unable to process what's happening, but my body doesn't care. I melt into the hug—*my first one in six years*—cringing slightly when I begin to cry.

Damn it, I lied to myself.

"I've got you," he soothes. Over and over, he rubs my back and doesn't let go. He makes me feel wanted, a feat I have no idea how he managed to do since I've never felt this way since that day.

His energy relaxes me, the light humming from his chest reminding me of a time where my life wasn't this bleak.

He's safe. I just don't understand how I can feel this way.

When I stop crying, humiliation sets in, and I step back, ducking my head. I feel sick and dizzy, but he doesn't seem to realise.

"You're okay," he says, his usually smooth voice sounding husky.

"She's going to lose her job," I whisper. Okay, Nora, good job hiding from your breakdown. A better solution, though, would be not to have one. I wring my hands, glancing up at him. "She's made a mistake, and she's going to lose her job. Her nana relies on the income, and I have no idea how I'm meant to help her."

He doesn't reply, still rubbing my back. His ocean blue eyes are raking over my face, a brief flash of something indiscernible across his face when he locks in on the redness of my eyes. He seems troubled, but I don't know if that's just my imagination.

"And then you come and offer me a job, a get out of jail free card, and I know if I leave, it's going to look like I did this to benefit me. That I fired a very hard-working colleague and then got a promotion because of it. I'm going to ruin her life, ruin her amazing nana's life, all because I was nosey and got involved in something I shouldn't."

"What if there was a way she could keep her job?"

This sobers me entirely. "You mean, there's a way she could keep her job? Even after... sleeping with a client?"

"I'm sure we can find one," he offers, tucking my hair behind my ears and giving me a hesitant smile. "Do you have time now? I can help you devise a plan."

"I, uh, yeah, absolutely," I stutter out, and he grins. "Thank you."

"The health, safety, and happiness of my people is important to me," he says softly before dropping his voice to being barely above a whisper. "Even those not part of our world."

If only I could hear the wolf within, I might have been able to truly understand the meaning behind his words.

3

ATTICUS

The lion within me is finally sated. He's picked a mate, a fucking perfect mate, and I couldn't be happier. I glance across the table where she's sitting, barely able to hold in my purrs.

She's got thick, long brown hair that I can just imagine wrapped around my hand as those deliciously full lips work their magic. Her dark brown eyes are filled with pain, and I can't wait until the day where they glisten with pure happiness all of the time.

She's tiny, only about 5'2", which is hilarious next to my 6'5" frame. I'd be scared to break her, with how dainty she is, but my lion would rather tear out his own throat than do that.

She's slim, but scarily so. She's underweight, and it only adds to the fragileness of her.

I want to take her home with me, where I can keep her safe in my den. I'd feed her, love her, protect her. She needs me.

She should have a pack, and she doesn't, which confuses

me, but that's fine because I have a giant fucking pride that will welcome her with open arms.

Persuading her to come out for dinner with me was hard but worth it. She's scrutinising the menu, and based on the scents she's giving off, I can tell she's embarrassed and slightly nervous. I'm not sure why, but the scents don't lie.

Maybe I've picked somewhere a little too upscale. Our budgets are vastly different, so maybe she's just never been able to come somewhere like here. The restaurant is quite lavish, the artwork and tasteful decor combined with the low lighting makes it romantic. There's fresh flowers on the centrepiece of our table, linen tablecloths and napkins in a royal gold and navy, along with freshly lit candles.

The classical music is kept quiet enough that the buzz of conversation from other patrons can still be heard, but not so that you can't hear it at all.

Still, despite the way I relax in this familiar environment, I should've expected she may not. They don't make any effort to hide the expense.

And why would they? That's how they get away with charging the extortionate prices.

Nora is interesting. On paper, she's a smart, confident, empathetic woman. She's risen through the ranks at my law firm very quickly and has a strong work ethic. Her bosses and her subordinates have nothing but kind things to say about her.

But in person, she's so much more than that. She's shy but still strong enough to tell me no. She's skittish but willing to take my comfort. She's strong-willed but broke down in the most heartbreaking way.

My lion has refused to pick a mate in the ten years that we've been eligible to have one, and I've always thought there was something wrong with him.

But today, he proved me wrong. I'm an Alpha lion with a giant pride, and they're going to be so fucking excited when I bring home my queen.

"Are you ready to order?" the waiter asks, his footsteps light but still audible. Nora was surprised, though, and she quickly closes her menu and straightens her back.

I give him my order, pausing to see if Nora wants to order for herself. She's tense, but I don't know if it's me or the place. Being able to smell emotional changes is a helpful skill that shifters have, but I'd much prefer mind reading.

She flicks her long dark brown hair over her shoulders, the light making it seem the shade it is rather than black, and her dark brown eyes light up as she places her order with only a little bit of hesitance. There's a genuine smile on her face as she eagerly nods to whatever he's saying.

When he disappears, she shoots me a tense smile. *So it's me making her uncomfortable.*

"So..."

"So?" I query, grinning.

"What do you do?" she asks before a red tint covers her cheeks. "I mean—"

"I know what you mean." But I don't want to answer too honestly. I don't want to out myself as Alpha, not just yet. It's not often someone in our world doesn't recognise me, and it's nice having this freedom to let her discover the me she will always know as opposed to the rumours. "I make the tough decisions. So, back to that job..."

"Maybe we should talk about something other than work," she suggests. What a good idea. "How long are you in town?"

"It was meant to be a few days, but I've extended my stay." A fact that's pissed Mal and Orson off since I didn't explain why I was going to be here longer.

"Oh." I watch as she tugs down the sleeves of her dress, and it causes my lion to get pissed off. *At me.*

"I can see you're nervous."

She gives me a weak smile. "I don't... I've never done this before."

"What? Eaten out?"

"Not with another person," she murmurs, shrugging like it's no big deal, but I'm completely gobsmacked. "Add in the fact that I barely know you, and I'm feeling a little out of my comfort zone."

"Well, what do you want to know?"

"Your name."

Holy fuck. No. Surely... surely I've told her my name. But by the blank expression on her face, I know I haven't. My lion lets out a grumble as I groan. "I'm an idiot."

"Just a little one," she teases, an adorable chuckle falling from her poppy coloured, heart-shaped lips. The full bottom lip is drawn between her teeth, a glazed look in her brown eyes as her head shakes, and her hair flies out. In my mind, I flash to a different scenario where those desirable looks are from a different kind of happiness.

My cock throbs in my pants, and I'm so grateful for the table to hide beneath.

Fuck, Atticus, get your mind out of the gutter or you'll scare her off.

"I'm genuinely an idiot," I mutter. "My name's Atticus... I thought you'd have guessed."

"Not a mind reader," she replies. "But I like your name, so you pass that test. Point regained."

"Oh, so I'm on a points system then?"

She nods, reaching for her glass of water with shaky hands. She takes a sip, unaware of how desperately I'm holding onto the hope that I've got lots of points. "So far, you have two points."

"Two?" I scoff, sitting back, and I know I'm scowling. Where the fuck is two points going to get me?

"One for having a pretty name," she says, using her straw to make the ice move in her glass. "And one for letting me borrow your handkerchief."

"Who has the most points?" I demand, and she bursts into giggles. My competitive attitude fades away as I watch my mate completely dissolve into a giggle fit. She's clutching the edge of the table with one hand and trying to cover her mouth with the other.

Her giggles are infectious, and I can't help but chuckle, too. "What's so funny?"

"You got so offended," she says, getting more comfortable in her chair. "Especially since I've never awarded points to anyone else."

So whilst two is not enough points, I'm winning, *and* I'm special. I don't think Nora fully understands how much her words affect my lion and me, but they soothe us. Alpha's are possessive and competitive by nature, and I love how receptive to that she is. *She truly was made for me.*

"You are dangerous."

She winks, "You don't know the half of it."

"I'd like to."

I hear the waiter coming, recognising he's ours based on the smell of my food, and I sit up a little straighter as I switch over to the Alpha persona. Nora gets to see me relaxed, but perception is everything to everyone else.

"What's wrong?" she asks, glancing around anxiously. *Can't she smell that our food is headed our way?*

"Nothing," I reassure her. She turns to me, her breathing uneven as the stench of fear hits me full force. I use a calming voice as I murmur, "Nora, I told you, safety is everything to me. There's nothing here that can hurt you."

Well, more accurately, there's nothing here that can get through me to hurt her.

She nods, but her shoulders are so fucking tense that my lion is raging in my mind. *Damn it.* The waiter comes, placing down our food, and I frown at Nora's plate.

I was too distracted watching her when she ordered that I missed what she ordered. There's no meat whatsoever. She's a wolf, and yet... she's not eating meat.

Is my mate a vegetarian? How does her wolf cope with that?

But there's also barely anything there. My side dish has more calories than her food.

The waiter pours a bit of the wine I chose into my glass, and I taste it, but I don't take my eyes off my mate. She's completely retreated into herself, and it hurts me. I give him a curt nod, and he quickly pours the two glasses before hastily making his exit.

"Do you want to leave?" I ask gently. I reach over for her hand, but she pulls it off the table and out of my reach.

This annoys the lion within, but he's smart enough to not let her know.

"No, it's fine," she whispers. Even though her head is ducked, I catch her looking around suspiciously.

It's not fine, though. I catch another waiter, and even though I can imagine me doing this is going to create more panic in the short term, I hope it'll build trust in the long term. I need her to be able to come to me when she's panicked so that I can fix it.

If she's anxious here, we leave. It's that fucking simple.

"Can I help you?" the waiter asks, glancing between us

with a nervous expression. He knows who I am, and is desperate to make me happy, but Nora doesn't. It's freeing.

"Can you grab the bill?"

"Is the food not up to at—"

"It's fine. We'd just like the bill."

He nods, rushing off.

"Atty, please, it's okay," she says, shocking me with the nickname. She gives me a pleading expression as tears appear in her eyes. "I'm fine."

No, little queen, you're not. I don't know why she's trying to lie to me. Even if I couldn't smell the distress radiating from her, she's completely closed herself off. Her feet are tapping against the ground, and she's gripping the fork in her hand extremely tight as she moves the food around on her plate instead of eating it.

The waiter comes back with the bill, accompanied by the manager, much to Nora's chagrin. I deal with it quickly, reassuring him that it's nothing he's done. We didn't even touch the food. How could that be a problem?

Finally, once they're both gone, I help her into her coat and lead her outside. She's silent the entire time that she gets in the car and buckles herself up. I pull off, and she sighs.

"You didn't need to make us leave. I would have managed."

"Nora, one day, I hope you come to me with every issue you have. But how do you expect me to sit there when you're in so much panic and just ignore it?" She shrugs, and when I glance at her, she's looking out the window. "When you come up with a good reason, I might change my attitude."

Doubt it, but at least it'll open up a dialogue so that we can talk about it.

"You're impossible," she mutters before turning to me with a half-hearted grin. "What day are you leaving again?"

I've never been an arrogant man, but the way she's done a complete one-eighty and relaxed in my presence does wonders for my ego. Pride is my downfall, and I know if I was in my shifted form, I'd be throwing my mane about as I prance back and forth in front of her.

"Don't remind me," I tease. But, aware that she's not eaten anything, I ask, "So, want to try the food thing again? There's a great place close to here... and it does drive-through."

"Kinny's?" she asks, and I nod. "Sounds good to me."

"Want to talk about it?"

"Not really." I nod, and she pulls her knees up to her chest. Her heels are kicked onto the floor, and it's just another thing that makes me smile. She's getting comfortable in my presence. "Thank you."

"For?"

"Being willing to leave the restaurant without me even asking."

I smile, reaching for her hand with my left one, leaving my right on the steering wheel. "You never need to thank me for that."

"So, what do you like to eat here?"

She's immediately deflecting, but tonight is not the night to push. I've got forever to get her to open up.

∞

"No!" she exclaims, giggling. "I don't believe it."

"I'm telling you. My brother really did share that video to the entire company," I say, laughing. "The house was at war for over a month."

"And I suppose you just sat back and watched the chaos?"

"What? Are you kidding? Fuck that. He screwed me, too."

She loses it at that, using me to hold herself up. We've spent the last few hours sitting in this random-ass park, and it's been amazing. I've not been the Alpha, I've not been the boss... I've just been her mate. It's been a very welcome change of pace.

"So, what about you? I've rambled about my brothers for the last hour, and I bet you're sick. Do you have siblings?"

She sighs, leaning against me as emotional pain assaults my senses. It's an unconscious move, one she's been doing all night, and it's made my lion ridiculously happy every single time. She might be skittish, but she can feel our connection and is using it to keep her centred.

"I've got a brother and a sister."

"I take it you're the middle child?"

She laughs and nods. "That obvious? Yes. My sister is a couple years older; she'd be twenty-eight now. My brother's nineteen."

So she doesn't talk to them anymore. I wonder why. "A good mix."

"Not really. We weren't a very close group growing up," she murmurs. "So, how many—"

I sigh when my phone rings, cutting her off. I pull it out to see it's Orson. *Fuck.*

"Do you mind if I take this?" I ask gently.

"I don't mind," she replies, and I nod, answering the call. There's no point moving away for some distance because she'll hear it anyway, but I hope he doesn't out my status just yet.

"Hey, what's up?" I ask.

"We've got a problem." Despite his panic-induced words, his gravelly tone doesn't sound too worried. Orson's like that, though, able to remain calm no matter the situation. It's a strong trait, and one I respect in my second.

"My favourite words," I mutter, tugging Nora closer to me. It's an innate feeling to protect her, even when there's likely no harm to her. "What's wrong?"

"Well, the fox has brought in two separate bounties."

I sit up, alert, causing Nora to groan as she gets moved around. I balance the phone between my ear and my shoulder as she gets comfy again, and she rewards me with a breathtaking smile.

"Whoa, who the fuck was that?" Orson demands.

"None of your business. Back to the bounties. Who?"

"One friendly, one foe."

"Fucking yes!" I exclaim, excitement racing through my veins. "The elephants?"

"Even better. The selkie."

"You're shitting me," I whisper, my jaw dropping, and it causes Nora to turn to me in alarm. I mouth that I'm okay, but that doesn't get rid of her confusion. I've gone from happy to excited to shocked in a matter of seconds, and the emotional whiplash is probably giving her wolf some anxiety.

"The problem... is they need transport."

"Then organise it," I command, a sharp snap to my usually crisp tone. I'm frustrated that he's interrupting this date with Nora to deal with something he can handle, even if the news makes me happy.

He sighs, and I know his next words are going to piss me off further. "They need you here to do it."

Shit. The selkies need our help... but I can't leave Nora behind. *Fuck.*

"I need..." I trail off, looking at the woman in my arms. She's wary, but is doing her best to not show how badly she's listening. I need to figure out a way to get her back to Oxley with me because as much as I want to spend all of my time here with her, I've got responsibilities I can't continue to neglect. "Shit, okay."

"What's going on down there? We've been trying to sort this out for months now. I thought you'd be happier about the news. I can get Kai to send someone else over to take over what you're doing there." Amusement fills my brother's tone as he adds, "He'd piss himself to be able to do it for you."

"Yeah, well, I've found something I've been searching for for years here. It's not that simple." I look down at Nora, smiling softly as her eyes twinkle under the moonlight, and ignore the gasp from the bear. "I'll call you later tonight, okay? Don't make a move on this without talking to me."

"Got it."

I hang up, giving my full attention to my mate. "Sorry about that. I should've had it on silent."

"Don't worry about it," she says, shrugging. "Should I ask?"

"If you want to know," I reply. Other than the species of the shifter—something I'm hoping her enhanced senses didn't allow her to piece together—there's nothing I'd need to keep from her.

And the species is only until they're settled because it's extremely dangerous for mythicals to be out and about. I can proudly say we've got the highest percentage of mythicals outside of their compound and that's because we can keep them safe and offer them a life they wouldn't normally have.

Freedom is their goal, and I offer that in spades.

49

"No. Not really. But it sounded urgent. Do you need to head back?"

"I'll figure something out," I reassure her, and her sigh of relief makes me smile. "But it's nearly midnight, and you've got work tomorrow. Can I drive you home?"

"My car is still at the office."

I nod. "Well, I'll come and get you in the morning." Which will be an extra chance to see her.

I'm so fucking smart.

She shakes her head, though, and I can feel myself pouting. "I'd prefer if you dropped me off there, please."

"If that's what you want." Because I'm not a fool, and after already managing to convince her to let me take her out for dinner, I'm not going to push her even further on the very first day.

"It is," she replies. She bites her lip, deliberately not meeting my eyes as she stands up from the blanket we were sitting on.

"What's wrong?"

"Thank you."

"You're doing a lot of thanking tonight," I say, standing up to follow her lead. I grab the rubbish and toss it in the bin before folding up the blanket as she takes the time to work through whatever she wants to say. I take her hand in mine, and we start walking over to the car..

"This is new..." she says hesitantly.

"What is?"

"Dating. Not that we're—"

"No, I like that," I say, swinging our hands together. "Dating." Dating my mate. It's fucking amazing.

"I don't really have friends. I work, and that's it."

"I get the workaholic life," I say quietly. "But having a balance is good."

"Atty, I don't need you criticising my life," she teases, but I still detect the hint of sadness in her words. "I love my job."

How arrogant is it to take credit for that? Legal Pride is my company, and even unknowingly, I've been providing a safe place for my mate. I can already hear the jokes from the guys about me being whipped. But I honestly don't care. Nora has me wrapped around her little finger, and I wouldn't want it any other way.

This woman here is mine—my mate, my future, my love.

4

NORA

*T*hings over the past week have been... different. Atticus has been a permanent figure, doing his best to monopolise all of my time when we're not at work, and even kind of at work. It's nice. *He's nice.*

But the situation right now is very much not nice.

"Repeat that again for me please," I say softly. I'm keeping my hands firmly at my sides in order to not fidget, but I feel light-headed, and I'm genuinely worried I might pass out.

"You have two choices," Kim says. She's annoyed that she's been asked to talk to me about this, but she's doing her best to appear happy for me. It's a tenuous balance, but she's pulling it off. "You can either take the position at the Oxley branch, or go up with the others for redundancies."

Apparently, it's been decided that we're overstaffed by two members of the management team, and the position as a senior partner that was open has now been closed so we can't just move someone up. Now, every junior partner— and there are only three of them—are facing redundancies.

My department is overstaffed by a manager, and also a

paralegal, but I have a golden ticket to escape it. Atty offered me a job, and now it's fast becoming like it's my only chance to keep my life the same. Even if that means moving to a new city.

I don't understand how this has happened, and so fast, too. The mysterious Mr Phoenix—our company's CEO, or maybe CFO, I'm not too sure—has decreed it, so it must be so.

"You've got the shortest tenure at the company, and despite your stellar records, I...," she trails off, looking at me sadly. "Nora, this is a scary time for us. You've got a chance to do something better, to keep your job and maybe help more people like you've always wanted to do. Don't let this be your story. Don't let a company downsizing put a stop to the good you can do."

So, despite not outright saying it, I can either take the new job or I'll be fired. That's the decision I get to make.

"Then, it seems like I accept," I say quietly. As if I have any other choice. I have sizeable savings, but not enough to live off for the rest of my life.

She grins, that tense grin where you're pretending you're happy but your teeth are ground together so tight because you're seething with jealousy. But she takes a minute to compose herself, and starts outlining how things are going to work. I've got four days paid holiday to pack up the house and arrange for my stuff to be transported over to Oxley, where they've got a house waiting for me. Her bitterness reared its head a little when she showed me photos of the house, but I barely heard her or took in anything she said through the pounding noise in my head.

This is very quick, very sudden, and I don't cope with that level of change.

I don't know if I've made the right decision—even if I

didn't have a choice. The small town life has kept me safe for years... do I really want to risk it all so that I can continue in my career? I can get a new job... I don't get a second chance at life.

I arrive home in a daze, my mind hung up on the fact that Atticus, the man I let console me during a breakdown last week, is the reason I'm safe from losing my job. It's surreal.

Surprisingly, or maybe not surprisingly, I've not seen him all day, which should've been a warning in itself. He's normally doing his best to be glued to my side. I pull out the number he gave me, and give him a call. I need answers... answers only he can give.

"Nora," he greets, sounding happy. "Hi."

"Hi," I murmur, rolling my eyes at myself through the tiny mirror on my side table. Why am I acting so meek? "Did you decide that people were going to lose their jobs?"

"Yes." Firm, unapologetic... powerful. Fuck, even without his smile to con me, he's still causing feelings.

"Why?"

"I'm sorry," he says, sighing deeply.

"Well, I'm safe," I whisper, and I hear his sharp inhale of breath. I can imagine him waiting, not even breathing, as he waits for what he wants to hear. "I'm taking on the position... I'm moving to Oxley."

"Good," he replies, and there's a calmness of his words that sort of settles me. Even just a little. "Do you need help getting things packed? I'm still in town, and have no plans."

"I, um, yes?"

Yes. Why did I say yes?

"I'll be over in an hour with lunch," he tells me. "Bye, Nora."

I didn't give him my address... I've still not shown him

where I live. When there's a knock at the door twenty minutes later, I put the kettle on and open the door, unsurprised to see him standing there.

"Hey," he says, smiling. How can he look so relaxed, so joyful, in that stiff, grey suit? "I brought food."

"Thanks... however, to come inside you've got to give me something," I tell him, leaning against the door frame. "Nothing big, I swear."

"See, I think I'm the one in the position to barter," he teases, his ocean blue eyes looking brighter in the harsh November sun. "I have food *and* I'm the help."

"Okay, I get that, but you do want entry into *my* house," I say, shrugging. "Take the chance, and we can see how things go." He hands me the bag of food, which I put on my coffee table, and I grin deviously. "Now you've really lost your advantage, Atty."

"Come on then, what do you want me to give you?" he asks, pulling me towards him without a care in the world. His actions show that despite him being willing to humour me... he's really the one in charge.

Why is that so hot?

"This is cheating," I offer, gripping his shirt as his hands are holding my waist.

"Is it?"

A surprised expression is on his face, but the amusement is clear in his eyes.

"It is," I murmur, a carefree smile on my face. "I think you should lose a point."

"You don't seem upset by it," he counters, but he does. He's been very anal about collecting his points, and threatening to remove one—or actually doing so—makes him very upset.

I groan, resting my head on his chest. "You're always

making things so hard. Just answer one tiny little question, and we can have lunch together. See, it'll be super easy."

"But I can just as easily do this," he says, and I pull back as I gaze up at him in confusion.

That only gives him the ammunition he needs to throw me over his shoulder and enter the house without my permission. I should be annoyed, but all I can do is laugh, and wiggle to try and get down. His grip on me is too tight for escaping, though—thankfully, too, since it would hurt if I'd fall to the floor.

"Now, since I'm already inside, why don't you ask me the question, and if it truly is *super easy*, I'll put you down. Otherwise, you'll have to watch me eat from up there."

"How did you know where I lived?" I ask through my giggles. "That's all I needed to know."

He freezes, and a little grumble escapes his throat before he places me on the ground. "I'm an idiot."

"Just a little one," I tease.

"I'm genuinely an idiot," he sighs, and amusement fills me because this is how he reacted when I didn't know his name. "I read your file when I was filling out the paperwork for your transfer. I thought you'd have guessed."

"Not a mind reader," I murmur, shrugging. I'm glad it's something as simple as that, though, because my paranoid mind was freaking a little thinking he'd been following me home or something.

Got to love the intrusive nature of my brain.

He grins, hanging his jacket on the back of my chair as he walks around the table to start unpacking the bag. "Let's eat some pasta, we've got some time before the company gets here and I want to see you eat."

Normally, I'd tease him about his obsession with feeding

me, but right now I can't because I'm trying to wave off the panic that he's just instilled in me.

"The company?" *He invited people over? To my house?*

"The packing company," he replies, and I nod slowly, trying to calm down after the mini panic attack he just gave me. *Deep breaths, Nora, you've got this.*

"You arranged for a moving company to come help me pack my things?" I ask softly, grateful he waited in silence for me to calm down.

"Yes..." he trails off at my expression, and sighs. "Was I not meant to? I thought that's what... I'm sorry, I really didn't mean to overstep."

I get the impression that sorry isn't a word this man uses often, and he's used it twice in the last half hour. "No, I appreciate the help." I think.

"Good. Take a seat."

"Atticus," I argue, but he presses a finger to my lips, cutting off my complaint.

"Don't bite me," he says, winking before heading to my kitchen. For a man who has never been in my home before, he's extremely comfortable moving around in it. He comes back in a few minutes later with bowls of fettuccine alfredo, and two mugs of tea.

It's cute seeing him balance this all, and it gives me the perfect view of him in his tight shirt. His arms are bulging, and it's clear how much effort he puts into maintaining his body shape.

He's massive, much bigger than me, and I just want to be wrapped up in his arms again.

"Thank you," I say, shocked once more as he seems to pull off Domestic Master just as well as every other part of his life. "I... seriously, thank you."

"Anytime," he replies before starting with his discussion. "So, talk to me."

"What do you want me to say?"

"Well, what inspired you to become a paralegal?"

"I wasn't in a great place, and I wanted to help people."

Simple. Doesn't give away too much, but also isn't a lie. By his calculating expression, I think he understands the parts I'm not saying. I really hope he doesn't. Nobody should feel the way I feel.

"And I've seen your record," he says, sipping at his tea. "You really are helping people."

"I try."

"Are you excited to move?"

As we eat, we discuss the city, and the job, and spend time talking about work. The thing is... I want to get to know Atticus the man, and not Atticus my boss. Every time we meet up, he tries to get to know me, but is super reclusive on parts about him. I love everything he's done to help me with Morgan, and I really appreciate him organising the packing company, but I want more.

I just can't ignore this magnetic pull I have towards him, and I'm scared that I'm seeing something that isn't really there.

"Tell me about you," I demand, and although he raises an eyebrow at my tone, he nods. "What do you do for fun?"

"That's your question?" he asks, laughing. "I do what normal shifters do, Nora. I hunt, enjoy time with the pride, spend time in my shifted form."

No.

No. No. No.

No.

"Why have you paled?" he demands, scooting forward and reaching out to touch me. I can't help flinching away.

"Nora, what's wrong? What did I do? Do you not like hunting? That's okay, it's not a deal breaker, sweetheart."

"Look, I have no idea what you're on about," I say softly, pleased that despite the way my legs are trembling, my tone is firm. "You're freaking me out, and I think you need to leave now."

"What?" he snaps, a glare on his face. "You're kicking me out?"

"You're scaring me," I offer in return.

I left the shifter life behind. I'm a wolf who no longer has access to that side of me, and I can't go back there. I don't know what kind of shifter he is, but I don't care. I can't do this. I won't do this.

Whatever connection Atticus and I had, I now understand it was because that tiny little part of me recognised he was a shifter, and the sense of belonging helped me realise he was safe.

But that's not true.

He's dangerous for me.

We're not friends, we're barely even colleagues. I don't owe him anything, least of all this.

"I'm scaring you?" he scoffs, but I can see the aggravated tone is to cover up his hurt. "I don't scare my people. I protect them."

The doorbell sounds, interrupting us, and I jump up to go get it.

"I can smell your relief," he gasps, panic in his eyes. "Why are you acting this way? What did I do?"

That second question was a broken plea, and the guilt I feel is crazy. How has he managed to worm his way into my life this fast?

I don't reply, heading to the front door to let in the movers. Their timing was amazing, but sadly, they're professional. They immediately get to work without hovering around us. Damn it. I need them to hover. I need them around so that he doesn't talk to me.

"Okay," he says, drawing my attention. "Let's forget that. Let's go back to being happy and relaxed. Can we do that?"

"We're colleagues," I tell him, not meeting his eyes. "That's all we are to each other. I'm sorry if you thought differently."

"Nora," he begs, an action I know is unfamiliar to him. Regret, guilt, neediness. I've really done a number on this man today.

"It was amazing for you to help this way, but this is my home," I say, ducking my head so that I don't give in to the guilt. "You're no longer welcome here."

He roars, his eyes flashing amber, and I can't stop the scream that leaves my throat. I don't know what kind of animal he is, but he has the ability to hurt me. I can't... I need him gone. Tears well up, and his hand covers my mouth as he pulls my body into his chest.

"Please, don't cry," he whispers, once again soothing me with his actions. I was terrified he was going to hurt me, but I can feel his tears dripping onto my head and know he's in pain, too. "Please, Nora. I'd never hurt you. Your fear kills me because I'd set the world ablaze before I let anything touch you. You are the one thing in this world I need to protect. You're my—"

"Stop," I gasp out, pushing away. "Please, stop with the lies. Stop with these words. Just leave. You're lying to me, and I don't want you here."

"I don't know who has hurt you to have you think this way, but they're wrong," he says quietly. "I can see I'm hurting you right now, and that's something I'd never want to do. I'm going to leave, but I'll be back here tomorrow for breakfast so that we can talk. You have my number—use it. Don't suffer alone."

He presses a kiss to the top of my head before walking out of the house. I hate that the movers are here because my coping mechanisms can't be employed. I sit on the sofa, and count down the minutes for them to leave. I appreciate their help, but I don't want it. I need to be alone.

"We're all done," the man says. He told me his name, but for the life of me, I can't remember what it is. I look up at him, and hope he can't see how pathetically miserable I am.

He's wearing a pair of coveralls with paint splashed on them, despite the fact that he's a mover and not a decorator. He's got dark brown hair, kind green eyes, and a smile that could make an older woman blush.

"Tomorrow we'll pick up the large items like your sofa and bed, and get them taken over to your new place for you."

"Thank you," I say softly. "How do I go about paying?"

"Already taken care of," he replies, and they leave before I can argue. One more kind act from Atty.

I watch from the windows until the car has disappeared before collapsing on the floor in a slump as I let everything out. My way of coping might not be healthy, but I keep everything in, until I can't anymore. Then I fall apart.

It's better than murder.

It's also better than suicide—even if my mind tries to convince me otherwise.

My phone rings on the hour every hour until one in the morning when I decide to shut it off. Atticus said he'd be coming over for breakfast, and that's not something I want to happen.

Instead, when I wake up, I turn on my phone—ignoring the missed calls and what I'm sure are some pleading text messages—so that I can phone the moving company to arrange for them to finish packing up my house without me. They need my keys to get in, but I won't be here to help them. I hope he's booked a good company... because I'm not waiting around.

It's time to start afresh.

I'm not strong enough for this, I know I'm not.

Atticus might think he has a right to be in my life, but he doesn't. We're not mates. We're not friends. We're colleagues.

And that's all we'll ever be. I wipe away the lone tear that has dripped down my cheek, and close the door behind me.

I'm truly not strong enough for this.

5

NORA

*A*tticus called seven times during the drive, and sent too many text messages to count. I stopped trying after the fifteenth and instead turned off my phone. Which makes this the second time I've had to do this in twenty-four hours because of him. I should have done it immediately after calling the moving company, but for some sick reason, I wanted to punish myself.

Or maybe, maybe deep down, I just wanted to see if he'd try.

It's not until I reach the new place I realise how badly I fucked up by fleeing. I don't have a key to the new house. I have the address, and it looks amazing on the outside, but I don't have any keys to get in.

For fuck's sake. Nothing ever goes right for me, not when I'm running away out of fear anyway.

Decisions, decisions. Do I call Atticus and ask for help—because even though I've ignored him all morning, I know he'll help me—or do I drive to the branch and see if they have any idea where I could get a key, or do I sit here in my car and continue to cry?

Eventually, there's a time where crying is not going to cut

it, where you've actually got to stand up and stop accepting crappy things happening to you and demand better.

I've been alive for twenty-four years, and yet I don't think I've ever truly lived. I had a sheltered life back in the pack, and since moving out from there, all I've done is do my best to get through the day. I stopped trying to challenge myself. I've stopped trying to enjoy myself. My only goal in life is to get from morning to night without breaking down and giving up the jig. I do my best to leave each person a little lighter than when I met them, and my career really allows for that.

I just haven't had the chance to do something for myself. My goal for each day has been survival and not enjoyment.

Then I met Atticus. It's been nine days since we met, and he's been amazing. We talk, we spend time together, and he makes me smile. Really smile, too, not just my usual fake one. I started to let down my guard, to let him in.

What a mistake that was.

I clearly don't deserve happiness. I never should have let Atticus get this close.

He's my boss, but, also, he's a shifter, the very life that tried its best to ruin me. I can't do this again.

There's a knock on my window, and I flinch as I very quickly lower it down.

"Miss?"

I jump in surprise, not having expected him to speak, and look at the man in front of me with a sheepish smile on my face. His dark eyes are narrowed in concern, and his thin lips are tilted upwards in a hesitant smile. He's got light brown hair that's neatly cut, with no facial hair on his face.

"I'm so sorry. I was lost in my own world," I murmur, raking over his figure. He's wearing a pale blue polo shirt and a pair of jeans, and seems at ease here. Is he a neighbour?

"No worries," he says, smiling properly now. It's a genuine look, and warms me to him. "You okay?"

I nod, smiling. "Yeah. You?"

"Good, thanks," he finishes, already walking away. I watch him for a moment longer, making sure he's truly leaving me alone before sighing in resignation. Only one move left to make.

I dial Atticus's number, hating myself for being so weak. He did arrange this, so he's got to know what to do. *That's good justification... right?*

"Hello," he answers, his voice curt. He's distracted... I hope it's not my fault.

"Hi," I murmur.

"Nora," he says, relief causing his tone to drop a few octaves. "Where are you?"

"Oxley."

"Of course you are," he sighs. I can only imagine him rubbing his temples as he thinks of a less commanding way to phrase his next sentence. "Is there any way you can head over to the office? Your house keys will be there, but I'm still a few hours out."

There we have it. Instead of saying go to the office and pick up your keys, he phrases it in a way that makes it seem like I have a choice in the matter. It's something I've noticed he does when he's holding back... his animal. *Fuck*. There's no ignoring it; there's no pretending.

Atticus is a shifter, and I'm not anymore. There's no future where we can be friends or anything more than that.

He's lured me in, trapped me in his stupid web, and once again I was so fucking stupid.

I don't deserve a fairytale ending. There isn't one in the

65

cards for me. Fate tried, she really fucking did, but I'm too unlovable.

"Nora?"

"Okay," I say. I wind the windows back up, the chill starting to make its way into my bones, but I still don't move.

"Go to reception and tell them Atticus has left keys for you and to check with Malachi."

"Okay."

Malachi? A pretty name, I suppose, but that's another man I need to talk to that I don't actually know. Chances are, if he's friends with Atticus, he's a shifter, too. This move was stupid.

I'm stupid.

"Nora, I'm sorry you felt you needed to flee the fucking town to get away from me."

"Atty," I plead, hating how desolate he sounds, and I hear his gasp.

"Atty? You were scared of me last night, and today I get nicknames?"

I've fucked up. Again.

"Silence, I see," he drawls, sounding exasperated. But not upset. "I'll be in Oxley within a few hours. Can we please meet up and talk?"

"I've got to head over to the office and get my keys," I say quietly.

This isn't fair to him. This back and forth all because I can't decide how I feel. I like him, I really do, but he's a shifter, and that's something that's not going to change.

But cutting him out of my life hurts me so badly. But not as hurt as I was when I was kicked out of the pack and lost my wolf. I've got to hold onto that.

The shifter life nearly destroyed me, and I'm not going back.

I can't go back.

"Okay."

I turn on the car, switching him to the internal car system instead of my phone, and we're both silent as I make the drive. He's content to listen to me breathing, and aside from one very small swear word that made him laugh, it was easy to forget he was even on the phone.

I can't even lie to myself without blushing.

Fine. I'm able to acknowledge that I want a man who is going to be so bad for me, so incredibly bad, that I don't know if I'll survive it. Logically, I don't feel like I'm going to be able to deal with that, but my heart... my heart wants him.

"Nora, I'm going to need to go," he says with an angry tone of voice. "We'll talk soon, okay, little queen?"

Little queen? He hangs up before I can argue, and I shrug off his strange behaviour because I've reached the office building. As I park my car, I'm unsurprised when a man is standing waiting for me, knowing Atticus would've arranged it to help with my nerves. He's bald, a good ten or twenty years older than me, with a large frame. He's wearing a security badge, and a black t-shirt and trousers.

He's pretty intimidating, which obviously makes him good for security.

"Malachi?" I ask a little hesitantly.

"No," he says, frowning at me like I'm stupid. *Oh.* "Kai's busy, but Atticus has asked me to give you these. They're your keys, right?"

"Yes," I reply, smiling. "Thank you."

"Mhm."

As soon as they're placed in my hand, he turns and stalks away. Well, he's extremely friendly.

When I get back in the car, I go through the messages

Atticus sent because I'm pathetic. I'm weak, and even though I know we can't be together... I want the connection we shared. The first few are worried until he realises I've arranged with the packing company to come over to Oxley today. The drastic change in the tone makes me feel like shit.

A text comes through as I'm reading, and I roll my eyes.

ATTICUS

Drive safe. Don't just sit outside the office all day.

He's clearly got a pack member spying on me.
Another text comes in, which causes me to giggle.

ATTICUS

Or do. It'll make it easier to find you.

Fuck. I'm going to need to do better at denying the shifter lifestyle because I refuse to be drawn back in. Ignorance is the only thing that will keep me safe.

Even if the dark side comes with a sexy as sin shifter who makes me laugh.

∞

Someone knocks at the front door, and I sigh, knowing exactly who it is. Time to be brave and end it. The it being my relationship—*friendship?*—with him.

I open the door, and I'm immediately wrapped into a hug by Atticus before I can even blink. I can't help myself and wrap my arms around his neck as I inhale his cedar scent. *I'm weak.*

"Hey," he whispers, sounding so relieved as he cuddles me in as close as he can. "I'm glad you got here safe."

"Me too."

He lifts me off the ground before carrying me into the house. I shouldn't let him do this to me... I shouldn't be letting him get close.

"I can feel your panic, little queen," he says sadly, sitting on the sofa with me still in his arms. I push back off his chest, and he looks me in the eyes as he supports my back so I can't fall. *Or escape.*

Putting it bluntly, he's an absolute mess. His hair is sticking up all over the place as if he's ran his hands through it numerous times. His suit is wrinkled, the jacket nowhere in sight, and the top few buttons are undone.

His tie is on, but loosened and crooked.

His ocean blue eyes are filled with pain as he regards me in the same way I'm doing with him. He gives me a grim smile, his thin, down-turned lips are pressed together in a straight line, and there's a lot of dry skin on the pale petal colouring.

"Talk to me," he pleads, lowering his head and pressing our foreheads together. "Let me understand what went wrong last night."

"There's nothing to talk about," I reply, moving backwards so our breaths are no longer intertwining, and I'm no longer relying on the arm he has around my back to keep me in place. I shake my head. My hair is currently thrown together in a bun, and it comes loose with the movement. It's a mess anyway, I'm a mess, so I don't bother fixing it. "You're my boss, or my boss' boss' boss or however many levels higher than me, Atticus. We're not on the same level. There's no future here."

He grins as if something I said was good news to him. What the fuck is going through his mind?

"Nora, you're considering what our future would look

like—a future with me by your side. You have no idea how happy that makes me."

"I'm telling you there's no future here," I remind him, but my harsh words haven't dimmed the light that has reappeared in his eyes.

"And to decide there is no future, you're imagining me in your future," he says slowly, his expression showing he thinks I'm dumb. "I don't think you're dumb, so get that offended expression off your face. I think that you're an incredibly smart young woman, and I believe if we talk through your issues, we can figure them out together. Just remember, we've known each other a week. There is a future here, I know that just as much as you do, but it doesn't need to happen overnight."

I roll my eyes, moving off his lap, and go to the farthest end of the sofa. Only I'd try and break up with a guy whilst sitting on his lap. I have no experience in this area.

I've never been the dumper...

"Look, the issues between us can't and won't change," I reply, shrugging as if this is inconsequential when that's further from the truth. "There's nothing to discuss. We can be colleagues, and I'm sure you're capable of being professional if we run into each other at work. That's all there is to it. There's *nothing* to discuss."

I keep repeating that there's nothing to discuss, and yet the hopeful look in his eyes doesn't diminish.

"Okay," he replies. "Colleagues it is. I'm capable of being professional—are you?"

"Yes," I mutter.

"Your feet are in my lap," he says, pointing to them with a grin on his face. "I'd move those if you don't want me filing for sexual harassment."

I can't help but laugh, and he grins. His flirtatious

70

banter, the kind that wouldn't even truly be flirting if it weren't for the heated look on his face, only makes me like him more.

"See, little queen, I'm so good at being professional. I think you're going to struggle the most."

"Nicknames aren't professional."

"Do astronauts not nickname each other?"

"Wait, that's the first place your mind went?" I ask, pulling my feet off his lap and focusing on him properly. "Like instead of a footballer or something, you chose an astronaut. Why?"

"I was thinking of *The Big Bang Theory* and the episode where Howard was going to space."

"Never seen it."

He gasps, and whilst dramatic, it wasn't faked. "Okay, well, I now have our plans for the night. I can't believe you've not seen it." I open my mouth to argue, and he shakes his head. "Don't even try it, Nora. There's no getting out of this. Colleagues can watch shows together, so sit back, I'm getting food delivered, and we're going to chill. If I know you as well as I think I do, then I know you're going to be going into work tomorrow despite having off until Monday. So tonight, we're going to do anything except discuss work."

I know a lost argument when I see one. "Okay, but, we don't have my TV here."

"Have you not looked around?" he asks, confused. I shake my head. I literally checked there was a bed, and that was all I cared about. I had a shower, and then sat here pretty miserably as I read the messages Atticus and I shared over the week, just to make myself feel worse. "Nora, I wouldn't move you here without having items ready for you. The company will swap out your items with these ones, and then donate them or something, so stop panicking."

I know he can tell my emotional shifts because he can scent them, which is frustrating. But we're colleagues, not friends, so that's okay.... right? Once we're at work, he'll stay at his department, and I'll be at mine.

Other than the people on my floor, I hardly saw any of the other people who worked at my building, and there were only seventeen of us. This branch is a lot bigger, and I bet there's going to be more than twenty people on my floor.

It's going to be okay.

I need the distance to remain strong against him. One more day, and then we can go to the plan I had in place of distance and avoidance.

Sounds perfect.

Well, it actually sounds pretty miserable, but I'm always miserable, so at least I'll be getting back to normal.

"I'll order food," he says. "Want to change and head through next door?"

"Next door?"

"Into the sitting room."

"I, um, may not have brought any clothes with me," I say, looking at my clothes with a sigh. I really didn't think this one through, did I? "I didn't... I didn't plan that far ahead. I need to go buy some to get me through to tomorrow when my stuff arrives."

"Fair enough," he replies. "Do you want some company? I'm quite familiar with the city, and I even know a good place for you to get some clothes from."

"Of course, you do," I tease, but nod. "Okay, yes, please. Thank you."

I grab my bag, and as we head out, he locks up, making sure to double-check all of my windows for me.

"I noticed you had cameras back at your old place," he says softly. "Is that something you'd want here?"

"Yes."

Without cameras, there is no chance I'm going to be able to sleep. My therapist recommended this when I finally gathered the courage to seek help, and it's something I'm going to continue doing.

She helped me deal with the changes that had come about due to me being kicked out of the pack, and despite being human, she helped me work through my grief of losing my wolf. She also helped reduce my paranoia with a lot of helpful coping mechanisms, and they're the only reason I can still get through the day.

It doesn't surprise me that Atticus noticed. Where it concerns me, he seems to notice *everything*.

"I've found the cameras I need," I say, showing him my phone, even though he's driving.

"There's a tech store close to the office that can probably give you a better deal than that shop," he says. "We could drop by if you want?" There he goes again, phrasing it like a suggestion, but he's already changed the direction of the car. I'm totally figuring this man out.

"Sounds good."

I know his game, and yet I'm still playing it. I have issues. I say I want to have some distance, and then I let him drive my car. He never even asked. We never talked about it. I instinctively just got in the fucking passenger seat for him to drive.

"I can almost hear the gears turning inside your head," he says, a soft tone to his voice as he tries to encourage me to open up. "Want to let me in?"

"I don't believe sharing my thoughts is something I do with colleagues."

He laughs a hearty chuckle, and glances at me quickly before his eyes go back to the road. "No, probably not. But, right now, it seems like I'm more of a chauffeur. You talk to those, right? Like your taxi driver or something?"

"You don't give up," I groan, and I can see his smug smile. "You locked up my house."

"Did you want me to let you get robbed?"

I facepalm, and he snarls quietly under his breath. "Well, no, obviously not. I just mean, I say I want things to be strictly professional between us, and then I let you lock up my house. You're driving my car—something we never even talked about—and I didn't even question it."

"I'm not the submissive kind of guy," he says, frowning. "I'm sorry if I'm not acting how you'd like. I do respect your boundaries, little queen, but it's going to be an adjustment for me. One of my brothers quite often takes time to himself. He'll go stay at his own place, something the rest of us don't have, and he'll go off the grid for a few days. That happens far too often."

"Okay?" I blink, taking in his words as I try to follow along with the random as fuck change of topic.

"My point is that on those days, me and my other brothers turn up at his flat. We'll do dinner with him, we'll play on the Xbox or each sit and do work whilst there. He needs the facade of distance, but he also needs us. My point is that sometimes I might overstep, and I might act like I know better than you—that's not the case, and you just need to remind me of those times. I don't make the same mistake twice... but I might make it once."

Why is he such a good guy? Why did I need to meet a shifter and mistake the connection we share to a cosmic connection rather than a familial connection?

When I was younger, every wish I had was to meet my mate. I wanted to have my happy ever after with an amazing guy, have a family, and be happy. I never had big dreams of

74

being rich and famous or of being at the top in my field, I'd have been happy with a simple life.

Kennedy ruined that.

Then I meet Atticus, the first man in my entire life to turn my head. He's powerful—in terms of his career, I mean —but he's also caring. I enjoyed spending time with him, I loved working together to help one of our colleagues, and I really love the time we spend outside the office. He's hard to get to know... but I could have seen a future with him.

That's until I learnt he was a shifter.

Something so simple to tell a wolf... except, I'm no longer a wolf.

He pulls up outside a tech shop and looks at me seriously. "Tell me when I'm overstepping. If you wanted to drive your car, I'm sorry. It's your car. I should've talked to you. Can I... can I be honest?"

"Yes."

"I don't think that you're upset about me driving," he says, holding his hand up to stop me from interrupting. Once again, he proves he knows me so well because I was about to jump down his throat. "I think you're more upset about the fact that this feels normal to us... that it already feels like a routine." I roll my eyes, and he smirks. "And even more so, I think you're truly upset by the fact that you don't really care. You want to care—for reasons I don't understand —but you don't actually care, and it's frustrating you."

"Well, you're wrong," I mutter, climbing out of the car. He's wrong. I do care.

He takes my hand as I round the car, and the two of us head inside to get the things we need.

"Al—" the man in the store starts, jumping up with a grin on his face. He's about 40 years old, latino, and has black hair that genuinely looks like he used a bowl to cut it.

He's got laugh wrinkles around his eyes and lips, and the smile he's bestowing on us now shows why. He's taller than me, probably only about 6'0", with a slim figure. Not overly muscular, but as with all shifters, there's minimal fat on him.

I've never seen a fat shifter before, because we transform calories into power once we hit our cap of fuel.

"Hudson, hi," Atticus says, smiling as he easily cuts off whatever greeting he was going to say. Slightly rude, but I've noticed Atticus is abrupt. "This here is my *colleague,* Nora. We need some cameras set up for her home. Could you help?"

"Of course!"

I roll my eyes at the way Atticus emphasised the word colleague. We're holding hands... I wouldn't believe the colleague lie, so I'm not expecting Hudson to.

However, Hudson just nods and leads the two of us over to where the cameras are situated. He's good, able to rattle off stats without even needing to look them up. Almost like it's a test, and he's desperate to pass.

"These ones are what I use," he says, gesturing to a different model than I came in for, but that's what sells me. If the tech store guy owns these cameras, then I think they're the best ones they have.

"Sold!"

"That easy?" Atticus asks, grinning. "I was prepared to be here all day."

"Atty, you're the driver," I remind him, grinning at his fake offence. "Shh."

"I see how it is." Hands raised in submission, he goes to sit on the chair. "Take your time, *little queen.*" Once again, he's emphasising his words, but this time it gets a reaction from Hudson.

"Oh, fuck, I, shit," Hudson gasps.

"Calm down, Hudson," Atticus drawls. "It's all good. She wants those."

"Yes," Hudson says, nodding. "Got it. We can have someone over to set them up for you. I'll get someone now."

Now?

"I'll get the set up arranged," Atticus replies, glancing at me wryly. "My brother works in tech. He can get it done whilst we're buying work clothes."

"Sure," I say, shrugging, before once again realising how badly I keep fucking up. *Distance, Nora, distance.* "That works."

"Amazing," Atticus replies.

As Hudson and I go over to sort out the payment, I notice Atticus doesn't even pull out his phone when contacting his brother. It's these little shifter-like details that remind me why we can't work. We live two different lives.

And yet, I'm so torn up inside. He can't ignore his shifter side, and that's something I'd never want him to do, but it's a life I can't be in. We really can't be together.

Why is this connection between us so fucking confusing? I wish I had an eyelash so I could wish it away... then again, all my wasted eyelashes were precisely that. *Wasted.*

Once we leave, he reaches for my arm, stopping me from walking past. "Back there... something made you sad. Your despair was overwhelming. What was going on?"

"Nothing," I whisper, biting my lip as his eyes darken. They don't go amber, meaning his animal doesn't take over, but he's still angry. "Where do you live? I'll drop you off. Don't worry about getting your brother to help. I'll manage."

"Nora, no," he begs. "Let me help."

"We live two very different lives. It's taken me a long time to get where I am, and I can't have any setbacks."

"I don't understand."

"No. You don't. Hopefully, you will never need to," I reply, and as I'm speaking, I loosen his grip on my arm and walk away from him. "I'll see you at the office."

As I walk around and get into my car, he doesn't move. His eyes are now amber, letting me know his animal has risen to the surface, and when I pull away, he lets out a roar —potentially a growl—and it tugs at something inside of me. A part of me I shut down a long time ago.

Why are you doing this to me, Atty?

6

NORA

"So, this is going to be your office. It's pretty minimalistic right now, but you do have a small budget to redecorate," Molly says as she flicks on a light, which illuminates the space that is now my office.

In the left corner sits my desk, and it's actually pretty beautiful. I step towards it and run my fingers over the edge, a wistful smile in place. It's a dark oak with fancy detailing that shows it was carefully crafted. It's heavy, and it even smells right.

Yes, okay, clearly I'm sad if this little thing makes me so happy.

The desk chair on the other hand can go. If my redecoration budget won't cover a chair that won't break my back, then I'll buy one myself. This one even has a wheel missing.

Other than the beautiful desk and the terrible chair, there's no other furniture. Well, unless you count a tiny pedal bin that's just to the right of my desk.

There's space for a couple chairs and a coffee table, a

bookshelf or four, and definitely a filing cabinet, but there's nothing here.

Hell, even the windows are bare, with no blinds or curtains.

"What do you think?" she asks, looking around with a carefully composed expression on her face. I saw her shock when we entered, though, and I know she's not impressed. "We want you to be happy here."

Me too, Molly, me too. I want to be happy here. I really want to be happy here.

But honestly? I'd take being happy anywhere.

It just doesn't come when you're this fucked up.

"It seems amazing," I reply, giving her a fake smile that I know she's none the wiser to. Unfortunately, when you fake your smile for six years, you get real close to even fooling yourself. "It has a lot of potential."

"Good," she says, and a genuine smile flits over her face. "You've got a good team of people here, too. They're great, the energy is great."

She believes what she's saying, and I truly appreciate her effort. But every time she shows me a new room or a new floor, I can't help but search for Atty, even though I know he's not going to be there. And the pessimist within me has been right, he's never there. I'm looking for him, despite cutting him out of my life because I'm absolutely pathetic.

Last night, Atticus called, and I stupidly answered. But after some ridiculous back and forth—*flirting, we flirted for an hour*—we finally managed to talk things through. No matter how badly it ripped my heart out, we finally reached a common consensus.

It was rough on us both, but I made my position on us dating crystal clear. I can't do a relationship, *and* I'm not a shifter, so I don't want to frolic with him in the woods. A fact that was hard to deny whilst playing ignorant to the shifter world completely, but I'm pretty sure I pulled it off.

Maybe.

But despite arranging it so I could come in today to be properly prepared for Monday, he's not been by to see me. Not that he would. Why would the CEO of a company this size be interested in the pathetic paralegal who has only been out of law school for two years?

Way to not sound bitter, Nora.

Just because I was the one to end things doesn't mean that I'm not hurt by it.

"If you head down to the tech department, you can pick out which brand of computer you want to use, and they can get you set up on the system," Molly says, drawing me out of my intrusive thoughts and centering me back to my favourite topic. *Work!*

Wait... brand of computer? Don't we all just get the same company issued one? This is such a different kind of environment to the one I was in back in Callent. It's strange to think we're part of the same company when even the uniform requirements are so vastly different.

Molly looks around my office once more just as her phone beeps. "Any questions?"

"No."

No questions that are acceptable to ask my boss. I want to ask what that message was and why she's so worried. I want to ask how things are going back at my old branch. I want to demand the knowledge as to which floor Atticus is on so that I can track him down.

I need to get my head on straight.

"Great. You've got a meeting in forty-five minutes, but someone will direct you there, which gives you time to go visit the tech department now. Do you remember where that is?"

"Yes, thank you," I say softly. She nods curtly and surveys the room... my new office, one last time before leaving.

"Yo, newbie," a voice exclaims, the penetrating tones already causing me to panic. I take a deep breath and turn with a fake smile on my face, despite wishing that Molly closed my door so that I could have a few minutes to myself.

The man who enters has a slimy walk and the smirk to match. He's got short, dark brown hair, and is about two heads taller than I am. He's wearing a pair of fitted, dark blue trousers and a white shirt. No tie, no jacket.

He's got narrow shoulders, narrow hips, and slender limbs. A runner, maybe?

He blinks, his dark blue eyes disappearing beneath a glimpse of long, luscious lashes that any one would pay good money to have. Until he rakes those eyes over my figure, and disgust fills me.

Great. A womaniser.

He falters, sensing my unease, and stops in front of me. Up close, I see the acne scars on his cheeks, barely hidden by the facial hair he has. They don't humanise him enough, though.

There's a panicked feeling within me, one that won't go away now that he's looming over me. He tries to smile, but his tongue seems weird—*well done, Nora, perfect thing to criticise on someone*—and I can't settle.

This isn't nerve-wracking at all.

"Whoa... nice to meet you. I'm Seb."

"Hi." I step forward and offer him my hand to shake, but he ignores it and focuses on my boobs instead. It's amusing since I barely have A cups, and there's more cleavage on his chest than mine.

But I don't get good vibes from this man—one of the very limited senses I have left—and I make a mental note to stay away from him the best I can. It's common decency to shake someone's hand when you meet them, and even without the internal warning, I'd never respect someone who doesn't do that.

He's still staring, and it's making me hesitant. Channeling my inner boss—so, Atticus in this instance, since I'm a terrible boss. "What can I do for you?"

"Just popping in to say hi to the newbies," he drawls, elongating the s sound like a hiss, despite me being the only newbie here. I don't like how his eyes settle on the lock on my door before snapping back to me with a smirk. "I'm the floor leader, and so I like to keep a close eye on those under my watch... especially the women." My eyes narrow, and he smiles. "You know, with this being a male-dominated environment and all."

I wish he kept up with his statistics because it would aid him when he's making these wildly inaccurate claims. I also don't think that he got the memo that I'm now his boss and not the other way around. It was made clear to me that everyone on this floor reports to me—both the paralegals, and the few interns.

"Hilarious," another man says. He doesn't pause to knock, just comes straight to stand by my side.

He's grinning, his wide, plump lips rising on both sides, but it's a cold look on him. His dark brown hair is short on the sides, but long on the top, and it's fluffy, as if he's run his hands through it one too many times. My head reaches his shoulders, even with my heels on, but when my eyes trail down to his feet, I see the slight heel to his shoes, too.

Makes me think he's ashamed about his height—you know, all 6'3" or 4" of it—and is trying to overcompensate.

He's wearing a suit, which doesn't really give anything away to his position here, but his stance is unwelcoming as he glares at the man in front of me. *He doesn't like Seb, either.*

"Just ignore this tool, Nora," his silvery voice says, and his Northern accent is quite clear. "I think he missed the fact that you oversee this floor—including shift leaders, which he isn't yet, despite his claims—which means you actually outrank him."

"She does?" Seb hisses, the leering gone as he now glares at me with pure hostility. Whoa. I mean, it's not my fault that I outrank him, but with his attitude... I am happy about it.

"Yes. Nora is your new boss," the man says, and I can hear the amusement in his tone this time. Dismissing Seb, he smiles at me, and it's such a contrast to the one he gave Seb a few moments earlier. His dazzling smile gives me butterflies. "Ready to head down to get your tech? I'll walk you down."

"That would be great," I murmur, edging past Seb who doesn't move to make things easier on me, and follow the mysterious man out.

"You seemed uncomfortable with Seb," he mentions as we walk past the bullpen and head to the lift.

"I'm okay." I try to keep the snap out of my words, but based on the way his thin, straight brows narrow playfully, I know I didn't succeed.

I don't take the lie back, though.

"If you say so," he replies.

"I'm sorry if this sounds rude, but may I ask your name?"

"It's not rude," he says, shrugging as the lift arrives. As one, we step inside, and as the door shuts, he turns to me properly, and I watch in time to see his eyes glow amber. *For fuck's sake.*

I knew from the moment Atticus outed himself to me that I'd meet more shifters here. I just didn't expect it to happen on my very first day.

He takes a deep inhale, stepping into my space. I try to keep breathing normally, but I don't think I manage.

"Although, I'd like you to explain why you didn't greet me properly," the man says, a hint of a growl to his usual silvery tone.

"I... um... I have no idea what you're on about," I whisper, taking a step backwards. Denial is the only thing that will keep me safe.

I left this life behind for a reason, and no matter how attractive this man is, he's not a good enough reason to break my vow. Atticus should have been the reason, he was everything I could've ever wanted, but I'm too much of a scaredy-cat to accept him.

I'm not strong enough to do it, there's no shame in that. *Isn't there? I'm a coward, pure and simple.*

"Sure you don't," he drawls, annoyance flickering in his light blue eyes. "I can feel your wolf, no matter how weak she is, and no matter how much you deny it. So, the real question is why can't you feel my tiger?"

"Are these euphemisms for your dick or something?" I ask, cringing at how weak that comeback was. *Really, Nora?* I need to become a better liar if I'm going to survive here.

His hand darts out to grip my arm, and despite it being a quick movement, his grip is tender and doesn't hurt. "Who hired you?"

"I was transferred here."

"Who organised the transfer?"

"There was a visiting manager, and he offered me the promotion," I say. I'm not going to use Atticus to help me this time. I need to do it on my own. If I want a life without him, I need to actually commit to that. "I didn't want to take the job, but I was told I either had to transfer or I would be fired since our branch was downsizing. What's it to you?"

"Where was this visiting manager from?" he asks, and the growl has disappeared from his words. "What was his name?"

Thankfully, the lift reaches the basement, and the doors open. I've never been more grateful for an escape in my entire life, and I move to step out, but he's still gripping my arm.

I look down at it pointedly, and he smirks.

"This conversation isn't over, little wolf," he murmurs, caressing my arm before letting it go. A cheeky grin is on his face, and his light blue eyes seem to sparkle in the new light. "Ask to speak to Micah when you reach the desk. He's my younger brother, and he'll sort you out. He's good people, I promise."

I cock my hip and cross my arms as I cooly regard him. "And if I don't want his help?" I am not trading Atticus out for another controlling cat, not even a little bit.

"Oh, baby, believe me, you're going to want his help," he says, grinning.

"You never told me your name..." I trail off as a door slams down the corridor, and we both turn to see a man walking towards us.

This man is quite familiar, but only because he looks just like the man I'm with. He's got shorter hair, and there's much less confidence in his walk. Unlike his brother, he's dressed so much more casually.

I'm not sure what the quote on his hoodie pertains to, but it's nice, and he's wearing some navy jogger bottoms to match with it. He's wearing a pair of trainers, and legit looks so out of place.

I low-key vibe with it, though, because if you're not going to be around clients, why not be comfortable? I don't wear these tight dresses and high heels for my own comfort.

"Bro," he greets, and even his voice is different. The accent is the same, but his voice is more fruity. If I had to pick a brother, I'd pick this one. "Oh, hey, good timing. I'm coming up."

The man I'm with groans quietly and moves his hand above my head, to block the lift doors from opening.

"Get back to work, Micah," the man says, and I'm not sure whether he's mad or what. "Nora here needs a tech set up; she's a new hire up on floor sixteen. Sort her out."

"And a wolf," Micah murmurs, stepping closer and sniffing deeply into my hair just like his brother did. As a tiger, he really should not need the closeness to determine my scent, but the close contact is something that shifters do anyway.

We're touchy feely creatures, bonding with more than just our words, and it's never normally a big deal.

Unless, you're a wolf shifter without a wolf, and you're denying your connection to that world.

"I love the nickname, but I have no idea what you're implying," I say, stepping back from him, but that only puts me closer to the other man.

Denial will be the only thing that keeps me safe. I have no wolf anymore—I lost her the day he took everything from me. I have the scent of one, I have very limited skills because of the animal I used to have, and I have an extended lifespan. That's it.

I no longer get to go on runs when I'm stressed. I no longer get to live within a pack. I no longer get to speak to my family. He took my entire life from me, and now I'm forced to live a life where I'm a constant outsider.

Because despite my wolf being one minuscule step above dead, humans can still sense I'm not like them. Wolves can scent that I'm not whole, and other shifters, well, I've never really been around them, so I don't know what they can sense.

My pack was secluded and exclusive to wolves, and then after living the small-town life for eighteen years, once I was not allowed to be in the pack anymore, my parents dumped me in another small town.

I went from being a shifter from a strong lineage, to being nothing. I can handle that. I've come to terms with it, and I get by. Now I'm in a very big city, full of shifters, and this office building seems to be full of cats.

Two tigers are currently here poking into my business, but I won't allow them to learn about me. They don't want the burden that learning my secrets come with.

Fuck my life.

Every time I find something to hold onto... fate fucks with it. Between her fucked up games, the deadweight inside me, and the voice constantly beating me down... how am I meant to keep going?

"Sure, you don't," the man taunts, stepping into the lift. "See you around, Nora."

"See you around," I reply, half-hoping that I won't... but just as equally hoping I do. Dismissing the mysterious man, I look up at Micah with a hesitant smile. "Hi, I've got to come sort out tech for my office, but you don't need to help me if you don't want to. No matter what your annoyingly overbearing brother thinks."

Micah catches onto my game and grins, two dimples

appearing on his cheeks. *Adorable.* "I don't? Amazing. It's lunchtime, and I'm absolutely starving."

"Yes, he does," the man snarls as the door to the lift closes. His snarl hits me deep in my core, and I can't help but cringe. No. I already have one shifter that I can't get rid of, I definitely don't need another. *Hormones aside.*

"Ignore Kai, he's an asshole, but he seems to like you," Micah says, shrugging. *That's him liking me?* "So, let's get you fitted out with the best tech this company can offer."

"That's his name? Kai?" I ask. It's hard to talk about tech when there's a mysterious tiger that makes sounds that give me butterflies, with an equally as attractive younger brother.

Damn it.

My life is a mess.

"Well, his full name is Malachi," Micah says, sounding a bit nervous. "Now come on, let me help you out."

Ah, that now makes all the sense. Malachi is the man Atty wanted me to pick my keys up from yesterday. Typical. *Of course, they know each other.*

Micah doesn't really seem interested in his brother, and since he's helping me—even if unwillingly—I don't want to mess him around.

I follow him down the corridor, casting one last longing look at the lift, before entering a dark room dimly lit by computer screens. He leads me through into another large room at the back that looks like it's every tech person's dream. I spot cabinets full of phones, computers, laptops, tablets, and then a bunch of things I can't even recognise. It's crazy, and by the manic grin on Micah's face, I think he knows that.

With a gleeful hand rub, he says, "Let's get to business..."

7

MALACHI

I'm in trouble—big, big trouble in the form of a doe-eyed wolf.

Fucking hell. It's been nine years since I was eligible to find my mate, and my tiger has never picked someone. Nobody has ever been good enough for him, and now... now he picks a weak ass wolf who is pretending she's not a wolf. What the fuck is happening?

"What's got a storm cloud over your head?" Atticus asks, and I dip my head in respect as I slide into the seat opposite him. He closes his laptop screen and gives me his full attention. He takes up so much space behind the desk, and with the untucked shirt, he's clearly been sitting here for a while.

It's not often he's dishevelled, especially not in the office, so he must not have many big meetings today.

Which is most definitely for the best. He's just got back from his business trip, and he's been in a mood bigger than even my current one, which is rare for the King.

When I don't immediately answer his question, the lion

within rumbles, and he demands, "Mal? What's wrong with you?"

"Some damn new hire," I mutter, rubbing my forehead. "She's got my fucking tiger all twisted up."

"Nora?" he asks, sitting forward, concern etched into his face. "Is she okay?"

"Nora," I confirm, nodding.

"She's my mate." Fuck. *Of course, she is.*

"Wait, are you the reason she's here?" I demand. He nods, getting a guilty expression in his blue eyes. "She's my mate, too."

"Congrats, brother," he says, smirking.

"She's weak."

He laughs, but it's bitter. "The day I met her, she helped a little girl, found out her dad was having an affair with one of her subordinates, and then suspended her."

"Standard practice..."

"She cried in the lift, full on broke down because the subordinate's nana or someone relies on the income, and she felt guilty about it."

My eyebrows raise, and I let out a low whistle. "She's perfect for you then."

"We worked together to find a solution," he says, and I roll my eyes. Atticus owns the company. There's no way he needed to "come up with a solution." "And we got to know each other on a personal level. She cried, Mal. Full on broke down, and sobbed in my arms, a stranger."

"I..."

"The reason I extended my trip was to spend time with her. She's sweet and kind, and yet she's pushing me away."

"She denied having a wolf to both Micah and me."

"Yeah. For days we've been getting on, flirting—*don't look at me like that*—and genuinely bonding. Then, I mentioned that I hunt in my spare time, and it's like a switch flipped within her. She backed off, she's constantly scared, telling me we can't be together, but I can tell that she feels the bond. Last night, she decided that we can't talk anymore, and made sure I knew she wasn't a shifter in no uncertain terms. I don't fucking know what to do. She's mine, but she doesn't want me."

"Well, there's now two of us to worm our way into her heart," I tell him seriously. "What do we know about her past?"

"Nothing. The company paid for law school, which is surprising, but she's the youngest senior paralegal within the firm. Despite her branch being small, it's still a big achievement. She's smart, meticulous, and all her reports say she's the first in the door and the last to leave."

"What do her subordinates say about her?"

"She's friendly, always willing to help them, and going so far as to take on tasks that will get them home sooner. Nobody at her old place had a bad word to say about her— not even Morgan, the girl she suspended."

"Nobody is that clean."

"They assume she suffers from anxiety."

"Really? She was so strong with me..."

"That doesn't mean anything," Atticus says, and I nod. Yeah, that's not how it works. "But she had a major panic attack at work eleven months ago. I looked into it, and guess what I found?"

"No idea." But the smugness radiating from my Alpha makes me want to punch him.

"A jaguar shifter was visiting," he says, sitting back in his chair. "I don't think it's a coincidence that our mate who is denying our world had a major panic attack—note the emphasis on the word major—the same day a jaguar shifter was visiting her office."

"She needs us," I hiss, barely holding onto my tiger. Atticus glares at my hands, noting the claws are out, and I roll my eyes but take them off his furniture. "I don't know what the fuck is going on, but we're not leaving her. If she's this terrified of us... what about her wolf? Her poor fucking wolf. Someone has hurt her somehow. Who? Do we know yet? I'm not against killing a wolf today. I already have a bear's ass to kick into shape, I can deal with a wolf, too."

"The day you kick Orson's ass into shape is the day I'll step down as Alpha," he taunts, winking at me before sighing. "No. I have no idea what has happened. We're going to figure it out, though. She says she doesn't want me in her life, and yet, I'm not leaving. She doesn't need to accept me in a romantic capacity, not if she doesn't want me, but she's never going to be alone again."

Well, damn. Our leader has fallen... and I couldn't imagine a better man to share my mate with.

"What did she do to get your tiger's attention?" he asks, a rue smile on his face.

"Despite how nervous I make her—I think that's her extremely dormant wolf recognising I'm a threat to her, by the way—she still stood her ground. I don't know, I don't think it was anything other than her being her. It's been nine years without a mate. She's something new, something that appeals to both my tiger and I. There wasn't anything I could do to stop him claiming her... and I don't think I want to."

"Do you know how she's settling in? We've got a meeting together in roughly ten minutes, and I wanted to gauge her mood before explaining it's my fault she's here," he says.

"Roughly?" I scoff with an eye roll.

Atticus is our Alpha, and that's not just because he's the most dominant animal. He's powerful, and he has the respect of every shifter within the city. He expanded the territory his dad had, and has made it into a safe haven for all shifter kind. We used to be a pride exclusive to cats, and when Atticus took over at nineteen years old, we started expanding, and now the entire city of Oxley belongs to him. We have very few humans here, which is rare, and they're aware of the shifter world. It's something that's never been done on this big a scale before, but there's a reason Atticus is the King.

He's meticulous with the background checks on any new pride member, something I aid in, but this careful way of planning is something that's been adopted into his everyday life, too. There is no way he only "roughly" knows the time of the meeting.

I bet he's got it down to the exact second.

"Fuck off," he mutters before straightening in his seat. "Go make yourself scarce."

"No. We share Nora, and if you're meeting with her, you can't cut me out." He rolls his eyes but relents. This isn't an area where he'll pull rank, and it's another thing I respect him for. I quickly text my assistant, Cara, to organise for my next meeting to be cancelled. I'm not being called out of this meeting with Nora for anything short of someone dying.

Atticus's phone buzzes, and he grins because she's about to come in. "Is it wrong that I'm excited?"

"Let her in," I say, shaking my head.

The door opens a minute later, and our beautiful mate enters the room. Her dark brown eyes flit between us, and she flicks her ponytail over her shoulder as she sighs.

She's wearing a light grey dress that clings to her figure, highlighting the minimal curves that she has. It seems to be made of cotton with a black belt around her petite waist. The heels she's wearing add a few inches to her height, but still, she could comfortably fit in my arms.

You know, once she puts the claws away, and I can trust that she won't try to rip my throat out.

"Of course, you know each other," she groans, but there's no true sadness about it. I'd know—I can smell both her arousal, and her happiness. To my surprise, she turns her frustrated look to Atticus, and I hold in my smirk that he's the one in trouble. "Atty, this wasn't what we discussed."

"I mean, did we really discuss things, little queen?"

Subtle, Atticus. Real fucking subtle.

"Malachi, nice to see you again," she says, sliding into the seat next to me. The cherry scent I've already associated with her assaults my senses with her movement, and it takes everything in me to stop my tiger from taking over so he can get another whiff.

"Kai works," I offer, unsurprised that Micah blabbed on my name.

"Or Mal," Atticus says, grinning at me.

"Nicknames aren't really a thing you do with colleagues."

"Well, I'm going to be offended that Atticus got one but not me," I say.

"So, what's this meeting for?" she asks, consciously making the decision to change the subject.

"My surname is Phoenix," Atticus says, and I burst out laughing at the fact that her face doesn't change. Her emotions don't change. There's no recognition to his words. She has no fucking clue what she's getting into. "Fuck off, Mal. My name, little queen, is Atticus Phoenix."

"I got that part," she says gently. "But I don't get what effect that should have."

"I own the company."

She goes completely still, apart from her eyes. Her gorgeous brown eyes refuse to settle on one single thing as she tries to understand. All I can scent is her panic, and it's making my tiger furious.

"I asked for your ID. In your own company," she says, calming me down. She's anxious because of a social mistake, not a security one. "Atty, I threatened to kick you out of a building you own."

She's embarrassed, which caused her panic, not scared. A big distinction, and one that I'm glad I took a minute to wait out before reacting to. She groans, much to my amusement. I think if my tiger didn't already choose her in the lift, he'd have picked her right now. She tucks her hair behind her ears, composing herself.

Another round of laughter escapes me, and she shoots me a look, desperately trying to shut me up.

"I love that, little wolf. You're hilarious."

"If it helps, it made me happy that you took the safety and confidential nature of the company seriously..." Atticus says, trailing off when she hits her hand against her forehead. "Nora, come on, it's okay. Stop panicking. I'm not mad. I called you here so you could hear it from me firsthand. This is my home base, and I didn't want to upset you."

"I, um, appreciate that, sir," she murmurs, ducking her head. She's embarrassed, and I hate that. I hate that we're making her feel anything but positive emotions.

"Drop the sir," Atticus demands.

"Okay."

"How were things with Micah?" I ask, getting comfortable in my chair. "Did he help you?"

"Yes," she says, nodding. "He was accommodating."

As if he timed it, the office door flies open, and Micah rushes into the room with a giant grin on his face. He spots Nora—though, to be fair, he never had eyes for us at all—and pales. "Oh, shit. Sorry. I didn't realise this was where your meeting was, pretty girl."

"Speak of the devil," I taunt, motioning for him to sit down.

"Three for three," she says dryly. "If we're done here, I've got work to get to."

"It's your first day, though," I say, frowning. "How can you already have work to do?"

"I'm now in charge of managing twenty-six people," she says. "That's twenty-six files I need to read through. Each of those twenty-six people has different clients, and whilst I don't need to know each of the ins and outs, I do need a little knowledge. So, I've got a lot of reading to do."

"You're going to read their files?" I ask, taken aback.

"Unless you have a better way for me to get history on all those people without forcing them to undergo an inquisition to a random stranger," she replies, a single eyebrow raised. At my stunned silence, she nods. "I didn't think so. I might not do things how you do, and believe me, I'll learn fast, but until a time where I can learn, I need to get on with things."

"I wouldn't have promoted you if I didn't think you could handle it," Atticus tells her. "Your methods work, and I'm more than happy for you to keep doing them."

"Great."

"I'm here if you need me," he adds.

"As I said, we're colleagues. Well, technically, you're my boss. Remember the part about levels?" she asks, and he gives one sad, resigned nod. Pathetic, but my tiger is feeling the same way. "Well, it was lovely meeting you, Micah, Mal. I have no doubt that I'll see you all later."

She leaves, the door slamming shut behind her.

"I take it I'm not the only one to find my mate?" Micah asks, glancing between us both.

"Not even a little bit," Atticus replies. "Welcome to the team, brother."

"Welcome to team taming the wolf," I murmur.

That's a shit team name because I don't think our little wolf requires taming. Unlike the wolf in the story *Little Red Riding Hood*, I think this time, the wolf is the one who was hurt.

I think that our little wolf needs saving.

And we're going to be the ones to do it.

8

NORA

"Excuse me," a man calls.

After my meeting with Atticus, Malachi, and Micah earlier, it's been a quiet day. A few staff members popped their heads in to say hi but, overall, I was left alone. Well, aside from lunch, where Malachi came to eat with me, and he asked me eighty-seven questions. I started a tally after the third to try and keep myself calm.

"You there," the man snaps.

I turn, despite the feeling inside of me urging me to run away. He's wearing a black hoodie underneath a long coat, and it covers most of his face. I can see dark brown hair peeking out the side, but that's it. He's wearing jeans and a pair of ratty trainers, his hands shoved in his pockets.

I smile at him, trying to be friendly, despite his annoyance but, sadly, that gives him the ammunition he needs to walk over and engage in conversation. He hands me a piece of paper, which is a bit weird, and when I look down at it, my confusion only rises.

"What is this?" I ask, furrowing my eyebrows as I try to make sense of what's depicted here. There's a drawing of a dead... I want to say dog, but I have absolutely no idea if that's accurate. It's definitely dead, though—the red ink being a clear imagery for blood. Why is this something he's showing me?

"That's you," he scoffs, tapping the paper once with his muddy fingers. "Dirty scum."

He turns, very dramatically, since his coat flares out and hits me, before stalking away in the opposite direction from which he came. I've met some really weird people in my life, but I don't think anyone has ever given me a drawing before.

I glance down at the piece of paper again, trying to decipher it. I don't understand why some random man is giving me a drawing of a dead dog.

"Nora," I hear someone shout, and I crumple up the piece of paper and launch it into the bin. I don't have time for cryptic people.

"Hey, Nora," Micah says, falling into step with me. He's slightly out of breath, which makes me smile. Micah is not an athlete, despite being very in shape. "How's your day been?"

"Not too bad. Yours?"

He sighs, and I pause, looking up at him, hopefully in a reassuring gesture. His ebony eyes are distant, and his shoulders are rigid. His hair is messy atop his head as if he's constantly been messing with it. He's stressed, it's clear to see.

His hoodie is clean, but the joggers have a stain or two on them from his lunch. We were sitting very close as he set up my computer for me, and he just smelt clean and maybe there was a hint of lavender.

That's changed, instead, he just smells musky, masculine, even, if that can be classified as a scent.

"I know this might be a little weird, but um, do you want

to go for some coffee? I've had a rough day," he says, rubbing the back of his neck as he gives me a sheepish kind of look.

"Sure." If this were Malachi, or Atticus, I'd not hesitate to say no. But coming from Micah, I can't help but say yes. It's the sweet, nerdy kind of personality he has.

He steals my bag, and I don't even fight him on the issue. I'm weak. I'm so very weak. He's had a bad day. Yeah, I don't know why I'm trying to lie to myself. It's one thing lying to these men about not being a shifter, it's another thing trying to convince myself that Mal and Micah don't give me the same fuzzy feelings Atticus does.

"Want to talk about it?" I offer as we walk.

"I messed up," he groans and starts filling me in on the drama within the technology department. I don't understand a lot of it, and the names of people—I think, but they could also be types of software—are going over my head, but I can listen. I can be here for him as a friend. We spend over an hour talking, and I only pause the conversation when my phone buzzes.

Only three people have my number—*only one of them who I actually gave my number to*—and one of them is sitting in front of me. You know, the same man I'm convinced gave my number to his brother.

I frown, not liking that it's an alert from my security cameras—the ones Micah admitted to setting up for me, even though I told Atticus not to bother. They've detected movement at the front door, which is weird within itself, but it's the fact that there's nothing there. There's nothing there at all. It took me less than thirty seconds to open the app and for it to load from me getting the notification. If someone or something was there... how did it disappear so fast?

"What's wrong, pretty girl?" Micah asks, and when I

don't reply, he cups my cheek gently. "Nora? I can sense your panic. What's going on?"

"I think someone was at the house," I say, leaning into his touch. "But the app isn't showing anything."

"Your house?"

"Yes. I... I need to go home."

Should I go home, though? Should I stay at a hotel? I can't tell if the dread I'm feeling is because something is wrong or if it's because my brain recognises the fact that I'm being paranoid, and yet my body can't.

"Calm down," he soothes, standing from the table. "Let's go."

He's reassuring the entire drive over to the house, and I'm grateful that he drove. Once we get out of the car, he does a deep inhale before grinning.

"Nobody is here, pretty girl. I promise you—it's okay. Do you want me to check inside the house first? Or I could come in with you if you don't want to be left alone out here."

"Nobody's here?" I ask, and he promises again that nobody is home. I might not have my own extra senses, but for the first time, I'm grateful that he has his. "No, that's okay. Thank you for driving me over."

"Always," he replies, and when I still don't move, he squeezes my shoulder. "Are you sure you don't want me to come in?"

The hesitance in his questions is quite refreshing. Atticus would phrase it like a question whilst doing it regardless, and I feel like Malachi would just go in without even asking. Micah's not like those two, though, and I quite like that.

You know, if we were going to be friends.

But we're not, so it's irrelevant.

"I'm okay," I say, squeezing his hand before walking up

my path. As I open the front door, the automatic lights turn on... and there's a piece of paper on the floor. I crouch down, and pick it up, and a terrified shriek leaves my mouth.

It's a very familiar picture, and this time I can see it for what it is. *Fuck.*

A dead wolf—not a dog as I assumed earlier—with the words "this is you" on the top. Someone knows that I'm a wolf, and that's only reaffirming the fact that I need to pretend I'm not one. The shifter world is dangerous, and a lone wolf will never make it alone.

Micah's out of the car within a second and has me behind him as he scans the room for a threat. I manage to count to seventeen as I take deep breaths in and out before the tension fades from his body.

Keeping hold of me, he spins, looking down. "What's wrong?"

"Nothing..."

He raises one straight, bushy brow, and I sigh and show him the picture. I know it might make him and the other two more overbearing, but I'm not stupid. This is above my abilities, and I don't fight this hard every day to stay alive to have someone threaten me with a badly done drawing.

"Fucking shit." His eyes are darting around the room, searching for something. His breathing is heavy, and his eyes are wide. When he's finally reassured, he looks down at me and gently asks, "Do you want to head to a hotel? To my place? We'll get some clothes and get you safe. Then I'll find the person responsible."

"Micah," I whisper, unable to look away from his ferocious amber eyes.

"What do you need, pretty girl?" he replies, cupping my cheek as he holds me tight to him. "I want to throw you over my shoulder and drag you to my place and keep you there.

But I can see that'll only scare you more, so I need you to work with me and tell me how I can help."

"Thank you for being honest."

He rolls his eyes, pursing his heart-shaped lips. His full bottom lip looks like a pout, and it takes away from the stern expression he's going for. "I'm counting to five—"

"Let's head inside," I say, and he groans. "Sorry."

"Don't be sorry."

He takes the sheet of paper, pocketing it before leading me inside. Like Atty did, he locks up, double-checking both doors and the windows, and makes his rounds around the house. I love how thorough he's being, and it really helps me feel safe... but he's locked himself inside the house with me. I don't think it was an accident.

"All clear," he says, not even ten minutes later. "Now, you are still too stressed for my liking."

That scent thing, I swear. "You locked yourself in."

"Good thing about locks, pretty girl, is you can undo them." He teases, winking at my gaped expression. "Once you're calmer, I'll head home, but for now, you need me here, and you need to feel safe. So, what do you do to relax?"

"Um..." I usually cry. I don't have good relaxation methods other than breathing properly and crying.

"Atticus mentioned you've not seen any *Big Bang Theory*," he says, tugging me through to the living room. Like Atticus, he doesn't shy away from making himself at home. "So, let's start that."

"I don't know..."

"About the show or me being here?"

"Both?"

He rolls his eyes, pulling off his jacket, before placing my feet in his lap. He gently takes off my shoes and gestures for me to take off my coat. It's relaxing... it's normal.

But it's not okay. Not even a little bit.

"Well, if you hate the show, we can put something else on," he says, shrugging. "I don't understand why you're denying yourself... but I don't really have the right to demand answers. Pretend I'm a friend, who doesn't have a tiger, and you're just a girl without a wolf. I'm aware nothing really happened, but that scream, pretty girl, it tore through me. Your panic was real. Don't push me away."

I hate that he's speaking sense when I'm so panicked. "Okay. I'll make some tea."

"I'll order pizza," he says. "And set up the show."

"Okay... how many sugars?"

He lazily grins at me. "Is this a secret test?"

I shrug, but yes, of course. "No..."

"And if I say I have none?"

"I'll judge you." He laughs, a beautiful sound that has me smiling, too. "And also refuse to make you one."

"I have two sugars and maybe a three for milk on the scale."

"Oh, and I just know this scale, do I?" I ask, leaning back. His hands are rubbing my feet as we sit, and it just makes me want to stay here. Atticus has that enticing smile, Micah gives foot rubs... how the fuck am I going to convince the illogical part of me that we don't want these men?

"Well, you work in an office with clients. I presume you make them tea. Wait... are you one of those mean people who makes them have it your way? I can totally see that, with the way you judged me for having no sugars."

"Even worse, I don't offer them tea," I tease.

"I knew it! You're evil, pretty girl."

I roll my eyes, getting more comfortable. "I don't want to get up."

"I wasn't sold on the idea of tea, to be honest," he says,

winking at me. "And if you grab the remote from the table, we don't even need to move."

"You might just be my new favourite person."

"Big praise."

It really is. I grab the remote and hand it over, the action as instinctual as letting Atticus drive. He logs into a Netflix account that definitely doesn't belong to me and selects his profile. Once he sets up the show, he pulls the blanket off the back of the settee and wraps it around me.

"Food is ordered," he says quietly before reaching over to flick my forehead. "Don't think too hard, pretty girl. I texted Atticus to order it."

"You asked Atticus?" I ask.

"Well, we're normal people tonight," he reminds me, squeezing my calf. "And I couldn't resist making my boss do something for me."

"I just meant I thought you'd go to Mal."

He groans, causing me to giggle. "I was right. You are evil. Next time Kai's first on the list. It'd definitely be funnier if we made him go get it for us."

"Then he'd want to join us," I point out.

Micah shrugs, and I love the smile on his face. "That's not a bad thing. Kai's an ass, but he's a good brother."

"I wasn't—" He cuts me off, placing his finger to my lips.

"No, I know you weren't. But this only works if we're honest. I'd not be upset if both Kai and Atticus were here. Believe me, pretty girl, I want to steal you for moments alone, but I can share."

I snort, and he glances at me in a *well, talk* kind of way. "I'm not doubting your ability..." I'm just confused as to why he thinks I'd cut things off with Atticus to then accept all three of them.

"Atticus is one of the most selfless people I have ever

met. Kai's also one of the most protective. Both of them are dominant and leaders... but they're not selfish people." Clearly, neither is Micah. He's selfless, loyal... *too good for me.*

"Again, not what I meant. I'm not doubting that you're good at timekeeping, but emotionally... I don't think they're very good at that."

"Neither are you," he says, and I sigh. "Let's play a game."

"But they've just met a hot neighbour," I argue, pointing at the TV. "I need to see what happens."

"Pretty girl, you can't fool me. You're not watching it because you didn't laugh at the entire first part and it's hilarious. So, favourite colour?"

"Orange."

A dramatic gasp is all I hear. "I would not have guessed you'd go for such a mundane and boring colour."

"I know for a fact yours is something mainstream like green."

"Well, accurate, but not completely. It's 1BFF0E." I pause, confused, and he roars with laughter. He's carefree in this moment, completely and utterly relaxed. But I'm missing the joke.

"Sorry," he says, rubbing the back of his neck with red tinges across his cheeks. "That's the HEX code for my favourite colour."

That's actually kind of adorable. "Cute. Okay, so if you were in a fight, what animal would you want at your back?"

"A dragon."

"Dragons aren't real."

"Neither are shifters."

"I said animal," I argue before rolling my eyes. *That was a stupid question on my behalf.* "You're very literal. Okay, new question, if you could only eat one food for the rest of your life, what would it be?"

"Pizza," he says, pushing my legs off him as he stands up. I frown, but he points to the door. "Pizza is here."

Oh.

There goes his shifter senses. I count the seconds he's gone, straining my ears to try and hear the click, scared to be alone. I don't think the threatening letter was anything more than one of the other shifters playing a prank... but my anxiety doesn't like to listen to logic. No, instead, it likes to creep in on the moments I'm alone and overwhelm my system.

When you're alone, it's so much harder to fight the demon that is your own mind. I just wish I could tolerate being around people and showing my weaknesses.

When you have to put on a front all day, you develop the friendly alter ego. Work me is a completely different person to home me. That bitch is so perky and nice, and me... I'm one breath away from a mental breakdown. *Always.* It's scary how easy it is to slip into the mask, the fakeness.

If I want to have someone around during the weak moments... I'll need to learn to let down my guard and let them in.

But when this mask has been my protection, the way I can compartmentalise life so that I can make it through the day, it's not as simple as playing the get to know each other game.

Micah returns with food, and even though I'm more subdued, he doesn't let that phase him. He's still chatty and friendly... he's just being himself.

If only I could do that, then maybe things would be simpler.

∞

Micah

"She's asleep."

"Good. Now what the fuck has happened?" Atticus demands, the panic he's feeling at his mate being targeted is shared across our pride bond.

The Alpha is terrified for his mate, and I don't pity the fool on the other end of things. I quickly fill him in on what happened, making sure to explain how extra spooked it made her. I don't understand the level of terror she had when she found the note because it's not even that scary.

It's enraging, but it's a pathetic attempt to hurt her. *But it worked.*

"Orson's away, but once he's back, I'll get him to help me work some shit out," Kai says. *"Check the cameras. See what you can find out."*

"We need to change the locks here," I say, already having the plan to go through the footage. The problem is that I'd need to move to do it, and I don't want to risk waking her up. She's gorgeous, and she's sleeping so peacefully. I really don't want to fuck with that.

"I'll get someone over tonight," Atticus says. *"Potentially tell her that it was me who did that. I'd rather she's only pissed at one of us at a time, and I can take the hit."*

"Most mates would want their mate to not be pissed at any of them."

"I'm her Alpha. There is going to be many times when she gets pissed at decisions I make. Add in the fact that Mal is a complete and utter jackass, and well, you're probably the only one ever safe from her being mad at."

"Hey," my brother protests, although I know he's

probably smirking about it. *"Anyway, check the cameras. I'll be over in fifteen with Paul, and we'll make some upgrades to our girl's place. It should help her feel more secure."*

"Get her into bed," Atticus adds. *"I don't want her sleeping on her sofa."*

"Ah, isn't he cute," Kai says, and I don't need to be there to know Atticus either punched him or threw something at him depending on how close together they're sitting. My brother lives to wind up our Alpha, and Orson, but that's an entirely different game for him.

I disconnect and heave a sigh before picking up my mate. She's so fucking tiny, but she cuddles in closer. In her sleep, Nora knows she's my mate. Her dormant wolf—a phrase that even thinking only confuses me—understands the connection. In fact... she welcomes it. Why can't Nora feel the same way?

A tiny whimper from her has my tiger furious, and I sigh. Someone has done damage to my girl, but I won't let it be irreparable.

Malachi, Atticus, and I are here to stay. Even if it takes a decade to convince her, we're not letting her go.

But first, her house needs an upgrade. We're going to make sure she's safe, one step at a time.

9

9

NORA

*D*o you ever have those days where you wake up, and absolutely nothing has happened yet, but you still think it would be better off if you were dead?

Like, sure, it sounds dramatic that the moment you open your eyes you're already thinking about offing yourself.

But that's not necessarily what I mean. It's 6:43 am, and I didn't get to sleep until around 4, when my brain finally shut off. I've got 2 minutes, literally, until my alarm goes off to tell me to shower so that I don't look like a mess at work.

A mess that I most definitely am, but I need to work on hiding because I can't give these people another reason to doubt me.

Then, I've got a fifteen minute window to shower, with thirty minutes to then get dressed and leave the house so that I can make it to work for my start time of 8 am.

Which brings me to my actual day of work where Atticus, Malachi, and even Micah, to a degree, will beg for my attention as I try to get my footing with the new place. Seb will inevitably get on my nerves somehow, and I need to pretend that I don't mind his repeated questions, whilst the rest of the staff judge me and make me feel unwelcome.

All the while, I'm trying to remind myself that living is the best thing.

That if I were dead, I'd not be happy or sad or tired. I'd just be dead.

I'd be nothing.

But damn, on this bleary morning in the middle of winter—well, autumn, but it's so close to the beginning of December that it's practically winter—does nothing sound better than just not existing.

And that is true mental illness. It's not the obvious sign, not really. It's not like the crying, or being unable to get out of bed, or the panic attacks. Not the insomnia, or the under-eating, or the struggling to do self-care.

It's the hidden thoughts, the ones nobody can see or truly understand, the ones that would get you locked up if anyone could hear them.

It's the genuine belief that, even just for a moment, you'd be better off being nothing than just being alive.

The fact that this kind of thought is my first thought should be mildly concerning, but it's not. Because this morning is still somehow a good morning because when the alarm goes off, I manage to haul myself out of bed to get dressed for work.

And that's a win.

Another win is the fact that my clothes are finally here from Callent, and after being washed, dried, and ironed, they're ready to be worn. It's a small dose of happiness, the familiarity of being able to wear clothes that I like, and one I truly need to get through the day.

I put on a black blouse, and pair it with the knee-length plum skirt. My heels are the required length, although I've noted when reading the employee handbook that there's no actual requirement for this branch like there was at my old place.

Still, I like to keep things the same, and these help with that. Even if I'd be more comfortable in a pair of flats.

I tell myself, though, that the heels help people take me a little more seriously. I'm short, I know that, and the four inches on the heels give the impression I'm not *as* short. 5'6" is better than 5'2", even if it's just so that I can reach the cabinets to get a mug for my tea.

Because I refuse to ask for help, even if it would be given.

The drive to work doesn't take long, and unsurprisingly, Malachi is waiting for me as I pull into my bay. You know, the bay that has a sign on it with my name, despite the fact that nobody else has their own personalised space—not even Atticus, the CEO.

But when I left the building on Monday at, like, nine PM, Malachi was furious that I was parked so far away, and then this showed up on Tuesday.

I decided not to park in it, my little act of rebellion, but it was a futile attempt because Malachi came and took my keys and moved my car for me. I'm not sure if he went out to check or if someone reported on me for him, but either way, it's invasive as fuck.

Good job lying to yourself, Nora. We don't appreciate the nice gifts from the pretty men who want to be your friend.

"Good morning, little wolf," Malachi murmurs, sniffing my neck as I brush past him. "Cherries, as usual."

Overbearing, as usual.

"Morning, Mal," I reply, looking him up and down with narrowed eyes. Something is different about him, and I don't know what. "You look nice."

"As do you, baby," he replies, swiping my bag from me

and the box of files that I have in my boot. "Atticus isn't in today—"

"Is he okay?" I bite my lip, my cheeks flushing as he gives me a knowing look.

"He's fine. Pride business, you know?"

"Pride is normally in June, so I don't know, actually," I say, avoiding looking at him because I know my expression will give me away, and instead smile at Keely, one of the paralegals on my floor.

She's kind of sweet, but she doesn't return the gesture, instead going to meet up with another member of my team.

"I wish you'd stop with these games," he mutters, opening the door for me without dropping my things, a skill I'm pretty impressed by. "But Micah is in, and I'm here, too, if you need anything."

"If I need HR or tech support, I'll be sure to reach out."

"Ah, I love the chase," Malachi says with a smirk. We get in the lift, and he immediately grumbles under his breath when Seb gets on with us.

"Nora, hey," Seb says, smiling at me. He's wearing his usual business attire, today's suit pants being a dark grey. There's a tiny stain on the left side of his chest, some kind of red—wine?—that he's not got out properly. "You were in such a hurry to leave last night—"

"Do you classify an eight-thirty finish on a Tuesday night, hurrying out of here?" I ask, tilting my head in fake confusion. Mal might not be my boss, not the one I directly report to, anyway, but he is the head of HR, and I refuse to let Seb paint me as a terrible employee.

Malachi snorts, clearly not bothered, but Seb just shakes his head with wide, dark blue eyes.

"No, of course not. I just meant when we were talking—" His tone grates on me, but I don't know if that's just because of the feelings he ignites when around me, or if it's genuinely an annoying voice. He over accentuates the vowels, dragging them out longer than they need to be, but I suppose I can't hate the man for that reason.

"Ah, maybe she just didn't like the topic of conversation," Malachi says as we come to a stop on mine and Seb's floor. Mal smirks, barging past Seb and holding the doors open for me. As I step off the lift, Mal goes, "Or more accurately, the conversation participant."

Seb flushes, a bright red covering his cheeks. "See you later, Nora," he mutters, holding onto an envelope. Mal and I walk over to my office, and I do my best to not feel guilty over the scene with Seb.

He makes me uncomfortable, and I don't like spending time with him. Plus, I didn't do anything, so I have absolutely no reason to feel guilty.

But that's not really a reason to evade guilt. It actually makes it worse. I should've told Mal to stop, to intervene on Seb's behalf. If I truly cared, I would have.

"What's got your mind whirring, little wolf?" Mal asks, his arms flexing as he drops the box of files onto my desk. He heads over to the fridge in the corner and grabs an apple juice.

I watch in surprise, since he always seems to steal my water, and he pierces the film before passing it to me.

"What?" I ask, looking at the juice before him in confusion. "Do you need me to hold it for you?"

"I want you to drink it," he replies. He walks around my desk and knocks on the space heater, the room immediately starting to warm up. "Now, Nora."

The sharp tone has me instinctively obeying, and I know it's more than that when I see his stupid amber eyes. He has used his animal's magnetism to make me obey, and the teeny, tiny part of me that used to belong to his world recognises that.

Damn it.

I finish the juice, though.

"Good girl," he murmurs, his voice low and husky. I don't know if he's deliberately trying to make himself seem seductive, but I've decided the feelings it ignites within me —you know, the tingles in my core, the weak knees, and the desperateness for his touch—are *not* because I like the way he sounds, and are simply just because I'm glad I pleased him.

My colleague—not boss—who is several ranks higher.

I'm totally not the virgin with the praise kink. No, I'm not that cliche.

Mal's phone rings, and he sighs. "It's Cara." His personal assistant. "I've got a meeting. Call me if you need me, or get Micah." Then after a longing look that I can't understand, he disappears so that I can actually get on with my day.

I protest, maybe even a little too loudly, about their company, but I kind of like that they're still around.

But that's a tiny but because deep down, I know that's stupid. I refuse to let hope build in my chest, since I know this is never going to work.

Not when I'm as damaged as I am.

∞

"Hey, are you free for lunch?" Seb asks, and I barely manage to pull my eyes away from the screen before there's a snarl from someone behind him. Relief fills me, and I hate myself for it because that snarl belonged to Atticus.

You know, the man who isn't meant to be here today, and

so to hear him, I get a little thrill run through me. A thrill I want no part in because Atticus and I are merely colleagues, and it should fill me with dread that the CEO is coming to see how I'm doing.

"Sir," Seb says, spinning with a surprised look on his face. I catch another stain on the back of his shirt, and wrinkle my nose. He's not very put together today. "It's so good—"

"Nora's busy," Atticus says, his crisp tone sounding sharp and annoyed despite winking at me over Seb's head. "Please see yourself out."

"Yes, I understand." With a jerky nod, Seb practically knocks Atticus over on his way out of the building.

I sit back in my chair, a cool smile on my face. "What can I do for you, Atticus?"

He's wearing a pale blue shirt with a dark blue jacket and trousers. His tie is the same shade as his suit jacket, but it has white dots on it. He's pretty hot, and I didn't realise that suits were my type.

But they are, especially on him.

"No Atty today?" He doesn't wait for a response, though, closing the door behind him as he saunters over to my desk. "I've not seen you all day, so I wanted to come and say hi."

"Hi."

"Hi," he murmurs, dropping his lips to my forehead in a chaste kiss before leaning on my desk. His buttocks, the toned, meaty cheeks, are sitting on my desk, and I'm so tempted to touch them. "How has your day been?"

"Good," I reply, turning my chair to look at him properly. "How is it that the CEO of a very busy company has the time to come down and bug little old me every day?"

"I've got very good staff who work for me who can handle the day to day without me micromanaging, which gives me plenty of time to spend with you," he replies with a shrug.

"I see. So, they're good at their jobs and I'm not, is what you're saying?" I say, smirking when his eyes widen and panic fills his gaze. "I'm kidding, calm down. I get it." Well, I don't, which is our big issue.

I can't understand why a man like him—and, surprisingly, my issue is that he's a lion shifter and not a *billionaire*—would want anything to do with someone like me.

But he sighs in relief at my words, grabbing my coffee mug from the desk. I watch with narrowed eyes as he brings the rim to his lips, and takes a sip before exhaling like it's the nicest thing ever.

"You little thief!" I gasp, and he chuckles as he places it back onto the mug warmer. "Go bother someone else."

"I will. Soon." I frown, the push and pull upsetting me as it always does when jealousy rears its ugly head, and I think about him going to see other people. He sighs, and that's when I realise that today's visit might not be about me at all. His next words only confirm that. "I had a shitty meeting, and I just wanted five minutes where I don't need to be the boss."

I nod slowly, taking him in properly. There's tension in his shoulders, his frown lines prominent from where he's spent all day with a glower on his face. He's stressed, and I immediately feel guilty for being mean when he's not really asking for anything but a few moments of my time.

"What did you do today?"

I fill him in on my very boring morning, but he listens like it's the most fascinating thing he's ever heard. It's nothing exciting, but he makes me feel important when he gives me his full attention.

As I watch some of the tension fade out of him, I feel warm and happy. I did that. I helped.

Even if I don't want whatever fake connection Atticus thinks we have, the feeling of being able to help someone will always make me feel good.

"Thank you," he murmurs a few minutes later.

"Anytime."

His phone buzzes in his hands, and he sighs before saying goodbye. He heads out and the fact that I need to turn my space heater on to warm the room has nothing to do with the absence of him.

∞

"Hey, Nora!" Seb's voice hits my ears a moment before I see him, and I paint a fake smile on my face as he jogs over to me. How he can jog in those loafers, I have no idea. "I've been trying to catch you all day."

"I've been a little busy," I say, glancing up to the left corner of the room where a camera is. I spot the red flashing light, reassuring me to know they're on and someone is on the other end.

Not that I expect anything to happen, but just on the off-chance.

"Totally get it. It's hard being the boss," he says, puffing out his chest. "I'd know."

Mhm, so he claims. Except his employment records show different.

But it's not worth getting into it. "Yes, sure."

He opens his briefcase, pulling out an envelope that he hands to me. I frown at it, and when I look back up at him, he seems the exact same as always—slimy and overly eager.

"What's this?" I ask. "An invitation?"

"An invitation? You mean, if I offered one you'd accept?"

Ignoring the eagerness in his tone, I ask, "So if not an invitation, what is this?"

"Someone put it under your door yesterday whilst you were out."

"If it was under my door, how do you have it?"

He avoids looking at me, instead, motioning to it and changing the subject. "So, what is it?"

"Private," I snap, walking away from him.

"You should've said thank you," he calls, the cold, detached tone causing me to freeze. Tingles race down my spine, and when I turn back around, he's gone.

What the fuck?

I hurry into my office and open the letter before sighing. Another one. Pulling open the bottom drawer of my desk, I throw this into the pile of graphic images that I've received.

I first received an image six days ago, on Friday of last week, but I seem to get one or two a day. I've hidden them in here, not sure what to do about it.

I keep denying that I'm a wolf, that I've got no contact with the shifter world, so hopefully, eventually, people will stop looking deeper.

A knock on the door has my attention darting upwards, and I guiltily slam the drawer. Micah is on the other side, a frown on his face.

"Hey, Micah!" He's got on the same clothes as yesterday, and I get the feeling he's not gone home since I last saw him.

"Hi, pretty girl. You done for the day?"

I look at the piles of work before nodding slowly. I don't want to be here anymore, not alone where I'm vulnerable. "Yeah."

"Amazing. I'll walk you down," he replies.

Normally, I'd fight it, and based on the surprise on his face, he expected that. But I don't have it in me. Not right now.

I woke up this morning thinking about being dead.

I never considered it wouldn't be by my own hand.

10

NORA

"Nora?" Atticus calls, and I hold in my frustration as we run into each other for the fourth time today.

As the CEO of a very large business, I can't understand how he has time to come bother me *every single day*. Yet without fail, he comes to say hi, he bumps into me in the coffee room—we're on two completely different floors, and considering he's the very big boss, I'm sure he has someone whose job it is to get him coffee—and seems to have a sense of any time I need to use the lift *because he's always in it*.

And don't even get me started on Malachi. With him being only the floor above, he's got even more chances to come down here. Micah is the only one who seems to act normal at the office. Imagine the carefree, energetic techie being the normal one. It's crazy.

I've been here for just over two weeks now, and it's been an adjustment. I'm still trying to find my feet, something they're annoyingly helping with.

"Yes, sir?" I ask, turning to look at him when he knocks on my door frame again. He looks nice, the messy look with the hot as fuck dark suit that contrasts against his sandy skin.

His beauty is something I'm sure he knows, but his nostrils flare when I call him sir.

"Are you free this evening?"

"For?" I don't want to be free, but I am, as he well knows. *Damn it.*

"A work event." By the smirk on his face, I highly doubt this is purely a work event. He's not that slick, despite him thinking he is.

"What kind of work event?"

"A kind whereas your boss, I can demand you be there."

"You know, I could always file a report with HR," I mention, and his eyes flash amber as he steps in and closes the door.

"I'm more than happy to get a representative to come speak to you. Mal's free," he offers, and I groan. "But why don't you talk to me about your concerns first? As the boss, I like to take a hands on approach to dealing with my staff."

"Well, last time I talked to you about my concerns, you fired half the office and forced me to move here." Okay, he fired one person, but still.

"And now that branch is doing amazingly well, and employee satisfaction has risen. I'm good at my job, Nora, and I like my people to be happy. That includes you."

I sigh, closing the document I was working on and stand up. "I appreciate the concern, but I'm fine. What can I do for you, *sir*?"

As expected, his nostrils flare, and his eyes are now purely amber. His cat is on the surface, and I still don't know what kind of predator he is. He's a lion... but that doesn't narrow down the game he's playing.

"Believe me, Nora, there's a lot you could do for me," he

murmurs, his voice deeper... more primal. *Fuck.* "But for now, you're going to go and buy a dress ready for tonight. We've got a gala to attend, and I need you by my side."

Who throws a gala on a Wednesday?

"Don't you already have a date?" I ask, my voice small. A twinge of something unfamiliar slices through me, but it's gone almost as fast as it appeared.

"Yes."

My face drops, and I nod. "No worries. I'll head out now."

I turn away from him, hating how messed up that made me feel. I grab my bag and rifle through it to check I have my purse. I have absolutely no right to act this upset, and yet, it hurts. Why is he bothering me every day if he has someone else? Do I even have the right to be upset if I can't ever be with him? He knows I was a wolf, despite me denying it, so why is he playing this game when he has a mate out there that will be perfect for him?

He can't be mine, even if I had a wolf and wished it to be true. I'm not able to be loved anymore.

"Wait, Nora, that's not what I meant," he says, frustration lacing his tone as he storms forward.

"Don't worry about it," I say, chirpily. I pull my bag onto my shoulder and turn to look at him with a fake smile on my face. He steps into my space, and before I can step back, his hand immediately reaches up to cup my cheek. His ocean blue eyes bore into mine, reading something from me that I don't even realise I gave.

"I would like it if you'd be my date," he says quietly. "Please?"

"Atticus... I can't," I whisper, shaking my head as tears well up in my eyes. "You're my boss."

"And?"

I've made so much progress over the past few years, but when I'm around him... I can feel my mind plotting against me to undo it all. It's terrifying. All my hard work in putting myself back together can be undone by this man—these men because Micah and Malachi are just as good at giving my brain ammunition.

The three of them could be so good for me. If they weren't shifters, that is.

"And?" he asks again.

I groan but still don't move away from him. I can't move away from him. "Atty, please."

His gaze softens, and as my bag slips, he rights it on my shoulder before placing his hand on my waist. He's trapping me in his arms, and my body loves it. "No matter how much you push me away, little queen, I'm not going anywhere."

"I can't have a relationship," I tell him, my voice shaky despite me trying to be strong. My body is betraying me. My mind is betraying me. *How am I meant to keep going?* "I can't do this with you."

The door opens, and I try to pull back, but Atticus doesn't move. He doesn't even glance at the door, which only confuses me.

"Is she being difficult again?" Malachi asks, and I hold in my groan. Here is problem number two, and surprise, surprise, *he's not working*. It's a wonder these two make money because they never seem to do anything.

"As usual," Atticus teases, grinning at me. "But she's going to come to the gala as my date."

"Sounds good," Malachi says, walking over to us. He's wearing a navy suit with pinstripes, and I hate to admit it but I don't like it. He still looks delectable, but it's just not his style. He presses a kiss to my forehead, something that has me confused, before grabbing a bottle of water from my fridge.

"You two have no boundaries."

"Where you're concerned, we have no need for them, little wolf," Malachi says, sitting on top of my desk. At least he was kind enough to move the documents out of the way. "Now, what colour are you going with for your dress? I want to match."

"She's my date," Atticus argues, letting go of my cheek and giving me some breathing room, even if he doesn't let go of my waist. "You should have asked her first if you wanted to match outfits."

"And risk your wrath?" Malachi drawls. He winks at me, showing me he truly is just teasing. "You're hilarious."

"I never agreed to go as your date," I say, cutting off their fighting.

"You cited some reason like me being your boss," Atticus says, shrugging. "I don't really care about that reasoning. I'm the King around here, little queen, and that's always going to be how things work. Any other arguments?"

"You're not King."

They both burst out laughing, and I hold in my frustration. They're gorgeous, and I have absolutely no idea why they're wasting their time with me. I can't be their mate, and that's the only reason I can think of for their actions. I had a mate who left me, and I'm not worthy of a second chance.

Who would want the mentally unstable wolf-less wolf?

"Fuck, you're funny," Malachi says, grinning. He grabs his wallet from a secret pocket inside his suit—something I'm extremely jealous about since my suit jacket has two *fake* pockets. "But for now, here's the company card. Go buy a pretty dress."

"I have my own money."

"That you get from working here?" Atticus asks, and I nod. "Then, either way, you're spending my money. Why does the account it comes from matter?"

"Atty, that's really not how earnings work," I sigh, looking into his earnest gaze. "I get paid for working here. You're not just gifting me the money. My pay check might come from the business, and ultimately you, but that doesn't mean it's not mine once it hits my account. I worked for it."

The surprised expression on his face makes me giggle, and Malachi hands me the card.

"Think of it as a company expense," Mal says, rubbing the back of his neck. Yeah, he doesn't believe that lie either.

"Why is my name on this card then?" I demand. The card isn't your average bank card either. It's a Coutt card that is purple in colour and has world written all over it. It's like the next level for bank cards, and he's just gifting it to me for nothing.

Not for nothing. And there goes my mind, trying its best to create even more friction.

"Do you want the truth, or do you want to continue pushing us away?" Atticus asks. I sigh and place it into my purse. It's not worth the fight. I can take it and just never use it—*way to go, standing strong against the men, Nora.* "Now I have got a car here that can take you to some places that can get a dress fitted in time for tonight... if that's okay?"

Malachi scoffs, and Atticus punches him. Children. Immature little children.

"Sure," I say, massaging my temples. "That would be great, thank you."

"Have you got a headache?" Atticus asks, his eyebrows drawing together as he lowers his voice. "I'm sorry, little queen."

"Are we being too loud?" Malachi asks, his tone equally as quiet as Atticus's. "Here, have a drink of this. It'll help if you're dehydrated."

Atticus pulls out his phone and dials a number, his eyes raking over me in concern as he does.

"Who are you calling?" I ask.

"A doctor."

"Atty, hang up. I'm fine." They're intense. They're so fucking intense, yet it's hard to be mad when it's super sweet how they both care about me. "I promise, I'm really okay. Please, hang up."

"Fine," he mutters, petulantly tucking his phone into his back pocket. "I was just trying to help you."

"I know, and I really appreciate it," I say softly. *Peacekeeper.* "But I've got to go buy my dress for tonight."

"Want me to come with?" Atticus offers. "I can help. Fuck it, I'm coming. Mal, cancel my meetings."

"Sounds good," Malachi says, grinning at my confusion. He beckons me to come forward, and I frown but edge closer. He bends his head, and with his lips hovering at my ear, he whispers, "I cancelled them before coming down here."

"What?" I gasp. The whispering was for show since Atticus can hear him, but I'm surprised he took that initiative.

"Have fun with Atticus, baby, I'll see you tonight," he murmurs, kissing my cheek.

"Let's go," Atticus commands, and I'm surprised, but let him lead me out of the office. Nobody even looks up as we exit—something I know is to do with Atticus's animal—and it's not until we get into the back of a car that I feel myself relax a little.

"So, you can just take afternoons off to take some

random manager shopping?" I ask softly. I'm scared he's missing important meetings to cater to me, and I hate that.

"You're not just some random manager," he snarls, reaching over to double-check I did my belt properly. "I can smell your confusion... why do you pretend you don't know about our world?"

"Of course I know about the world," I say quietly, looking out of the window. "We live in the UK—"

"—that's not what I meant, and you know it. Talk to me, Nora."

"Atty, this isn't fair," I sigh. "You're not even on my level."

"You're right about that," he says gently, rising to the bait this time. He reaches for my hand, ever so gently lifting it to his lips, and presses the sweetest of kisses to my knuckles. "You're way above me, Nora, I know that."

Why does he need to be so sweet? Why does he need to drop his tasks to take me shopping and buy me a dress to accompany him to events? *Why does he care about me?*

It's the chase, isn't it? I'm making things harder on myself by letting them chase me. They're predators, and this is the ultimate hunt.

"We're here," the driver says, pulling in front of a very expensive boutique. The driver's wearing a suit, and one of those cute little fedora hats. Atticus gets out without even thanking the man, and I hold in my sigh.

The driver grins at me through the rearview mirror, a soft smile on his face that matches his kind eyes.

When Atticus appears at my door, opening it for me, I can't help but smile despite my frustration at him being rude to the driver.

"Thank you very much," I say to the driver, giving Atticus a pointed glare. He shrugs and offers me his hand.

The action is extremely foreign to me, but it still gives me butterflies.

"Any idea what kind of dress you want?"

"Oh, not even a little bit," I say, not able to keep the smile off my face. "I think we could be here for a few hours whilst I try dresses on."

"That's good with me," he replies, opening the door for me. "I told you, little queen, there's no place I'd rather be."

Looks like my plan backfired.

$$\infty$$

*N*ot only did we buy a dress, but he made sure I had shoes, jewellery and even organised for someone to come do my make-up. When I argued—which, sadly, I didn't do a good enough job of doing as is the theme lately—he reminded me it was a work event, so the business would cover it. He still can't wrap his head around the fact that people's earnings are not actually his money either.

I have absolutely no idea who his accountant is, but I guarantee he's not going to be able to write off my outfit as a business expense. Then again, I wouldn't really bet against him, so I'd just not argue and agree that it was needed if I was the government. I'd be a terrible government agent.

Now I'm nearly ready for tonight. My hair is done, my make-up is perfect, and even my nails are painted a midnight blue colour to match the dress. All I need to do is put the dress on, and I'm ready. I'm nervous because no matter how many times I asked—*once, I only asked once*—Atticus wouldn't reveal what tonight was about. He says it's a work event... but nobody at the office mentioned it.

I really hope this isn't a pack event because I might lose

my shit. Not in an angry way, either. No, in a major panic attack-type of way.

Is it too late to call things off?

Someone knocks at the door, and I sigh. This is probably him. I grab my iPad to check the doorbell app, but I don't recognise who is at the door. There's a man, short and stodgy, with a balaclava covering his face. It doesn't instil confidence in me at all. He knocks again, and I can see the iPad starting to shake.

I dial a number I never thought I'd use first, grateful he input it into my phone.

"Hey, little wolf," Malachi greets. "What's up? Need helping zipping up your dress? I love that you called me and not Atticus or Micah."

"I, um, that's not... I really need your help."

"I'm on the way," he replies, his tone serious. "What's going on?"

Another knock sounds at the door, and Malachi curses as there's a low murmuring in the background. "Fuck. I'm going to transfer you to Micah, okay? I need to shift. I'll be five minutes. It's going to be okay, baby."

"Hey, pretty girl," Micah greets not even a second later. The forced cheeriness is barely heard over my heart palpitations. "We're on our way, too. Atticus is driving, which is going to be hilarious. I had no idea he had the knowledge to drive himself."

"Me neither," I whisper, which isn't true. Atticus has driven me on more than one occasion, but I appreciate the fact that Micah's trying to keep me calm. There's another knock at the door, causing me to jump. "Micah, I really don't know who it is. I can't... don't have the abilities to protect myself."

"That's okay, Kai's nearly there," Micah soothes. "Are you

ready? Unless this guy turns out to be a serial killer, we're probably still going to the event. Are you excited?"

"For a boring work event?" I whisper, my eyes not moving from the screen in front of me. "Not really."

"See, it's boring for the big wigs, but we get to drink champagne and have a fun time," he replies. "We're only forced to go because Atticus—whoa dude, slow the fuck down."

I hear Atticus snarl, and he mutters something unintelligible.

"Kai's here," I say, diverting to Micah's nickname for him, as my eyes lock in on the tiger. Without hesitation, he pounces on the man at my door. The hood flies down, and before I can tell Micah I know who he is, a shriek leaves my throat because Malachi rips out the man's throat. *He rips out the man's throat.* Micah starts yelling, but I can't focus on his words, unable to do anything more than watch Malachi kill the man.

I called him here to help me, and he responded by murdering someone.

"Nora. Pretty girl, I need you to talk to me," Micah pleads, his fruity voice rising in pitch with his panic. "Atticus is losing his shit, and we really need you to let us know what's happening. Nora, please."

I hear his words, but they're going in one ear and out the other. I can't focus. I can't breathe. I'm an accomplice to murder.

As shifters, we're perceived as being dangerous. That's true, we can be dangerous, but humans are just as capable of doing harm. They have guns, we have claws. It's not a matter of the species as a whole being bad, but it depends on the person themselves. Our animals are primal, but it's up to us to control them.

We're not bad people.

I'm not a bad person.

Malachi is.

"Open the door, Nora," he says, after shifting back. Somehow, his silvery grey suit is still pristine, which is the only sign that he's not rattled. The heavy breathing, the angry glare, the flickering of his eyes between amber and light blue, however, all show that he's pissed off. "You have one chance before I rip it off the damn hinges." The tiger within him is echoing his words with a deep growl that gives me shivers.

"Nora, baby, open the door for Mal," Atticus says gently. I can't move. I can't hang up the phone. I can't run away. I'm rooted to the spot.

There's a bang, and when I hear something hit the wall, I know that Malachi is forcing his way inside.

I still can't move. I still can't react. My brain is trying to catch up with the horror my eyes just saw.

Malachi is a murderer.

11

MALACHI

"Is she coming?" Micah asks, sitting in front of me as I do his tie up. He's a fucking pain in the ass, but he's my brother. My baby brother at that. Our dad was never interested in teaching us how to do ties, and Micah has never bothered to learn, so it's always down to me.

Micah's suit is a dark grey three-piece that looks good on his seashell coloured skin tone, and he's paired it with a pair of tan loafers.

He hates the shoes, but like the suit, they're the same ones he wears *every single time* we have one of these events. He found one he liked, and has refused to buy a different kind.

It's extremely annoying."Yes," I repeat for the fifteenth time, trying to keep the annoyance out of my words. I don't know why he thinks she's not coming, and I really don't mind reassuring him, but I'm just ready to go.

I wipe away the spec of blood on his jaw from where he cut himself shaving. He might have been shaving for the last ten or so years, but he still manages to cut himself nearly every time. I swear, he needs a damn keeper.

"Her dress is pretty," Atticus says, spinning around with a grin on his face as I snarl at his words. Antagonistic prick. He's a fucking asshole, and he knows it.

Like Orson and I, Atticus tries to wear a different suit every time we host one of these events. As ridiculous as it is, clothes are a staple of success, and it's something people will scrutinise.

We're always broadcasting how good our pride is, and our wealth is a big part of that.

Atticus tends to keep his suits in the realm of blue—navy, royal blue, whatever his stylist decides is best—because he claims that they make his eyes look better. No, he clearly just likes the colour blue and pretends it's not his favourite colour.

Today's suit is a three-piece royal blue with a silvery white tie. His cufflinks are gold, a lion head just to be flashy, and so is his watch. You know, the watch that cost nearly the same amount as Micah's shitty car.

"We ready to go?" Atticus asks, still smirking over what he decided was a funny joke.

I'm surprised that he hasn't shaved. Atticus always keeps his beard neatly shaven, but today it's a little more rugged. *Hm, is he trying to impress Nora?* If facial hair is the way to do it, I'll grow my own out. Surely I can grow a better one than Atticus.

"Sure," I reply, straightening Micah's tie as he stands up. How the fuck he managed to mess it up by standing, I have no idea, but at least now it should be perfect. "Is Orson meeting us there?"

"He's going to be a little late," Atticus replies, and I nod despite the flash of irritation that rushes through me. If I were second... I sigh and shut that thought down. *I'm not.* "But, yes, he'll be there."

We make our way out to the car, me getting into the driver's seat. Atticus is a reckless driver and I don't really want our mate in the car with him behind the wheel, and Micah is far too slow. He's a fucking tiger, a car crash won't kill him. There's a difference between being safe and being a grandma—Micah is a grandma.

My phone rings, and I frown when I realise it's Nora. I answer it, ignoring Micah's frustration. If he knew it was her, I doubt he'd care about me being on the phone.

"Hey, little wolf," I say. "What's up? Need helping zipping up your dress? I love that you called me and not Atticus or Micah." Atticus growls, and I wink in response. Payback for him taunting me about her dress.

"I, um, that's not... I really need your help," she says, her voice shaking. If I was there, the scent of her fear would drive me crazy, but I'm not.

She's alone and in danger, and it's my fault for leaving her. I watched her house as the stupid hairstylist was there —make-up stylist, whatever—and when they left, I did, too. I thought she'd be okay for an hour until she met us at the gala. I was wrong.

"I'm on the way." I pull over at the side of the road and ask, "What's going on?" A very loud fucking knock sounds on the door, and I have my answer. Someone is going to pay for scaring her, and I'm going to be the one to dole out justice.

"I'll go," Atticus hisses.

"She called me," I remind him. Out loud, I can't hold in my curses as I see the figure at her door. "Fuck. I'm going to transfer you to Micah, okay? I need to shift. I'll be five minutes. It's going to be okay, baby."

I'm out of the car and shifting before she can reply,

making sure to focus so that my clothes remain in tact, and as much as I know Atticus is going to be pissed, we need to protect our mate. She's in danger. It's my job to fix it.

I make it to her house in record time—beating the five minutes I told her despite being at least fifteen minutes away—and when I see a hunter at her door, I don't hold back. I could smell the wolfsbane coming off him a mile away, and combining that with the other arsenal of drugs he has, I know he was going to try and hurt her.

Picking on the weak wolf is usually an easy kill. Picking on the weak wolf with three mates is a death sentence.

I rip out his throat, hating how easy it is, and start chewing his body. I hear her scream, and I know it's because she saw me murder someone, but the animal within doesn't care.

To him, this is the perfect way to show off his skills, to prove to our mate that we'll protect her from everything.

Part of me agrees with his logic.

The area is silent. She's unknowingly living on the outskirts of the pride's land. We're fucking idiots. She should've been at the centre where we could protect her.

The pathetic human makes a noise, and it only reminds me that I need to make this hurt. I need to make him suffer.

When he finally stops moving, I know he's dead. *Good.*

I shift, avoiding the blood as Atticus will whine about me making a scene at his event, and knock on the door.

"Open the door, Nora," I roar. I need to see her. I need to make sure she's okay. "You have one chance before I rip it off the damn hinges."

When it's silent, I shrug and kick down the door. I didn't hold back, and when it splinters against the wall, I barely pay it any attention as I walk forward. I round the corner, where she's sitting unresponsive. Her eyes are glossed over, but she's fucking gorgeous.

Her dark brown hair is in some kind of pattern with lots of little diamonds embedded in it, and around her neck is a matching necklace. She has earrings in and even bangles on her super slim wrists. She's wearing a short black robe, which I think will be better than her dress. My mate is fucking beautiful, but I hate the terrified look on her face. A look a fucking hunter put there.

I edge forward, not wanting to startle her, and hang up the phone. I don't give a fuck about Micah's complaints. She comes first. She always comes first.

"Hey there, little wolf," I coo, kneeling in front of her. "It's me, it's Kai."

"You killed him," she says, her tone as emotionless as her face. "I watched you kill him. You didn't stop. You started ripping his arms from his body. His legs are deformed. You mangled the poor man."

"That man was a hunter, baby," I reply, and it still doesn't snap her out of this. For someone who has been denying that she's a wolf, I'm surprised she's admitting that the tiger she saw was me. "I needed to protect you, little wolf. I'm sorry you saw it, but I won't apologise for the methods I use to keep you safe. You are the most important person in my entire fucking universe, and if I need to kill every threat that comes your way, believe me, I'll do it with a smile."

"You killed him," she whispers.

"I did."

I get up from my position and sit down next to her on the settee, pulling her into my side.

"Malachi, you're not a good person," she says quietly. "I called you for help, and you killed someone."

"I'm not going to apologise," I reply, shrugging. "He was

a hunter, Nora. I know you're pretending you're not a wolf, for whatever reason, and that's fine, but we both know how much danger you were in. I'm never going to apologise for protecting you."

I hear a car, which has me immediately back in defensive mode for less than three seconds. It goes on top of the grass and hits a rock, alerting me to it being Atticus and Micah.

He's a fucking terrible driver.

"Who broke the door?" Atticus snarls, rounding the corner.

"Guilty," I say, raising my hand. My girl's lips don't even budge into a small smile. *Fuck.*

He rolls his eyes, focusing on Nora. "Go put on your dress, Nora. I'm sending over pride members to pack up your house. You're not staying here."

"You don't get to decide that for me," she snaps, jumping up. Her spirit is admirable, but she's facing off against three more dominant males who all care about her. She's not winning this one.

Atticus storms forward, his lion having risen to the surface. "You misunderstood. This wasn't a choice I was giving you. You're a member of my pride, and as the King, as the Alpha here, I make the orders. *Now go put on your dress.*"

"This isn't over," she hisses before heading to her bedroom. At least she's no longer unresponsive.

"Well, she's going to be fun to live with," Micah exclaims. He's grinning, and I glare at his tie. Once it's on, if he stopped fucking fidgeting with it, it'd stay tied properly. "I'll organise for a team to come over now."

"No men," I demand, and he nods.

We wait in tense silence until Nora exits, her face pained, but she looks gorgeous.

She spins and asks, "Can someone zip me up?"

I don't try to fight Atticus for it—not that I'd win—because he needs this.

"I'm sorry," Atticus murmurs, shocking Micah and me. He's not one to apologise, and definitely not on the subject of safety. Although, we're probably going to be seeing a completely different side of him, now that we have her.

"You're sorry?" she asks, sounding breathless as his head dips to kiss her very bare shoulder.

"For shouting."

"Oh." The dejected tone is upsetting.

"What did you think he apologised for?" I ask as he zips her up.

"Thinking he can decide where I live," she says, spinning to look at us. She's breathtaking. The dress is hugging her figure and has flowers embroidered on it. It's dark blue and sparkles in the light. It's pretty, but she makes it look ethereal. All she's missing is a crown…

"Didn't you move here because I made it happen?" he asks, an eyebrow raised.

"Atty, if you want me to come to this event, I'd drop the attitude," she says, not backing down from his glower. "You are not my boyfriend, you're my boss. You forced me to move because of a new position at another branch, and I'm going to this stupid event because you said it's a work thing. Let's not blur the boundaries any further."

"Like I said, little queen, I'm the King, and you will do as I say," he murmurs. "Safety is a non-negotiable topic. You're weak right now, and that makes you vulnerable. Do you know what would happen to me if I lost you?"

"You'd find someone else to bug?" she asks, her face twisting at her own words.

Micah glances at me, confused, and I shake my head. This is Atticus's time with her, not ours.

"That's not even a little bit true," he says gently. "You're the only person I want to bug. You're the only person that could ruin me, Nora. If something happened to you, I'd go feral, and the only person able to bring me back would be you. We can talk properly after the gala, but just know you mean everything to me."

"I don't understand," she whispers, glancing at me and then Micah.

"You said you didn't know this man. Is that true?" I ask, changing the subject. Atticus found her first, so he gets to spill the beans on the mate subject. "We've got a team coming over, but any information you have can help."

"Wait here," she murmurs, walking into the kitchen. Her heels click on the tiles, but she returns a moment later and hands me a piece of paper.

"What the fuck is this?" I demand, not able to figure out the drawing.

"A dead wolf," Atticus snarls.

"When Micah and I went for coffee the other week, that man was waiting for me," she says quietly. "He gave me the paper, and I was confused and just threw it away. Micah and I—"

"Shit. You got the security alert," Micah gasps, slamming his hands onto the counter as he grabs the paper with a huff. "I can't fucking believe I left this here."

"And this was under my door," she says, acting as if Micah's not spoken. Micah's eyes turn amber as he pulls Nora to him. "Calm down, Micah, it's okay."

"It's not fucking okay," he snarls, taking in deep breaths as he inhales our mate's scent.

141

"It is," Nora says quietly. "Because that's not the only one I've been given."

"What?" Atticus snarls, anger radiating through him. My tiger tenses, waiting for our Alpha to calm down, but it doesn't happen. "What the fuck do you mean this isn't the only one you've been given?"

"Do not talk to me like that," Nora says, and I'm very proud of her for standing firm, even though her voice shakes.

He blinks his amber eyes away, and some of the tension fades out of me. "I'm sorry. You're right. That was inexcusable," he says, a soft tone to his voice that he only ever uses when talking to her.

"It wasn't," Nora counters. "You're worried, I get it. But if you asked me rather than shouting at me, I would've told you." He nods, and she sighs as shame fills the air. "Every day I get one or two of them."

"How?" Micah demands, looking around the room. "I've got cameras monitoring every inch of this place and haven't seen anything."

"At the office mostly," she says, looking down at her hands.

"The same man brings them?" Atticus asks, and she shakes her head, explaining how they often come in envelopes attached to her car, given to a different member of staff, or even just taped to doors.

"I want to know how," Atticus demands, and Micah nods.

"Him coming here was a sacrifice," I say, looking at Atticus for confirmation. "They're moving onto the next stage of their plans."

This was the hunters testing our response and seeing how fast we'd get here to protect our girl. *Fuck.* That hunter was a sacrifice, and now they're going to be ready for attempt number two.

Hunters are thick as fuck. They originally were formed because they thought that killing a shifter would award them the powers of a shifter. *Which is ridiculous.*

But now, their goal is to kill off shifters, so we don't take over the world. Again, they're thick as fuck and don't realise how integrated into human society we are.

"I'm sorry I didn't tell you," Nora says, looking between the three of us. "I didn't... I forgot about it, which is reckless, I know... I'm sorry."

"Don't apologise." It's not her fault. It's ours. Micah told us, and although he dropped the ball by leaving the drawing behind, we did look into it. We changed her locks, reinforced her security, and searched for the person. But Orson and I found nothing. That's on us. We should've done a much better job of protecting her.

"Let's go," Micah declares, his high energy infectious as she sends him a weak smile. "The party will be fun, pretty girl, I promise."

"Okay," she says, sighing. "But my front door..."

"Will be monitored," I promise, asking Micah my silent question. *Did he get people to start looking into the hunter?* At his nod, I feel myself relax a little. "We've got people looking into the hunter issue."

It takes a few more minutes of convincing before we manage to get her in the car. She's sitting in the passenger seat, despite insisting she should take the back. It's surprising to see Atticus this... domestic, but I suppose it makes sense. We're all going to be different now that we have her.

"So, who wants to play a card game?" Micah asks, and I hear Atticus hit him.

"Don't hit him, Atty," Nora says, without even turning around. "Use your words to voice your displeasure, not your fists."

"You're my new favourite, pretty girl!"

"Thank you," she murmurs.

"So, how come you acknowledged my tiger today without freaking out?" I ask, not even pretending to be subtle.

She rolls her eyes, letting out a huff. "No idea what you're talking about."

"Sure you don't."

"Let's say you have no idea, don't you think that those of us who are acknowledging their animals... can tell that you're a wolf?" Atticus asks curiously.

"What happened to make you cut off your wolf, Nora?" Micah asks softly. "Why are you so insistent that the shifter world doesn't exist?"

She doesn't reply, but we can all smell the pain she's in. Emotional pain gives off different markers to physical pain, and it hurts. It hurts so fucking bad. Someone hurt our girl, and I'm not going to give up until I find out who. But she's already suffered through one traumatic event tonight, I'm not that much of a dickhead that I'll make her suffer through another one.

I pull up to the front of the gala, parking the car, knowing that the valet will sort it for us.

"I'm sorry," Nora says softly. "I know you're trying, and I'd really love to be friends. I just can't acknowledge that part of things, okay?"

"Good enough for tonight," I reply, my voice equally as soft.

The four of us climb out of the car, Nora's arm through Atticus' as I toss my keys to the valet. We're not asked for our tickets, and when we enter the ballroom, all eyes turn to us.

Over ninety percent of the people here are shifters, but the very few humans that are here do know about us. It's a good way to live.

"Ready?" Atticus asks quietly. She nods, and we descend the stairs as one.

I don't think she knows what she's getting into, but our King has just made the announcement that he's found his Queen, and now the prominent figures of our society know this. The news will spread like wildfire, and that will only solidify her safety. Nobody will be able to hurt her now.

"Alpha," someone greets. I don't care who, that's not my job.

I lean in close to Nora, whispering, "Be strong, little wolf. Micah's gone to grab drinks, and I'm making the rounds. Stick close to Atticus, okay?"

She nods, a cute little glare on her face as I walk away. She's going to be just fine, Atticus wouldn't have brought her otherwise.

"Voss," I greet, sitting opposite the only fox that resides in pride limits.

Voss is six foot even with a lithe figure. He's slim, little to no muscle mass, and that's pretty much all I can tell. His feet always look like he's wearing two different shoe sizes, and I don't know if they're that way because his feet are two different sizes or what, but it's weird.

His hair is bright red and is shaven short around the sides, but atop his head is a mass of curls.

His small, down-turned lips rise in a half-snarl as he slowly speaks my name, enunciating every syllable. "Malachi."

Voss's hazel skin tone matches the red suit he's wearing,

even if I'm surprised by it. The fox always aims to blend in, his work done better because of that, but tonight he's dressed to be seen.

I wonder what his goal is.

"How are you?" I ask, attempting to make small talk.

"What do you need?" he drawls, and I don't know why I bothered when dark green eyes are trained on Atticus and Nora. Okay, fine, his eyes are very clearly only on Nora, and it pisses me right off. "Who is she?"

"None of your business," I reply, and he smirks. Foxes are sly little fuckers, and he's one of the worst. *But also the best.* "Now, we need your help."

"What's going on?" he asks, his tone serious for once. Normally, he switches between cocky, charming, and sly depending on the need for it, but right now his voice is taut. "Is she in danger?"

I hate his curiosity in my mate, but I really do need his help. I nod and explain what happened tonight with the hunter, and include the details of the images she's been receiving.

It's extremely fucking annoying that the hunter that came to her tonight is the only one she's seen because he's now shredded to pieces and can't answer any questions.

"I'll look into it," he promises, and I know that he will. He might not be my favourite person to spend time with, but he's very good at what he does.

"Your usual fee?"

"Not this time," he murmurs. I frown, not liking the sound of that. *"I just want to talk to the wolf."*

"If she's cool with it," I reply, doing my best to keep my face steady. Fucking hell. I want to refuse, but I'd do anything to keep her safe, even let her talk to Voss just once.

He rolls his down-turned eyes but nods. *"I'm not going to do anything, I just need to see something."*

I make a mental note to mention it to Atticus and make sure he's cool with it, but I don't see the harm. He didn't ask to see her alone—a stupid loophole he should have seen coming—and he's not going to risk my wrath by harming her. It's relatively safe, and when he gives us information to help her, it'll be worth it.

She'll be safe.

12

NORA

"*I*t's time for food, little queen," Atticus says, placing his hand at the small of my back. "You hungry?"

"I'm tired," I say, leaning into him. It's been two hours and whilst we've spoken to a lot of people, I'm pretty sure we still haven't seen everyone yet. It's absolute madness, but Atticus seems to be on top of it. He's actually a very popular man, which shouldn't surprise me, and he's very good at networking.

Some of the guests are here because they want a favour from him—and most of them aren't very subtle when asking —but some seem to genuinely like him and want to catch up. Unsurprisingly, this isn't just a work event.

I was mad, but these people aren't his pack either. His business associates are other shifters around the world so it's *technically* a work event. My boss is a very powerful man, and sneaky.

Let's not forget the sneakiness.

"Let's get through dinner and we can leave," he says softly. "Thank you for being here."

Grinning, I look up at him. "You really didn't give me much choice."

"Well..." he trails off and shrugs, sitting me at the head of the table. *Oh no.* He's on my right, with Malachi in the seat to my left, and Micah sitting next to him.

Everyone, and I do mean everyone, is looking my way. I duck my head, not able to handle the stares, but I bet Atticus can feel my fury.

"Chin up, little queen," Atticus says in my mind, and I gasp out loud, looking at him. *"What's wrong?"*

"I... you're talking in my mind."

"I am."

Tears well up in my eyes, and he panics, but for the wrong reasons. I'm not upset that *I can hear him,* that his voice is in my head. It's amazing that I can hear him.

My wolf... I've never had the ability to form this kind of connection with someone for over six years. It's been years since I've been able to bond with someone on this level, and I can't believe that he's the one to give this back to me.

I don't let my tears fall, blinking them away, but I reach under the table to squeeze his hand. He might not realise what he's given me, but it's something I never thought I'd have again. *Something I never thought I'd want again.*

"Nora," Malachi says, and I glance over to him. His blank face doesn't reveal anything. "I'd like to introduce you to Devoss." He gestures to the man with unruly, curly red hair sitting next to Micah, and I smile at him. He's pretty, with high cheekbones and a cheeky grin on his face. I don't know who he is, but I get friendly vibes from him.

"Nice to meet you," I murmur, offering him my spare hand to shake. Surprisingly, Atticus doesn't argue, something he's spent the entire night coaching me against. Apparently, I shouldn't touch the common people—okay, he phrased it more diplomatically than that, but that was his point.

Voss's hand is warm, and quite small. Sparks travel up my arm when our hands collide, and heat rushes to my core as the tingles spread all over me. I tilt my head, noting the flush in his cheeks, confused at what's just happened.

"As I thought," Devoss muses, dropping my hand. "Nice to meet you, *Nora.*"

"Sorry, I'm late," another man adds, sliding into the seat next to Atticus.

He's got to move the seat over a bit to be able to sit down comfortably, due to the sheer size of him. He's got to be about 6'7" or 6'8" and as wide as two men. His thighs are thick, like probably the same width as *me*, and his arms aren't much thinner. He's not fat, though, not even a little bit. He's pure muscle.

The man is wearing a black suit, and his white shirt isn't done up all the way, so I see a little bit of blonde chest hair peeking out the top. He's so masculine, it nearly kills me.

Why do I find it attractive? He's a good foot and a half taller than me, I guarantee he benches more than I weigh, and still my brain is conjuring up images of us doing the dirty things.

They're vague, with little idea of what the dirty things actually entail because I've never done them before, but the arousal is simmering away regardless.

I've never imagined myself with a lover—Atticus, excluded—but there's a part of me that would love to just give him a try, even if he might break me. I'm not even exaggerating here, he's *massive.*

"What have I missed?" he asks, giving Atticus a sardonic grin. *Fuck, never mind.* Any friend of Atticus's is most definitely not a friend of mine. Not because he picks bad friends, but because they're all of the furry kind. The man's hooded eyes lock in on Devoss, and a feral grumble leaves his throat. "Who invited the fox?"

"Foxes are cuter than bears," Devoss argues, glaring at the newcomer.

Foxes, bears, tigers, lions. Why did I seek out so many shifters?

"Enjoy this, little queen. The fox is now going to be vying for your attention, too," Atticus says, the humour etched in his tone despite it being said across the mental connection. I don't even want to know what he means by that, even if I do have some inclinations.

"Hello," the new man says, glaring at me. His hooded eyes are trained on me, the hazel colouring pretty, even if a little unnerving. He blinks, and I take in his short, fair eyelashes. I'm not sure what I've done to upset him, so maybe it's just my presence. "Name?"

"Lose the attitude," Atticus hisses. Despite his clear annoyance, his face stays the same. He's not showing his fury to the guests.

But can't they hear us?

"Sorry," the man says, sounding anything but. He's got a gravelly voice, and a strong Northern accent. "I'm Orson. I'm presuming you're the weak wolf these goons can't shut up about?"

"No," I reply, shrugging at his confusion. "I think it's cute you refer to yourselves as your favourite animal, but it's a little strange."

Devoss and Orson both gasp, but I ignore them in favour of glancing down the really long table.

"Cool it on the judgement, pretty girl," Micah teases, spotting what holds my attention. "We use long tables so we don't need to talk to anyone further down. Atticus might need to pretend to like people, but Orson and Kai scare everyone away."

"Why doesn't that surprise me?" I ask, looking up at Malachi with a small smile on my face. "You don't have great people skills, Mal."

"Hey, I never claimed to need them," he says, shrugging. "People do as they're told or I kill them. Super easy."

My heart rate slows as he presses a kiss to the top of my head.

"I'm sorry," he murmurs. "I don't kill *everyone*. Just some people." Orson snorts, and Devoss starts laughing. "Shut the fuck up."

Thankfully, servers start bringing out food for us. Conversation dies down slightly, but with eyes constantly focused on me, I struggle to choke down more than a few bites of each course. It's tense, at least for me, but the men surrounding me seem to be having a good time.

"Just dessert, then we can escape," Atticus says softly.

"You've not spoken to Alpha Newitt," Malachi reminds him, and Atticus groans. "He specifically made a point to request an audience with you."

"Alpha Newitt?" I ask. *No. No. No. I need to go. Fuck.*

"You know him?" Micah asks, but I don't reply. "He's a small town Alpha, but he's expanding pack lands. Kind of annoying, but he's a decent guy. A wolf, like you."

He's talking as if the entire table can't hear us. Yeah, fair enough, people are talking, but they're shifters. They're going to be listening in.

"Why are you scared?" Orson demands, edging forward in his seat. He lowers his head a little, and I can see the flickering emotions raging through his eyes. "I can smell the fear from you. Why are you so scared, Nora?"

I don't reply. This can't be happening. This isn't fair.

I've done as I was told. Even though I stayed in a small town, and avoided other shifters, some found me anyway. I met some amazing men, who despite me not being willing to allow a relationship to form, they're sweet and funny, and they care about me.

I messed up by letting them get close. I knew it was a mistake.

"I'm going to need to leave," I whisper.

"Okay," Atticus says gently. "We don't need to see him."

"No, you misunderstand," I murmur, not able to meet his eyes. "I'm going back home, back to Callent. This was a mistake. I'm sorry."

"I'm sorry, little queen, but that's not something I can let happen," Atticus says slowly. "You're not leaving me, or the others. I'm sorry, but you're ours."

"I can't be."

"Do you need me to spell it out for you?" he asks.

I shrug before nodding. "Yes."

"You're my mate, Nora. My lion has marked you as his."

"As has my tiger," Malachi adds.

"My tiger is equally as possessive," Micah says, a red blush tinging his cheeks when I look at him. "We're mates, Nora."

"You felt the sparks," Devoss adds, and I'm shocked by that. I didn't think...

"Now, you've got until the end of this meal to tell me why you're so scared of Newitt, before I beat the answer out of him," Malachi says, deathly calm.

"You don't understand," I whisper. "We can't be mates... it's not possible."

"Trust me, it's very possible," Atticus replies.

"It's not," I say, shaking my head. I stand, every eye in the

153

room falling to me, and it's extremely hard to ignore the rumbling sounds that Atticus' lion is making.

"I'll see you at the office," I whisper before turning and walking out the room. I don't even make it to the door before I'm pulled into a firm chest. I don't need heightened senses to know it's Atticus.

"You don't ever walk away from me," he says, his tone scarily quiet. He spins me in his arms, and I gasp at the fury on his face. "You are my mate, and I don't care if you think otherwise. You don't get to leave me, Nora."

"I'm sorry."

His mouth descends on mine, and his tongue instantly invades my mouth. He bites my lip, drawing blood, and I moan as his hand grips my hip. *Fuck.*

"You are my mate," he murmurs against my lips. "Now, why am I hurting Newitt?"

"Atty, no," I plead, raising my hands up to cup his cheeks. "Just leave it. Please. Let's go, and we can talk about us somewhere else. Please."

He shakes his head, and presses another kiss to my lips, before licking my blood from his lips. It's a very inappropriate time... but that was kind of hot.

He storms over to where people are watching. I so hope that they didn't hear. It's bad enough they saw us kissing. I scoff internally. *They're shifters. Of course they heard.*

"Dessert has been cancelled," Atticus roars, and I flinch. "Time to go home."

Malachi and Orson stand, flanking his sides. It's a very impressive trio, and the people here seem to figure that out too as they all start to clear out. As people stand, Devoss gets lost in the crowd, and I don't move from where I'm cowering against the wall. Atticus is listening, and since he's making things easier for me, I need to do my part. He really believes we're mates, and when I clear things up, he'll understand.

"Alpha Newitt and his mate," Devoss introduces them the moment the room is clear of people, and I hold in my tears. Not only has Devoss not listened to what I wanted... but he's dragged Kennedy over here.

The man in front of me has barely changed from when I knew him years ago. His eyes are still that shade of bright green—not as pretty as Voss's jade green eyes, though—and his hair is a reddish-brown.

It's shorter now, so I can't see if it's still as curly, but even if it were, it has nothing on Voss's.

He's more tanned now, his skin used to be so pale he couldn't look at the sun without burning, and it just seems to match the fake smile on his face.

Kennedy used to be one of the fittest members of the pack, and sure he's still pretty in shape, but he looks puny compared to the men surrounding me. Between Orson the giant bear, and Atticus the powerful Alpha, Kennedy just looks pathetic.

Kennedy, my *ex*-mate, who is now standing in front of me with his new mate by his side. I know I can't judge, considering I'm standing here with four of my new mates, but it doesn't take the sting away.

Unlike me, he *chose* his mate. Not that I'm complaining, since fate has not only given me a second chance, but she's picked some absolutely *amazing* men for me.

The worst part about all of this, is seeing the woman in front of me who carries the mate bond I should've had, and recognising exactly who she is.

My sister. Kennedy has replaced me with my sister.

He rejects me, ruins my life, and stands here with her on his arm, acting as arrogant as he used to be. I might not have seen them here tonight, but I doubt they missed me or who I was with. They could've left and reached out to Atticus another way. That's what I'd have done.

But no. They're terrible fucking people. *How could they do this to me?*

"Nice to see you again, Alpha Phoenix," he says, smiling like they're old friends. His voice is still the same baritone that I remember—it's hard to forget it. I'd know, I've tried—his Northern accent is still as strong. "I really appreciate you still taking the time to—"

He's cut off when Malachi kicks the back of his legs, causing him to fall to the ground. He groans, but when Orson's hand grips his hair, he doesn't fight the hold.

"You only speak when spoken to," Orson hisses.

"What did you do to Nora?" Micah asks, and I can only focus on how serious he sounds. Micah's one of the most laid back men I know, but twice now tonight he's lost his usual cheer because of me.

Be brave, Nora. I walk over to where they're standing, hesitantly taking my place beside Atticus, and he leans down and presses a kiss to the top of my head.

"It's nice to see you, Nora," Neve says quietly, and my eyes rise to meet hers. Her eyes are identical to my dad's—a light brown colour—and the brief flash of pain that fills me is awful. I refuse to mourn parents who did this to me.

She looks good, I hate to admit. We've got the same dark brown hair, but hers is cut similar to how our mum used to wear it—shoulder-length and straight. She's gained a little weight, which is unsurprising considering it's our twenties and she's bonded properly with her wolf, and she's a good five or so inches taller than me—even with me being in heels and her in flats.

Her dress is a gorgeous, but simple, silver, and she's

carrying a clutch bag to match. It's nothing flashy, and definitely doesn't carry a price tag as high as the one I'm wearing. But then again, the pride I'm in now has a lot more finances than the pack I used to belong to.

She seems comfortable, happy, even, and even though I hate her choice of mate, I'm glad that she's healthy and thriving.

With a soft voice, she says, "I've missed you."

I shoot her a tense smile, already counting down the minutes until I can leave and pretend this night never happened. "Atticus, this isn't how I wanted to discuss things."

"You didn't want to discuss things, little queen," he reminds me. "If you want to change your position..."

"I'd prefer you didn't torture my sister's mate," I say, looking at Malachi directly. "Can you both stop that?"

"But—" Malachi starts, and when Atticus growls, he groans, and both Orson and he let *him* stand up.

"Thank you, Nora," *he* says.

"Don't speak to her," Devoss snarls. "You don't get to speak to her. You don't look at her. You don't even get to think about her. You wolves might have decided you're better than us, but I'm pretty capable of murder, and I don't care about the fake hierarchy you've created."

My sister gasps, and I hold in my annoyance.

"Devoss, please," I sigh, looking at the redhead who also claims he is my mate. I went from being a rejected wolf, to having *four* new mates. Fate really is testing me. "Can you please stop with the threats?"

"She's your sister?" Atticus asks, confusion clear in his face. I nod, and he glances between the two of us. "I'm missing something. I don't understand how your sister is... strong and you're so weak. I don't get it."

"She's been exiled," *he* hisses. Even thinking his name hurts me, and the tiny flicker from my wolf only makes my head hurt. "That's why she's so weak."

"Ooh, spicy," Malachi exclaims, grinning at me with pure excitement in his gaze. "What did you do, little wolf? Beat someone up? Steal from someone? Murder someone?"

"You think she murdered someone and you're excited?" my sister sneers, disgust lacing her tone.

"Less of the attitude," Malachi snaps before winking at me. "Come on, I won't think less of you, baby."

"No, I didn't murder someone," I tell him, wanting to end this. There's no way I'm getting out of this without telling them something. "I was exiled because I was rejected by my mate." And they freeze. "So that's how I know we can't be mates. I had one, and he's still alive, so I don't get another." I don't deserve another.

This causes them all to snarl, and even without my wolf senses to smell it, I know they're furious.

"You were exiled because your mate rejected you?" Orson hisses. "What the actual fuck is going down in your pack, Nora?"

"Not my pack," I say.

"That's the procedure when they lose their wolves," *he* says. "It's a safety thing. It's only done in the most serious of circumstances, and the person becomes a shell of themselves. They lose what makes them a wolf, and they're no good to the pack that way."

It wasn't even twenty-four hours before they dumped me in a new place. I didn't even make it until it was no longer my birthday before they stole everything from me. It wasn't long enough for them to determine if I'd be a threat. It wasn't long enough for them to determine what would happen to my wolf. They didn't wait. *They didn't fucking wait.*

They ignored policy and got rid of me as quickly as they could, as if it was my fault that my wolf couldn't handle the pain, as if I was a disappointment in the worst of ways, and all I did was scent my mate for the first time.

"You're a fucking idiot," Atticus says, laughing. I glance up at him, confused by why he's laughing. "Believe me when I tell you that your pack lost out big time."

"I'm confused as to why you're laughing," *he* says, echoing my thoughts.

Micah takes my hand, and pulls me into him. I'm surprised Atticus lets it happen. "Every shifter has a mate. Wolves can sense their mates at a certain age—sixteen or something, I don't know or care—and once they get a whiff of their mate's scent, that's it for them. Cats are different. We get our mates through an act. You impress a tiger, or a lion, and if our cat is interested, they mark you. If your mate never had rejected you, you'd never have been able to be our mate. That jackass all but handed you to us on a silver platter."

"Foxes can sense it via touch," Devoss reveals, winking at me. "And the sparks at dinner... well, I'm not happy about needing to share with your cats, but I can adapt."

"So you're saying that her mate rejecting her has let her be the mate to the most powerful cat pride within this country?" *he* asks, frowning. He looks to Neve hesitantly, and that brief look they share doesn't hurt me like I expected it to. I have those same exact looks with my men, even when I'm pushing them away.

"Yes," Atticus replies, smiling. "So I want to thank you, you worthless piece of shit. Thanks to your pack's negligence, Nora's going to be happy with us. I was going to hurt you, as it would be very well deserved, but instead, I think I'll be happier leaving you with your pathetic life."

"Nora," Neve whispers. "I'm sorry. I'm so sorry."

"I wish I could trust that, but you came here with him," I say, my tone hesitantly soft. "I wish you all the happiness that I can, but I hope we never need to see each other again."

"David's mated now," she offers, and I hate to admit that that hurt. Even deeper than her coming here and flaunting her new mate in my face. "Him and Crystal found out a few months back. Do you remember her?"

"I think it's time for you to shut up now, wolfie," Devoss declares, and I don't know whether he can smell my hurt or if it's that clearly painted on my face, but I'm glad he's interrupting her. It's killing me to hear. "Off you pathetic people go. Bye bye."

"But you were meant to help us," *he* snaps. "And you don't speak for Atticus, fox."

"And you don't use his name, wolf," Devoss hisses. "Believe me, I'd love nothing more than to cut out your tongue, so I'd shut up if I were you."

Atticus seems amused, but looks at me. "Do you want us to help your sister, little queen?"

"Don't let her decide," Neve squeaks out, looking at *him*. "Babe, tell them."

"Tell us what?" Malachi demands. "We don't give a fuck if you're pregnant, we can already smell that."

"You're pregnant?" I whisper. This day is getting better and better.

"Yes," she says, her voice equally as quiet. "Nora, I'm sorry."

"Help them," I say, my voice trembling, as I look up at Atticus. "I... just help them with whatever they need."

"As you wish, little queen," he murmurs.

"I'll wait out there," I say, gesturing to the exits before I all but run out of the room. I head to the giant staircase and sit on the second to bottom step, kicking off my heels. This is all too much. I should've known fate's test included more than just happiness.

"Why didn't you tell them who he was?" Orson asks, startling me. He raises his hands in defence, and I sigh. His blonde hair is tied up in a bun at the top of his head, small tendrils framing his face.

Up close, I can see that his thick beard has a ginger tint within the blonde colouring. Unlike Micah and Mal, who have shaved prior to this event, Orson definitely has not. His beard is spiky, very full, and covers from just in front of his ears, all the way down underneath his jaw, connecting with the moustache.

His bright hazel eyes are guarded, as is his body language. He's tense, but he's trying desperately to hold onto his emotions.

He moves to come sit near me, and I turn slightly to look at him. "Fuck, why did you tell Atticus to help them? He was your mate, right? He was the one to reject you."

"I'm sorry you're caught up in my drama," I say quietly, deliberately not answering his question.

"Do you know how bears find their mates?" he asks. I shake my head and he smiles. "Bears are protectors. When our mate is in danger, or she's suffering, her animal will call to our bear, and if we're able to prove ourselves worthy, that solidifies the bond."

"That's sweet."

He nods. "You're in pain, and that means you're suffering. I need to help you, Nora. Please don't let me fail my bear." I tilt my head, and he sighs. "A hunter showed up at your house, obviously wanting to hurt you. Your ex-mate is now here, rubbing it in your face that he's happy and moving on without you. Out of all your pack members... he chose your sister? I need to fix your hurt. Please, let me fix your hurt."

"I appreciate the offer, but I'm okay. There's nothing to fix."

A grumble echoes from him, and it's strangely soothing. "I'm one second away from ripping out his heart. Give me a reason why I shouldn't. Give me a way to help you because my bear's furious, and I'm barely holding on to control."

"My niece or nephew," I whisper, reaching for his hand. I don't know Orson very well, but I can't have another death on my conscience. Not tonight. "I don't want them growing up without a dad. No matter what kind of person he was to me, I'm sure he's a good Alpha."

A snarl leaves his throat, and I can see my words aren't helping calm him down. I edge even closer. "Tonight, I called Malachi to help me with the hunter, and he killed him. I had to watch as he tore that man to pieces, and as much as I know the hunter was going to hurt me... I still feel guilty. Please don't make me add another death to my conscience. Not tonight. Please."

A whine leaves his throat and he pulls me onto his lap. I can curl up whilst in his arms, and he's big enough to surround me. I feel safe and comforted in his tight grip. The tension radiating in both our bodies fades as his earthy scent overwhelms me.

"Thank you," I murmur, kissing his chest.

"You don't believe we're mates, do you?" he asks.

"I don't," I reply, shrugging. "But after tonight, I'm not even sure it matters. I think I'm just grateful that you're here... all of you."

"We've got you," he says, tightening his arm to demonstrate physically. "We're never letting you go."

13

ATTICUS

"Help them," she utters, looking up at me. Her dark brown eyes are filled with tears that she stubbornly won't let fall. "I... just help them with whatever they need."

"As you wish, little queen."

I'd rather kill him. It doesn't take a genius to put two and two together who he is, even if she's not going to say it. I'm honestly surprised that she told us she was rejected, but now... now I understand why she's been pushing us away, and it's all because of this man in front of me. He rejected her, and he's not getting a fucking thing from me until he explains why. I'll help because she asked me to, but I'm not making it easy on him.

"I'll wait out there," she says, pointing to the doors. I nod, but she's already turned and disappeared.

"I'll—" Micah starts.

"I've got her," Orson says instead, jogging after her.

"At least the bear's not boring," Voss says, grinning. "We've got such a cute little gang here."

"Shut up," I snap. The fox is not a welcome addition—his skills are, but his voice is annoying me.

"Sure thing, King," he replies, wandering over to the couple in front of us. "If I were you, wolfie, I'd sit down. Your mate is going to have to answer some questions, and it would be easier if you moved."

She looks to me for confirmation, and I roll my eyes. Pathetic.

"Sit down, babe," Kennedy says. He stands with his chin up, and when I meet his eyes, he gives me a strong nod. For someone so undeserving of his title, he sure has an awful lot of confidence. Then again, he also seems to lack any kind of brain cells, and doesn't realise how stupid it is to try and challenge me.

Is he really this fucking delusional?

"You know, for a jackass, your name is very girly," Voss points out.

"You know what, it actually is," Micah agrees, his tone rising a few notches. It doesn't surprise me that Voss and Micah are hitting it off, but a quick look at Mal's narrowed eyes shows me why they've been kept apart. There might only be a year between the brothers, but Malachi definitely likes being the older brother. "I couldn't place it, and I'm sure it's a unisex name, but I definitely agree."

"Do you know what it means?" Voss asks, an eyebrow raised, and Micah shakes his head. "Ugly head. It literally means ugly head."

"Not inaccurate then, is it," Micah cackles, looking down at the Alpha.

If I wasn't here, this would go down very differently. Any Alpha worth his title wouldn't stand for disrespect coming from those beneath him, but then again, he's not worth his title. It's embarrassing.

"Children," Mal mutters, winking at me. "So, Ken, let's talk about the shit you put our girl through."

"Our girl?" he asks.

"Look, the replacement is pregnant," Voss says, glaring at Kennedy, and I hold in my laughter. He's very annoying, but I can't say I hate his behaviour. I can't act like this, but it doesn't hurt that the loose cannon can. "The pup is my girl's nephew, and if the replacement loses the baby after needing to watch us hurt her sister's mate, well, she's going to feel guilty and sad, and we've just found her, you know? I don't want her to be sad."

"Your point?" I drawl, content to let him run the show.

My lion is furious, and as much as I want to make the baby grow up without its father, Nora will not be happy. I don't understand why she wants us to help them, when they definitely don't deserve it, but I won't deny her anything.

"My point is that he's going to answer our questions, and fast, or else I'm going to get mad. I don't want to get mad, but we all know he's the OG mate, so let's cut to the chase. Understood?"

"Kai, you've been keeping the fox from me," Micah whines, turning to his brother with a pout on his face. "I'm telling Nora. This is actually the worst thing you've ever done to me."

"I once clawed your stomach and you had to be hospitalised because you weren't healing fast enough," Mal deadpans. To be fair to Mal, Micah was being whiney as fuck. Like now.

"And?"

"I'm a bad influence," Voss stage whispers, even going as far as to cover his mouth with his hand like he's telling a secret. "He was protecting you."

Neve sobs, and I glance at her, but I don't feel any

sympathy. Her sister was exiled from her pack, and instead of supporting her—an act she should've done as her older sister—she stole Nora's mate. I don't give a fuck if this is inconvenient for her, or upsetting.

"So, why did you reject Nora?" I demand.

"She's weak," Kennedy whispers, refusing to meet my eyes. This act only cements him as the biggest piece of shit in my mind. Only a coward can't face up to the decisions he's made—good or bad. "I needed a Luna who was going to be able to handle the position without constantly fucking it up. Nora is pretty, but that's her only talent."

"Where did you come into this arrangement?" I ask, looking at the sister.

"I'm Nora's older sister," she whispers. *Obviously.* "My mate is dead, and my parents and Ken's parents thought I'd be a better match for him. We weren't aware of the effect rejecting someone would have, but we needed to take the risk."

"Because you thought she was weak?" Micah asks, confused. "Nora handled losing her wolf. Nora's handled losing her pack, her family, her friends, her life. Nora is the strongest woman I've ever met, and it's taken me till tonight to realise that. You fucked up her life so badly, and she still tells Atticus to help you."

"We didn't mean to hurt her," Neve says. Unlike her cowardly mate, she meets my eyes, and I'm so fucking grateful they look nothing like Nora's. "You have to believe me. We thought she'd be upset, but she'd be free to live her life, find a new mate, and be able to be happy without fucking up the pack. It wasn't a matter of us wanting to take this from her, but about us putting the pack first."

"How didn't you know the effect it would have?" I ask.

This sounds very well-rehearsed to me, and I hate that I

don't know enough about wolf culture to verify it for myself. Cats don't reject their mates because it's always a joyous occasion. I can't wrap my head around this being something they were doing for their pack.

Nora's fucking perfect. She's strong, empathetic, and kind. Qualities that are needed in a Luna. How can they come here wanting to expand when they see those qualities as weak? *What the fuck is their pack like?*

"Because it's a barbaric thing used in the most extreme of circumstances," Voss reveals, and I turn to him in surprise. I didn't realise he had insight on wolves, which is pretty ignorant of me. The fox has his fingers in a lot of pies, pies that have come in handy more than once for our pride. "It's usually used for cases where the mate is abusive, or a criminal. It's not something that's done commonly. It's thought that those being rejected lose their wolf because the actions that caused their mate to hate them are usually severe and worthy of such punishment. It's pretty interesting, actually."

"How do you know so much about wolves?" Mal asks, saving me from doing it later in private. Can't let the enemy be clued in on my ignorant status.

But in my defence, they're secretive fuckers, and the only time they're really out of the pack life is if they've been exiled. As you can guess, that's usually for bad people, and they're not usually the kind to talk about their culture. For animals not on top of the food chain, they sure act like it.

"Ex-girlfriend," Voss says, shrugging. "What? I'm going to tell Nora about her. I mean I was going to wait until she was more secure, but she started the ex discussion tonight, so it's only fair that I loop her in on mine."

"She did her best to get out of it," Mal reminds him, but Voss waves him off.

"So to cut a boring ass story short, you rejected her because you thought she was weak, mated with her sister, and now want our help to expand your pathetic and neglectful pack?" Micah says.

"Yes."

I admire his backbone, but he's lucky his pregnant mate is here. Even I have limits.

"As I told Nora, we'll help," I say, hating myself for this. This goes against every single fibre of my being, but Nora asked, and I won't ever deny her something that she wants —that she needs. My strong, beautifully kind mate asked me for this, and I'll give her her wishes because I know how hard it was for her to ask in the first place. "You'll come to my office at eight tomorrow, and we can go over your plans."

"Thank you."

I don't reply, and as I walk out the room, Micah offers to show Neve to where their coats are. It doesn't take a genius to know what's about to happen, but clearly Nora got the looks *and the brains*. Neve hesitantly leaves with Micah, and I can't help but smile.

I can't do what I want, but there's nothing stopping the two loose hinges. And if Kennedy comes to the meeting tomorrow with a broken jaw, well, at least I won't need to listen to his voice.

I leave via the door Nora used, and I smile when I see her cuddled into Orson. She's wrapped up in his arms, her dress flowing around the two of them. She's gorgeous, and I can hear her even breathing, telling me she's sleeping.

"Is she okay?"

Orson nods, not moving from his position. The bear is infatuated, something I guessed would happen, and it's really been a bright spot in the midst of this night. My mate has a pride to back her now, and she has many mates who want nothing but the best for her. We've got her. She's going to be okay.

"Exhausted. Tonight was one problem after another for her."

I sigh. *"I want you and Mal on the hunter issue first thing tomorrow."*

"But... she's moving in."

I hold in my snort. Of course the bear is more interested in decorating her bedroom, the one we've already been preparing, than anything else. He's a homemaker at heart.

"And you can sort her room soon," I say. *"Her safety takes priority."*

"Nobody's getting through me to her," he says, snarling as he pulls her even closer.

"Nora," I call, ignoring his frustrated glare at me waking our mate up. "It's time to wake up, little queen."

"What?" she murmurs, sounding groggy. She sits up a little and sleepily rubs at her eyes. "Are they gone?"

"Micah's getting their coats now," I reply, walking forward to crouch in front of her. "We've got a lot to talk about, little queen."

"I know," she whispers, reaching up to cup my cheek. "I'm so sorry, Atty. I wasn't... it was easier to pretend that it wasn't real than to admit how damaged I am. I never expected them to be together, or for him to be here, or any of this shit. I'm sorry. I'm so fucking sorry that I caused all of this."

She turns into Orson, and her quiet sniffles are all I can hear. I move to take her from him, and a disgruntled grumble emits from Orson. *Fucking bears.*

"You're a jackass," I say.

He shrugs and starts rubbing her back. We're not getting to touch her at all tonight, not unless we want an angry bear stopping us. Nora's panic caused their bond to start, and he's not going to be content until he's proven himself to her.

"Nora, I'm not upset with you," I soothe. I hate that I can't comfort her. "I get it. I really do. I'm not mad at you. You don't need to cry."

"You don't need to cry?" Orson scoffs, and if she wasn't on his lap, crying, well... I'd do something to him. "Let's head out to the car, Nora. The others will meet us there once they're gone."

"We won't all fit in the car," she says through her cries. "How are we meant to leave if we won't all fit in the car?"

She's so fucking precious.

"Leave that to me," I murmur. If it were up to me, any problem in her life should be left to me. I'll move heaven and earth to fix shit, and believe me, my methods can be creative.

"Can you organise for a car big enough for seven people to meet me at the location of the gala?" I ask, speaking to Jeremy, one of my assistants.

"Of course, Alpha."

"There you go, it's all handled," I tell her softly. "Now, please, stop crying. It's okay."

Orson rolls his eyes, and after moving her slightly, he fixes me with a pointed glare. "I know you don't have much experience with women"—a fact I love he said in front of her—"but they're not able to stop crying on command. Just like you don't tell them to calm down when they're mad. Fuck, I'm giving you all my tricks for nothing."

"I think that applies to everyone, not just women," Nora says before giggling. "Today has been a long day. I know you said I can't go back to the house..."

"And that is still true," I say gently. Crying isn't going to sway me on matters of safety. "There's space at my home, or

I can set you up with a house within the centre of the pride if you'd rather." She nods slowly, and I give her a weak smile. "I'd really prefer you live with us, but I get that things are going to need to move a little slower than normal between us all. I want you to understand that you're safe with us, and that there is no pressure for anything."

Okay, the last part might've been exaggerated. We want to be her friends, we want to be there for her. The last three weeks have been spent with me and the tiger brothers worming our way into her life.

But there's no romantic pressure. We won't move faster than her pace—even if our animals disagree.

"For the first six months or so, I didn't leave my house," she says, looking at her hands. The smell of shame and despair fills the air, and it takes everything to stop my lion from taking over. "I stayed home and cried at every noise. I was terrified, and I was alone. It took a really long time before I could do anything without having a panic attack, and then we met, and..."

"But you're here now," Orson says, kissing the top of her head when she trails off. "You got through something extremely hard, and you're a better person because of it."

"My wolf is dead," she says, pushing to get out of his arms. A smile forces its way out, and I can't stop it. She's fighting a bear to get out of his grip. It's cute, but it's never going to work.

"Even Atticus is laughing at you right now," Orson taunts, not even flinching as she pushes his arms. "Say your piece without running away, and then we can drop the issues for tonight? How about that? One last piece of honesty, and I promise we'll go home and forget about it all for tonight."

"Promise?"

"Promise."

She takes a deep breath, and juts her chin out. She's radiating confidence and pride, and I couldn't be fucking prouder. He may have attempted to ruin her spirit, but it failed.

"My wolf has all but died. I'm not a better person without her. She was the other part of me, and he took her from me. I'd have made an amazing Luna, and I know it even if my family and the pack didn't. They fought to diminish every good part about me, and no, I'm not a better person because of it. I'm still me, I'm still the same person I was back then. All minus my wolf. No more shifting. No more pack links. No more heightened senses. My body is a shell of what it once was, but I haven't changed. I could have let the situation harden me, or take away my joy, but then I'd be the person my pack wanted, and not the person I am. So, please don't ever say I'm a better person because of what they did to me. I'm not. I'm still me."

Well, fuck. Seems my little Queen is going to be the one to give pep talks when they're needed.

They fucked up when they lost her. They really fucked up.

"Time to go home," I say, standing up and grabbing her heels. Orson can carry her—a statement I needed to think so that my lion still felt he was in control. I know the power balance has shifted, but until her bonds are cemented with her other mates, my lion is not going to care.

My only hope is that she can still feel our connection, even without her wolf.

Orson stands, and she tries to wriggle free, but he doesn't let her. *Good.* She's nothing but persistent in her efforts to remain alone, but we're not going to let that fly.

Nora Nouvel Hart has five mates that are going to fight until the end of time to make her happy.

She says something to Orson that I miss, and he laughs, causing her to join in with her infectious giggles. She sounds so happy, and although I know that doesn't mean she's okay, I know that it's a good thing.

Maybe... maybe even if she can't feel the bond, then that'll be okay, too.

14

ORSON

"She's out," I say, my voice quiet in the back of the limo. I'm sitting at the back where seats would be if this were a normal car, with Atticus sitting right by me. Then on the right seat, the longer chair, are Malachi, Devoss, and then Micah, in that order.

From my position, I can see everyone. It's great seeing the jealousy in their faces, especially when I can smell it, too.

"This night has been one epic disaster after another," Kai says before sighing deeply. His pleading blue eyes meet mine, and I smirk inwardly because I know what's coming. "Can I hold her?"

"No," I snap, infusing a bit of my bear in the word. He's asked so many times tonight, and I've had it. I swear to fucking god, the only thing that saved him from broken wrists was the way Nora giggled each time he asked, and after the night she's had, any kind of happiness from her should be celebrated. She's asleep now, though, so I'm more than willing to make good on my silent promises.

The pathetic fucking tiger couldn't take me in a fight no matter how badly he wishes he could.

"She cried," Atticus says, his crisp voice sounding amused. I don't need to look at him to know he has a smug expression on his face. "I think it's going to be a while before we get our turn."

I'm not going to agree because it'll only rile them up further, but the only time she's leaving my arms is if there's danger and I need to protect her. She's accepted the bond between us, something I don't think she's done consciously, and I'm not giving her affection up. Not even Atticus can take her from me right now, and by the way he's smoking a cigar with a chilled out look on his face, I don't think he gives a shit about trying.

"Well, he's probably going to cry tonight, too," Micah says, leaning over Voss to smirk at his brother. "I'm sad I missed out on the fun."

"Don't tell lies," Kai drawls, glaring at his younger brother. "Seriously, shut the fuck up. You're whiny, and it's annoying me."

"Stop taking your frustrations out on him," I say when Micah gets a sad look on his face. The guys tease me quite often about being a mother hen—it's the instincts from my bear, not that I actually care for their feelings—and this is one of those times.

"As if you care," Kai says, rolling his eyes. Someone is a little tense right now. *Me. That person is me.*

"No, I really don't," I reply, ignoring Micah's offended expression. He knows the score. "But the girl in my arms will, and she's already had to watch you kill someone tonight. I don't think she wants to have to visit your brother in a hospital bed because your temper got the better of you. *Once again.*"

"What did she say to you?" Kai says, sitting forward in his chair with his hands clasped together.

"That she feels guilty about you killing the hunter. That his death is on her conscience. She's sweet, and nice, and she takes shit like that personally. Even when she doesn't need to."

He nods, and leans back in the chair, looking at Voss with a grin on his face. The fox is sly, and dangerous, but he's also loyal. I know he's going to be a good mate for Nora, even if he's not the most rational of men.

"Are you wanting to move in with us?" Micah asks Voss after a few moments of silence. *Wow.*

"You want him to move in?" Kai asks, glancing between us all with narrowed eyebrows. "Like, into the house?"

"Nah, the woods," Micah says, with an eye roll. "Where else?"

"They're mates," I say, cutting off the fighting as three pairs of eyes dart my way in surprise. "We adapt to his sneaky ways because she needs all the love she can get. I don't care."

Atticus is still looking out of the window, not commenting. I know he's listening, he always is, but he's more interested in the night passing us by.

"You're so fucking sappy," Kai says, amusement in his tone. "I wonder what Nora will think about that." I ignore his pathetic taunts, but that doesn't stop him from continuing.

Occasionally, the fox or Micah will counter back, but I just tune him out.

Luckily, we arrive at the house not too long later, and I'm saved from enduring his taunts or arguing back with him. I make sure that Nora is settled properly before I climb out the limo. She doesn't wake up, something that makes my bear and I happy, and, instead, she just cuddles closer into my chest. She feels safe with me, safe enough to trust me to guard her whilst she's at her most vulnerable, despite barely knowing me.

This is a way my bear and I can prove our worth.

I won't let her down.

"Are her clothes here?" I ask, once we're inside the house. Atticus nods. "Someone get her something to sleep in and bring it to my room."

"Her stuff is already in *her* room," Atticus says, emphasising the word her whilst smirking at me like this is the funniest thing he's ever seen. "Why don't you put her in there? I'm sure she'd love to spend the night *alone* in her new room, and get comfortable."

"Wolves and their dens," Voss says with amusement in his eyes but a straight face. *Fucking cunt.*

"Believe me, I'll fight you over this," I hiss, directing my words to Atticus, who laughs.

"You'd have to put her down first."

Fucking prick. I ignore the laughter coming from them all, and I make my way upstairs, going into my bedroom instead of hers.

I'm not stupid enough to go into a wolf's den without permission, even without Voss's reminder.

I hope she'll feel safe in here, though.

I place her onto the bed, amused as she gets comfortable in my scent. I give her a few as I kick off my shoes and throw my jacket over the armchair.

Once I'm a bit more settled, I feel bad about it, but I reach over to turn on the lamp. She's in her dress, a fucking stunning dress that looks like it was made to fit her, but she'll not be comfortable at all if I let her sleep in it all night.

After her safety, her comfort ranks number two on my list.

"What's happening?" she mumbles, rolling away from the light with a frown on her pretty face. She's bleary eyed as she looks at me through slow blinks. "Orson?"

"You can go back to sleep soon," I murmur. She groans, and I give her a soft smile. "I'm going to grab you some pyjamas so you've got something to wear tonight."

She sighs, and clumsily gets off the bed as I watch in trepidation. I don't want her to fall. "Can you unzip this, please?"

I don't hesitate in undoing her dress, and it drops down her body into a pile surrounding her feet.

"Can I borrow a t-shirt?" she asks softly, and I caress her naked back before grabbing her what she needs. I try not to look in the mirror opposite where I could see her front, but I can't help myself.

She's fucking gorgeous, and she's my mate.

But, more than the attractive lines of her body, the swell of her breasts, the pubic hair covering her mound, is the clear sign of neglect. Nora is tiny standing next to Atticus, and then even smaller next to me. We're all big men, but she's not.

She should've connected with her wolf and had the bulking out and the growth spurt that comes along with reaching maturity not long after her eighteenth birthday, but hers clearly didn't happen. *Is that why her wolf was so weak to the rejection from her mate?*

But even without that, she's small by human standards, too. At 5'2", she's tiny, and it makes sense her body would go with that. Except, her weight seems unnatural. She's skinny, like, very skinny. And it seems to come from neglect of her body versus her natural frame.

178

It causes the bear within to grumble as he claws at my mind to take over. We're not near a fucking lake, though, so it's not like he can go catch her a fish. *Even if he could, she's not going to eat a raw fish.*

So he's useless.

But I agree with the sentiment. She needs to eat more. I note the bruises on her arms, just small ones where she's clearly banged an elbow or knocked her hand, showing she's likely anaemic.

She needs care, and my bear and I thrive on offering it.

I grab the shirt and walk back over to her. I move to stand behind her, and instead of taking the shirt from me to put it over her slender frame, she raises her arms.

"Getting demanding, aren't we?" I murmur, a warm feeling filling my chest as I pull the shirt over her head. It's not till it's secure over her body that I pick her up from behind and throw her onto the bed.

She starts giggling, a sound that makes my bear really happy, before righting herself amongst the pillows. "I need a mirror."

"You're beautiful." An instinctual response, but apparently not the right answer.

"Thank you," she says, almost shyly. "But I need to take all these diamonds out of my hair, and it'll be easier if I can see them."

"I'll do it," I offer, already moving towards her.

"You will?"

I don't reply and get comfortable behind her. I'll do anything for this woman. Anything at all. She starts pulling out these weird things, and shows me one.

"I need all these out," she says, and I tilt my head, trying to see what it is.

"What are those?"

"Granny clips." I can't hold in the laughter, and she turns to look at me over her shoulder. There's amusement lighting up her dark brown eyes, a little twitch of her button-nose as she slowly blinks through her long, thick eyelashes. "I'm not joking. They're called granny clips."

"Nah, that was funny, but tell me, what are they really called?" I ask, desperate to know.

She lets out a little huff, and turns back around. "I told you. Granny clips."

I shake my head, knowing she's not going to give up the secret, and start taking out these granny clips and the diamond twirlies. Who the fuck put so many in her hair?

"Do you think I'm going to lose my job now?" she asks quietly.

What? I'd really like some insight into her mind because I get the feeling I'm going to constantly be surprised by what she comes out with.

We were discussing the 'granny clips,' so how did we get here?

"Why are you worried about losing your job?" I ask, continuing to take her hair out as she silently muses it out. I hope she opens up, but I'm not going to pressure her.

"Because Atty thinks we're mates?"

"Remove the word think from your sentence," I caution her, and she gasps. Atticus wouldn't take his annoyance out on her at the constant rejection, but I don't feel like going a few rounds to rein in his lion. That bastard has sharp teeth. "But, of course, that's not going to make you lose your job. Do you like your job?"

Some of the tension fades from her shoulders, and her head rises a little more. "I love it."

"Then you'll always have it," I promise, rubbing her shoulders gently. "Stop worrying, Nora. That's our job."

"Then what's mine?"

"To let us," I reply, kissing her shoulder before going back to her hair.

"You and Atticus are a lot alike," she says, messing with the loose thread on the bottom of my shirt. It's cute, the way she's avoiding looking at me even in the mirror, but it angers my bear that she feels the need.

"We are?"

"That's something he would say."

She's not wrong. Our protective instincts are something we both share. I finish pulling those diamonds out, and she thanks me before heading into the bathroom to get cleaned up. This whole thing is very domestic... it's like she's been in my life for years and not just a matter of hours.

Is this how fate feels? This easy, this simple, this powerful?

I change out of my suit, and pull on a pair of shorts. Normally, clothes are not a requirement in my bed, but I don't want her to be uncomfortable sleeping next to me.

"All done?" I ask. I heard her leave the bathroom a minute or two ago, but I gave her time to get her fill of my body, the scent of her arousal hitting me right in the centre —well, that would be true if your centre is your dick.

She nods before climbing into the bed. She goes to rest on the left, but I scoot her over and take that for myself. I won't have her close to the door, not when I'm her last line of defence in case something happens. I expected there to be a fight about her sleeping in here—because it would be a fight if she wanted to stay elsewhere—but she doesn't seem upset about it.

"Why am I so comfortable with you?" she asks as she cuddles in even closer. Her hair is sprawled out over my chest, her right hand resting on my nipple, and it's so fucking intimate.

"Because you've accepted that we're mates," I reply softly, and I hear her catch her breath. "Whatever is left of your wolf accepts me as her mate, and this is how easy it feels."

"It never felt like this with Kennedy," she whispers.

That makes me happy, but I don't think she's emotionally ready to hear me diss her ex. Instead, I press a kiss to her head, and my bear keeps me awake until she passes out, rumbling away in a soothing manner.

Only then do I let myself drift off to sleep.

∞

"*I*'ll see you tonight," Nora whispers, pressing a kiss to my cheek.

My eyes fly open, and I'm surprised that she's fully dressed. She's wearing a white dress that reaches her knees, and some kind of black scarf ribbon thing. I don't know, I just know it blocks my view of her tits, and I find it offensive.

She's got a blazer on, and a pair of heels. They're not tall enough to be *fuck me* heels, but I'd still appreciate having them at my ear.

She's fucking gorgeous, but based on the bashful look on her face, I don't think she realises it.

"Are you okay?" Nora asks.

"Where are you going?" I ask at almost the same time.

"Work," she says, smiling. "I didn't mean to wake you—I'm sorry. I just didn't want to leave without saying goodbye. I'll be home around six, though."

"What time do you get lunch?" I ask groggily as I look at the clock on the side. 7 am. *Fuck me.*

"Um, one-ish?"

"See you at lunch then."

"See you at lunch," she replies, heading out. She sounds cheery, which is very reassuring after our night together. Our very PG night.

I close my eyes, preparing to go back to sleep when a bang sounds on the door.

"What?" I snarl, sitting up and glaring at Atticus. He doesn't like the challenge and emits a feral roar, causing me to submit. *Fucking prick.*

"Get dressed. We leave in ten."

I nod, the sleepy fog having disappeared at my Alpha's roar, but he doesn't hang around to see what I think.

Fuck's sake. I wanted to sleep in and surprise Nora with lunch—well, she knows about it, but the thought is still there—and then make her some cookies. But I forgot about her piece of shit ex-mate who needs a beating or twenty-seven.

I quickly dress before heading into the kitchen where they're all sitting around drinking coffee and tea, with the remnants of breakfast on the counter. Voss is half asleep like me, a scowl marring his face, but the other four are wide awake as they chat. Seems we're all being forced to go in for this meeting.

Micah's wearing his usual attire of joggers and a hoodie, as are Atticus and Malachi who are in their work suits. Voss is dressed a lot more casual like me, in a polo shirt and some jeans.

But it's Nora who steals the show. She's wearing a cotton dress that hangs down to her knees. It's long-sleeved with a high-neck, and she's got a pair of tights on, too.

Despite them not being overly provocative, the dress

clings to her, showing off her curves and body. She's beautiful.

Her clothing choices are the biggest draw for me finally taking up a position at Atticus's firm.

"Why are you an early riser?" I groan, teasing my mate. Nora grins, and gets up to make another coffee. I'm surprised when she hands it off to me, though. After all the bitching from Atticus and Kai, I didn't expect her to be so palpable.

But we know her secrets now, so I think they'll find things a bit easier from here on out.

"Drink," she commands, the stern tone jolting my dick. *Is she a secret domme? Fuck, yes.*

"Why is that commanding tone hot?" Micah asks, and I roll my eyes—*mighty hypocritical there, O, you did the same thing*—and press a kiss to her forehead.

"Thank you."

"Anytime," she murmurs, glancing nervously at my mug. I take a sip, seeing her shoulders lose their tension. She gets very anxious over little things. Normal shyness or something more?

"You didn't make me any coffee," Malachi says with a sullen look on his face. *Fucking baby.*

"You were already drinking coffee when I came in," she says slowly, and I pull her to stand between my legs. She fits against my chest, the heels causing her head to rest at the top of my chest rather than lower, and it shows how well she's made for me. Kai's light blue eyes flash at the challenge, and I wink in a taunt to him as I lean forward to kiss her neck. The positioning is awkward with how short she is and my back twinges, but it's worth it to rile the moody bastard up.

It's even more worth it when she gasps slightly, a small

piece of her arousal flooding the room. Kai doesn't respond, not even a twitch in his monolid eyes, so a tiny little bite on her neck is my next taunt. She moans, and every eye moves to us.

Micah's barely breathing as Nora's eyes flutter closed, and I do it again.

"Nora, stop doing that shit at the table," Kai snarls, slamming his fist on the counter, and she freezes in my arms as her panic overtakes her arousal. "Go get your bag, it's time to fucking go."

She nods, and rushes out the room, embarrassment the primary scent coming off her now.

"You're running to work," Atticus says, his tone deadly calm as he stares at Malachi. The King is daring Kai to argue, but luckily for the tiger, he's smart enough not to. "I want you in my office ready for the meeting at eight. Orson was riling you up, but you don't take your shit out on her."

A knife flies through the air, and I can barely hold in my grin when Kai's hand darts out to bat it away, but he still stays silent.

"We don't throw knives around here," Micah warns, looking at the mischievous fox with a grin on his face.

"We also don't talk to my mate like she's a dog to be ordered around," Voss says, twirling a second knife around with a deadly look in his dark green eyes. "So, the stupid little tiger is going to go for his anger management run and will make sure he apologises to her. Otherwise, well, I know more knife tricks than just throwing them, and believe me, some of them can hurt. I'm very creative."

"Welcome to the team," I say, reaching out to fist bump him. He doesn't take the offering, and instead fixes me with my own glare. *What did I do?*

"You're hardly any better," he says, and I raise my hands

in submission. Atticus smirks, not used to me bowing down to another man—a lesser creature at that—but I ignore it. Nora's the only creature I take orders from now—well, you know, in terms of my personal life and not pride business—and her happiness comes before my pride. "Don't use her in your petty fucking displays. She's a person, not a tool for you to wield."

I nod, breaking eye contact, but I can still feel his glare burning into the side of my face. Holy shit. I think I really like the fox. Who would have thought it?

"I'm ready," Nora says quietly, walking into the room. The cheerful mood she was in has been replaced by a level of anxiety. I pinch the bridge of my nose, trying to ward off the headache my bear's attempting to give me. "Are you all coming with?"

"We're coming now, little queen," Atticus says, giving her a giant grin. With an icy tone he adds, "See you at the office, Malachi."

Damn. Atticus only uses Kai's full name when he's pissed.

"He's not coming?" Nora asks, confused, looking at Kai when nobody replies to her. "You're not coming with us?"

"No."

She nods and ducks her head as panic overtakes her in stronger waves. I fucked up. I really fucked up.

"What are you doing today?" Micah asks, grinning at her as he places the mugs in the sink.

"We've got the mock trial tomorrow," she says, looking at him. "So I've got to prep the floor on that."

"For Brian?" Atticus asks.

"Yeah. We've got all his witnesses coming in, too, it's going to be a long day," she replies, seeming happy about that.

"What's he on trial for?" I ask. They all turn and look at me like I'm stupid. Even the fox. Fucking hell. Can I do nothing right today? "What? Was it in the news or something?"

"There's this little thing called client confidentiality," Nora says, grinning up at me as Micah helps her into her coat. It's a real grin, too, that helps soothe me. "But the vast majority of our clients are needing criminal lawyers, so I think that might help narrow it down for you."

"Smart ass," I mutter. "Let's go."

The ride to the office doesn't take very long, and Micah and Voss spend the entire time making our girl laugh. She's adorable, and her laugh is like wind chimes. It's amazing the things you notice about a woman when you actually care about her. When we get out, some jackass is standing with two cups of coffee, watching our car with beady eyes.

"Nora," he calls, giving a half wave. Who the fuck is this snake? Literally, too. He's a snake shifter, and he's pathetic. I can deal with the fox living with us, but I can't deal with a snake. She better not have mated him, or I think I'm going to need to permanently move into my apartment.

"I'll see you inside, Seb," she replies, not even looking at him. That simple act cools down my possessive bear. There's no way she'd disregard a mate that way.

"Who is he?" I murmur, smirking when his eyes flash a bright green at the way he's been dismissed. It's impressive that his snake is attempting to challenge us for Nora, but it's embarrassing. The fox could hurt the snake, never mind the motherfucking King.

"One of the managers on my floor."

"One of yours?" I demand, an irate feeling building up within me.

"Yes, I'm his boss," she murmurs, reaching up to kiss my

cheek but settles for an under jaw kiss since that's all she can reach.

"I wanted to talk to you about the—" Seb starts, following us just a little.

"She said not now, little snake," Voss snaps, and on our way past, he bats the coffee out of Seb's hands. *Yes, the fox can definitely stay.*

"That wasn't nice," Nora admonishes, but she's grinning and clearly feels no guilt about it. "I get that he's a little annoying, but he's an employee here. Stop causing trouble."

"I'm a fox, baby, I'm never not going to cause trouble."

"I'm not going to lie, but I don't know enough about foxes," she says quietly. "Wolves I have down, but the others..."

"Don't stress about it," Micah says, reaching for her hand and squeezing it. She looks at him like he's her whole world, but unlike the moment with Seb, I feel no jealousy. She does the same thing to me. "We know hardly anything about wolves since you're all so damn secretive. It'll be a nice learning curve for us."

He's got a point. Wolves always live in packs exclusive to wolves. Them and birds are the only types of shifters that stick to themselves. They hoard their information, they keep to themselves, apart from the Alphas, and it's extremely rare to find a lone wolf.

Bears, on the other hand, tend to live close to prides now, so that we're able to stay alive. We're not one of the rarest animals, but there's not an abundance of us either. Many years ago, we were one of the first targeted by hunters. Bears are solitary animals, and so despite our large size, we were easily taken down. Now, we're still major introverts, but we do have the safety of being surrounded by other shifters.

Adaptability has kept us alive. It's a scary world, but I'm happy where I am.

"See you guys later," Nora says once the lift doors open on what I'm assuming is her floor.

"Are you going to be okay?" I ask, my heart hammering in my chest.

She laughs, and without answering, exits the lift.

"Do I need to be here for this meeting?" Micah asks once the doors close. "Or can I go to work?"

"Go to work," Atticus says.

Micah nods, and when we get out on the top floor, he stays in the lift and cheerily waves us off. "Have fun."

"He's a brat," I mutter.

"He really is," Atticus says. The three of us walk down the corridor into Atticus's office. He doesn't acknowledge either one of his secretaries, but they're used to it by now.

Once we're in his office, he takes point in the arm chair. "Okay, we've got thirty minutes before Kennedy will be here, so we need to talk about the hunters."

"Fucking great," I sigh, dropping into the seat closest to the door. It's instinctual, the need to protect my Alpha, even when it's not warranted.

"Fucking great," Voss repeats.

The difference between our statements was in the tones we used. One of us was worried and the other sounded like Christmas came early. I definitely was not the excited party.

"Nice to have you on board, Voss," Atticus says, smiling tightly.

Malachi storms in, his suit a little dishevelled from his run, before I can start to recount what I've discovered. The cloud over his head is visible, but he still dips his head in respect to Atticus as he stomps over and throws himself down onto the same sofa as Voss. He's so fucking dramatic, but at least he's smart enough to not take his anger out on Atticus.

"Good run?" Voss chirps, and I can't help but snort.

"Don't fucking talk to me," Kai snaps, falling into his seat before meeting my eyes with a nervous energy. "Is she okay?"

"Fine," I tell him, and just like that, our anger at each other fades.

He runs his hand through his hair and asks, "Does she know about the meeting with Kennedy?"

"No," Atticus says, shaking his head. Voss purses his lips, but I don't protest. Keeping her safe covers more than just her physical wellbeing. The woman that I held in my arms last night needs protecting mentally, too. "So, before we get onto it, I want an update on what the two of you found out a couple weeks ago, so that we can go forward from there."

Great. Time to share one of my failures.

15

DEVOSS

"I've got contacts that I can get working on this," I offer, the upcoming fun time already racing through me.

Nora's in danger, and I am fucking furious about it. I've finally found my mate, and hunters seem to think they can take her from me.

I'm pissed we didn't meet sooner, especially since I've been watching her since she stepped foot into Oxley. The mysterious wolf who rolls into town and is super close to the Alpha, of course every eye within the city has been on her.

We've all had our theories on their relationship. Fuck, I'm part of a betting pool that's trying to figure out how she knows Atticus.

There's been guesses ranging from secret sibling—no idea how that one would work when we all know the previous Alpha only had two kids and they were both male —to his scorned mistress. I don't think anyone guessed mate, which is kind of dumb now that we see them together.

But the rumour on the street has been that she can't stand him, so fated mate was a guess nobody picked.

I wonder if it's too late to change my guess. I could use those favours.

"That works," Mal says, glancing at the clock again as if willing the time to go faster. I don't know if he's wanting the meeting to start with the pathetic ex-mate or if he's wanting it over so he can go make amends with our girl.

"It does," Orson echoes. "Whatever favours need cashed in, make sure they know it's us doing it."

I nod because as much as I can do a lot, having the King at my back will get me even further. It might be a blow to my pride knowing I can't protect my mate alone, but, clearly, fate knew more than I did, and that's why Nora has multiple mates.

"They've approached her more than once. It's clear that they're taunting her," Kai says, his straight, thin eyebrows furrowing together. He's pissed off, his taut tone would send tingles down a weaker man's spine. "That's not something a single circuit would do."

"No, it's not," Atticus says, sighing. "The city is locked down the best it can be, but he still got through. So, we need patrols amping things up, and the pride on high alert. At the moment, I'm not keeping Nora on lockdown, but if we can't keep the city protected, then that will change."

"I don't want that," Orson says, looking sad.

"That's how it will need to be," Atticus says with a shrug. "I want the pride notified, so that they know to be on alert."

"That seems like it'll only spook the hunters, though," I say with a frown.

"And if we let everyone continue going around unaware, they're going to get hurt," Atticus says. Whilst his words are kind of dismissive towards my opinion, his tone is not. He's got to make the tough choices, and he's not led us too wrong before. "I'm not saying we hold a press conference and let everyone know we've got issues with hunters. I'm saying, we let each group leader know what's happening and make sure precautions are in place for the vulnerable groups. Whilst that's happening, I want patrols working overtime, and I want every angle being exhausted so that we can find the network of hunters and get it neutralised."

"Understood," I reply. I don't. I still think it's a stupid idea, but whilst I have one person to look out for, he has eight million.

"You have no idea, do you?" Kai taunts, and I shoot a frosty glare his way.

"Shut the fuck up," Orson snaps at him, surprising me by having my back. "You're just whining because you're in Atticus's bad books."

"I'll talk to her after the meeting with this dickwad," he says, and Orson nods. "So can we drop it? I fucked up, but you weren't an innocent party."

"No, he wasn't. You need to both start acting like better mates. She's already had one dickhead in her life—one I'm still pissed off about the fact that we need to help. So I need us all on the same page from the moment he walks in the room. I don't care how we get to that solution, but we're on one side. Once the meeting is over, you can apologise and fix the issue, or believe me, Voss and his knives will be the least of your issues. For now, though, we're all friends, and we're all ready to make things as hard as possible for this jackass."

I think I might really like Atticus.

"This is going to be great fun," I say, grinning as I lean back more comfortably on the sofa. Kai looks at my legs with a glare that would burn if he could, but that only makes me happier. "I hope he doesn't bring the pregnant chick with him today."

"Nora's sister," Orson reminds me, and I roll my eyes. I'm not stupid. I just don't value her as a person, so I don't think my mate should either. "We're not going to hurt her, even if she deserves it. We have lines, Devoss."

How rude of him to assume I don't have lines, too. And this is actually one of them—especially after what happened to my mum.

But I'm not going there.

Pregnant chicks are the exception to my bloodthirsty nature. That and kids. You never hurt kids. Oh, wait, that's totally the same rule. Pregnant women are just human incubators for the tiny little humans within.

I don't give a fuck about hurting women, or even old people. I quite enjoy making old people bend to be perfectly honestly.

You be a dick, you're fair game. It's that fucking simple. Well, I should say, you get on the wrong side of me, *or* the people that hire me, well, then you're fair game.

Money may be a driving force—don't worry, I accept favours and I.O.Us as well—but I do have some morals.

And potentially causing a miscarriage is something I can't fathom. That shit fucks people up. And doing it when the unborn baby in question is Nora's niece or nephew is something incomprehensible.

I won't ever let my mate suffer the way I did—even if it's only a fraction of the pain.

"You're very weird," Orson says, an eyebrow raised as he regards me with his bright hazel, hooded eyes. "You went from excited, to what I think is your version of upset, to excited again to angry, and then—"

"Everyone has emotions, bear," I reply, holding a scowl

on my face. I don't like that he's reading into my emotions. I don't like it even a little bit.

"Yeah, but yours occurred over the space of like thirty seconds. Do we need to hook you up with a psychiatrist or something?" The weird thing is, he actually sounds like he cares. I'd expect this to be a teasing comment, with a flippant kind of attitude, but he's genuinely asking.

Hm, the bear is intriguing.

Atticus rolls his eyes, but I'm cut off from needing to reply when his phone dings. It's one of those big office phones, and clearly it's an intercom or something. I don't know, I've never really used them other than to bug them so that I can spy. Speaking of bugs, they're a pain in the ass to use with shifters. We can hear the near silent buzzing noise they make, and it causes them to be caught very quickly.

Unless you're creative.

"Alpha Phoenix, I have Alpha Newitt here for you," a woman's voice says. The woman is between forty and forty-five years old, she's a smoker, and she's recently cried. I don't know if this is one of his regular receptionists—secretaries, whatever—but she needs replaced if she is.

Nora doesn't need to be around smokers, even with our shifter lungs, that shit is damaging. I want my mate to live a full, healthy, happy life. Not die years before she should because she's got lung cancer.

"Send him in," Atticus commands, the shift from friend to Alpha becoming very apparent. The green light goes off the phone, and he glances between the four of us with a cool expression on his face. "It's go time."

"Hey, Alpha Phoenix," Kennedy says as he enters. He dips his head as a sign of respect, which is a little embarrassing. He should be greeting Atticus *as an equal* and not as a subordinate. They're the same position, the same rank, and although Atticus is more dominant, that's not a factor. *It shouldn't be a factor, anyway.*

He's wearing a suit, similarly to Atticus and Kai, but it's of cheaper material. I used to eat out of the rubbish, scrounging for anything I could get so that I didn't go hungry, so I'm not being snobbish here.

If he wasn't such a fucking pathetic weasel, I might respect him for trying to better his pack.

But he is, so I don't.

"Newitt," Atticus says, gesturing to the empty sofa. "Take a seat."

"Where's the wife?" Kai asks, and whilst it sounds like he's just making small talk, I know he's asking so that we can try and protect Nora from seeing her.

"Ah, my mate is downstairs," Kennedy replies as he sits down on the sofa opposite me. "She's a bit under the weather, so I gave her permission to get some coffee rather than come up here."

Kai nods, and I know he's dealing with keeping the replacement busy so that our girl doesn't catch wind of her being here. It's the last thing Nora needs, especially when she's got a busy day today.

"You gave her permission to get coffee," Orson deadpans, anger in his tone as he regards the wolf in front of us. "You gave your pregnant *wife* permission to get coffee."

"I don't understand," Kennedy says, looking between Orson and Atticus with a frown on his face.

Atticus laughs, but it's a dry sound. "I do believe you've insulted my second, Newitt."

"How?" Kennedy chokes out as Orson grumbles under his breath. I'm not afraid of the bear, I think as long as he doesn't catch me, I could outwit him. But fuck me, is he someone you never want to go up against.

It's not often a bear is a second to any Alpha, but to an Alpha with a pride the size of Atticus's? It's unheard of.

It's very clear to see why, though.

"He believes that his woman shouldn't need permission to do things," Kai says with a dry tone.

"Coffee!" Orson snarls, and Kennedy jumps at the anger in his tone.

The mild amusement on Atticus's face only worries Kennedy further.

"I'm sorry," Kennedy says, cowering as the scent of his fear fills the air. "I... can we get on track?"

"Sure," Atticus says, sitting up properly. "I never really got the chance to hear what you wanted from me the other night."

"We're wanting to expand into the neighbouring pack," Kennedy says, and I narrow my eyes. A hostile takeover. Fucking coward.

"Why?" Kai asks, grabbing a notebook.

"We've heard rumours about abuse in their pack."

Orson frowns as Kai jots that down, but there's still no change from Atticus. The King has his poker face down.

"Which pack would that be?" Kai asks. "Diamond Heart, Ocean's Moon or—"

"Crystal Blood," Kennedy says.

"Gone are the days of being respected by using a normal name," I say, causing Orson to snort, and Kennedy to glare at me.

"Are you insulting wolves, fox?" he sneers, but he falters when I nod. Because yes, I am, and no, I'm not afraid of the repercussions of doing so to an Alpha.

He's much stronger than Nora, but he's still weak as far as shifters go. Wolves have this ideology that they're the top of the totem pole, but they're barely above preys.

Not because they're weaker biologically, but because they're stupid. Wolves are pack creatures, but who says they need to be so discriminatory?

If they bonded with lions and tigers, and even a rare mythical or two, they'd be unstoppable. Or at the very least, they'd be taken seriously.

"We can't all be part of the Phoenix Pride, Voss, come on," Kai says, smirking at me.

"Wolves would never join a pride," Kennedy scoffs.

"No?" Orson asks, titling his head. "Well, Nora will be a good first to deviate from your pathetic tradition."

"Nora?" Kennedy scoffs. Is that all he can do? Sneer and scoff as if we're beneath him? It's a bit embarrassing since he's the one who has crawled here with his tail between his legs to ask for our help. "She's barely a fucking wolf anymore."

Atticus roars, and Kennedy flinches as he slowly raises his eyes to meet Atticus's angry amber gaze. "Do not disrespect my mate."

"Yes, sir," Kennedy utters. The scent of his terror fills the air, and I roll my eyes.

"You want to take over Crystal Blood?" Kai asks, getting the conversation back on track. Kennedy nods. "Okay, we've got information for them, but I'll want you to go through and verify it's all correct."

"Can't you get an assistant to do that?" he asks.

"No," Kai replies. "We don't send our people into dangerous situations without information. If we're going to help you, then you need to help yourself."

"Why do you want one of our people to do it?" Orson asks with a frown marring his face.

"Because he can't get access to the lands," Atticus says

dryly. "How do you plan on taking over the land if you can't even get one person there?"

Kennedy sighs. "We received word seven weeks ago about the abuse. We sent two wolves —they volunteered, just to make that clear—and they've not come back. We lost contact with them at the five day mark, and so we sent in a second person. They've not come back, but did send a letter informing us they met their mate and wouldn't be returning."

"Don't you need to give permission for that?" Kai asks. His tone shows he's mocking Kennedy, but his question is genuine. They know so little about wolves, and it's my bad for not giving them a crash course with all the information I know.

"No," Kennedy says, shaking his head.

"Elaborate," Atticus commands.

Kennedy jumps in his seat before hastily explaining what I already know. "When true mates are found, their bond to each other overrides their bond to the Alpha once it's formed. They've got to re-join a pack, and if they're part of the same pack it's very easy, if they're part of different packs, then they get a choice."

"And these two wolves chose Crystal Blood?" Orson asks, and he nods.

"The Alpha is holding people hostage." Kennedy's voice is a deadpan accusation, but his heart rate speeds up a little. I narrow my eyes, not liking that.

I'm not sure if that's because he's lying or because he's anxious about it.

"Didn't you send your best in?" Kai asks, writing another note. Kennedy nods. "So how are they so pathetic that they can't leave?"

That stumps Kennedy for a moment.

"I see," Kai replies.

"Well, I've got a plan forming," Atticus says, spreading his legs as he gets more comfortable in his chair. "But if you'd like my help, I've got some requirements."

"Which are?" Kennedy asks, looking around at us all nervously.

"I want anything that your pack kept of Nora's," he says, sitting up properly. "She told me your pack left her in a town with some measly belongings when you rejected her. I want anything that was hers that was left behind because it has no right being in your pack."

"I can't guarantee there will be anything," Kennedy says. The frustration is easy to see on his face. "Her parents; they weren't happy with how weak she was at the rejection. They likely threw it all out."

"Well that's the first requirement," Atticus says, and Kennedy nods with a sour face. "If you want us to do anything for you, you ask, and you better damn hope there's something."

"What's the second one?" Kennedy asks with a sigh.

"David. Neve mentioned him last night, and it made Nora sad, and I want information on him and his mating," Atticus replies. "If my mate would like to attend any ceremonies or whatever the fuck you are doing for them—if anything—I want the information so she can decide if she wants to go."

"Are you joking?" Kennedy demands, shaking his head. "She's been exiled from our pack, she can't come."

"She can as a guest," Atticus replies with a shrug. "If you want my help, you'll make it happen, won't you?"

"You're making demands for your... for Nora—"

"Get her name out of your fucking mouth!" Orson snarls, slamming his fists down on the arm chair. Another flinch from Kennedy as he gapes at the bear. "She's not to be tainted by you any longer"

Kennedy is pale as a sheet as he nods.

"What were you going to say?" Atticus asks with a smirk.

He promised Nora we'd help with whatever Kennedy wanted. I love that Atticus is holding up the promise of not making it easy on him.

"I just... you're making demands for things for your... mate rather than being willing to help solve an abusive situation," Kennedy says. "I came to you because of your reputation."

"My reputation is one of someone who comes in, handles it, and then fixes it," Atticus says, and Kennedy nods. "I don't take demands from wolves, pup. I solve it, and handle it the way I see fit."

"I'm not a pup."

"Hm," Atticus says. "Regardless, *pup*, I don't normally do this. But my mate asked it of me, and so I shall. Now, final requirement."

"Yes?"

"You'll sign this," Atticus says as Kai hands over a stack of papers. There's about thirty sheets here. "Take it to a lawyer, of course, but I want that returned to me by the end of the week if we're going to go forward with anything."

"What's this?" Kennedy asks, reaching for them with shaky hands.

"The terms of the agreement," Atticus replies. "And the penalties for anything that should go wrong."

"You drafted this last night?" Kennedy asks with disgust in his eyes.

"No," Attics replies. "I got this drafted when you initially reached out for help on the off chance I wanted to be benevolent. But the first two requirements were something I added after learning of your relationship to *my* mate."

Kennedy nods slowly. "We'll not be back in pack property until—"

"I don't really care," Atticus replies with a shrug. "It's Thursday today. I want the documents back in my hands by say... Wednesday. There you go, six lovely days to make a decision."

"And if I choose to not sign?" Kennedy asks, a tiny bit of fake bravado in his words.

"Then we'll dissolve the partnership, and maybe we'll even offer help to Crystal Blood," Atticus replies as he stands to his feet. "Orson, would you like to go check on Neve?"

Orson nods and disappears as Kennedy frowns.

"Why is he checking on my mate?"

"Because as much as we hate the woman for what she's done to her sister, she's still a vulnerable woman," Atticus replies. "We'd like to check that she's okay before you leave with her."

"I see." Bitterness laces his words, and he nods. "Can I... can I ask how Nora is?"

"No," Kai replies. "You got one look at her yesterday, and if I have my way, that's all you'll ever get. The Queen of our pride has no need to take up space in your thoughts."

"You made the worst mistake someone could ever make when you threw her away," Atticus says with a shrug. "But that's something I will reap for my own benefit. Nora's everything I could ever want in a mate. Everything my pride could ever want in a Queen."

Kennedy falls silent, shame and regret burning my nostrils.

I don't like the pathetic wolf, so I'm very happy to see him suffer.

Kai takes his leave, and I move over to sit on the same sofa as Kennedy.

"I've got to take this," Atticus says, gesturing to his silent phone, and he's out the office.

"I've got a word of warning to you, wolfie," I murmur, leaning into the Alpha wolf. He turns to me with hatred burning in his eyes. "Nora might not want her revenge—"

"Revenge?" he snarls. "I lost everything that night. I suffered. She got off fucking easy. I was the one who had to mate a woman I couldn't stand. I'm the one who spent weeks battling my wolf, until finally, I had to be tied down and injected with medication just so that we could consummate our bond and be rid of the loyalty my wolf showed her. I'm the one who suffered. I'm the one who deserves revenge."

I blink in surprise, just once, before a smile appears on my face. "Ah, wolfie, you've made me a very happy man."

It's his turn to look surprised. I pull out my favourite pocket knife, and his eyes track the movement. I reach up, him sitting very still, and cut off a small lock of hair. His eyes narrow, but he doesn't pause, as I *accidentally* cut his ear.

"Hm, this will be very handy," I say, putting it in a little baggy right before his eyes.

"What for?"

"Do you know what foxes are good for?" I ask.

"Hunting?" he asks, and I nod.

"We're amazing hunters," I reply, sitting up properly. "And whether you work with Atticus or not, whether you give Nora her things or not, fuck, whether you run away and hide because you know I'm coming for you or not... that won't change anything."

"Coming for me?"

I nod as I rise to my feet. I hear the bear in the corridor, his feet stomping as he walks back to us. "I'll get Nora's revenge for her one day. It won't be tomorrow, and probably not even next year. You'll spend the rest of your life looking over your shoulder, wondering if every bit of bad luck that comes your way is because of me, if that's me finally getting my revenge, or if there's still more to come."

I smell his fear, his anger, and I hear the grinding of his teeth as he holds himself back.

"But I can promise you that no matter what happens to you, I'll never stop until you're a ruined, pathetic mess. I'll never let you be happy because you don't deserve it."

The door opens, and I turn to grin at the bear. "Hey, Orson. How's the replacement?"

"Ready for her mate to join her," Orson replies, and Kennedy jumps to his feet. In his haste, he doesn't grab the papers, and I chuckle.

"Kennedy?" I call, and he turns to look at me, even paler than he was when Atticus and Orson shouted at him. Hm, I like being the scary one in the group. I like knowing that even with Atticus's own brand of torture, I'm the one he truly fears. "You don't want to forget these, do you?"

He shakes his head, and Orson kindly passes them over.

Only when his footsteps are gone does Orson turn to me with a raised, blonde eyebrow. "What was that?"

"What?" I ask in fake confusion.

"His reaction."

"Hm, we had some words," I reply, placing the pocket knife and the baggy of hair into my pocket. "Well, I've got some leads to chase down. Have a good day."

With the roaring laughter from the bear filling my ears, I

cheerily leave Atticus's office. I spot the chain smoker, and make a note to dig up something on her.

I want her gone from Atticus's desk.

But first, it's time to unleash some of this bloodlust on the hunters who think they're clever by trying to take my mate from me. Fools.

Nobody who threatens Nora will ever live long enough to carry it out.

Not as long as I exist.

16

NORA

"So, we've got the client coming in tomorrow," I summarise, glancing around the room. I've explained exactly how things are going to be going down, and what every person is going to be doing. It should go well, which will give the client a clear picture on how things will go on the actual day—albeit a lot smoother. That gives me an idea, actually. "We're going to be doing the mock trial, and making sure he's ready. Any questions?"

Seb's hand raises, and I hold in my frustration. *He is a pain.*

I hate saying it, but it's true. I don't know what he wanted from me this morning, but it agitated the men with me. Orson in particular, but I don't know if I'm just sensitive to his moods since we're further along in our relationship. Crazy, considering I've known Atty for weeks, but Orson for less than twenty-four hours. I feel closer to them all after last night... but I've been nervously checking the clock all morning.

How long is the meeting with my brother-in-law going to take? I thought one of my men would come let me know once it was done, but maybe not. Maybe it was so easy, and they didn't think I needed to know.

"What about the daughter?" Seb asks when I call on him. At least he was polite enough to wait his turn—even if that meant waiting for me to pull myself out of my thoughts.

"She's not going to be here tomorrow, since she's on their witness list and not ours," I remind him. Something I've already covered. "Anything else?"

The door opens at the end of the room, and Malachi walks in grinning. He's wearing a pair of beige trousers that cling to him, and I marvel at his thick thighs. His white shirt shows off his broad shoulders, his toned chest, his lickable abs.

I start to feel embarrassed, but I quickly diminish that urge. He's my mate. If I want to imagine licking all the way down his chest, getting my fill, I damn well can.

I'm relieved he's here, though, and it's made me happy that he's the one who came to let me know how things went with the meeting.

Things were a little tense this morning, which is completely my fault, but it's just been another thing to worry about when I've been here. Work has kept me a little busy, but not enough to stop my mind wandering. Mal is smug as he leans against the wall, his broad frame hard to ignore, so at least the meeting with my sister and her mate went well. Hopefully, we can discuss this morning, and we can go on to have a lovely day.

He doesn't say anything, and when everyone's eyes fly to him, I wink.

"How can I help you, *sir*?" I ask when he stays silent.

"Just making the rounds," he says, shrugging, and it causes his arms to flex. *Wet panties, check.* "Making sure the staff are doing their jobs, you know? Some of them hide out in conference rooms rather than working, so I like to have a more personalised touch."

"I do," I say, not backing down from our intense staring.

It seems someone is still grouchy over our small disagreement this morning. I won't tolerate a second mate treating me like shit, but that wasn't what this morning was. He was tired and grouchy and clearly didn't like me and Orson being slightly sexual at the breakfast table.

I get it. Not everyone is open with bedroom activities, and I can respect that now that I know it's a boundary. I don't need him dragging things into my meetings because I was never going to avoid him. I *want* to talk to him. I want to figure things out and apologise for upsetting him.

There's no point fighting the bond anymore, not now that my past has come to light, so it would be good if we could be happy together—with or without the wolf within.

"So, how are things?" he asks, his light blue eyes surveying the room. The people in the room are glancing between the two of us, aware something is happening, but unsure what.

"Well, it is a high profile case, and only those on it are going to be included in the details," I say, smiling. "So, rest assured we're working diligently, but unless you want to be on the case and work underneath me, just trust that I'm capable of doing the job I was hired to do."

It's my job to prepare this so that our solicitors don't need to. Come tomorrow, they'll be the ones running the show, and I'll be stepping back into a more legal assistant sort of role. But today, the show is mine, and these people are mine to organise.

His nostrils flare, but I look away, dismissing him. I want to talk properly, and that needs to be done without witnesses. "Now, does anyone else have any questions?"

"I have one," Malachi says, even going as far as to raise his hand. *Of course he does.*

"Well, since nobody else does, why don't you take a seat, and we can go through them together so everyone else can get on with their day, Mr Romero," I offer, shaking my head slightly.

I get that the childishness is part of his personality, but I don't want our relationship to be founded on underhanded tactics. I want to have a healthy relationship—something I've never experienced—and that means when we fight or someone does something that upsets someone else, we can handle it properly.

I wait for his nod before dismissing everyone else. "Thanks, everyone. I'll be here until late, so any questions, you know where to find me."

As the room clears out, Malachi slides into the seat at the head of the table, something that doesn't escape my notice. I sit opposite him and wait for him to speak. Clearly, he's doing the same thing because we sit here in silence for seven hundred and thirty-five seconds. I only know the time because the clock ticks for each second, which is kind of relaxing despite the tenseness between my mate and I.

"What can I do for you then, *sir*?" I'm more than capable of broaching the silence, especially since it seems he's more content to just look at me instead of speak.

"Stop with the *sir*," he sighs, running his hands through his oily, dark brown hair. "I came to apologise, little wolf."

"You came to interrupt my very first giant meeting, where a very large client has a mock trial happening... to apologise? You couldn't wait until the meeting was over?"

I don't understand this man. He's flustered, I can see that, but I don't understand why.

"I didn't think of that," he says slowly, his brows

furrowed. "I was an ass this morning, and again just now. I'm sorry, little wolf. I'm trying to make things right, but I... I suck at this."

"Your apology is heard and accepted," I reply, walking to slide into the seat next to him. I squeeze his knee, and he meets my eyes. "I get that what Orson and I were doing was making you uncomfortable, and I'm sorry about that. You were right, it was the breakfast table, and it was inappropriate. I can't fix it, but I can let you know that I understand your position on public displays and that I'll do better in the future."

His frown alerts me to his confusion, and I smile knowing he's the one feeling a little lost right now. I can help with that.

"For whatever reason, the bond between Orson and I has developed faster than the one we share," I say, almost apologetically. "I don't know why, but that doesn't mean I need to flaunt it in front of you. I'm sorry, Mal. You don't need to apologise to me because I get that some things are uncomfortable to talk about, but I want you to understand that I'll learn and do better. PDA isn't your thing, and I get that."

He stands without saying a word and moves to the door. I've just bared my heart... and he's leaving. Tears well up in my eyes, and I drop my head so I don't need to watch him walk out of the door.

"Calm down, little wolf," he soothes, his tiger rumbling in his chest as an added soothing tactic. "I'm locking the door so nobody can interrupt us. Then I'm closing the blinds, and we're going to talk properly, okay?"

"Okay."

He does exactly that before kneeling in front of me. His head reaches my shoulders as he looks up at me in earnest.

Mal reaches up to wipe away the few tears that have fallen, and he smiles, but it's a sad look on him. "I fucked up, little wolf. I never should have snapped at you this morning because I took it out on the wrong person. I was pissed at Orson and not you. I'm not upset that your bond is more developed with him than it is with me. I'm not upset that you stayed in his bed or any other actions you two did together."

"Then why are you mad?"

"I'm mad because for the last five hours, whilst I've been upstairs with your dickhead ex-mate, you were here thinking you did something wrong. You were already panicked about today, for the big meeting, and having to have him in this building where your future is going to be, and I added to it."

Men are confusing. This man at least. He's saying words and talking around the issue, but he's not telling me what's actually wrong. He's apologising, and he's saying that he directed his energy to the wrong person, but... he's not once said what was wrong. Even when I was a wolf, mind reading was not a skill I possessed. I need him to open up just a little so that I can understand.

"Little wolf, I can smell your frustration, but why are you getting annoyed with me?" he asks, hurt etched into his face. He threads his hand with mine and squeezes them together.

"Because I was open with you. I told you my issue, I talked about what I had done, and what I was going to do to fix it. You're just talking around the bush, and I'm so confused. What are you thinking? How are you feeling? Can you let me into your mind... just a little?"

He grins and squeezes my hand again. "Before I do tell you the issue... you do know it's beating around the bush, right? I can't have you embarrassing yourself thinking it's talking around the bush. Who talks around a bush?"

I roll my eyes, and motion for him to get on with it. He's not funny, even if he thinks that he is.

"Orson is number two in the pride. I'm close to his level, but I'm not *on* his level. It's not something that bothers me ninety-five percent of the time... but that other five percent, well, that other five percent is a problem. He's not a pack animal, I am. He doesn't care that he's number two, whereas I would. He spends more time away from Atticus than he does with him, but he's still in the position I want to be in."

"And today aggravated that?" I ask gently.

I think back to when Atticus told me about when one of his brothers—who I now guess is Orson—takes time away from the group. He'll head to his own apartment and need some time, and I kind of get it a bit more now that I know Orson's a bear and likes the solidarity. So this dynamic helps me understand Mal's frustration this morning.

Okay, so I was wrong about what upset him, so I'm glad he opened up to me.

"The two of you acted so effortlessly, so easily. We've had weeks of built-up frustration, of banter, of a connection, and yet, when it came to it, you bonded with him first. I'm not upset about that, believe me, I'm not because like Orson said, you deserve all the love we can give you, and clearly Orson's brand of safety was something you really needed last night. You really do deserve the world, baby. You've had a hard life, and now that we're here, I want you showered in love. I want you smiling and making coffee and just being comfortable in my home, in your new home."

He presses a kiss to my hands before sighing. "Orson, however, knows of my jealousy issues, and this morning, the kissing you on the neck and biting you wasn't him being sweet towards you, but it was him using you to taunt me. He knew exactly what he was doing, which isn't funny. It's not cute, it's immature, and it pissed me off."

I frown, but he doesn't stop talking.

"And, yeah, I was a little jealous, but that played no part in my anger. It was the way he used you in our dominance battle that pissed me off. Your parents used you. Your sister used you. Your fucking mate used you. We're meant to be better than them because you deserve better. I'm not saying we're perfect people, little wolf, because we're not. We're never going to be perfect, but we are *good* people. And we're going to be good mates, and it pissed me off that Orson thought to use you like that within the first twenty-four fucking hours of him knowing you. That's why I got pissy, and I acted out. So I'm sorry, I'm so fucking sorry that at our first breakfast together, we fucked it up."

I pull my hand away, and he doesn't even fight me, but instead of walking away like I think he expects, I wrap my arms around his neck and let him pull me into him. I'm cradled into his chest, and he starts pressing kisses to the top of my head as we both sit on the floor together rather than one of the forty chairs in the room.

A tear drips onto my head, but before I can react, a knock sounds on the door, interrupting us. A loud roar leaves my tiger, and his grip on me tightens. It's a good thing he has advanced senses and can tell who was on the other side, or I'd be annoyed he could have outed us.

"Easy tiger," I murmur before bursting out laughing at my accidental joke. "Sorry, bad pun."

"I'm honestly just grateful you got that one right," he teases, and stands up without dropping me, and sits into the seat I vacated. "You're amazing, you know that?"

Instead of answering, I move so I'm straddling him and

press our lips together. The kiss is hesitant on my end, but a soft growl leaves his throat as he takes over. His tiger is clearly close to the surface as he's been very growly today, and I'm kind of nervous about meeting his other form. Mal's hands cup my ass as his tongue invades my mouth. It's sloppy, wet, but oh so perfect. Until I accidentally bite his tongue, and he hisses.

"I'm not against pain in the bedroom, little wolf, but that hurt," he groans, pulling away. He taps me on the nose, humour evident in his eyes. "You don't bite tongues."

"Would you believe me if I said it was an accident?" I ask, ducking my head the best I can in this position.

"Whoa, that's a huge whiff of embarrassment. Why are you embarrassed?" he asks, humour lacing his tone. I don't move, so he tucks my veil away from my face by moving my hair out of the way.

"I've never done this before." I press my lips together, and he beams.

"Kissed someone?"

I roll my eyes and look at him properly. "I wanted to wait for my mate. Is there something wrong with that?" And then once I met him, I was too busy trying to put myself back together than focusing on getting the mighty O.

And no, I don't mean Orson.

"Oh, baby, you have no idea how happy that makes me," he says, leaning forward to kiss my cheek. "No idea at all."

He presses featherlight kisses along my jaw before his fingertip moves to tilt my chin up.

His kisses trail down my neck, still as gentle as the ones he left across my jaw, and his teeth hover around my jugular.

"I want to bite you," he murmurs, his hand that was

cupping my ass grips it a little harder. "I won't bite hard enough to mark you, but I really need this. Please."

I don't reply, and he stays in that position, hovering at my neck, waiting for me to give him permission. Even with knowing he's more dominant than I am, and knowing how easily he can overpower me and take what he wants, I still feel in control. He *lets* me have that control. I let my right-hand trail up his back, very lightly, before gripping the back of his neck tightly. I hope I'm not hurting him, but it makes me feel powerful... it makes me feel in control.

"Yes," I say, it escaping as a breathy moan.

With the permission he needed given, he bites down on my neck, hard, but the initial pain fades into pleasure, and I let out a moan. It still hurts, but a little spark of something hits me as heat travels down to my core. A very quiet howl sounds inside of me, so fucking quiet it was barely loud enough for me to recognise it, but I did. My wolf hasn't fully left me... *fuck.*

I can't help the tears that appear in my eyes, tears of gratitude and relief, because I know he helped bring her back—even if just a little—but I also can't ignore the panic from setting in. When his teeth don't let up, I rock into him a little. Our positioning sucks, but I don't care. I need friction, I need something.

"Please," I murmur, being driven by a need within me. A need the hazy mess inside my head can't understand. "Please."

"Please what?" he asks, rocking ever so slightly, and I moan in both want and frustration. *"What do you want, little wolf? Do you want me to kiss you? Do you want to taste your blood on my lips? Is that what you want?"*

"Please."

It's the only word I can think of because I don't know what I want. I don't know what I need. I just need to dispel the built up frustration, the built-up energy between the two of us. I have no idea how to express that into words, but I think he knows.

He pulls away from my neck, licking the open wound. His teeth elongated slightly when he cut into my neck, but he didn't fully morph his mouth. If tigers mark the same as wolves, then that explains why I wasn't marked. I trusted him, and he didn't let me down.

"When the connection is open like that, I can hear what you're thinking," he says softly, and I frown when the desire thrumming between us both dissipates. "I'm pleased you heard your wolf, little wolf, but I'm not going to rush our relationship for you to have more of her. You're a virgin, and that's completely okay, but you waited to do the act so it could be meaningful. I'd love nothing more than to fuck you in this office, but not for the first time, and not for this reason."

I... as much as he says with the connection open like that he can hear what I'm thinking, he's misunderstood. Now that the arousal has dimmed, I can understand the jumbled mess of thoughts, and I know how wrong he is.

I don't want to rush our relationship to get more of my wolf back, to become whole with her again. I don't even think I want her back in my life. I wasn't trying to rush things between us, I was just enjoying the moment together. I respect him for cutting it off before we took things too far because we are at work, and I know there are shifters here, but he's wrong about the reasoning.

I don't want my wolf back.

Not now, not ever.

"I'm sorry," I sigh, sitting back to look at him. "I loved

that we had an intimate moment, and I may have gotten just a little carried away."

"You don't need to apologise," he replies, kissing the top of my head. "I loved that we were intimate, too." He squeezes my waist before sitting back in the chair. "Atticus wants to talk to you about your bedroom."

Quick change of subject, but I think the erection pressing into me might have something to do with that.

"I'm at work. We can discuss my bedroom tonight once I'm finished." I flick my hair over my shoulders, grinning at him. "We now have a new rule."

"Oh, we do, do we?" he asks, a teasing grin spreading across his face.

"Yes," I reply, earnestly. "Only one mate can come and interrupt my work per day, so you've used the groups allotment just now."

"Oh, so this is my day?" he asks, winking at my exasperation. "I accept, as will the others, but, baby, a better rule would have been to not let any of us come and interrupt your workday."

Well, yeah, obviously, but then I'd not get to see them all day.

"But I know my men," I tease, seeing my opportunity to play it off like I'm doing them a favour and not myself. "You're all needy. I don't think it's a coincidence that Atty comes down three whole floors every time he needs a cup of coffee."

"I can't speak for him," he says, shrugging. "Maybe the coffee here is better. Did you make it?"

"No."

"Oh, then yeah, he probably just wants to see you," he says, laughing. "I did my best to help a brother out, but his obsession clearly can't be explained away."

I lean forward to kiss his nose, loving how his eyes flash

amber. It's such a pretty colour, one I can now appreciate rather than hate, and it makes me happy to see his animal coming forward.

Even if the thought of meeting the tiger within gives me hives.

"I told you, I'm figuring you all out. But for now, I really do need to get back to work. Tomorrow is going to be a very long and trying day, and more than half these people don't like me," I say, sitting back in his lap slightly. "Did you know five of them applied for my job, and yet, I never even applied for my job? I'm the youngest person here, and I'm in charge. That doesn't lead to many friends."

"We're only a few years older than you and in managerial positions," he says, shrugging. "Atticus is twenty-eight, Orson is twenty-six, as is Micah. I'm the middle at twenty-seven. I think Voss is your age, though, maybe a year or so older." My jaw drops a little, and he grins. "Close your mouth, little wolf. It gives me bad ideas."

"You're incorrigible."

"But, yeah, we're all close to your age," he says softly. "Atticus has been running this pack and making it a safe haven for shifters since he was nineteen years old. So don't let these close-minded people think you're not good at your job because of your age."

"They don't think that."

His hand darts up faster than my eyes can follow and flicks my forehead. My eyes widen, and he smirks. "We're going to work on this poor self-esteem of yours. Atticus might have realised you were his mate and wanted you here, but he'd never risk his company—and the livelihood of our pride—by giving you a job you couldn't handle. There are many positions at this branch you could have taken, but if you weren't a fit for any of those, he's King here, baby, so he could have made a position for you if it were needed. So, go be a boss. Shout at someone, it always makes me feel better."

"I think our management styles might be slightly different," I reply, ducking my head to wipe away the tears that have appeared. It's been too long since someone has found any good in me, since someone has cared to even look.

"We've got you now, little wolf," he promises, pulling me in for a hug. He repeats the words Orson said the night before, and it's reassuring to know they all feel the same. They're so fucking amazing, and I can't believe fate was kind enough to me to give me a second chance. Multiple second chances to be precise.

Another knock sounds on the door, and he sighs before placing me on the ground.

"I'm glad we talked," he says softly. "But duty calls. Some annoying fuck"—he raises his voice slightly on the *annoying fuck* part of his sentence, and I'm not sure why—"wants this office. I bet it's Seb."

"Is he a snake shifter?" I ask, and he nods. "Ah. He annoyed Orson and the others this morning, and I didn't know if it was an insult or not."

"Let me guess, he tried bringing you some coffee again?" Mal growls, and I nod, smiling. "Someone better have knocked the damn cup out his hands."

"Voss did."

"Good man, that one," he says, grinning. "He's a little fucked up, but he's a good man."

Interesting. He walks over to unlock the door, and it flies open to reveal Orson, not Seb. Mal ushers him in, shutting the door and locking it once again.

"Why do I smell your blood?" Orson roars, storming forward, and tilting my head to the side. "Oh." He leans forward and licks it off my neck before pressing a kiss to my pulse.

"Nah, you can't talk to her today," Mal says, grinning. "She has a new rule."

"Oh, yeah?" Orson asks, looking down at me. "Going to fill me in?"

Tongue-tied, I can do little more than gape at him. I didn't pay good enough attention this morning, but he's wearing a very nice suit today. Dark blue, which looks good against his tanned skin, and the shirt is low cut enough that I can see his chest hair.

"Only one mate is allowed to interrupt her workday," Mal says, drawing my eyes away from the beauty that is my bear mate. "I think we'll need to take turns on keeping Atticus busy because he'll try and steal all the slots, and then we'll never get to see her during the day."

"I agree," Orson says, nodding seriously. "And keeping Voss away. He's annoying. Let him babysit Atticus, and the rest of us can hang out here."

"Stop being mean," I sigh, and I reach for Orson's hand. "This morning was rude, especially since I didn't understand you were using me to taunt Mal. Don't do it again."

"I know," he murmurs, regret on his face. "I'm a dick, but that's no excuse."

"Great. Glad that's all sorted. Time for me to go to work," I say. "Have a good day."

With that, I exit the office and head to the toilets, luckily not running into anyone. If Orson could smell my blood, so can the other people in the office. That's not something I want to add to my already tense position here.

I might have mates in high places, but I can't rely on them to fix every problem I have. Especially since I know they'd do it, no questions asked.

I can do this.

Because I'll have them at my back, not covering my front.

17

NORA

"You did this?" I ask, glancing around at the room Atticus has got set up for me at the house. I never had the chance to see it yesterday, since I spent the night in Orson's room, but I doubt it looked like this previously. It's... perfect.

"Do you like it?" he asks nervously.

Stupid question. The room is beautiful and reminds me a lot of my old place. The walls are a similar shade of green, but instead of the poor attempt at mixing glitter in that I did, this looks professionally done. Whoever did this room knew what they were doing and it shows. There's a reading nook in the corner, fitted with a pillow fort and blankets. There's a giant bookshelf that runs alongside the sidewall, adjacent to my bed.

Speaking of the bed, I know it's got to be custom-built. I had a double at my flat, but this, this is even bigger than a super king. By the wry smile on his face, it doesn't take a genius to put together why. The bedsheets are a dark brown that actually complements the green theme. There's a canopy of leaves, well a leaf effect woven into the fabric, surrounding the bed, and it's perfect.

Shifters are very into nature because a small part of us loves the freedom it provides. When I lost my wolf, that's something that stayed with me. The connection to nature remained, and once I sorted my mental health out, I regularly spent time camping in my backyard—I'm not stupid enough to do it overnight—and going hiking so I could keep that feeling of freedom.

I love that he's made it so I can have the semblance of this within my bedroom. It's genuinely perfect.

He claps his hands, causing me to jump, but the lights just shut off. We're enveloped into darkness, and my heart begins to race.

"Now, clap three times fast," he murmurs, somehow now standing right behind me. *Damn shifters and their speed.* "Do it, little queen."

Unable to ignore his command or his excitement, I clap three times and grin when all the little fairy lights turn on.

"This is perfect," I gasp, looking around in amazement. The fairy lights are a mixture of bulbs and little butterflies, the warm glow of the light making everything so much more homey.

"Go lay down and look up." I do, and look up at the ceiling as he commanded. "Clap twice, hard."

When I do as he says, I start to cry seeing the way the stars light up bright. I can't help it. How could someone who barely knows me go to this much effort—yes, he didn't actually do it, but he did organise it for me—to make me happy?

I don't deserve this.

He climbs onto the bed with me and pulls me onto his chest. He's wearing a shirt, but the buttons are mostly undone, showcasing the little bit of chest hair he has between his pert nipples. I undo them further, ignoring the amusement on Atticus's face, before resting my head on his chest. I love being able to hear his heartbeat, and the skin-to-skin contact soothes me.

We lay this way for a little bit, me taking comfort from my Alpha mate, and him just content to offer it.

I really don't deserve it.

"You are worthy of our love, Nora," he murmurs, his tone soft but passionate. "I hate that you feel you're not worthy of it, but you are. You deserve this."

That stops my tears, and I push away to sit up and look at him properly. "You heard that?"

"Yes."

"Atty... you didn't open a connection." He shakes his head in the negative, not understanding my surprise. If he didn't do it, that means *I* did. "That's twice today I've felt her. She howled earlier when I was with Mal. Now she's sending you thoughts. She's still with me."

My voice cracks at the last word, and the tears flow again.

Losing her was the worst thing that ever happened to me. It wasn't an immediate thing. It would have been so much fairer if when Kennedy said that he rejected me, that she died off and left me immediately. She didn't. That's not how it goes when you lose your soul.

She cried for days. She'd howl and plead and beg for her mate. She was suffering almost as if he was dead because she couldn't feel him. She couldn't feel the connection between the two of us anymore. She didn't get it. She had no choice.

Her mate didn't love her.

We went through all of the stages of grief, and it was

awful. I suffered with her, but I at least understood what happened. I was kicked out of the pack, I lost my family, and I lost my entire life. My wolf was crying, she was mourning, but at least she had me to help her through it. I had nobody there with me.

It would have been kinder to put a bullet to my head. That's how I felt then, and that's still how I feel now. I learnt how to deal with things. I learnt how to live a life without my wolf. I don't wish that fate on anyone.

So for her to now start to resurface, I'm so fucking happy, but I'm so, so scared. I don't know whether she can handle being around again. I've been elated every time I've felt her, but within me has been doubt. Doubt that she's not going to be able to handle life again. Doubt that she's going to be as weak as she was the first time. Doubt that she's going to be whole again.

My parents and my mate thought I was weak. My compassion, my light, my joy, were traits they thought would ruin our pack. My wolf wasn't those things—she's primal, she's powerful, but she wasn't the light. She left me, and I had to find myself again.

It took months of therapy before I could go outside. It took weeks before I felt like I could continue to live. I wanted to die. I was alone and depressed, and I wanted to die. *I* put myself back together. I did it all with no help from her.

Now she wants to come back when I'm whole again. She wants to come back now that there are men to love her. I wasn't good enough to be the reason she kept living. I don't want her back. I can't have her back if she's going to be as weak as she was the first time.

I need strength. I need to still be the light, the compassion, the joy.

What if she can't handle that? What if she comes back and realises there's nothing worth living for again? What if she leaves me again? What if they leave us, and I have to suffer that pain quintfold?

I don't know if I'm going to be strong enough to put myself back together a second time.

"I don't think quintfold is a word," Atty says, his voice thick with unshed tears. "I've told you, little queen, you are my mate. I know we've got a while to go before we earn your trust, but we will earn it. We're not going anywhere."

I can't stop my tears, but he doesn't budge from holding me.

This is what a mate is meant to do. A mate is meant to be there for you in your weakest moments... not cause them.

I give in to the dark thoughts in my mind, and I let them all out. I cry, I scream, I plead, I suffer. Atticus sits with me the entire time. He doesn't say a word, he just stays with me. She's whining in my head, not very loud, but it's louder than she was yesterday. She's going to keep getting louder until she takes over, and I'm stuck with her again.

I'm not strong enough to put myself back together for a second time.

Eventually, I stop crying. I haven't stopped because I'm over my grief, or my panic. I stopped because there's nothing else in me to give. I'm empty and exhausted... but so is she.

And that's something I can live with. If I'm running on empty, so is she, and she can't take over if she's this weak.

Atticus pulls a tissue, from where I have no idea, and wipes at my eyes and cheeks before lifting me off the bed.

"Atty put me down," I whisper, not able to talk any louder with how sore my throat is. I don't want to see the others because they'll worry about the state I'm in. I can't handle the inquisition. Not tonight. He listens and steadies me on the ground before kneeling in front of me with his head bowed.

"What are you doing?" I ask, my voice shrill.

"Submitting to my queen," he replies, bearing his neck. "I can't prove that I'm a good man, but I can show you how our relationship will work. I'm the Alpha—the King—but you are the queen. You're the compassion to my rage. You're the joy to my misery. You're the light to my darkness. *You are my mate.*"

Silently, I cry once more. I thought I had nothing left to give... but Atticus proved me wrong. He heard my worries, and he reassured me in a way that only he can. He picked up on the qualities I was scared to lose, and he made sure I knew that they were good enough for him.

I kneel, too, and kiss his neck before wrapping my arms around him. No more words need to be said. He gave me the greatest gift of all tonight. *His submission.*

18

NORA

$\mathcal{A}$tty carries me into the living room, placing me into the empty spot between Malachi and Micah on the sofa. The former hands me a plate, and Micah places two slices of pepperoni pizza onto it. It's smooth, like we've practiced it a hundred times, and nobody asks any questions about what I was doing upstairs with Atticus. I look like shit, but they don't ask, just trusting that Atticus handled it— handled me. I love that.

"How did the mock trial prep go?" Atticus asks when Mal hands him a plate next. He grabs his own slices of pizza, five to my two, and takes a seat on the arm chair to the right of us. "I never got the chance to touch base earlier."

"It was fine," I tell him. "We're ready for tomorrow. Oh, um, don't be alarmed, but I've scheduled a fire alarm test."

This was my idea earlier, it'll help make the situation not go as smoothly. It might do more harm than good, but we don't know until we try.

"To go off during the trial?" Mal asks, his thin brows furrowing as he tries to work out what I mean. I nod, a small smile on my lips.

He's sitting with his legs crossed, a pillow over his lap, and then his plate is resting on that. He's got grease on his fingers, that he licks off, before taking another bite of food.

He's so aggressive in the way he eats it, and I can't help but just watch.

"Why?" Atticus asks, drawing my eyes away from Mal's eating habits.

I wink but don't reply, and Atticus rolls his eyes.

"Where's Devoss and Orson?" I ask before taking a bite of my pizza. It's nice, but my appetite has disappeared so I place it back down. Atticus's eyes narrow on the movement, but he doesn't comment.

"Voss is probably digging a hole in the garden or something," Malachi says, and I giggle, even though it's mean since he's not here to defend himself. "And Orson is busy with pride things."

"Oh."

"Now, back to this fire drill," Atticus demands, leaning forward in his seat. His pizza plate is nearly knocked over, but somehow he manages. He's concerned, but I don't know whether it's for me, his building, or something else entirely. It's kind of cute seeing him this riled up, though. "What are you doing?"

I take a bite of food, taunting him a little since I truly don't want to eat it. His ocean blue eyes darken as exasperation fills him, and it's kind of funny to let him simmer for a moment before I explain. The fire alarm is just something that will go wrong—the real trial will be filled with hurdles, and so one this drastic will help them be prepared. It might be silly, but I like to be prepared, and when I mentioned it to the solicitor who was acting as the judge, she loved the idea.

"Need any help with tomorrow?" Mal asks once we've cleared away the plates. "I can be free."

"And I can handle it," I say. He nods, and that's that.

"Time to watch a movie," Micah says, tugging me upstairs with him. "They're going to do boring shit, and you've got a new room I want to utilise."

"Sounds sexual, and that's not okay," Mal calls, but Atticus tells him to shut up.

"He's my brother," I hear Mal whine, but Micah pulls me into my room before I can hear the response from Atticus.

He closes the door, leaning against it with a smirk on his diamond shaped face. His full lips are in a sort of pout as his ebony eyes rake over me with a mixture of lust and amusement.

It's a look nobody should be able to pull off, but Micah can.

He's ditched the hoodie he wore today but is still in the same joggers and t-shirt. You know, the t-shirt that is so tightly moulded to his chest, that I hate the thought of anyone but me seeing him in it.

Micah's the first to admit that he's not the most athletic man around, but his body doesn't agree with that statement. He's got a slim build, sure, but his chest is toned, and his thighs... when did thighs become my biggest turn on in a guy?

That's weird, right?

"What's got that look on your face?" Micah asks, raising one of his bushy brows. *I'd love to get near them with a pair of tweezers.* "Nora?"

"Nothing. Just thinking about Mal's teasing."

"You know, there are only eleven months between Kai and me," he says, pushing off the door and stalking forward. Mal didn't go into the specific time frames when he told me how old everyone was, but I knew there was a close gap between the two of them. "He acts like I'm twelve and he's fifty, but there's not even a year between us. Hell, we were even in the same school year, much to his annoyance."

"You two are close, though, it's sweet."

He nods and does a complicated clap, and the floor moves slightly to give way for a TV screen to rise from the floor. *What the fuck?*

"This is high tech," I mumble, my eyes not wavering from the giant screen appearing from my floor. "Like, I think it might even bypass that stage and go straight to the obscene level."

"I work in the technology department," he reminds me. "Our rooms are all like this. Technology makes your life easier, and the lights are great for our... never mind. Grab some pyjamas so we can get comfortable. What kind of movies do you like?"

"I'm not picky."

I don't like how he brushed past talking about how the lights are good for our animals because he was scared it would upset me. I might not have mine fully, but she's kind of here. I care about theirs, too, so I'd love to know what the technology does and how it helps. He's focused on the screen, though, the conversation made him uncomfortable, so I stay quiet.

I grab my pyjamas from the dresser and change into them before throwing my work clothes into the washing chute. Apparently, my mates are rich enough to have a washing chute. It's crazy.

"Stop being judgy," Micah admonishes, and I grin as I climb into bed. "I don't get what you're judging, but I can smell it."

"Judgemental isn't a smell," I argue, and he winks.

"Sure, it's not, pretty girl. But was I wrong about the judgement?"

I roll my eyes and swipe the remote to start flicking through shows.

"Was it the TV in the floor? Humans have them, too. They're not that obscene."

"I kind of like my floor TV," I reply, settling on a Disney movie called *Zootopia*. He doesn't argue and pulls me into his chest as his tiger begins to purr. My mates constantly manhandle me... but I kind of like it.

"Then what?"

"The washing chute," I murmur, closing my eyes. "Who even does the washing? Please don't tell me you have a maid."

"Nothing wrong with having maids," he argues.

"No, there's not. I'd just feel very uncomfortable having someone you pay to clean my clothes."

"That's fair enough. Well, luckily that's not the case."

"Then who does your washing?" I ask.

"You might laugh, but Orson," he replies, kissing the top of my head. "The bear nests a lot. It's weird as fuck, but he enjoys the housework. He cooks, cleans, and bakes. If he ever mentions spring cleaning or deep cleaning, run far away, pretty girl. He goes mental and even pulls out toothbrushes to get right in the grout. And we can never do it right, he just shouts and gets mad before taking over. It's easier to hide out."

I giggle and listen as he outlines some of their quirks. Atticus is apparently a billionaire—I know, it's so shocking. How I didn't have a heart attack when Micah shared this information, I'll never know—who does a lot of rescuing with his money. Buying houses for pride members, adding extra people into the pride so he can look after them, and he funds a lot of projects from the pride. It's sweet and doesn't surprise me.

Malachi is apparently a gym buff, another thing that doesn't surprise me at all. He works out a lot and is the only reason Micah is in shape—according to him. He also does self-defence sessions for the pride, making sure that everyone knows how to defend themselves against hunters, and other types of shifters.

He knows very little about Devoss, which makes me a bit sad. I've missed my fox mate tonight, but there's time to learn everything about him. We do have forever.

"What else do you know about Atty?" I ask quietly because the little fact about him having lots of money wasn't enough.

"I know we say it a lot, but Atticus is the King. He might have his home base at the criminal law office, but he's got his fingers in all of the pies. He's the reason that the tiny convenience store is still thriving because they don't make enough money to cover their rent, but they provide a service that Atticus encourages. He's the reason the otters still have their home because they're currently not working whilst they figure out their situation. Atticus knows everyone— even if they don't know him—and he takes care of every person he can."

My mates are good men. Really good men.

I cuddle in closer, and it doesn't take me long to drift off to the sounds of a police chase on the TV.

"Good morning," Voss says. My eyes fly open when a slender finger with slightly too long nails rakes down my cheek. I turn my head, and spot my red-headed mate smiling as he kneels next to the bed. "I know you've got your big case thing today, but could we have breakfast together first?"

"That would be amazing. I really missed you last night." Micah answers before I can, and I have to hide my face in the pillows to stop my giggles.

"I don't know why you're laughing," Voss teases, tickling my sides as he comes onto the bed. "I did come to invite Micah to breakfast and not you."

"Mhm," I choke out through my laughter. He doesn't let up on the tickles, and I'm wriggling around on the bed desperate to not piss myself. "Stop! I need a wee! Stop!"

"Sounds like she's not begging enough," Micah says, and I groan through the laughing.

"Please!"

"You beg so prettily," he replies, stopping his attack. He leans down and presses a kiss to my lips before sitting up. "But go put some clothes on. We don't have long if you're going to be at your meeting thing early."

"Sounds good."

I edge out the bed and grab some clothes before heading into the bathroom. I take a quick shower, get dressed, before going down to the kitchen where Voss and Micah are sitting. Micah's had a shower like me, which is evident by his wet hair, because otherwise I'd not have known.

He's wearing identical clothes to the ones he was wearing yesterday, and if I didn't know any better, I'd think they *were* the same ones.

"Where are the others?" I ask, looking around.

"They already went into the office," Micah replies. "They've got an early meeting, and they knew you were going out with Voss, so didn't wake you."

"Oh."

Why does that make me so uneasy?

"Text them on the way," Voss says. "See you soon, Micah."

"Bye," he replies, grabbing my wrist as I try to walk past him. I look up, and he smiles softly. "Have a good day, pretty girl. I'll see you shortly."

"See you soon," I reply, ducking my head to kiss his cheek. I then follow Voss out to the car.

"Is this yours?" I ask, taking in the Tesla in front of me. It's sleek black, five doors, four wheels, you know a standard car from someone who knows absolutely nothing about them. What I do know, though, is that it's most definitely *not* Voss's type.

"No," he scoffs, proving my point. I open the front seat, and get comfortable as I do up my belt. He takes his seat to the right of me, and does up his own belt. "It's one of Atticus's, but he said you couldn't ride in my usual ride, so loaned me this."

"What is your usual ride?"

"Well, it has two wheels, so let's just go with that."

"Yeah, probably for the best," I say, giggling a little. "Cars aren't my thing. I'm just happy when mine turns on."

"Yeah, it's a piece of shit." I gape at him, and he shrugs. "What? It is. It won't be long before Atticus replaces it."

I roll my eyes, and decide to change the subject rather than fighting with him. "So, how old are you?"

"Why?"

To get to know you, obviously. "Kai mentioned you were around my age, but wasn't sure of your exact age."

He smirks, and indicates to turn right. "He wouldn't."

"Why's that?"

"Did you text them yet?" he asks, and I shake my head.

NORA

I missed you this morning.

I send the message to Atticus, Malachi, and Orson separately, before turning back to Voss. "Why are you being so secretive?"

"It's the nature of a fox, little mouse."

"Little mouse?" I query just as my phone buzzes. A smile ghosts over my face when I see it's Orson.

ORSON

I'm sorry, little cub. Blame Atticus. He sent me on an errand.

I missed you, too. I'll be home tonight, though. Can we do something?

NORA

Absolutely.

"Who was that?" Voss asks.

"Orson. He's making plans for tonight," I say, and he nods. "Why did you ask me to breakfast if we're not going to get to know each other?"

He sighs, turning the car around another corner, and shoots me a nervous look before his eyes go back to the road. "I should've grown up in a skulk, but I didn't past the age of eight."

"Did you join a pride?" I ask, a little confused.

"No. I was a rogue for the majority of my life," he replies, and my eyes widen. "My parents were both killed, and it left me alone."

"Shit." Tears well up in my eyes, imagining the young

boy of the man sitting before me, alone. I reach out and place my hand on his knee, offering him the only bit of comfort I really can.

"They were murdered," he says, pulling into a parking space outside a cafe. He doesn't turn to look at me, instead, staring out at the road in front of us as people walk by. "My mum was only a few weeks out from giving birth. Fox pregnancies are about 110 days, not even a third of a year, and they killed her before she could deliver my brother."

I gasp, tears now freely dripping down my cheeks, my hands covering my mouth in horror.

"My dad made me hide. I burrowed my way into the ground just in time," Voss says, his tone still devoid of any emotion. "They tortured my mum, and made my dad watch before they killed him, too."

I close my eyes, trying to keep my sobs quiet. My phone buzzes, but I can't grab it to look. I really can't.

"I was only eight," he says softly. "I left the skulk that day, knowing I'd be dead if I remained." He sighs. "I got my revenge. I was eighteen when I went back and murdered my leader, and nearly all of his family."

"Nearly all of them?" I ask, my voice shaking. I asked to get to know him, I just didn't really think his past was full of these horrors.

"His daughter was pregnant," Voss says, choking out the words. "I couldn't kill an unborn child. I spared her and her mate. Luckily, every other member of his family were adults."

"What happened to them?" I ask, wiping away my tears.

"They took over the skulk and have a gorgeous six-year-old daughter," he says, turning to look at me. I see the tears in his eyes before he blinks them away and sadness overtakes his face. "I didn't mean to make you cry."

"Don't try to apologise," I say, shaking my head. "I'm glad you shared."

He nods. "I was homeless until I was thirteen. I was taken in by a rogue bounty hunter, I'll spare you that story for another time, but he trained me and taught me everything he knew. At 18, he died, and after getting my revenge, I sought out the best pride around."

"This one?"

"Nah, the one down South rejected me so I had to come here," he says, winking at me. "Kidding. Yes, I sought out Atticus, and I've been here ever since."

"Bounty hunting?"

"Among other things," Voss replies. "To answer your earlier question, I'm 25. Just a year older than you."

"When is your birthday?" I ask, and he laughs but shakes his head. "What?"

"You're perfect, little mouse," he murmurs, bringing my hand to his lips and kissing it. "You've got enough of my secrets for today, though. Let's go eat."

I nod and grab my purse as we exit the car. I check my phone as we get seated at the table, and smile at the two messages.

MAL

I missed you, too, little wolf. Hurry up and come see me.

NORA

Why should I come see you when we both know you'll come find me?

He doesn't reply, and I laugh as I flick over to Atticus's message.

ATTICUS

I missed you, too, little queen. Have fun with
Voss. Make sure you eat something.

NORA

I will.

I silence my phone and grin at Voss. "So, want to hear
about the time I got kicked out of the ballet group?"

Mirth fills his eyes, and I mentally pat myself on the
back for distracting him even a little, and he nods.

I can't relate to the horrible childhood my mate had, and
the murdering of people is not something I love about him,
but a big part of me is happy he got his revenge.

∞

"*E*nough fighting," I snap, glancing between the two
groups that are *already* arguing. Hell, they were
already arguing before I even arrived.

"You might be in charge of us, but you're a weak wolf,"
one of the men says, a growl in his tone. I can't tell his
animal, I can't even remember his name. I don't care,
though, I just need the fighting to stop. "Shut the fuck up
and keep out of this."

"I said *enough*," I hiss, standing and looking between
them all, hoping that the disapproval on my face is enough.
"This isn't a zoo where you're all going to shift and do
dominance battles. This is a workplace, and we've got a
client—*a human client at that*—coming here in less than an
hour. So, if I need to get a higher up manager that will stop
the fighting, just let me know."

Two people shift, and I sigh and pull out my phone to
call one of my men. It's slightly embarrassing having to rely

on them this way, but I know they don't mind. Even if I had my wolf, I doubt I'd be more dominant than the shifters in front of me.

I don't know much about the pride side of things with Atticus, but I know he's a very strong lion, and it makes sense his pride would reflect that.

"Hey, baby," Mal says, a smile in his tone. I can just imagine the way his full, pinky coral lips are tilted in a grin, the cheeky glint in his light blue eyes as we talk. *Why did I hesitate to call?* "I thought we were banned from calling you today."

"Well, normally I'd impose that, but I currently have a lion about to fight a cheetah, and I'm not sure I should get in the middle of that."

"Fucking hell," he groans. "On my way."

He hangs up, and I look around at the groups cheering them on. This kind of thing happened at the pack all of the time. It's a good way to get aggression out, and both sides usually made up afterwards. Our animals ride us, and this calms them enough that we get a clear head and can handle things like the rational humans we sometimes are.

The issue is we've got things to do in the next hour, and if the client turns up early or any of the witnesses do, we've got nobody to greet them because there's a giant fight happening.

A giant male lion saunters into the room, and something in me recognises him as Atty. He's a gorgeous colour, yellowy-gold, but his mane is where the true beauty lies. It's light around his face, a light gold turning to brown, before being a big thick black. He's magnificent, there's nothing else to say about it.

He's broad-chested, with a round head and round ears.

His tail is long, with a hairy black tuft at the end that matches his mane.

His paws when he walks thunder through the room, and by looking at them, the pads seem bigger than my head. He's massive, his head definitely my height without heels, but his back will probably reach my mid-chest. He's bigger than a normal lion, his shifter genes giving him the boost.

He's flanked by two tigers, both the same build but differ slightly in their colouring, and I know the one on his right is Malachi based on the way his eyes are locking in on me.

Micah is gorgeous, truly, and looks just like a normal tiger. Well, if normal tigers were as big as he is. Both he and Malachi are the same height, and about a human head shorter than Atticus's lion. Although, it might be a bit more when you take into account the lion's mane.

Micah's eyes are where things alter. When he's in human form, his eyes flash amber to signal his tiger trying to take control, but in his shifted form? His eyes are an emerald green.

There's a little huff as Malachi scratches at the ground, and I fight a smile knowing he was trying to get my attention. I'm shocked to see the colour of his fur. Unlike Micah, Mal is a golden tiger. It's beautiful, but not expected. His ears are slightly shorter, too, much more round.

Their tails are nearly the same length, but Malachi is a bit fluffier. I'm tempted to run my hands through their fur, to truly get to know my mates in their primal form.

A loud roar echoes through the office, and the two animals that were circling each other fall to the ground in submission.

I might not have my wolf... but that doesn't make me weak.

Mal and Micah head to the two animals, both of them

growling low, as Atticus strolls over to me without a care in the world. He's gorgeous, and I can't help but run my hands through his mane. I lean forward and kiss his head, and he purrs loudly.

Tears well up in my eyes, and I let them soak into his fur. I'll never have the ability to shift and go play with my mates.

I'll not get to run away as they chase me, or lounge around in the sun with two tigers by my side. I'll not get to chase Devoss through the mud, or bounce around in a lake as Orson hunts for fish.

I'll be confined to a human form, and it kills me.

She whines in my head, but I ignore her. That's all I can do to survive.

The four men in front of me shift back to their human forms, sadly, meaning I no longer get to look at my two tiger mates, and I sit back up properly.

"Feeling better?" I drawl, looking between them both. I get two glares and a shrug. "Get yourselves home, you're done for the day."

"You don't—" one starts, but the other one kicks his leg and gestures to Atticus. The lion by my side chuffs as if he finds this funny. "Right. Sorry."

"This isn't a punishment," I say softly. "Go for a run, go hunting, go spar. Do something to get control of yourselves. Your animals are acting up for a reason, go figure it out. Take today as a paid holiday or whatever, and just call me before the end of the day so we can see if it needs extended through next week."

Mal's jaw drops and turns to me, confused. I ignore him. These are my people, and I'll manage them how I see fit.

"Thank you," the second man says quietly. I nod and they both head out, the mood a little more subdued now.

"Is everyone else able to work today?" I ask, and nobody

replies. "Great. Sarah, Dan, get your two groups set up and make sure the two who left are both covered. I'll be with you in ten."

The room clears, Seb hovering, but with a glare from Mal, he leaves the office space, too.

"Thanks for coming down," I tease, looking at Mal, who shrugs. "Bit overkill, but I appreciate it."

"You gave them paid days off?" he demands. "I'm now going to have to sort those out."

"I run my floor, you run yours. When I start getting applications from your people, do you want me to let you know?"

He storms over, and I burst into giggles, and it causes some of the fight to leave his body. "They're no good to me if they're going to fight over the littlest of things. I can't force them to submit like you guys can, and when there are fights, it riles up the entire office. I don't need to explain myself to you."

Atticus shifts, and I frown at his lack of shirt. "Where is your shirt?"

"What's it to you, little queen?"

"Nothing, clearly." I roll my eyes and scoot off the desk and shimmy my way between Atticus and Malachi since they've both annoyed me a little. "Have a good day."

"The fire alarm will go off at eleven, pretty girl."

I grin, and rush forward to hug Micah. "You're the best, literally. Thank you!"

"You're welcome," he says, kissing my head.

"Point to you!" I say, squeezing his hand. "And a bonus point for being so pretty in your shifted form."

"Wait—" Atticus starts, but I wave him off and head into the giant conference room that my team have gotten set up in. Atticus growls, a deep roar echoing through the space that sends tingles up my spine.

I don't engage, knowing we'll be able to continue this fun tonight.

Because, apparently, I allow myself to look forward to things nowadays.

And it's all thanks to them.

19

NORA

"You're covered in blood."

Devoss came home today with blood coating his shirt and sprayed up his arms. He's got a cut on his cheek, that surprisingly hasn't healed, and he's missing a shoe. Has he really walked home with only one shoe?

What the fuck has he been doing today that he'd come home like this?

"I know," he replies, pressing a kiss to my cheek. "Sometimes things get messy, but it's all part of the gig. I'm unhurt, though, so no need to worry your pretty little head."

"Aside from your cheek."

"That'll heal," he says, winking at me. "Besides, the other guys are worse off."

"So you've hurt someone," I reply, confused but also a little hurt at how dismissive he's being. "Do you need a lawyer?"

"They're not going to be able to press any charges."

I look to Atty for help, where he's sitting in the arm chair in the living room, but he's doing a good job of avoiding my gaze. Looks like it's on me to deal with Voss.

"So they're dead? You killed someone today?"

He gently cups my cheek, lowering his forehead to mine. "That's part of what I do, Nora. I handle messes for the big wigs who can't handle them themselves."

"And these messes are...?"

"Ask Atticus, I was dealing with one of his today," he says and kisses my forehead before heading upstairs to shower. He doesn't look back, humming a song as he goes, and it doesn't escape my notice that he didn't apologise for hurting my feelings.

"Atty."

"Yes?" he sighs, looking at me with a wary expression. "It's pride business, little queen. Don't worry about it."

I hate that that is an answer. He's right, unfortunately. I'm not a high-ranking pack... pride member, and so I'm not in any position to demand answers from my Alpha—even if he's not my Alpha because I have no wolf, and he's my mate.

Damn it.

"Okay," I murmur, moving to sit down with everyone.

"Okay?" Orson asks, an eyebrow raised from where he lounges in the seat next to me on the sofa. "You're dropping it?"

"Yes."

"That easily?" Atticus asks, sounding just as sceptical as Orson.

"I was in a pack before, I get how things work," I reply as Orson pulls me into his lap instead of letting me sit on the sofa alone. Atticus gets a calculating look on his face, but Orson presses a kiss to my neck, distracting me.

"What's your plans tonight?" Orson asks, his voice barely above a whisper as his facial hair tickles my ear.

"I don't have any," I reply, with a teasing lilt to my voice. We made plans together this morning, and he knows it.

A grin appears on his face. "You still want to come with me somewhere?"

I glance at Atty, unconsciously, but not really for permission, and he nods in reassurance.

"Of course," I say.

"Go change into something less office-like," Orson commands, a bit of glee infused into his tone. I stand up, and he smacks my butt, causing me to gasp.

"Good requirement," I tease, but head upstairs to change. I pull on a dress, some tights, and a pair of boots before going down to where he's waiting for me at the bottom of the stairs. I don't run into Voss, so I make a mental note for when I'm back so I can check if his cheek has healed up.

"We'll bring back food," Orson shouts, tugging me out the door. He seems eager, but I don't get why.

"So, where are we going?" I ask as I buckle myself into the car. I don't know what the plans are, but his excitement is evident.

"You'll see. Atticus shared your employment file, little cub," he says.

"Oh, he did, did he?" I mutter, picking at a loose thread on the bottom of my dress as my tone turns surly.

"You're our mate. There's no such thing as privacy."

"I get that," I reply, facing him as he drives off. "But you could've asked, or even mentioned you were reading my personnel file. The file that belongs to a company you don't work for at that."

"Hold up, are you mad at me?"

"No," I sigh and run my hands through my hair in a frustrated move. "I think I'm annoyed about the fact that

I'm not annoyed." Or maybe I am annoyed. I don't really know.

"Women," he teases, his hand falling to my knee, and it takes everything in me not to throw it off my lap.

"You know a lot of women?" I ask, and he groans. I throw my head back on the headrest, letting out a similar groan. "I'm sorry, I don't know why I'm trying to pick fights."

"How are you feeling on the inside?"

"Agitated, worked up."

"Could it be your wolf?" he asks tenderly, and the sweet tone only agitates me more. "I know you've been getting thoughts and feelings from her, so... could she be worked up and that's why you're feeling this way?"

I don't want her to be causing problems. I don't want her. It's that simple. She left when things got tough, she made my life even harder than it had to be. Do you know what it's like when your insides are warring? When the one part of you that's meant to protect you, that's meant to help you, is the reason you're suffering?

No? Well, I can promise you it's fucking torture.

I check inside, and the usual whining she's been doing for the past day or two isn't happening. *Fuck my life.* "Maybe?"

"Okay, we're changing the plan. I was taking you over to meet my niece, but I think this will benefit you more. Do me a favour and call Atticus and place it on speaker."

I don't argue, doing what he says. Atticus answers on the first ring, and I smile. "Hey, baby."

"Hi, little queen," he coos... he actually coos. "What do I owe the pleasure?"

"I miss you." Even saying the words reminds me of how much I actually do miss him. It's not even been twenty

248

minutes, and yet, it hurts that he's not here with me. Why didn't he want to come with me?

"Put him on speaker," Orson demands. I roll my eyes, but do as he says. "Someone has a little bit of attitude, so we're going to the clearing. Want to grab the others and come?"

"How much attitude?"

"Not enough," Orson replies, side-eying me before his bright hazel eyes go back to the road.

They continue talking without actually saying things, and I know they're discussing me, but I can't understand what they're trying to say. It's slightly rude to be honest.

"Think it was the fighting earlier?" Mal asks. *Hold up.* When did Mal join the call? He didn't even say hi. Why wouldn't he say hi to me?

I hang up the phone, and throw it to the ground, holding in the urge to throw it out the window. I can feel myself getting angry, really angry, and Orson just bursts out laughing. His hand is gripping my knee as he laughs about me. I fling his hand away, which doesn't quell his humour.

"You really are feeling bitchy," he drawls a few moments later. "It's okay, we'll help, I promise. Deep breaths."

"I am breathing."

Instead of engaging—like I want—he moves his hand back to my knee, and a little grumble leaves his throat. I close my eyes, and as he continues making soothing noises, it helps settle me down a little. Not a lot, and not even enough to take off the edge, but it reminds me that he's here and it's sweet enough that I don't want to punch him.

When we reach an open area, he pulls into the parking spot marked 'O' and gets out the car. He undoes my belt, and helps me out.

"Look at your hands," he murmurs.

I don't need to. They're in a tiny partial shift, where I no longer have human nails, but wolf claws. It's minute and so fucking pathetic, but it's something, I suppose. She's getting stronger.

"I can't," I gasp, pushing away from him with panicked efforts. "Take me away from here. I don't want to be here."

"Calm down," he soothes, rubbing my back, ignoring my futile attempts to leave. "It's a good thing, Nora."

"It's not," I cry, still pushing away from him, but also pulling him closer to me. "It's not a good thing."

I don't need heightened senses to hear the roar of a lion, and when a little reddy-orange and black fox bounds over, a howl leaves my throat. *My first howl in six years.*

Orson shifts, too, and I'm surrounded by my five mates. A lion, two tigers, a bear, and a fox respond to my howl, working themselves up, and it helps. It helps to have them surrounding me, and I fall to my knees, and start digging. I don't know why, but it's soothing the internal battle inside of me. My hands are moving superhuman fast, the claws easily digging into the wet mud, and it goes everywhere.

The digging is turning even more frantic, and I keep whining. It's like I'm here watching myself do these things, but I'm not the one doing them. I know it's me, but I don't recognise the person in front of me.

My dark brown hair has mud covering the ends, grass sticking to it. There's a trail of mud on my cheek, and based on the way my vision has strengthened, the view in front of me looking like it's in a higher-definition, I know my eyes have shifted.

They aren't their usual chocolate brown, instead, they are amber.

My eyes are amber.

If I go back into my body, if I become me again, she's going to take over. She's going to ruin my life... again.

I watch as my mates come to lay in front of me, all but Orson, who sits behind me. We must look a right sight to any onlookers. A crazy woman digging a hole surrounded by wild animals.

My lion lets out a whine, shaking his fluffy, magnificent mane, but it doesn't deter the wolf within. She's trying to take control, and I don't think I'm strong enough to stop her.

The bear's paw lands on my shoulder, and the crazy animal inside of me growls. She whirls around, no longer digging, and growls again at the black bear. The bear doesn't submit, but he doesn't fight her either.

Someone needs to fight her for me. I don't have the strength to fight on my own. I can't do this again.

But I can feel her anger, her frustration. She can't accept these men as her mates, even though she feels the bond just as strong as I do, because her mate is dead. *Dead.*

She came back, and she's mourning him again. I can't mourn him again. I can't do this. I've fought for the last six years to keep my head above water, to keep the dark thoughts away, and this moment right here has the potential to undo all of my hard work.

The normal coloured tiger edges forward, a soft whine leaving his throat, and with his paws moving to cover his eyes, it doesn't take a genius to see he's hurt. The tiger is in pain.

But what about me? What about my pain?

I can't help him. He needs my help, but I can't help him when I can't even help myself. The wolf within growls again, and when she raises her paws to attack the bear, I can see they're fully shifted now. Her human arm stops just below the elbow, where it's now a wolf paw. A giant midnight black paw with nails that can do harm.

The wolf within me is feral. I know this. I can feel this. *Why can't they?*

I whine again—and I've recognised that whines are me, not her. She growls, I whine. It's my way of begging my men, my mates, to come and help me, but they either don't realise that, or don't care enough to help. Orson brought me here, and now he's leaving me to suffer alone.

As she rises, I know I have a choice to make. There's a split second where I'm going to be able to overpower her and push her down again. Where I can regain control and subject myself to another year long internal fight. I've finally got the chance for happiness—real happiness—and my brain, and wolf, have let me down.

The second choice is just as scary. I can let her in. I can let her take over, and with her being this feral, I know the others are going to have no choice but to put me down. No matter how much they like me, I'm a risk to everyone.

I have two choices. I need to decide whether I'm going to try and fight the fight for another day, or I can give in, and hopefully I'll get put down.

Do I want to live a life not worth living for the chance, the tiny chance, that I'll eventually get happiness... or do I want to give up and die?

Each of my men take a turn shifting back to their human forms. A naked Micah is sitting looking at me, his eyes portraying his sorrow. An angry Malachi is sitting with his arms crossed as he glares at me, or more accurately, my wolf. A cheeky grin is on my fox's face, and Voss winks in my direction. He's amused, but I think that's covering his anxiety—the smell of it is so overpowering.

The fourth man I can see is my leader... my King. Atticus

is sitting with a blank mask, and the only part of him displaying emotions are his amber eyes. His lion is unhappy, and that means he is, too.

I can't turn to look at Orson, but the worry I can scent from him is enough.

I have two choices.

I want to live.

I need to live.

With a decision made, I close my eyes and let my wolf rise. The men can feel the power shift within me, and when Micah gasps, I push her down. I beat her back into her corner, and build the walls so damn high, not even a giraffe could see over them.

When they sense her retreating, I open my eyes and they fall to the extremely deep hole I made.

"That was fucking horrible," Orson whispers, pulling me into his chest. I don't fight him. I can't fight him. I need to save all my strength to fight the battle I have in my own head. I need to save my strength so that I can battle the voice —the feelings—of the wolf within.

"Nora, baby, what the fuck is going on with your wolf?" Mal asks, reaching for my hand. "How can we help?"

"You can't."

My emotionless tone surprises them, but I don't know what to say. How do I explain what's just gone down? How do I explain that this part of me—the animal inside of me— is broken? She's come back an even bigger mess than she was when she left me.

"Let's go home," I say after a few minutes. The mood is somber, but they don't deny me this. Orson motions for me to go into the car, and I don't look back, even when Orson and the others don't follow. I know they're going to talk about me, but I don't care. I can't bring myself to care.

I watch them huddle together and chat, each of them seeming concerned. I don't blame them after the way I just went on. I shed my shoes, and pull my knees up to my chest. Huddling in on myself, I press my head into my knees, closing my eyes.

My head is not a good place to be right now, but there's nowhere else I can be. It's down to me, and me alone, to make sure I survive this a second time.

My eyes dart between each of the guys in front of me. They're my future, I know this.

I just hope that we get our happy ending.

20

MICAH

"What the fuck was that?" I snarl, looking up at Atticus with fear racing through me. His face is twisted in pain, and the anguish I see in his blue eyes is exactly how I think I look, too. But too fucking bad. He's the Alpha, he's the one who always has the answers.

I clutch at his top, tugging at it, as I silently beg him to fix it. "Bro, what was that? What is wrong with my mate?"

"I don't know," he says, running his free hand across his face as he tries to calm himself down. "I really don't know." He sighs, and I let go of his arm as my own anxiety builds. "Voss? Anything you could share with the group?"

Voss slowly shakes his head, his curly hair bouncing around, and the tiny bit of hope that had built diminishes.

"I think her wolf is feral," Orson reveals, causing Kai to gasp. Voss nods in agreement. "I think her wolf has come back, maybe not fully yet, but she's come back enough that our mate can feel her. But she's feral—the wolf within is feral. We need to know more about what happened when she lost her so that we can figure out her wolf's state of mind and work on getting her the help she needs."

Our girl is going to struggle if this is the case, and I can't have that happen. I can't let her struggle because of something caused by Kennedy, the fucking ugly headed asshole who decided to go against fate. It's not fair.

Nothing about this is fucking fair.

She's already suffered something no shifter should ever need to suffer... and she survived it. *Alone.* Now that she has the chance to finally be happy, to finally get some peace, to be loved by her mates, she's got another obstacle to overcome.

It shouldn't be this hard. Not for someone like her.

Why can't the cunts of the world be the ones who get all the suffering? Why can't the murderers and the rapists of the world be the ones given a death sentence?

Why did it need to be my mate?

"Take a deep breath," Orson murmurs, placing his large hand on my shoulder. I look up into his hazel eyes, and his smile is grim. "Calm yourself, Micah."

"Okay. Okay. I think we need to get her a therapist, maybe, someone who can understand what she's gone through. If we can get her some help, maybe she can bond with her wolf," I say, my voice racing as I barely breathe in my rush to get the words out. I can't stand here uselessly. I need to help her.

"Calm," Orson repeats.

I force myself to take a deep breath, but it doesn't actually do anything. It appeases Orson for a moment, though. "Will she take that? Will she accept the help from us?"

"I don't know," Atticus sighs, looking at Kai for his opinion. My brother looks just as pathetic as I feel. His eyes are droopy, there's a fury in his eyes that I know is directed towards Kennedy, and his tiger is whimpering within.

"What do you think? What can we do to help her if not that?"

"I think we should wait for her to come to us," Kai says, his usually silvery tone sounds dark and miserable. "Let's see what we can do to help, see who we can bring in, and what kind support they offer. *Then* when she comes to us, we can give her the options and let her make the decision."

He rubs at his pale cheeks and nods. He's made a decision, and he's sticking with it. "Yeah, I think that's the best course. She's had so many choices taken from her, and I think she needs to start making them for herself."

"That's where I disagree," Voss says, and I frown. I thought Kai's argument actually made a lot of sense. "Yes, she needs to make decisions for herself. But I don't think this is one of those cases. We're her mates. This isn't a thing where we offer to help her. She needs us, whether she's in the position to ask for it or not. I just know that feral wolves... any feral shifter, to be fair, normally requires putting down. It's for their safety as well as ours. We're not putting down our mate. She's not going to die, so we need to figure this shit out so that she's covered."

We all turn to look in the car where Nora is sitting, defeated. Her eyes are closed, and she looks like she's gone through a major battle. Mud covers her gorgeous honey brown skin, her hair the worst of it, and her clothes are wrinkled and tattered.

She has gone through a battle—it's just this was a mental one instead of physical.

If what Orson and Voss say is true... then the battle isn't over, not for a long while yet.

She's gorgeous, even covered in mud and exhausted, but the empty look on her face breaks my heart. We can't put her down, I can't take part in a conversation that involves killing her.

I'd slaughter the entire world to protect her if I had to.

"Let's go home," I say, my tone as flat and dead as I think our mate feels. I need to be with her right now, I need to be by her side. Lists are how I get through the day. I'll make a list, and check things off, and she's going to be doing amazing. "She needs a bath and some food. She needs us around to help ground her. She shouldn't be alone. We can do some movies in her bedroom. Cuddles."

"That sounds good," Orson says, shooting Atticus and Malachi nervous looks. *Is he worried about me?*

"Voss you drive, take Micah with you," Atticus commands. I know he's turned silent as he gives Voss some instructions, but I don't care.

The two of us head over to the car, and I get in the back seat and buckle my belt in.

"Hey, pretty girl," I say softly, my hand gripping her shoulder from where I'm sitting directly behind her. "We're heading home now. Someone wanted to play in the mud so we need to get you all cleaned up."

She laughs, but it lasts less than a second before the blank look falls on her face again. Her long, thick, dark eyelashes are damp from the tears, and it kills me seeing those track marks on her cheeks.

The only time I'm going to be happy to see her tears is if she's happy.

Voss pulls away from the park, and I look back to see Kai in his shifted form, fixing the ditch Nora made. Atticus is on his phone, shouting down the line at someone, whilst Orson watches.

I'm terrified of what's to come, but I know we'll come up with a solution to help her. I know that we can.

Because that's what mates are for, and fate wouldn't have given her to us just so that we could watch her die only a fortnight later.

As soon as we get home, I help her out the car and carry her up to her room when it's clear she can't get there herself. She's unresponsive, basically, unable to talk, or maybe she can, but she doesn't want to. I don't fucking know.

I just know it's hard for her.

Voss starts the shower in her bathroom, testing it until it's perfect, and only then do we work together to undress her.

This is my first time seeing her naked. Seeing the swell of her breasts, seeing the perfect little mound covered in hair, admiring her toned ass.

This is also the first time I'm seeing just how slim she is, how fragile her tiny waist looks, how little fat is on her stomach and thighs.

She's gorgeous, truly a fucking masterpiece. But it's hard to appreciate her beauty, to fully let the desire within take over, when she's in this state.

This isn't a consensual admiring session where we're going to get to do all the things my dick is hardening at the thought of. This is us helping our mate who is broken and can't help herself.

She needs care. She needs gentle love. She just needs to be protected.

I strip off down to my boxers, a blush coating my cheeks when I see Voss has gotten himself fully naked because I can't bring myself to follow suit.

I know he cares very little about my junk, but it's a little awkward. Especially when I see the flash of silver in his dick, that mine doesn't have.

I grab her shampoo as Voss brings her under the spray

of water and wets her hair. Then we turn her so that she's still getting warmth as I start massaging the shampoo into her hair. I get whiffs of the cherry scent every so often as I diligently make sure I don't miss a single spot.

Only then do I turn her back around and start washing it out. She stands still, her eyes dazed and unfocused as she lets us get her clean.

Then we repeat the process again before doing the conditioner. This one I was less good at, but I tried my best. Voss gets out first, leaving me in the shower with our girl.

"I know you're struggling, pretty girl," I murmur, cuddling her into me as we stand under the stream of hot water together. "I wish I could fix it."

"You can't." Her tone is emotionless, dead, cold. A shiver wracks down my spine despite the heat, and I cuddle her in closer. "Nobody can." She's giving off no scents other than pain, and it's heartbreaking.

She sounds broken, and it only makes me angrier at Kennedy and his worthless pack for what they did to her.

I blink my own tears away, confident enough to know she won't realise I'm crying for her right now. Voss returns a few moments later with a towel and some clothes for Nora.

The fucker didn't bring me a towel, but I'm not mad about it. I can barely function past the pain Nora's going through, never mind thinking of someone else's needs.

I kiss her temple and head out to get myself changed, knowing that whilst I'm not there for her, that he will be.

Hopefully... hopefully, she'll be okay after a nap.

"She's not hungry," Orson says, putting down two plates on the counter with a dejected sigh.

"It's okay," I say reassuringly. "She might be come dinner time."

He shakes his head, his hair flying everywhere. It's usually tied up, but today he's left it down as if he can't be bothered to look after himself. I know it's not that, though. I know that his own needs are so low on his priority list that Orson can't even imagine taking time to go through his hair care routine when there's something he could be doing for Nora.

Even though there's nothing he can do for her.

"She's already underweight," Orson snarls, glaring at me. There's so much anger in his gaze, but there's equal amounts of pain. "She can't afford to not fucking eat. Her wolf is malnourished. *She* is malnourished. If she doesn't eat, she'll struggle even more because she has no fucking energy to do anything. She's deficient in vital vitamins that help her."

He whines, deep and low, and I know that's a sound from the bear within.

"I know," I soothe, and he sighs as he drops into the seat next to me. He pats my knee and gives me a sad smile. "It's hard on you, I know."

"I could've fucking helped Eden, and I didn't," he says, hanging his head in shame. His thin, blonde hair falls and covers his face as he sniffles. "I won't fuck up again, not with Nora."

"You didn't fuck up with Eden, either."

He shrugs and sits up straight before reaching over to grab the two plates from the middle of the table. "Here, eat these. I've got a curry simmering for dinner, but I don't want you going hungry until then."

Fucking mother hen. I don't argue, though, and take the plates of food. I've got a chicken pie with chips and peas on one plate, and then a waffle with fruit on the other.

"I didn't know if she wanted savoury food or sweet food," he says in explanation for the two very different meals. "So I thought if I made both, she'd have an option, you know?"

Fucking hell. He sounds so pathetic right now, but I fully understand it. I feel the exact same way. If the bear would let me in the kitchen, I'd try and make these kinds of things for her.

Sure, she'd get food poisoning, since I'm a terrible cook if it doesn't involve a kettle and a pot of noodles, but I'd try.

"Well, I'll enjoy both," I reassure him, and he nods with a ghost of a smile on his plum coloured lips. "Is Atticus still with her?"

"Yeah," Orson says with a nod. "Voss left about an hour ago to handle something, and Kai's in his room moping."

Yeah, my brother isn't taking Nora's mood easy either. Fuck, none of us are. But when Malachi is in a bad mood, he's a fucking asshole, and right now, I need to avoid that.

"I'm going to clean her car for her," Orson says, sitting up in a sort of *aha* motion. "I've got nothing else to do until it's my turn to sit with her again, so I think she'll really appreciate a clean car."

"Yeah, of course she will."

"Thanks, Micah. If you want more food, come give me a shout."

He's silly if he thinks I'll interrupt him once he gets started. The bear is an obsessive man, and once he gets into something, you'd be stupid to try and get him to stop. I nod, though, and then he leaves to go clean.

We can't do anything for Nora, not really. We can't fix her mental health, and we can't make her wolf go back to normal. But we can sit with her, and make her food in case she gets hungry, and we can clean her car in case she decides to do a midnight break away from us.

I finish my food, the full tummy making me feel lazy, and fill up a bottle with some water and a second one with some isotonic juice. Nora's not been drinking much, so stealing a page from Orson's book, I take both so she's got options.

I just want some fluids in her, to be honest, so as long as it's something hydrating, I'll get her anything she wants.

I knock on her door gently before letting myself inside when there's no response. It's pretty dark in here, and I notice that the drapes are closed. Her fairy lights are switched on, though, and it gives the room a warm glow.

Atticus and Nora are laying on the bed, cuddling together. Atticus looks at me with bleary eyes, a tired expression on his square-shaped face, but Nora doesn't even move to acknowledge me.

My tiger bristles, but I don't even flinch. She's not here mentally, her brain whirring, so she's not ignoring me on purpose.

She's a tiny figure huddled next to Atticus underneath her duvet, so I've got no idea what she's wearing. I see a mop of dark brown hair, and that's it. I doubt anyone has gotten her changed, though, not with how exhausted she is.

Atticus is wearing a pair of joggers, some high-end brand, of course, unlike my cheap ones, but no top. Nora seems to like lying with us without a t-shirt on. Maybe the heat from our bodies feels good for her or something, I don't really know.

I raise an eyebrow, a silent question about our girl's state of mind, but Atticus shakes his head. She's not spoken since he's been here, likely not even have moved.

"Hey, pretty girl," I say, keeping my voice low as I walk over to the bed. She moves, rolling onto her back to give me a small smile. It's all she can really manage, and it means the fucking world to me that she's done it.

"Hey," she croaks out, her eyes closing briefly in pain.

"I brought water and juice," I say, sitting on her bed. She nods, and I help pull her to a sitting position before handing the isotonic one over. "Orange good?"

"It has to be if that's all you brought," Atticus teases. There's a hint of sadness in his words.

"It's perfect, thank you," Nora replies. Still polite as ever, even with how badly she's struggling. I watch her hold it, messing with the straw on the bottle as her eyes focus on nothing.

She's already disassociated, her thoughts stealing her from the present.

"Do you want the water instead?" I ask, and she shakes her head.

"I think Micah wants you to drink, little queen," Atticus says gently. His words are softer than I've ever heard them, and if the situation were different, I'd tease him for it.

Instead, I'm just grateful he can be that soft and steady presence she so desperately needs.

"Oh," she whispers, a brief look of shock on her face before she takes a tiny sip. Her mind is elsewhere, focusing on the battle in her head.

I wish I could fucking be there with her. I wish I could fight the demons back. I just wish I had a purpose.

"Mind if I chill in here with you both?" I ask, aware I'm encroaching on Atticus's time with her, but unable to help myself. Nora shakes her head and lifts the blankets a little so I can slide under them with her. I double check with Atticus, who also doesn't mind.

Nora takes a second sip of her drink at Atticus's insistence before migrating over to get cuddles from me. It's silly, with everything going on, but a small part of me loves that she came to lay with me over Atticus.

I kiss her temple and close my eyes.

"Do you think that I'm a good person?" The question from my mate's lips shocks me, and my eyes fly open. Atticus doesn't reply, so I take the question.

"Yes," I reply, my thumb rubbing circles across her hip. "You're one of the best people I know."

She nods, but I don't think she believes me. I begin to outline all the good traits about her, the things I love, the things that need cherished.

Like her smile, her thoughtfulness, her spitfire nature when dealing with my brother—and Alpha, but I'm not stupid enough to say that in front of him.

She's quiet, contemplative as I speak, and when I fall silent, wet tears absorb into my t-shirt.

"It would be so easy if I were dead," her mind screams, and I know she didn't mean to share it along the bond, but I flinch nonetheless. I hope Orson didn't hear that, the bear can't handle it.

I kiss the top of her hair as she drifts off to sleep.

"She's been sharing things across the bond the entire time I've been here," Atticus says. Ah, well I've not heard anything, so maybe her wolf is only sharing them with the people in the room. Maybe. I don't think even the wolf is doing it on purpose. *"I don't think she realises, so good job on not drawing attention to it."*

"I'm not sure what I could've said," I reply, and he nods because he gets it.

My mate thinks that death is the option.

Doesn't she know, we'd have no choice but to get revenge before following her to heaven if that's the option she chose?

21

ATTICUS

"*She's drifted off,*" Voss says.

"*Thanks for the update,*" I reply.

"*Is... is she okay?*" Micah asks.

"*As good as she can be.*"

She's still in bed. It's been two whole days since she smiled at me without having tears in her eyes. She's struggling, badly, and I have no idea how to help her. She's my mate, and I'm her Alpha. I'm failing her twice the amount of anyone else in this house, but there's nothing I can do to fix things. This isn't like stopping someone from abusing her, or paying her bills because she can't afford them this month.

She's suffering because of something within her, and I can't help with that. I don't have a fancy degree that can let me help with the mind, and I don't have the capabilities to force her wolf to behave. I'm useless right now.

Voss is lying with her at the moment, but we've each been taking turns rotating out so she's not alone. That's the only thing we can do. None of us want to push her and make things worse, but we're never ever going to leave her to suffer alone. Day and night she has company, even if all she can do is lay in bed and drift in and out of sleep, and cry from sheer exhaustion. No matter how scared we are, no matter how worried we are, she doesn't see that. The moment we step into her room—or she comes out—she's the only thing that matters.

We support each other, so that we can support her. If we go in there and let her see the effect her suffering is having on us, I'm scared she'll push it down and force herself to be okay to please us. That would be worse. No. She's the priority right now.

But that doesn't mean we're letting each other go unchecked. I know that Orson's been taking her struggles the hardest, but Micah is a close second. I've been checking in with them, just like they've been asking me. We're doing okay, we're getting through it.

It's Sunday today, and she's due back at work tomorrow. I don't know if she knows the days of the week right now, but I doubt she's going to be back to the office. I want her to let me in—hell, I'd even take her just letting any of us in—so that I can do my best to get her the help she needs. That's all I want. I want her to not suffer in silence anymore.

A knock sounds on my open office door, and I look up to see a red-eyed Micah standing there, his ebony eyes are dull and unfocused. He's wearing a rumpled pair of joggers with a long-sleeved t-shirt that has a few wet patches. Drool or tears, I'm not sure, but I know they're from our mate. His short, dark brown hair is in need of a wash, but I know he sacrificed his shower time to sit with Nora.

He's exhausted.

"I'm going for a walk."

"Okay," I reply, but he doesn't move from the doorway. He doesn't want a walk. He felt he needed an excuse to come and talk to me. We've stopped with our responsibilities over the last couple of days, focusing all our attention on our mate, but I know from tomorrow I need to get back on track.

Micah is probably worried that he's interrupting something important because his issues aren't worthy enough of my time. I understand his point, but it's silly. His issues will always be important enough for me.

"Anything I can do to help?" I ask as I gesture for him to come sit on the sofa where I'm sitting. I'm pleased when he strolls in and slumps into the cushions, very close to me. I don't speak, waiting for him to talk to me, and he hesitantly meets my eyes. His eyes are dull, full of unshed tears, and every few seconds they flicker to being amber. His tiger is suffering because his mate is suffering. *Fuck.*

"She's not okay," he cries, tears dripping down his cheeks. He scrubs at his hollow cheeks, but the tears fall fast so he just sighs, and leans his head on the back of the sofa. "She's so not okay, bro. How the fuck did we get here?"

I wish I knew. I wish I fucking knew.

I pull him into me, and when more wet tears fall to my shoulder, I pat his back. It's all I can do. I can't erase his pain. I can't take anything away from him. We're all struggling. But, just like Nora, he doesn't need to be alone whilst it happens. We sit together for a while, but I don't move until he stops crying.

"Fuck, sorry," he whispers, wiping his snotty nose on his sleeve. Normally, I'd chastise him and give him a tissue, but I'd prefer he opened up to me, so I stay quiet. I want let in to the thoughts that are rampaging in his mind.

"Don't apologise for that," I reply, squeezing his shoulder in a one-armed hug. Despite needing a shower, he still smells the same way he always does—clean, with a hint of lavender from the detergent Orson uses on our clothes.

The rest of us have overpowering smells, but Micah just reminds me of home, of pride. "Don't ever apologise for that."

"I want to help her, but I don't know how. She flinches any time my tiger makes noises, she's so fucking scared of me, and I don't know why."

That's something I've noticed, too. Any rumble or growl or even whimper, and she flinches away, retreating into herself even deeper than she already is. My lion has understood that he's scaring her, and he's so fucking good at being quiet whilst we're sitting with her. He doesn't want her to suffer anymore than I do, his love for her goes deeper than my own.

The problem is that I just can't connect the why. *Why is she scared of our animals?*

"Is he being quiet when you're with her?" I ask softly. Micah nods, throwing his head back to rest on the back of the sofa instead of on me. "We'll get through this, Micah. I'm not sure what's caused her to relapse, but the combination of her wolf and her mate reappearing in such rapid succession might just be a little too much for her to handle right now. We're helping her, Micah, and it won't last forever."

He sniffles, his convexed, lowered nose wrinkling as more snot drips down. It's a good thing Nora isn't here because I've never seen this particular Romero brother look so unattractive.

Although, women tend to fall for the sweet, nerdy vibe he has. But because it's his actual personality type, he never gets further than a conversation with them before they go running.

"We're here for her, and we're going to get through this," I say, making my usually crisp voice go softer. "It's a rough patch for her, but she'll get through it. We're stronger together, as cheesy as that sounds, and as long as we can rely on each other, then we're going to be okay."

He nods, seeming a little lighter. I don't know if it's just from the breakdown or the reassurance that we're here with him, but it's something that helps soothe my lion.

I love that Micah came to me for support, but I feel like Orson would've appreciated it more. The bear's mothering instincts need nurtured, and he would've thrived offering it to Micah.

"Okay," Micah says, nodding. His eyes light up, a bit of excitement racing through him. "Maybe we can buy some things that we can do together that might help her. Like things to stay home and do so she doesn't get bored whilst we're off." We never talked about her being off, but it's something that's been on my mind, so I'm glad we're on the same page. "What kind of things does she like?"

"I think at this point, anything you get, she'll like," I tell him gently. "Have a look on Amazon. Maybe buy her a dressing gown or something."

"Thank you. I needed that," Micah tells me, patting my knee with his hand, but he leaves it there for too long. I grin, and he shrugs with a bashful look on his face. There's eleven months between Micah and Mal, and nineteen between him and I, but he just looks a lot younger. Especially when he's grinning. It gives my lion a lot of pride knowing he's part of the reason his people can be so relaxed.

"What was that?" I ask with a smirk.

"Orson does it. I was trialling it out. Probably better that it was a one time thing."

"Dude, you caressed the fuck out of my knee," I reply, shrugging with a few chuckles. "If that helps you feel closer to me, though, I'd never take that from you."

"You're a dick." His eyes narrow for a moment before he smiles. "Voss needs a piss, and it's getting late. Go swap out, take Kai with you, and try and get some sleep."

"Are you sure you don't want to?" I ask, my lion grumbling at the offer. After Micah's breakdown, being close to her might help, and I'm not selfish enough to take it from him.

"You need her more," he says, giving me a warm smile. "And Kai is drinking his way through another bottle, so please, take him with you so I don't need to worry."

This is why I know we're going to be so fucking good for Nora. We look out for each other—even Voss, who is fitting in seamlessly with our group, despite not having the years worth of memories—and our bonds, the bonds between us men, are so important to us. Micah is more worried for his brother and me, than he is for himself.

Jealousy is never going to be a major issue. I'd be a fool to think it will never be an issue, of us wanting to monopolise Nora's time and affection, but I know we can handle it. We care about each other and will always make sure her needs, and the group's needs, are met *before* our individual needs.

As Alpha, that's something I do without thinking, but it really makes me proud of the men I surround myself with that they do the same.

"Thank you, brother." I stand, grasping his shoulder and look at him seriously. "I'll see you in the morning. Thank you."

He nods, and I head down to the kitchen, guessing that's where Mal is sitting.

"What?" he snaps, spinning in the chair to glare at me when he senses me hovering. He looks like fucking shit, and that's the nicest possible way I could describe him.

He's dressed similarly to his brother in a t-shirt and joggers, but unlike Micah, Mal's covered in pasta sauce from when Orson made Nora dinner, but she didn't want to eat it, so he scarfed it down. But clearly he missed his mouth one too many times.

"We're going to go and sleep with her," I tell him, wrinkling my nose at the stench of alcohol wafting off of him. "Go brush your teeth first, she doesn't need to smell the whisky on your breath and be worried you're drinking because of her."

He rolls his eyes, and without breaking eye contact, he downs his glass before smirking at me.

"Don't make me make this an order."

When he starts fumbling for the bottle to refill his glass, I sigh. He needs to be with her, he needs the stability, he needs her warmth. There's not a lot that I can't fix, but sadly, her mental health—or the mental health of her wolf—is one of those things. I can't stop her from hurting, and that means I can't prevent the hurt reaching my brothers. But I can do my best to make sure they're getting what they need to make it through the day, without turning to alcohol or fights—not naming names, but Voss is on house arrest right now.

The fox has made it his personal mission to destroy anyone who can even spell the word hunter since he can't help Nora fix her mental health, he's directing his focus to her physical safety.

"Get off your fucking ass, and go brush your teeth," I hiss, my lion's rage fuelling my words as I stare down the cat in front of me. It was barely a command, but he's so lost, he can't fight it. I follow him upstairs, his bare feet making me cringe. His nails are long, but his big toes are both a little hairy.

I prefer to groom myself a lot better than that. For all we know, Nora's got a foot fetish.

"What's got you huffing?" Mal snaps, but I just gesture for him to go into the bathroom. He brushes his teeth, washes his face, and even uses some aftershave before we head into Nora's room together. She's awake, cuddling with Voss, whose eyes are closed, but they open when I sit down on her bed.

"Okay, I need to shower," Voss says, kissing Nora's cheek. "Have fun with the cats, chick."

"He didn't want to tell you he needs a wee," Mal taunts, grinning at Nora's blush. Cradled in Voss's arms, she looks dainty, and that's weird since he's not that big. She's more fragile right now, and it's scary. "Move over, little wolf. I want to cuddle."

She does, silently, and we get settled in her bed as Voss leaves. She didn't giggle, or even laugh at his joke.

"Want to watch TV?" Mal asks. She shrugs, and whilst I doubt she does, she doesn't say no. As the background noise of the TV fills the room, I turn off the lights and get as close as I possibly can. Today has been another hard day, but I'm cuddling with my mate, and that's all I can ask for.

22

NORA

*A*tticus and Malachi are both asleep in bed, and I'm stuck here lying awake. I'm pleased they fell asleep as fast as they did so I could turn off the TV. The silence is bittersweet, but at least then I've only got to have one voice talking to me. My wolf is crying behind her wall, hating that I'm in bed with two men she won't recognise as her mate. She can feel the connections to them, but she hates them.

She hates my men.

I can't sleep in fear of her taking control whilst I'm unaware. I don't know the damage she'd do, and I'd hate to put any of my men in the position where they'd need to hurt me—*kill me, even*—just to subdue the feral beast inside of me.

But a small part of me is scared she'd hurt them, that she'd do something to try and remove the bonds from inside of us. It's terrifying.

My hand falls to Atty's naturally wavy, dirty blonde hair, and I run my fingers through it, trying to calm my breathing. My heart is beating so loudly, that it's even louder than the whines of my wolf, and I can almost hear the blood being pumped around my body in the near silent night.

There's nothing worse than being trapped with only your mind for company in the middle of the night.

Deep breaths, Nora, it's only seven hours until morning. Seven hours. I've only got to make it seven hours, and then things will be better again.

"Why are you still awake, little queen?" Atticus asks gently, his voice gruff with sleep.

When I don't answer, he catches my hand and stops me from playing with his hair before he somehow manages to flip us. The agility he uses is something I can't fathom, but I'm stopped from thinking about it when he lowers his bearded face to mine.

Normally, his beard is thin and neatly shaven. The same colour as his eyebrows, a shade or two darker than the dirty blonde of his hair, it covers his jaw, some of his neck, and rises to the middle of his cheeks. Over the last few days, where I've been locked in my mind, he's clearly stopped shaving.

I kind of like it, the scratchiness being soothing, even if it makes me feel guilty. He's too busy taking care of me to look after himself.

"Answer the question," he murmurs, his minty breath washing over me as he presses our foreheads together.

"What was the question?"

His breath warms my cheek as he blows out a little huff. He thinks I'm being pedantic, but I'm not. I just truly already forgot.

"Why are you still awake?"

"I have a few things on my mind," I say quietly. As has been the theme the past couple of days. I don't sleep unless one of my men are awake watching over me, and even then, it's only for a few minutes at a time. That's all I can afford to let myself have. "Why are you awake?"

"Because I felt your hands on me, and I was worried about you still being awake," he replies. His tone lacks the hesitance that mine does. "It's late, little queen. You have work early tomorrow."

"I think I need a sick day," I say quietly, avoiding his gaze. Do you know how hard it is to avoid someone's gaze when their forehead is pressed to yours? It's pretty damn hard, but I focus on the concaved shape of the bridge of his nose, looking at the little blackhead that's there. "I just need a day."

"That can be arranged." I nod, not even able to feel grateful because I'm running on empty. He presses a chaste kiss to my lips, concern in his gaze as he asks a question I think he's been afraid to ask this weekend. "*Are* you sick?"

"Maybe?"

You don't need to physically be sick to be sick, right? Wanting someone to end my pain by putting me down isn't something healthy people think about all day every day, right? Wanting to get someone to cut out a part of me that can't be cut out isn't normal, right? I've got to be sick because if this is my new normal, if this is how I've got to live the rest of my life... I don't want to live it.

If someone else is suffering the way I'm suffering, for this illness, this way of life to be normal, well that's not fair. Fate gives me a mate—mates—so it's hard to think the same thing that could give me all this happiness would make me suffer this much.

It has to be an illness. It has to be my brain or my wolf being sick. This isn't life. This can't be normal.

Atticus sits up, pulling me with him, being careful not to hurt my legs with the position we were in, and rests his head on top of mine. He's massive, and the way he can cuddle me in is so loving.

I know he can't read minds unless the connection between us is open—which it's not—but he can scent my emotional changes. I dread to think what he's getting from me.

"Okay," he says simply. "You can have the day off."

"Okay."

We sit in silence for a few minutes, the only sound is Mal snoring—something he wasn't doing before Atticus woke up—and I'm straining my ears to hear Atty's breathing, which is quiet and controlled.

"Things are hard," I say, opening up a mental connection with him.

Somehow thinking it silently helps. It's easier to say it in my head than out loud. Maybe because I don't have the shakiness of my tone, the sound of my tears choking up my throat, the shame that comes along with being so weak.

He nods, not arguing. *"Can I help?"*

"Asking for help is really hard," I say, sniffling as tears soak into his shirt. *"I... six years ago when he rejected me, my wolf didn't just give up immediately. She didn't just leave me immediately."*

He gasps, and tears start dripping down my cheeks. I explain my story to my Alpha, whilst crying silent tears. I don't let my sobs escape me, and I don't push away from Atticus like I want to.

"I had a choice then, and I'm faced with the same choice now. I need to keep fighting, I know that. But how am I meant to fight when all I want to do is die?"

Tears of his drip into my hair as his own pain fills the air, and his grip on me tightens.

I don't want to die. That's the most confusing part. I want

to live, I want to be loved, I want to be happy. I don't want to die. But my brain, and my wolf, is trying to convince me that I should. It's really hard to fight a part of you like this. It's really hard when all you hear every day is a voice in your head picking at all the bad things in your life, reminding you of all the things that you wouldn't miss when you're dead.

"Thank you for trusting me, little queen," he says quietly. "Now, for tonight, you're going to get some sleep. I know you're scared, but I'm going to be here, and I'm going to stroke your hair like you were doing for me, and you're going to cuddle with Malachi. That's all we're going to do for tonight, okay?"

"Okay," I whisper, still crying.

"Come here, little warrior," Mal say softly, tugging me from Atty. I knew he wasn't sleeping earlier, but I'm not sure what he heard other than my crying. I don't know if he heard me through the mental connection, or if I was just talking to Atty. I'm not going to worry about it, though.

"No more little wolf?" I ask through my sobs.

"Never again," he says gently. "You are a warrior, and it's in spite of your wolf... not because of her. So, come here into my arms and sleep."

"You heard that?" I ask. *Well, that not worrying about it only lasted for a heartbeat.*

"You projected it along all your bonds."

He pulls me in closer, and I rest my head on the pillow as his arms wrap around me. As promised, Atty comes to sit near me and starts stroking my hair. The soothing gesture lulls me to sleep, and I drift off between my two mates.

When a fox jumps on the bed and nestles his way between Mal and I, nobody complains... least of all me.

∞

Atticus

She drifts off to sleep, and I do exactly what I promised. I lay here awake, running my hands through her hair. Over and over I soothe her head the best I can, and whenever a non-human noise leaves her, my lion forces her wolf back down.

She wants to die.

I don't think she actually wants to die, but her wolf is causing her extreme pain to the point where she thinks dying is the better option.

The feelings I have for Kennedy Newitt and his entire pack are beyond murderous. They're beyond words. I don't think I can see that man without wanting to do very bad things to him. Things like breaking his bones over and over, laughing as they heal just so I can do it again. Things like carving off his skin, and cutting off ligaments, testing the boundaries of what he can heal whilst doing my best to cause him the greatest amount of pain possible.

I've never really thought of myself as psychopathic, but these thoughts lie within that realm, so maybe I'm closer to my brother than I thought.

I don't care, though. My mate is suffering because of actions Kennedy did, and he deserves to feel even an ounce of her pain and suffering.

Back at the gala, she told me she'd have made an amazing Luna. I believe her. She would have been everything that pack could hope to have in a leader. Something my pride is going to be grateful for. Her inner strength is admirable, and she's suffered more than any person I know, even Orson.

But I'm here now. I'm not so big headed to think I can fix

every single issue in her life, but I'm going to get the ball rolling. George Abbott, one of the best psychiatrists in the fucking world—okay, I don't have the figures to back that up, but he's a very good psychiatrist—is going to be getting a call in the morning, and I hope to all that is holy he's willing to work with her.

I'd never force her into anything, but having a chat with him can't hurt. Not when she's this low.

My lion's on guard all night, not letting me drift off, and making sure his mate is safe. I promised I'd stroke her hair, so no matter how sore my wrist is, I don't stop. I can't stop.

"She's okay," Mal says, his voice groggy with sleep. The sun rose an hour ago, something her blackout curtains stop us from seeing, but my watch's alarms went off. Voss left around then, too. "I've got her now. I'm awake. Go get coffee, and do whatever you've been planning all night. I've got her, Atticus."

"I promised I'd stroke her hair," I say quietly.

"And now I can do that," he replies, sitting up and manoeuvring our mate so he can do just that. His hands are large, still smaller than mine, of course, but they cover most of her head as he gives her some decent hair strokes. "Get someone to bring me in some coffee, too. Apparently, I'm not healing myself from this hangover."

"Can't say you don't deserve it," I taunt. I kiss her forehead, her brows furrowed, and leave the room. I want to fix her bad dream, but again, that's another field I have no fucking knowledge in. Malachi has her. She's okay.

"Morning," I say as I walk into the kitchen. Orson is cooking breakfast, wearing a pair of pyjama pants and nothing else, and he cringes as a bit of bacon grease hits him. He looks wide awake, and there's a fierce determination about him, as if today is the day he's going to fix Nora.

On the other hand, Voss is half asleep as he rests his head on the counter, his hair a mass of red messy curls, and whilst I can't see his face, I have no doubt there will be a sleepy dazed look in his eyes.

"Morning," Voss mumbles, a groggy fog of words. He yawns and sits up, rubbing at his green eyes with his fist. "Is she still asleep?"

"Still?" Orson asks, seeming happy about that.

"She's slept all night," I say proudly. Directing my words to the fox since Orson is busy preparing breakfast for Nora, I ask, "Can you take Mal some coffee up?"

"The tiger doesn't deserve coffee," he mutters, but gets up to pour it anyway.

"Ignore his whining," Orson says, smirking at my confusion. "Kai apparently found Voss's collection of whisky last night and made his way through a bottle."

Oh, shit. That's just great. Voss had *one* rule when he decided to come live with us. *Don't touch his shit.* Simple. Easy.

Unless your name is Malachi. Fucking hell. The tiger is a pain in my ass lately.

"Whatever he took, I'll replace," I offer. It's a hesitant offer because I know that he's not going to take me up on it, but I truly can't deal with the fighting.

"Oh, no, that would be far too easy," Voss says, grinning. "He'll make it up to me, don't you worry."

He exits the room with a manic smile on his face, and I dread to think what he's done to Mal's coffee. I'm not wasting my mental energy on it, I have more important shit to do.

"What's the plan for today?" Orson asks, his brain already whirring as he anticipates what I may need.

"She's taking a sick day," I tell him, and his relief fills the air, even if his face doesn't change. "And I'm arranging some time for her to talk to Dr Abbott. I'm not forcing her into therapy, not if she doesn't want it, but one chat won't kill her."

And, honestly, I'm a tad concerned she might kill herself if she continues down the same path she's on. Her thoughts are very obsessed with death, and it has my lion and I very nervous, especially since we can't help.

"That's a really good idea," Orson says. "Did she ask for a sick day?"

"She did."

He nods, bringing me a plate of food. "I keep making food, hoping she gets hungry, but she never wants to eat."

He's been cooking food for her at every meal, and she's not come out of her room to eat it. He goes up and asks if she wants food, but she's never hungry. Three days since she's sat and eaten with us, and it's hurting the bear more than anyone else. This is his department, and he feels like it's a personal failure that he can't get her to eat.

"I know," I reply, and he sits opposite me, waiting for me to take a bite. He's taking this the hardest, and as much as it doesn't surprise me, considering his sister, it's hurting me that I can't fix things for him.

That I can't fix things for everyone.

"I'll just keep trying."

"For what it's worth, this new way of cooking the bacon is really good," I tell him, crunching on the bacon.

He grins. "You think? I wasn't sure if it would make much difference or not."

"Well it does," I say. "So, congrats. Food experimenting is working."

He goes and gets me my laptop, and it's another reminder of why he's my second. He's capable of doing shit without me needing to constantly be on him. He knows I need a laptop, and he gets it. He knows I need teams scouting so we can try and identify the hunters location, and it's done.

Despite him struggling with Nora's mood, he's been on top of shit with the pride, something I'm so fucking grateful for. I've been slacking the past couple of days—something that's changing from today—but he hasn't. This is why he's my number two and not Mal, despite the tiger's desires.

As I open up my office emails, it doesn't take me long to read a very interesting one. I've got a lead. It might not come to anything, but there's something here. It's about fucking time. "Orson, go swap with Mal. I need him."

"Okay."

And he's gone.

"What's wrong?" Mal demands, rushing into the kitchen a minute or two later with worry etched into every one of his pores, his socks allowing him to slide into the room on unsteady feet. Orson's clearly made things sound worse than what they are. I show him the screen, and his eyes rake over the information before he nods. "I'm on it."

"Good."

I pull out my phone and call my secretary to let her know we're not going to be in today. That Nora specifically won't be in today because she's the only one who gives a shit about missing work. Whilst Mal's chasing up this new lead, I can organise with Dr Abbott a time for him to talk to Nora.

It's finally time to get our girl the help she needs.

23

NORA

"Good morning, little warrior," Malachi greets, kissing my forehead.

He really has dropped the wolf nickname, and I'm not sure how I feel about it. On one hand, I really love it, but on the other I feel like it's another testament to how weak and pathetic I am that he's had to change it.

He sighs, inhaling whatever scents I'm giving off, and it makes me feel guilty. He's been awake for longer than I have, but I've only been up about fifteen minutes before I'm already ruining the day with my toxic thinking.

I wish I could be a better mate. A healthier mate. One who doesn't cause them to waste an entire weekend laying in bed as I cry and whine because I can't handle living.

"How did you sleep?" he asks, and his silvery voice cuts through the darkness just for a moment.

I shrug, and nestle my head into his neck. "Can we cancel today?" I ask instead of answering.

"Consider it cancelled," he replies, kissing my pool of matted dark brown hair.

I slept great, but that's only given my wolf more

ammunition. She's butting her head against the wall, doing her best to demolish it. What's good for me, is good for her. When our body is fully rested and at full power, that makes it easier for her to fight me. When I'm exhausted, so is she.

I'm fighting a silent battle that nobody can help with.

I'm fighting against a part of me that should be working with me... not against me.

The worst part is nobody can see how hard it is. Nobody understands how draining it is to just be awake. I'm in a house full of people who love me, but I feel as alone as I did when I hadn't left my house in months.

Which is worse because then I've got to consider their feelings, too, and it's so hard. My feelings are drowning me, overwhelming to the point I can barely breathe, but then adding on them... it's too much.

I don't want to lose their company, though. I need them here with me.

"I can smell your pain," Mal says. His words barely register, but eventually his arms wrap around me. That helps. The contact helps.

We lay together for a while before he swaps out with Orson. I don't ask why, not when it seems normal now that they've been doing it for the past few days. I don't think I'll be able to understand why they keep trying, not even when I'm out of this fog of darkness.

My bear hugs better than my tiger does, though— *something I'll not be saying aloud*—and it's helpful at reminding me I'm not alone, even if it hurts me. My wolf hates their arms around me, which in turn, makes my head a busier place to be. She doesn't speak to me, but her thoughts and feelings take up a major part of my brain.

I drift in and out of sleep over a period of however long, unable to do anything more. Being awake is hard, but without having eaten or really drinking over the last few days, my body is running on empty.

I've not brushed my hair. I've not brushed my teeth. I've not even been to have a wee today. My body isn't able to do those things because it's wasting all its energy on fighting.

"Nora," Atty calls. I open my eyes, spotting him in the doorway.

He's changed from when he was with me last night, probably showered, too, since he's not confined to this bed. He's got on a pair of grey joggers, and even with how low I am, I can still appreciate the pure sex appeal that comes from my Alpha mate.

The grey seems to outline everything in further depth, the tightness on his thick, meaty thighs... I sigh with exhaustion when the wolf within growls, bashing her head against the wall in revolt at my arousal. *I can't have anything, not even for a second.*

Tears well up in my eyes, the sting of them burning the back of my throat, as I look away from Atticus.

Not one to lose my attention, he softly clears his throat, and my eyes snap to his face. His ocean blue eyes rake over my figure, a sad smile on his pale pink, thin, downturned lips.

"I've got the doctor here, little queen," he murmurs, and my heart races. "Can I come in?"

"Sure," I whisper.

I sit up with Orson's help, and Atty places a laptop in front of me, revealing a man double our age. He's got long-ish brown hair that's wavy, and maybe even different shades of brown. His eyes are a soulful green that seem to read everything about me, even through the screen.

His lips are a corally colour, grainy but very plump. He's

got a muscular frame under the white shirt he's wearing, but the most important part?

He seems nice.

It doesn't change how scared I am, but it's an important thing, and I like that he seems that way even now.

"Hi, Nora," he says softly. His voice is gravelly with absolutely no accent that I can discern. He sounds different from me, from the others, who have grown up in the North. But he doesn't have links to anywhere I seem to know either. "Can I call you Nora or would you prefer something else?"

I nod before shaking my head. With a nearly silent whisper, I say, "You can call me Nora."

"Perfect." Did his shifter senses help him hear me, or does he have subtitles on our call or something? "My name is George. I'm a psychiatrist here in town, and Atticus reached out this morning. Could we chat?"

"Sure," I whisper, glancing up at Atty in disbelief, in awe? He got me some help, and if I'm willing to take the branch... if I'm willing to accept it, then maybe things might go back to being stable.

Atticus listened last night... and he got me some help. *How can my wolf not see what I see?* Atticus, and the others, are good men, they're honourable men who just want what is best for me. They're so much better than Kennedy, the man she's stuck mourning.

"We'll head downstairs and give you the room," Orson says, kissing my shoulder before they both head out.

George waits a beat as I get comfortable in my nest of pillows and blankets before talking. "I know Atticus has arranged this for you, and he mentioned you weren't against it. Is that true? I don't want to force an appointment if you don't truly want one. Therapy only really works if you're willing."

"I told him I've had a psychiatrist in the past, but we never talked about this appointment."

He nods, making a note on his notepad, and my eyes twitch as I glare at it through the screen. That's something I hate. I hate knowing they're writing things about me, and that I don't know what they're saying. I know I can request copies... but when it's discussing how weak I am, I don't want to read that because it'll send me to an even more unstable place.

I never claimed my mind wasn't a complex place...

"We're going to do a quick questionnaire so I can assess both your mental state, and that of your wolf, okay?"

"Okay."

The 'quick' questionnaire took twenty-three minutes and fourteen seconds. Not very quick if you ask me, but it wasn't truly invasive. He'd ask a question and I needed to give him two answers, one for me and one for my wolf. He jotted everything down, and I'm sure he counted up my points.

I just don't know whether a low score or a high score is the desirable outcome to being healthy.

Then he goes through my history and asks countless questions about my mental health and my struggles, even making a note to get my files from my previous therapist. *Perfect.*

This is the worst part about therapy, I'd say. About needing to go through your past, and outline all the times where you've had relapses, where you go into crazy detail about the times in your life that you were weak and couldn't do anything but lay here.

My past showcases how badly I struggled to overcome a horrendous situation. I know that it makes me brave, and amazing, and all these words my men have been using to describe me. I don't feel brave. I don't feel amazing. I feel like a failure.

"Okay, I know that was difficult," George says gently. "But I appreciate you working with me. So, I think we have two different problems right now. Want to hear about them, or are you done for the day?"

"Our appointment has lasted for seventy-nine minutes," I mention, glancing at the timer for our call and watching the seconds rise. My last therapist only did fifty minute appointments, and that seems to be the norm.

"It has. Do you want a break? Do you want to stop?" he asks, placing down at his papers and giving me his full attention. Not that I've not had it this whole time, but still. "Nora, I'm not going to cut things off once we're finally communicating more than just tests. I have all the time in the world for you."

"How much is Atticus paying you?" My snooty tone should shame me, but I'm so lost in my thoughts that it doesn't.

"Nothing."

I edge forward, my brows pulling together in confusion. "He's not paying you?"

"No."

"I don't understand."

"Atticus pays for my two bedroom house that I share with my mate and son. He covers my living expenses, and makes sure that we're safe," he says, shrugging at the pure shock on my face. "That's it. That's all I need. I'm a psychiatrist here in the pack, and I do that to help people, not because I want to rake in the dough. Atticus provides us safety for my family and I, and in turn, I do my part to support the pride."

"I'm sorry... I didn't mean to imply—" I start. I don't

know what I was trying to say, but I do know I've come across as an asshole.

"I know," he says gently. "How did things work back in your pack?"

"I don't really know," I say, biting my lip. "I know we paid taxes to our Alpha—"

He lets out some kind of high-pitched screech, anger in his gaze. "Well, after everything I've learnt about him, that doesn't surprise me."

"What do you mean?" I ask, kind of glad to not be talking about me for a minute.

"I've been in a few prides, packs, groups, whatever they were called changed on the leader's animal," he says, sitting back in his office chair. I can see a little more of his office now that his face isn't pressed so close to the screen, and it looks a little dark, but cozy. There's a warm amber hue to the room, likely from the four... no five different lamps that he has switched on.

His furniture looks nice, and modest to suit his homely vibe, but I can't really tell what shade of brown it is.

"And what tells the good ones from the bad ones is the leader themselves," he continues, unaware that my mind wandered a little as I piece more things together about him. "Take your old pack for example, the taxing of members is shocking. It's abhorrent."

"I don't understand."

"Atticus pays my utilities, he paid for my house when I wanted to move, he pays for my car, and I get a living stipend each month so that I can get whatever I need," George says. He adjusts the computer a tad, and I can see more of him now. He's wearing a checkered blue sweater vest, and his trousers are either red or brown, I can't really tell. He gives off granddad vibes—*aside from his age, of course*

—and it's another reason I feel comfortable chatting with him about more than just my crappy mental health. "And in turn, I offer services like this to the pack. It's like a job where he pays me for my time, except this month I've got three clients who need me, only three. If I weren't in a pride, my family and I would struggle to make ends meet."

"I see." But I don't.

"I've got a client who is struggling a little, and is without a job, so has no income. If this were the human world, she'd receive the bare minimum on benefits and struggle to survive, making an impossible situation even worse," he says, and I nod with tears in my eyes. "In your previous pack, she'd risk expulsion because she can't pay her way."

"He'd not have kicked her out," I say with a frown. "She'd be punished."

A sad look crosses his face, and he nods. "But here, she gets the help she needs to get to a stable place, knowing she's got her bills paid, and food on the table. Atticus provides that. He's a great Alpha, and will be a great mate to you."

And that's when the shutters go back over my face, and I shut down. My wolf, who was furious at our old pack being dissed that way, is now raging that the man in front of us thinks Atty would be a good mate.

But me? I know he's perfect.

Sensing the change in me, Dr Abbott moves us back to what he gets paid for. "So, back to you. Do you want to talk diagnosis, or do you want a break?"

"Diagnosis."

"Your wolf is still grieving her mate. She's now got four —if I'm counting correctly—new mates, but she's still in shock of losing her other bond."

"Five."

"Five new mates, or five including the wolf mate?" he asks, raising one manicured eyebrow.

"Five new ones," I murmur, a blush coating my cheeks. "Atticus, Orson, Malachi, Micah, and Devoss."

"The fox," he says, nodding as he jots that down on his paper. "Okay. Your wolf isn't feral, at least I don't think she is from what you've told me. Obviously, once you're up to it, I'd like to meet you in person and get a feel for her myself, but that can wait. Your wolf is scared, and it's been years since she had the power to do anything more than lay there within you."

"That's how I've been feeling lately," I reply, pulling my legs into me and resting my head on my knees. "I spend all day containing her, that I can't do anything else. I get how she feels because she's making me that way, too."

And it's another thing that makes me hate myself. I'm mourning a man I couldn't care less about. I've gotten over Kennedy's actions, and sure, it's killed me seeing him with my sister, seeing them happy—well, as happy as toxic people can be—with a baby on the way.

It's devastating seeing my sister live the life I could have had.

But then I'd never have met my second chances. I'd not have Atty or Mal. I'd not get cuddles from my favourite bear, or have someone call me pretty girl every day. I'd not get my sneaky fox.

Things are looking up for me, if I can just kill the wolf within.

"How's your food intake?" he asks.

"I try to eat when the guys bring food," I say, but that's a tiny lie. I do try, I really do, but I'm letting him think that I try and put food on a fork or spoon, and digest it. I never get that far. But I'm probably already high—or low—on his

293

points system, and like Atticus, I like to keep mine. "I feel sick all of the time. I just feel... hollow inside."

"I'm sorry, Nora," George says, making a note of that. "How are you sleeping?"

"The last few nights have been hard, and I've done my best to stay awake. A few minutes of drifting off here and there. Last night, I slept fully."

"Why? What changed last night?"

"Atticus stayed awake to make sure she didn't take over," I whisper, looking down at my hands, grateful to see raggedy, bitten nails on my fingers instead of claws. Therapy sucks, and the shame filling the room is immense.

"I see. So you feel if you sleep, she'll take over?"

"I don't want to take the risk."

"Okay. What do you think she's going to do?"

I sigh and shake my head. How do I explain to him that I think she's going to take over, and be so feral, so destructive, that I need to be put down? How do I say that without him thinking I'm a danger to myself—that if I get so low, so unable to continue fighting, it's okay because I have this safety option? How do you tell someone that your back up option is to die? All without sounding crazy? I don't think you can, not if you want to live outside the walls of a mental hospital.

He waits for a few moments before nodding. That's one thing I like about him. He seems to get when I don't want to speak up about things and will still move the conversation onwards. "So, I have some ideas we can try, so that we can get you into a better headspace."

"I... what kind of ideas?"

He moves his files away completely at this point, and edges closer to the screen. "Your wolf thinks her mate is dead, and that you have five 'replacements.' She's scared of the bonds you share with your men. Terrified, even."

"And how do we fix that?"

"You need to continue developing your relationships with them," he says, causing me to gasp. The breath catches in my throat and just won't move. "You need to go on dates, you need to spend time with their animals, hell, get physical if you feel like it. If you strengthen your bonds with them, it'll help her come to realise that they're permanent fixtures in your life."

"You're prescribing sex?" I ask, my voice going high pitched as red coats my cheeks in the little box with my face in it.

He grins, but doesn't say no. "Nora, you're a wolf. She might have been vacant for the past few years, but *you are a wolf*. You need to bond with her again, and to do that, you need to bond with the men in your life."

"You mentioned two diagnoses," I murmur. I'm not discussing my sex life with my therapist on day one. There's lines, and much like the third date sex rule, there's a third appointment sex rule.

"In my professional opinion, you're suffering with PTSD," he says gently. "You've suffered a great deal of pain, loss, and trauma in your life. I think you're really struggling right now, and that's a result of your untreated PTSD."

"No," I argue. "I deal with people who have suffered trauma. I deal with clients who have dealt trauma to others. I lost my family, yes, but that's not trauma. I wasn't raped, or beaten, or sent to war. I've not suffered trauma. No. Thank you for this, but no. I think we're done here."

"Okay," he says, not even arguing with me. "It's a good point to leave off at. I'm going to prescribe some sleeping tablets, and one of your mates can come get them. I want you to take one a night, for the next week or so, so that we can get your body back at optimum levels. I understand your feelings about sleep, but I think it'll really help your body, and your mind, to be rested. Final thing, I promise. I've got a fit note for work, if you feel you should take some time off."

"I don't want to take the sleeping tablets."

"Why?"

I thought he understood my feelings about sleep? Instead of trying to explain it because I don't know if he truly cares, I resort to another truth. "They don't work."

He frowns before realising. "Because you'd have been taking tablets that are fit for a human. Even without your wolf being dormant, you are still a shifter, Nora. These are modified for a shifter, strong enough that one will knock you out for a good night's rest."

I nod slowly. "Okay."

"But you didn't share the full truth there, did you?" he asks. "Why are you so afraid to take the sleeping tablets, Nora?"

"Because then I'll be rested... and so will she. It's been so hard today to fight with her, to beat her back into her corner and to stop her from taking over. She gets rejuvenated just like I do. At least when we're both exhausted, she can't do anything."

"That's not healthy."

"That's all I have. It's all I can offer," I whisper, tears once again dripping down my cheeks.

"Try it my way. Just for this week, why don't you try my idea? We can see if spending more time with your mates—physically, or not—and we can reassess this day next week. Seven days of self-care."

"Today I've not even left my bed."

"Depression is a common illness linked to PTSD."

I know something is wrong with me... but it can't be that.

"Oh, look at that," I mutter. "Already gained a second diagnosis within three whole minutes. I'm good at this shit. How high did I score on the test?"

"Quite high," he says, not phased by me lashing out as he gives me a warm smile. "Trauma doesn't need to be abuse, Nora. It can be anything that hurts you, and the scale isn't objective. It's subjective to the person involved. If a situation happened, and it was bad enough to make you suffer, that's trauma. It's that simple."

"I was broken up with."

How can't he see how pathetic my "trauma" is compared to others? I've seen kids who can't even speak due to the abuse they've suffered. I've seen people unable to leave the house because of the mental trauma they suffered at the hands of abusive partners.

I suffered a break up, a bad one, yes, but a breakup nonetheless. I don't want to be one of those people claiming a diagnosis that isn't true. My struggles don't compare to theirs.

"I was broken up with," I repeat, wiping away the tears in my eyes.

"You were broken up with, and lost your mate. The person you have *a soul deep connection* with—the person that fate thought would be the best person for you. That's not a break-up, but someone ripping away all the best parts of you. Then you lost your pack, your family, your job, your life. You moved to a new town, where you told me you were terrified, paranoid, anxious. You struggled alone for months. The one thing you had left was your wolf. What did she do? She grieved the mate who ripped everything from you. She cried, and she whined... and then she gave up. She made you want to die. Your life was horrific, and you were so beaten down, you wanted to die. You could see no future for yourself, you could see no chance of life. But the human in you didn't die. You didn't give up, Nora. This now, the way you feel now, this is a relapse. Your wolf is finally ready to start fighting, which has sent you back to that horrible dark place you were in all those years ago. But want to know something?"

I nod, hardly able to see the screen through my tears.

"But this time you're not going to do it alone. You don't have a pack.... but you're the queen of this pride. You've got five mates, and you've got help. We're not going to leave you alone to struggle. So, yes, you might feel alone, and it might be utterly terrifying, but it's not true. You're not alone, Nora. I know I promised earlier that I had one last thing, but after talking just now, I've got another suggestion."

"Okay."

"But I want to speak to Atticus about it. Would you mind grabbing your mate, please?"

"No," I whisper before relying on the mental connection I share with my mate instead of having to go get him. *"Atticus. Can you please come upstairs?"*

The door opens less than a second later, and his eyes lock in on me. "Are you okay?"

"Therapy," I mumble as a way of explanation as I gesture for him to come sit by me. I'm not okay, but that's okay.

"Dr Abbott," Atty greets, his arm wrapping around my waist. The heat of his arm pressing into my lower back is soothing, and although his inner lion is silent, I can feel him strong and steady like I have all weekend.

"Nora's got a few tasks to do this week, but I'll let her tell you about those herself," George says, smiling pleasantly. "But after talking to her, I think Nora will really benefit from a pride link. So, my suggestion is that you and her other mates take some time over the next few days, and admit her into the pride."

"She's already in the pride," he says slowly, glancing down at me in confusion. "She's my mate."

"Yes, she is in spirit, but it's not yet official. Her wolf isn't in the pride," George replies, and whilst I can't see Atty's face anymore, I know by the way his hand has gripped by waist a little tighter that he's worried.

"So what do I do?"

"You need to admit her properly, like you would any new applicant."

Atticus frowns, looking down at me with a raised eyebrow. "Is this what you want?"

I shrug because, right now, I know what I want, but it's not an option.

"Okay," Atticus replies.

"I've got a prescription ready for Nora, if someone can come collect it," he adds.

"I'll go with whoever to get it," I murmur, and Atty nods, kissing my head.

"Great. If I'm in a call, my son can bring it out to you. We've got our next appointment on Wednesday at 11, if that works for you?" I nod. "Perfect. Please reach out if you want to talk in the meantime, and Atticus has my number if you have questions. Any time, day or night, call me if you're struggling," he says, and I nod again, it's all I can do, really.

He drones on a little more about things with Atticus before he finally hangs up.

"Want to shower first?" Atty asks, but I shake my head.

"No."

I know I've not showered in a few days, and that my hair looks like utter shit, but to shower, I need energy. I only have

299

a tiny little bit of energy, and I don't want to waste it on showering. I just need to go and get my meds, and have some fresh air. I need out of this house.

But that's not really something I can explain without sounding silly.

"Okay. I'll get Micah to drive you over," he replies, kissing my forehead. He scoops me up, literally. My bum is balanced on his forearms, and I groan but wrap my arms around his neck. I'm capable of walking, but I think my lion just wants to help. I can only imagine how powerless I've been making him feel lately.

"There you are," Voss exclaims, as Atticus and I come through to the living room. Pure happiness radiates through him from his place on the sofa. Correction: *I can only imagine how powerless I've been making them all feel lately.*

"Get some shoes, Micah. You're heading over to pick something up from Dr Abbott," Atty commands. Micah nods, standing from the chair, ready to despite his loungewear of joggers and a t-shirt. All he needs is some shoes. Atticus places me on the floor, and looks down at my own bare feet. "Want shoes?"

"No."

He shrugs, and turns to the others. "Nora's going to join the pride."

"Already?" Orson asks, looking at me from where he's sitting on the armchair, with a concerned expression on his face. "Are you ready for this?"

I shrug, wrapping my arms around my waist. *I really don't know anything right now.*

"That's okay," Atticus says, crouching in front of me. "You don't need to know. We're here. We can handle things. If I thought you'd let me solve every aspect of your life, I would, little queen. Go with Micah, and get some fresh air. We'll handle everything else."

"He said I need to go on dates."

"With us, yes?" Voss says, an eyebrow raised. I can't help the giggles that escape and nod, causing him to grin. "That's a yes. Dating can be fun. You have a job, though, so we're going to need to do ones later in the day."

"What part about less stress for her do you not understand?" Mal snaps, glaring at Voss. "Think before you speak, you stupid fucking fox."

"You don't talk to me," Voss says, angrily. I flinch, but he doesn't turn my way. "You are on my shit list, tiger."

"Please, stop fighting," I say. Mal nods, although Voss's glower doesn't drop. I shoot Atticus a nervous smile.

"Mal may or may not have stolen the fox's property."

"Oh."

He smirks. *"And the fox wants revenge."*

Kind of understandable, he did ask none of us—even me—to touch his things when he moved in with us.

"Okay, I'll not be long," Micah says, peeking his head in the room and giving me a cheeky grin.

"I'm coming with," I murmur, and he nods, no surprise on his face, as I follow him out. It's not until we're in the car that he speaks.

"I know you're not okay, but is there anything I can do right now?"

"No," I reply, squeezing his hand.

I love that he's trying, but it's a stupid question to ask when there's nothing he can do. There's nothing anyone can do. In the words of *Taylor Swift: it's me, hi, I'm the problem, it's me.* And until I change my way of thinking, it's the struggle bus for Nora.

"You look beautiful," he says, and I hold in my sigh. The

worst question is *are you okay* because how do you truthfully answer that? But the worst statement, well, he's close to having said it. The worst statement is *you look like you're doing okay*. Well, yes, I usually do look like I'm doing okay.

I used to time how long I can be this low, this trapped within my body, before I'm back to work after a holiday. I figure out the days where I can retreat in on myself without fear of others noticing. Every workplace has a required amount of holidays you need to take, and I'd use those to hibernate. I'd not leave my house, I'd not get out of bed unless I had to, and I'd pretend I was dead. All without actually dying.

It's therapeutic for someone as fucked up as me, and it helped me recharge just enough to continue living.

At the end of the day, death is the easy option, and on days where I'm not truly hating myself, I can admit I'm strong.

So, yes, I might look like I'm doing okay after my week's holiday, like I'm thriving and happy, but nobody saw what I was like during it. Nobody asked how many times I had to tiptoe to the toilet because my bladder hurt from how long it took me to gather the strength to go wee. Nobody saw the clean sink in the kitchen and wondered if I'm just really good at cleaning up after myself, or if I've not eaten in a week.

People only see what you show on the outside, and when you come across as a cheery, upbeat person, you don't give people any reason to look deeper.

These behaviours are what get me through the day, and the week, and then the month. I do my best to surround myself with people until I crash. I'm the world's biggest unpeople people person. I love people. I love helping them.

I love spending time with them and making them smile. I really love people.

But people drain me.

Micah has been driving around as I've been lost in thought, and it's been nice. It's quiet, but not silent, and it's soothing feeling the vibrations of the car underneath me as the breeze that's coming through the tiny crack in the window keeps blowing a loose strand of hair across my cheek.

We pull up to a standard sized house with two cars in the driveway. It's modest, and after what George revealed about his financial situation, it fits. He trusted me with that information, shared a lot and gave insight into my Alpha mate. It's only another reason why Atticus is a good man, why I respect him as much as I do.

"Want to come in with me?" Micah asks gently.

"Sure."

I look like shit, and I have no shoes on, but George saw me this way on the video call. I'm past caring at this point. Micah doesn't knock, which surprises me, and leads me through the house to the kitchen. He motions for me to stay still, and I hang around the corner, spying as my mate creeps forward and taps him on the shoulder. The man in question screams, and I gasp. *It's not George.* The scream was definitely not a George scream.

Fuck. He did mention a son... Why did I come in?

The man stands, and turns with a grin on his face.

"Micah! How've you been, mate?" he asks, and without waiting for an answer, he continues speaking. "You're an asshole, but here's the prescription and the fit note. He said to get your girl to check things over, and he'll change what he needs to."

His mellifluous tone is a balm on my soul, and for

reasons I don't understand, I find myself creeping a little closer to it. I want to hear him speak more.

"Nora," Micah calls, and I sigh and edge my way around the corner before trudging into the kitchen.

The man's eyes flash a dark red colour, and he moves super fast to entrap me against the wall. I freeze as his head ducks into my neck, and he breathes in my scent. He doesn't say a word, one arm underneath my head, and the other around my back at my waist as he presses me into the wall gently.

I've not showered in three days, and I've not even brushed my hair. *Why the fuck is he smelling me so much?*

"Micah," I plead, looking to my tiger for help. He sighs and shakes his head as the man inhaling my scent like it's a drug lets out a squawk. Okay, totally not the time, but is he a type of bird? An owl? They hoot, actually. An eagle? He could be an eagle.

The man lifts his head, locking eyes with me as he very, very slowly inches forward before connecting our lips together. *I hate myself in this moment.*

I respond to his kiss.

I *eagerly* respond to his kiss.

My tongue darts out, wetting my lips slightly, and he takes that as an in. He picks me up and my legs wrap around his waist as I press even closer to him. Heat travels down to my core, and all I can smell is cinnamon, a scent that suits him. It overtakes me, completely overwhelming my body, attacking my senses. I don't want to be anywhere else.

I want to stay in his embrace.

His hands grip my hips even tighter, and I rock my body slightly against him.

My hands raise up and tangle themselves in his hair as

he deepens our kiss. Tiny sparks appear wherever we're touching, and it only makes the kiss more frantic.

As my teeth start to elongate, I disconnect our kiss, and kiss along his jaw where there's a little bit of facial fuzz, loving the fact that his eyes are red... before sinking my teeth into his neck. My mouth shifts properly, into a partial shift, and I mark my very first mate.

Fuck.

What have I done?

I pull back, not even cleaning the wound, as realisation hits me like a bucket of icy water. *What the fuck have I just done?*

"Calm down," my new mate soothes, but this time, his beautiful sounding voice is like nails on a chalkboard. "It's okay, beautiful girl. It's okay. Take a deep breath."

He's talking to me like I'm a wounded animal. How... *then the shoe drops.* Of course, he knows how fucked up I am. He's my therapist's son, and he'll know all about how pathetic I am.

"Nora," Micah says, coming closer with concern etched into his face. "It's okay. Put her down, mate. Let her settle herself."

"I can't."

"Put me down," I beg. I should have known there was a reason for me wanting to come. I should have guessed something was going on. *Fate is a fucking bitch.*

"Okay."

I'm put on my feet... and I do the only thing I can think of.

I flee.

24

GRIFFIN

"She ran away," Micah says, seeming a little lost. He tried chasing her, but I stopped him, knowing that if anyone gets to chase her, then it'll be me.

And I will. As soon as I can understand why she ran away.

He slams his fist onto the table, a snarl leaving his throat. I don't know why he's so pissed off. My mate marked me, and was so horrified by the man she mated, that she ran away. She's got no fucking shoes on, and still thought being away from me was better.

Clearly, she's not okay. She's got a prescription and a fit note here from my dad. She's one of his patients, so clearly needs help with her mental health, and yet she's still had to run away. I have absolutely no idea how she's struggling, my dad never would tell me even if he knew we were mates, but that only makes it even more imperative that I find her.

I need to be able to help her.

"I'm going to find her," I tell him, the decision now made in my head. "Grab her prescription and go get it filled from the chemist. I've got her."

"You're not my boss," Micah argues.

No, I'm not, but I am more dominant, and I am a rarer shifter. A tiger has absolutely no way of defeating me. I can fucking fly.

Stepping closer, I let my eyes shift, and glare at him. "Want to rescind that?"

"She's got no shoes on, and she's struggling with her wolf," he says quietly, ducking his ebony eyes so that he's not looking at me in challenge. "Find her and fast, and get her back to the house. Atticus and the others will go crazy. I had one fucking job."

I nod and head into my dad's office. I don't have time to calm down the tiger.

"Did Atticus send someone over for the things for his mate?" my dad asks, not even looking up from his laptop.

"Nora is my mate."

He sighs and fixes me with a pointed stare. "Of course she is. Where is she? I need to talk to her."

"She marked me and ran."

"Fucking hell," he says, rubbing his fingers against his temples. What the fuck is he so stressed for? "Be cautious, but find her."

"I'll probably be out late," I say, and he nods.

My dad is an easy going guy, and it was a surprise to Atticus's dad when mine decided to move here. There are only nine of my species on record in the entire world, so to have three in his pride is a big thing. We've lived a quiet life, thanks to Atticus and this pride, and it's something I don't take for granted.

As soon as I leave the house, I shift and launch myself up in the air. My mate might have been overwhelmed enough to flee, but she did mark me first. That deepened our bond, giving me the ability to track her easily using her scent. She's not far from the house, sitting in some park. She's not alone, with two older women watching her, as they sit and drink their coffee. Time to be an asshole, it seems.

I land in front of them, causing them to shriek. "Sorry, little otters, but this park is currently occupied."

They squeak—very high pitched and kind of embarrassing to be honest—as they rush out the park, not even looking at my mate once. Good. That's how I like it. She's overwhelmed and really doesn't need any extra eyes on her during this tense time.

"Hi, Nora."

"Um, hi," she whispers, her brown eyes darting around nervously, unable to settle on me.

"I know we didn't get to introductions, so I'll start. My name is Fin. Griffin, actually, but as you saw, I am a griffin, so that was an awful choice of name from my parents. For parents who really do love me, I've been confused for my entire life about why they'd call me after my animal."

I apparently ramble when I'm nervous in front of my mate. Good to know.

"Orson's name means bear cub," she points out. Orson?

"Orson? Atticus's second hand man?"

"And my mate."

I nod, and edge closer to the table. "I see. How many of those do you have?"

"Six. Seven if you count the one who rejected me."

"I don't because he'll be dead soon."

Way to go, Fin. She's in a fragile mental state, and I'm discussing murder. I'm an idiot.

"He's mated to my sister," she says.

"What an asshole." Seriously, what a fucking asshole. Her sister is just as bad.

"She's pregnant."

Fuck. No wonder she needs a little extra support from my dad right about now. "I'm sorry, Nora. That must be tough."

She shrugs, and turns to look at me properly. Her dark brown eyes are filled with unshed tears, and her long, dark brown hair is tatted and messy. She's struggling right now, that's clear, but she's still beautiful.

"It is what it is," she says with a heavy sigh. "I'm sorry I marked you. I'm also sorry I ran away. That was childish, and it wasn't fair to you. I'm being honest, so you know what you're getting into. I'm a mess—which is clear by the fact that I need your dad's help—and it's not something that's going to be fixed overnight."

"No, your mental health usually isn't. Just like a broken leg or a burst appendix," I say, sitting on the opposite side of the table, despite my griffin's complaints. She's terrified, and I'm not going to make things worse by throwing myself at her—no matter how much I want to. "Did you know there are only nine griffins in the entire world?"

"I didn't," she says, looking a little curious at that information. "A griffin is a mix between an eagle, and lion, right? That's not offensive is it? I'm just..."

"No, it's not offensive. Yes, we're a hybrid of sorts, but technically, we're our own creature. My point is that you're not the only one who comes with 'problems'," I reply. I made sure to do finger quotes around the word problems, so she understands that it's not a problem—that she's not a problem.

"I don't understand how that's a problem."

I shrug, pulling out my knife to carve into the table as I talk. "And I don't get how yours is either, but you know. We're protected here in the pride, thanks to Atticus and his dad, but we're highly valuable creatures. There's a reason there are only nine of us. We're usually stuck living in some boring ass mythical compound, according to my dad, but thankfully, we don't. But we're at risk whenever hunters are involved because of our rarity. I'm just saying, you're not the only one who has 'issues'."

She rolls her eyes at my second use of quotation marks. "Okay. Well, I marked you. I've been having issues with my wolf... but in that moment, we kind of merged. We both wanted to, um, claim you."

"That's a good thing... right?"

She shrugs, reaching over and taking my knife from me. "Sorry, that was just making me a little nervous. Can we walk whilst we talk? Being stationary is not helping."

"Sure."

What she's yet to realise is that I'd do anything for her. Her ex-mate clearly didn't treat her the way she was meant to be treated, but now that means I get the chance to be there for her. Even if that means I've got to share her with five other people.

We walk, and it takes everything in me to let her walk on her own. I want the contact. I want to be close. However, the reasoning is because she's got her shoes off and there's stones on the ground. I don't want her to experience any kind of hurt, even if it's just standing on a tiny pebble.

When she cringes, I don't even wait to see if it's because of something other than her feet hurting. Instead, she gets picked up and placed onto my back, and I hook my arms around her thighs, to hold her in place.

"Seems you've got the caveman aspect of being a mate down," she teases, wrapping her arms around my neck. They're a little tight, but I don't argue. She's willingly touching me, I couldn't care less if it hurts.

"Seems you've got the appropriate footwear part of

being a hiker down... oh, wait," I tease, loving the way her twinkling laugh escapes her. The sound is foreign to me, but it's something I could listen to all day every day. It's light and sounds like little bells.

"Don't be mean," she murmurs. "But thank you for picking me up. I was getting tired."

"I've got you," I promise. She nods, and rests her head on my shoulder. "I'm going to start walking back to your home, if that's okay? Micah will be worried about you running off."

And as much as I want to keep her all to myself, she has other mates for a reason. If I don't respect the mating circle, it's going to make things very hard for my mate, and I refuse to do that.

She's already got one dickhead ex-mate, I'm not going to give her any reason to make it two.

"Thank you," she replies.

I start walking, the extra weight of her barely registers since she's so fucking tiny, and when her breathing turns soft, I pause to bring her to my front. It's so much fucking better to hold her in my arms like this. I brush her hair behind her ears, and pull her in as close as I possibly can.

I wasn't expecting to find my mate today. Hell, I wasn't ever expecting to find my mate. Griffin's can sense their mate via a scent that the animal within gives off. It's similar to that of wolves, but still unique to us. I sensed something weird when Micah came in, but it wasn't until my griffin was able to see Nora that I realised she was my mate. I couldn't hold back... I didn't want to hold back.

The walk through town is annoying because people keep looking at me—more specifically, they're looking at the dark haired beauty in my arms. That pisses me off. She's mine.

When a large black jeep pulls in front of me, I frown and

get ready for flight. That's until the window rolls down, and Micah's grinning face greets me. Fucking idiot. "Hop in. We'll get her home."

"She wanted to keep moving."

"The car will be moving, she was happy with it on the way over, I swear," Micah promises. "Get in the car, Fin." I roll my eyes, but climb into the back, keeping a tight grip on her. He pulls off easily, and doesn't hesitate in starting to talk.

"So, I'm not sure if you guys talked or what, but here's the deal. She's mated to me, Malachi, Atticus, Devoss, and Orson. Two tigers, as you know, and obviously Atticus is a lion."

"Orson's a bear, she mentioned that, which leaves Devoss."

"The fox," he replies, grinning at me. "He's a funny guy, not going to lie. You two will get along."

"Really?"

"Well, I like him, and you like me, so, it's not that big of a stretch to assume."

I don't reply and press a kiss to the top of her head. The drive continues in silence, and when he inputs the code to the gate, I hold in my snort. As if a gate can keep anyone within this city out. It's hilarious.

"I know," Micah groans, parking the car in front of the house. "I told him people would laugh at us, but Orson really wanted the gate. Even though he spends more time at his boring apartment than with us, he still got his way."

"Good job on not sounding bitter," I tell him, motioning for him to get out and open my door. He's rolling his eyes, no literally, he's rolled them about forty-seven times so that I can still see him doing it when he opens the door for me. I clamber out, but luckily she's still sleeping.

"She's not been sleeping properly," Micah says quietly, peering over at the beauty in my arms. His hands twitch as if he wants to touch her, or maybe even take her from me. I move over ever so slightly, just to make that itch a little bit easier for him to resist. He gives me a bemused look and, thankfully, doesn't comment. "So I'm glad she's still sleeping."

"Did you get her things sorted?" I ask.

"Yep. I got the script filled. Two weeks of sleeping tablets and a two week fit note ready to be handed into her boss."

"And that is?"

"Depends who you ask," he says. "She works for Atticus, as do ninety-five percent of us, but he's like two or three ranks higher, so they argue over it. Kai says he's her boss, too, but he's definitely not, but he does head the HR department, so he gets a bit of leeway with his claims."

Micah is not normally this chatty. I'm not saying it's a bad thing—considering it's like Nora cliff notes—but it's new. We're not close friends, but we have hung out a few times, and now we share a mate.

I've never spent any time around the others, not really. It's going to be an adjustment dealing with these people.

"Honey, we're home," Micah says, not raising his voice, but I know that they can hear him. "Don't raise your voice, we have a guest, and Nora is sleeping."

"A guest?" a voice demands, and when a red-head rounds the corner with a dirty look on his face, I know it was him who asked. "The griffin."

"Considering you're called the fox, despite being extremely common shifters, that's not the insult you think it is," I drawl.

"Considering you're in my house holding my mate, well, I don't think you should be resting on those laurels."

I roll my eyes—just the once, unlike Micah—and carefully free one of my hands. I have to balance Nora super carefully so I don't drop her, and I pull down my shirt to display my mark. "Since your nose is a little inferior to mine, I'll not say anything and let your eyes do the work."

"That was comment enough," Micah drawls, and I smirk. "The others are upstairs. Want to hand her over?"

"I can carry her just fine."

He nods, and the three of us head up the stairs. Nora moans quietly, and I pause to make sure she's okay. There's a little furrow in her brows that goes away when I kiss it. I'll always protect her—even from bad dreams.

"Griffin, hi," Atticus greets as the door opens to reveal a modern office. It's very high tech and very sleek. Doesn't surprise me that the billionaire has a nice office. He's got a blank expression on his face, not really showing any surprise at me being here, or about her being asleep in my arms. He raises one thick, dirty-blonde eyebrow, and asks with concern etched into his crisp tone, "Is she okay?"

"Fine."

"Put her down," Orson demands. I can only place who he is because Nora mentioned his name.

He's fucking massive, an inch or two taller than my 6'6", and a lot broader than I am. I'm stocky, a strong build from my shifted form, but he's just the same. He's wearing a pair of shorts, showing off his hairy calves, and a long-sleeved t-shirt that seems to cling to him.

It's a good thing I'm not easily emasculated because this man has the power to do that based on his body alone.

The only area I think I'd win in comparison to him is our hairs. Mine is shoulder-length and dark brown at the roots with a multitude of different shades of brown throughout. It fades to a lighter colour near the bottom.

Mine is wavy and soft, despite the wiry look to it. I look after my hair, I really love it.

And Orson seems to be the same. I can't really tell how long his is, but where mine is thick and luscious, his is thin and blonde. He's got it tied neatly into a knot at the base of his skull rather than letting it be free.

His hazel eyes rake over my mate, an assessing look on his face.

Micah's cliff notes kind of help. The bear is protective, as are all bears, and it helps to know that his gruff demeanour is not because of me but because of his instincts.

"No," I say, shaking my head. "We're mates, too, get over it."

"Marked, too," Atticus says, his tone and face giving nothing away. "How did that happen, and how did she react?"

"She did it, and as you can sense, I haven't returned the favour," I say quietly. "She ran, but we've talked, and now she's asleep in my arms, so I think that should be clue enough on how she's doing."

Despite my sarcastic tone, Atticus doesn't argue. He simply nods.

"She's collecting strong men," Orson points out. "Do you think that's her subconscious trying to protect her?"

"Then again, the jackass was an Alpha, so maybe she's just a powerful wolf," Malachi says, shrugging. My eyes narrow because I sensed the wolf within, and she's weak. Very weak. "Mate, can you at least sit down with her? He's not going to calm down until you do."

So dramatic. I can handle holding her, she's fucking tiny and probably weighs less than one of the bear's legs. I do sit, though, not wanting to fight with one of her tigers today.

"Who was her previous mate?"

"Kennedy Newitt," Atticus replies, his eyes locked on mine when I tense. "Know him?"

"I met him before the gala the other day. His car needed some touch ups," I mention, frowning. "He seemed like a nice guy, and his mate was super fucking sweet. Are you telling me I helped the fucking asshole who hurt her, and made her disgusting, backstabbing sister a cup of tea?"

"I like you," Voss coos with a sad nod. He's perched on the desk, sitting away from us, but still involved. Somehow, I feel like this is the norm for the fox. "Yes. Sadly, she doesn't want us to kill them. However, she does currently have a hunter problem that we're tackling in a very bloody manner, if you get me."

"I do," I murmur, tilting my head. "How bloody?"

"I came home covered in blood after murdering four hunters," Devoss declares. "We're going as bloody as possible. There's a nest of the fuckers, and we're trying to figure out who brought them here."

"And does she know?"

"She saw me kill one," Malachi says as he drops into a chair. He sighs at the look of disbelief on my face before explaining what happened when she called him for help, and he had to kill the hunter in front of her. He did explain how he mangled the dead body... and I hate to say that he didn't technically need to do that. Like I'd totally do that, but not in front of my mate. *Clearly, Micah got the brains in this family.* Which is saying something since the younger tiger brother is not the smartest tool in the shed.

Well, academically, sure. Socially? Not a chance. He's got no street smarts.

"And she didn't say anything when you came home covered in blood?" I ask.

"It's pride business, and we outrank her," Atticus replies.

When a sneer appears on my face, he leans forward in his seat, leaning on his knees properly, as he gives me a stern look. "I won't apologise for how I protect my mate. I won't ever risk her health—mental or physical—unless it's absolutely necessary. I told her we were handling the hunter issue, and that's what I was doing. So drop the fucking judgement."

I don't back down, my eyes shifting to challenge the motherfucker in front of me.

"You don't want to do this," Atticus cautions.

But he's wrong. I don't just want to do this—I *need* to do this. My griffin needs to know his place within this mini-pride of Nora's men. I need to know whether I'm first... or second.

Atticus responds to the challenge, as I knew he would, and his amber eyes meet my red ones. It's silent as the others wait with bated breath to see who will win. I might be a mythical creature, but as the fox pointed out, those laurels aren't ones I can rest on, especially when facing down an Alpha of a giant pride. I can feel the strain as my griffin starts to give in to the lion, but that only makes me push further.

It's a feeble attempt, though, because I realise he was holding back, too. His eyes glow slightly brighter before I avert my gaze with an embarrassed cough.

"Sorry," I sigh, looking at him again. This time my gaze is respectful.

"Dominant males, I get it," he replies, shrugging it off without an ounce of annoyance. "I have more staring contests—as Nora would call them when denying her shifter half—a day than I go to the bathroom. It's the way of life."

"It is," I say, nodding. I'm pleased he's unfazed, but I

wish my griffin was the same way. He's currently laying here licking his wounds like a little baby. That's the difference between Atticus and me. He's a leader, I'm not.

"Brief me on this hunter situation," I demand. "I'll help any way I can."

"You're a mechanic," Devoss points out, an eyebrow raised. "How are you meant to help?"

"Just fill me in."

Atticus nods and starts outlining the story, extra details added in by the guys as and when they can. It's helpful, and gives me a better picture of the threat we're currently facing.

"We're also helping Newitt with his pack's expansion as long as he delivers the paperwork and meets my demands," Atticus reveals, and I open my mouth to argue, but his look silences me. "She told me to help them, and believe me, it pissed me off. But what she wants, she gets."

"I don't know how shit went down, or how he ended up with her sister, but I can't wrap my head around the fact that she wants to help them."

"Just because we're helping, doesn't mean we're making it easy," Orson tells me.

"Hell, just because we're helping doesn't mean I didn't get to have a little fun..." Voss says, winking at me. "Did you know wolves bleed just as easily as every other shifter?"

"The sister is pregnant," Atticus tells me, giving Voss a wary glance.

"Nora said," I say. "I'm missing a lot of the picture, but I think she'll want to tell me herself."

"She might," Micah says softly. "She might not. She's struggling at the minute, and we're not adding to her stress."

"Your dad prescribed dates," Malachi says. "I don't get his game."

"I'm guessing that her wolf is struggling with the new

mate bonds, and he's wanting us to be intimate—get the grin off your face, Micah, he didn't prescribe sex—because it'll help settle her. She's currently facing six new bonds, and yet her wolf is likely still mourning the dead bond. Spending time with each of us, constantly touching her, whether that's playing with her hair or holding her hand, and genuinely just being there should help the wolf come to terms with it." I sigh, rubbing the side of my face before adding the extra bit. "Marking each other helps, too. She told me at the park that both she *and* her wolf wanted to mark me, and that they had merged in the moment. I think that's why she ran and not because she found out she was mated to me."

"How do you guess that?" Malachi asks, judgement clouding his tone. He's been mostly silent, aside from asking about the dates, which is a bit worrying.

"Because I know my dad, and I listen when he tells me things."

"That actually helps," Atticus says, nodding in thanks. "Thank you for explaining."

"So, looks like we're all taking a holiday from work," Malachi says, glancing at Atticus. "If we're home with her, that should lessen the guilt with her needing some time off."

He nods. "I'll head in and sort things out there. Orson, start doing dinner. I'm not sure if she'll be up to eating, but having food there will help. Voss, Mal, head over and grab one of the teams so that you can target the next nest."

"What about me?" Micah asks.

"You get to babysit the griffin," Voss stage whispers.

"Well, yes, but mainly Nora. I'm not sure how she's going to wake up, and I'd rather there was a familiar face," Atticus says, looking at me to make sure I'm not upset. I'm not because I get it. She might want me there since we're the furthest along in our bond, but she also might want someone she knows.

I hate not fully knowing what's wrong with her... but discussing our illnesses isn't really a first date kind of discussion. *Bold of me to assume this is our first date.*

"Come on, I'll show you her bedroom," Micah offers.

"Thanks."

I stand with her in my arms, and each of the men kiss her forehead, or touch her in their own way before heading off. She might not have her OG mate, but she is loved.

She is loved.

25

NORA

*W*hen I wake, I can feel all the different people around me. My griffin's bond within me burns the hottest, due to the completed bond on my end, but I can feel them all humming within me.

I'm pleased about that though... which is a little surprising.

"Morning, little warrior," Mal coos, and my eyes fly open. "Well, evening. It's eight."

"You'd class eight as being evening?" Micah asks, surprised. He's sitting on the floor, and he looks very content despite it being the worst seating arrangement. He's now wearing a pair of grey pyjama pants that are baggy, and some fluffy colourful socks. His t-shirt is a plain white, or it would be if Micah didn't have coffee stains on it. "I'd say eight is night time."

"Nah, like, five to, like, eight is evening," Voss argues, a smirk on his face, from his spot at the bottom of the bed. He's sitting with his legs crossed, and resting back on his arms a little. He's made himself very comfortable on my bed, and I don't want to think how long he's been sat here. "After that is night time."

"I've got to agree with Voss," Atticus says, surprising me that he joined in. My head flies to the left where he's sat, and I can't help but giggle at the expression on his face. They're all taking this debate seriously. "Nine is, like, night time. Unless you're old, then anything after five is night time."

"In the summer, it doesn't get dark until ten, roughly," Orson says, bringing logic into the argument, with no hint of discomfort in his tone. He's sitting at my vanity chair, a little stool with a short back—and that's when I sit on it, so when Orson's there it seems even shorter—looking cramped and uncomfortable. His ass is barely fitting on the rectangular seat, and there's no padding to even protect his toned cheeks. The lack of fat on his body isn't doing him any favours right now. I take back my statement about Micah having the worst seat—Orson's got him beat, even if he's not complaining. "So, I'd say five until ten is evening. Ten until, like, five is night, and then five until maybe lunch time is morning? Then afternoon is the time in between."

"Why is this the discussion?" Fin asks, laughing slightly. He's lying next to me on my right side, his hand propped up under his head as he rests on his elbow to see everyone, and I can feel the heat of his body next to mine. "It doesn't matter what part of the day you class it as. Either way, it's eight pm."

"Why did you roll your eyes twice?" Micah asks slowly as I sit up in bed. Atticus' arm falls to my shoulders, and he pulls me into his side gently. Almost fearfully as if he's worried I'm going to push him away. I rest my head on his chest, and he softly presses a kiss to my forehead.

We're okay.

I might not be. My brain might be broken, and my wolf

322

might be feral, but everything between my mates and I is solid.

"After you rolled your eyes forty-seven times earlier, I thought it was the way things were done around here," Fin remarks, winking at me. "How are you feeling?"

"Fine."

"Me, too," he replies. "My mark is a little red, since you didn't heal it—kind of mean by the way—but, otherwise, I'm okay."

"Sorry," I mumble, ducking my head as shame fills me. I bit him, quite visciously I may add, before running away and leaving him to struggle. He had to track me down and deal with another Nora pity party.

"Asshat," Voss says, glaring at Fin. "Ignore the griffin, Nora. Orson made us food. Are you frungy?"

"Frungy?" Micah asks.

"Hungry," he mutters, rubbing the back of his neck. I catch a tiny glint in his eyes, just before he glares at Micah. "Shut the fuck up, it's been a long day."

"Yes," I reply, surprising the group. "Do I have time to shower before we eat?"

"Yes," Orson replies.

"We've got some things to talk about, too," Mal says.

"What kind of things?"

They trade nervous glances, and I hold in my frustration. When someone says those words, nothing good ever comes of it. It's scary, and as someone who already struggles with her anxiety, it's even more daunting.

"There's nothing to worry about," Atty says gently.

"You guys are dumb as fuck," Voss groans, shaking his head at them all. "Kai, you don't start a conversation with 'we need to talk' because it panics the person you're saying it to. Those words usually mean there is a break-up imminent or that there's some kind of big decision that needs to be made. They're usually followed by something panic worthy."

"Oh," Mal says, glancing at Orson, confused. "Did you know that?"

Orson shrugs, and I smile. Okay. Clearly, there's nothing to worry about. That helps. That really helps. I lace my fingers through Atty's, and he looks down at me with an indulgent kind of smile on his thin, downturned lips.

"We're all on holiday for the next fortnight," he says gently. I wasn't pressing for an answer, but I like that he gave it anyway. "You don't need to use your fit note if you don't want to, and you don't need to use your holidays if you don't want to, either. We want to be off work to be here, but if you need to go, that's okay, too."

"Oh."

I nod and let go of Atty's hand and head into the bathroom in a bit of a daze. I don't know if the others leave my room, or what, but I can't focus on that.

Instead, my mind is splintering, losing the tiny bit of strength I've gained from bonding with Fin.

Atticus's words have petrified me. Giving up my job, even if only for a few weeks, will be a setback, one I may not be able to recover from. It'll be going back to the time when I was too weak to do anything. It'll mean giving in and accepting this diagnosis of PTSD. I'm terrified to give up, and this feels like giving up.

I've barely made any headway on the people in my department, they're all so judgmental, and they truly believe I'm unworthy of the role. I have my own self-doubts, my own hatred of myself, but I've never doubted my ability at work.

But people suck sometimes, and they manage to make life even harder.

I brush through my hair, cringing at all the breakages. Apparently, not brushing your hair for a weekend or so really makes it tatty. That's the issue with a low mood haze. You don't care about your image because you don't care about anything.

It sounds so frivolous, but when you spend your time focusing on how you'll be dead soon—whether you're fighting Death's call or not—then why waste your time brushing your hair or shaving your pits?

As I brush my teeth—scrub at them to get rid of all the fuzz, more like—I cringe thinking about how Fin and I kissed... I need to start taking care of myself. But what's the point in taking care of myself if I'm just going to give into my poor mental state by not going to work? One step forward... two, or more like five, steps back.

The warm water of the shower washes over me, and it feels so good, so refreshing to almost wash away the depression. I'm not sure if I can claim to be depressed despite what Dr Abbott says, but I do know I'm not okay, so maybe, just maybe I don't need to decide today.

I can just be me, and this version of me is struggling and needs some help.

A knock sounds on the door, and I raise my voice to call out, "come in" when it opens to reveal Orson. He's already seen me a little bit naked, after the gala, so it doesn't bother me that he's come in without permission.

"Hey," Orson says, almost hesitantly as he shifts from foot to foot. "I know you're showering, but I wanted to come and say something without the others overhearing."

"Okay..."

"My sister isn't around anymore," he says quietly, well as quiet as he can be over the sound of running water. "When she had my niece, she had something called postpartum depression. Have you heard of it?"

I nod, but since I'm rubbing conditioner in my hair, I have no idea if he can see me. "Yes."

"I thought so. She struggled for a very long time, and we missed it. When we were there, she was okay. She played with Olivia, she was a good mum who never seemed to let anything faze her, and her house was always so clean. I know that sounds ridiculous because, of course, none of those things matter, but I'm trying to paint the picture here. She was on top of things. She never had a hair out of place, Olivia was always smiling, and they seemed happy. There was no reason to doubt otherwise."

"What happened?" I ask quietly.

"She killed herself."

Fuck.

"My sister was a strong woman, and she was battling something we could never understand. It was years ago now. My niece, Olivia, she's nine now. It was a loss that hit my family hard."

"I can only imagine."

"So, my point in sharing this is that I will do *anything* to ensure you and my sister don't meet the same end," he says with a grim smile on his face. "Accepting help doesn't make you weak. Taking some time off work isn't regressing. You are so fucking strong, Nora, and we're going to help you deal with your wolf, and get back to being a little happier. I'm not saying we're going to fix you because you're not broken. I'm just saying, I've seen firsthand what it's like to feel like you're all alone and that you need to be "strong", but that's bullshit. That's not mental health, that's crap."

I open the shower, and he hands me a towel from the towel warmer in the corner without breaking eye contact. I appreciate that because I think the topic we're discussing is more important than my boobs. It makes me happy that he does, too.

"I'm sorry about your sister," I tell him as I tie a knot in my towel in the front of my chest. Tears well up in my eyes, and his gaze softens. "I've not been taking care of myself lately."

"I know," he says. "I take care of the home, little cub, let me help take care of you, too."

But as easy as that sounds... how do I do that? How do I truly give in and rely on another person?

How can I be so selfish and let him take over my needs? How can I give in control and let him bathe me and feed me?

Because that's what I need. I don't have the executive functions to do those things for myself, so if he's proposing that he'll take care of me, that's what he'll have to do.

His eyes narrow as he sniffs the air, and I dread to think what scents I'm giving off to prompt that look in his eyes.

"I was alone last time I felt this low," I murmur, speaking before he can, really. "It's going to be hard to break the habits of dealing with it all on my own. I want help. I want to not hate myself anymore, but I don't know how."

I walk through to the bedroom, and he follows.

"My sister felt she couldn't come to us for help," Orson says, pushing me to sit down at the vanity. "She struggled alone, and when she got to that really dark point, she had nobody there to pull her back from it. She gave in to the twisted lies in her brain, and she's dead. Do you feel that low? Are you a danger to yourself?"

"No." Not right now, anyway.

His shoulders relax, and a small smile appears on his

face. He steals my hairbrush and starts gently brushing through my wet hair. "Good."

"I'm low. Sometimes I struggle to remember why I want to be alive, and I might even have weak moments where I give up... but I'm still here."

"And I'll be there during those weak moments," Orson says. "Atticus, Malachi, Devoss, Micah, and even Griffin will be there during those weak moments. Just know we're never going to judge you. We're never going to think you're weak."

I nod, and as he starts drying my hair, I watch him in the mirror. He's gentle but focused. It's sweet, and it's a reminder that he cares. Once my hair is dry, he puts away my hairdryer and hands me a pair of pyjamas.

"Clean clothes should help, little cub," he says, kissing the top of my head before pulling out a second towel when I don't move. He dries my arms, ever so gently, and I can't stop myself from taking his comfort. I need his touch. I want his help.

He dries every inch of me that's on show before undoing the towel, and again, gently dries my body. It's not sexual, just caring—just like when Voss and Micah helped me shower the other night. When tears spring to my eyes, he gently wipes them away.

Over and over the word of the night has been gentle. He's a giant, and I know first hand how tight his grip can be, but he's shown me nothing but dainty hands tonight. He pulls on my clothes, and even goes so far as to pull on some socks.

"I love you," he whispers, pressing his forehead to mine. "Don't say it back. I don't expect you to believe me—god knows you've not been shown love in your life—and I don't expect you to feel the same way yet. Just... I needed to say the words. You're it for me, little cub, and I'm so glad you're in my life."

I... how the fuck can he say he loves me? I can see the sincerity in his gaze, but it's not been very long. How can he truly believe he loves me?

"No panicking," Orson murmurs.

I nod—although my panic is not something those two words can just erase—and wrap my arms around his neck a little because they wouldn't go around his waist. He laughs, picking me up, and heads downstairs. My gentle giant is sweet, and I love that he felt he could open up to me about his sister.

"At least some good came from the day Atty made me move here," I tease, knowing the others can hear me now that we're in the communal areas. "Well, technically, we met at the gala he forced me to attend."

"See I take offence to the words 'made' and 'forced'," Atty shouts, and a genuine smile flits across my face for the first time in a very long while. "I just knew what you needed, clearly."

"Don't argue with him," Orson stage whispers, placing me on the ground in the living room where everyone has gathered. They're sprawled out on different sofas and arm chairs, with Micah sitting on the floor as usual. "He's got too big a head to hear the truth."

"Hey, she met me all on her own," Fin adds, smiling. "You don't mind if I stay for the night, do you, Nora?"

"No."

I'd prefer he stayed to be honest, and by the way they all nod, I think they knew that.

"Okay, time for food," Orson declares. "In here or in the dining room?"

"Here works," Micah replies from his spot by the coffee

table. "Now, come sit down, pretty girl. I've got a jigsaw for us to do."

"A jigsaw?" I ask slowly.

"Hey, I'm on holiday. I get to spend my paid time off how I choose, thank you very much," he says, faking offence.

"Now you know how you don't understand that people's earnings aren't your money," Mal says, grinning at Atticus.

"Wait, what?" Fin asks. Mal catches him up to speed, and I'm amused as I figure out the end goal. "Fucking hell."

"How does it feel to be paying us all to sit here and do nothing?" Mal asks.

"Fuck off," Atty snaps, rolling his ocean blue eyes as he pouts a little. It only lasts for a second before happiness overtakes him. "It feels great, actually."

I turn to the expectant Micah, who is sitting patiently waiting for his time to discuss the jigsaw.

"What kind of jigsaw?" I ask, moving to sit opposite him on the floor, and he pulls out a box. On the box where the jigsaw image should be... is a black square. *Oh my god*. I really hope Micah is going to be sharing, the word *us* flitting through my mind before it gets drowned out by the dark thoughts because this should be fun. "Ooo, this is exciting!"

"It's a jigsaw," Mal drawls. "A boring ass jigsaw at that."

"No, see it's challenging because it's all black," I explain, a giddy feeling filling me up. "Like you can't spy at the box to get a clue from an image because it's just black. So you've got to find the pieces that go there without having an image to guide you. It's exciting."

"Ah, but see, this is my holiday project," Micah says, grinning. My face falls, and yet his good mood doesn't drop. "So I'm going to spend my full two weeks trying to complete this 10,000 piece jigsaw... all alone."

"I'm not working," I mention, and his teeth now show through his smile.

I can feel the relief coursing through the air as the others understand that I'm going to be joining them on holiday... I don't know if I can use my fit note, but Orson's right. It's okay to take some time off. It's not weak to take time for my mental health, just like it's not weak for me to take time for my physical health. I just need to keep reminding myself of that, no matter how hard it is.

"You're not?"

I shake my head, and he hands me the box as Voss turns on the TV. "Welcome to team blacks, pretty girl."

"Okay, I don't think that can be our team name," I say, sighing.

"Probably not. But this should be a fun project. We're going to need to clear the big table, though, so we can do it on there."

I nod and look at him properly. "How do you do jigsaws?"

"What do you mean?"

"Well, like, how do you do the jigsaw?"

His brows are furrowed, but I don't get why he's so confused. Is he a weird person who just matches random pieces together, or does he do the edges first and then systematically works his way through? This kind of thing is important, considering it's going to take hours. I don't want to start, and be excited about it, for him to ruin it.

"I match the pieces together and keep going until it's completed..."

"Do you do the edges first?"

He groans, throwing his head back to rest on the sofa. "Pretty girl, please tell me you're not one of those people who spend hours sorting the pieces between edges and middles, and then places the edge pieces together before doing the middle?"

"Of course I am!"

He grins sitting up. "So am I. God, it's almost as if you don't know me."

I grin, and when Orson hands me a bowl of stew, I thank him and sit with my crossed legs underneath the coffee table, and put my bowl on top. Orson then hands bowls out to the others, as Malachi hands out cutlery. I'm opposite Micah, with Voss and Atty at my back on the sofa.

Directly opposite us is Fin and Mal, with Micah on the floor in front of them. Once everyone has bowls and salt and pepper and more bread, Orson finally sits down in the arm chair with his own bowl.

The news is on the TV, and Atty turns it up, and I instantly remember about my client who has a trial coming up. *Damn it.* It really is one step forward and five backwards.

How are you meant to practice good mental health when life gets in the way? It's even harder when these obstacles appear because the thoughts in my head are always *if you're dead, you won't need to deal with this stress*.

When the internal part of you, the rational and logical part of you, is the one reminding you of this way out, of this loophole to finish the game early... how are you meant to continue?

"Wait, I've got the trial coming up," I panic, looking over to Atticus. "We did the mock trial, and it went well, but we've still got the actual trial."

"You weren't going to be in court anyway," Atticus points out, which stings a little, but I get it. "Make a document outlining things that need handled, and I'll make sure it gets done."

"Who will be doing it?"

"Seb, or another manager from higher up," he replies.

"Higher up," I murmur.

I'm sure Seb is good at his job, at some aspect of the company, but I won't be letting him take over my floor. He's slimy—ironic since he's a snake—and it's not something I like.

"What's wrong with Seb?" Atty asks. "For real, don't just brush me off."

"He's slimy," I reply, and Mal nods in support. "I've felt it since my first day, and it's becoming more and more apparent. I can't place the why... but it's an internal feeling I get. He also delivered one of the images to me from the hunters."

"Fucking snake," Orson snarls.

"I get what you mean," Mal adds, to Atty's surprise. "I've felt it, too. The first day, your first day I mean, I played down my worry to you being an unmated female, and then we ended up being mates. So I've been blaming it all on jealousy."

"But?" Atticus asks.

"But I think he's worth looking into," Malachi replies.

"I'll go into the office after food and have a spy through our servers," Micah says.

Devoss grins, looking at Fin. "What are you doing later tonight?"

"Nothing..." he trails off, looking at me for support, and I shrug. My fox is apparently sneaky, so I have no idea what his plans are.

"Then you and I are going for a drink," Voss declares. "I know where the snake spends his time."

"Guys," I start, but Atticus cuts me off.

"No. This is me taking measures to protect the pride," he tells me, his voice firm but still soft. "So, no backtracking. I need you to be able to come to me with things like this—and I'm really glad you did—because I can't be everywhere, and sadly, threats come at every angle, even from within. I'm Alpha, Nora. That means when you tell me a pride member is 'slimy' I need to check that out. It could be you overreacting, it could be he's sexist, or he could just be a major suck-up. It will make me really happy if it turns out to be one of those things because it means my people are safe. If it's something more serious, well, I appreciate the heads up."

"But I didn't mean to get him in trouble..." I say softly.

"And right now he's not in trouble," Atticus tells me reassuringly. "As I said, I'm Alpha. It's my job to protect you as not only your mate but your leader. This would be the same as if any random pride member came to me with a concern. I'd listen, and if it turned out to be a false accusation, no harm, and it doesn't go further than me."

"Things didn't work like this in the pack."

"That doesn't surprise me," he says bitterly. "Kennedy, and his family, are weak, and it seems they run their pack through fear and sheer strength. I maintain position because I'm the strongest shifter, but I maintain loyalty because I respect my people. You'll see, but this is how good prides, and packs, are run."

"Sounds a little egotistical, but he's telling the truth," Voss says. "I've been around some fucked up communities, and this one is a good one."

I nod, although I think this is one of those things I need to experience fully before I can understand. I know they're good men, and I have no doubt that they're telling the truth. That's all I need to know.

"Okay."

"Okay?" Atty asks, and I nod. "Okay."

"So, when are we doing my initiation thing?"

Fin frowns, leaning forward in his seat. I've noticed he's barely touched his food, and I don't know why. "You're joining the pride? Even with the hunter threats?"

"Joining the pride will only help increase her safety," Malachi says, placing his empty bowl in front of me. "She was an easy target when she was weak and living on the outskirts of the pride. She's now at the centre, stronger, and surrounded by powerful shifters. Adding her into the pride will only be an extra level of protection for her."

Fin nods, his jaw tense.

"We can talk about that later," Atticus tells him. "But it's completely up to you, little queen. How about we do it Saturday? We can do something together afterwards."

"Sure," I murmur. It's only Monday, so we have a few days yet. That's good. "I'm nervous."

"We know," Micah says gently. "But it will be fun."

I nod and go back to eating. I listen as they spitball ideas, not caring either way. Being part of a pack, and obviously a pride, is about community. The whole *it takes a village to raise a child* mentality really applies to shifters. I doubt that has changed just because the species has. It'll be nice to be part of a community again—really nice.

26

DEVOSS

"Two pints of *Snakebite,* please," I say, nodding at Johnny behind the bar. My drinks are always a code, and now Johnny knows to have a look into snakes. As soon as he sees me make contact with Seb, he'll have his eyes and ears out to get me the gossip.

"Sure thing, Voss."

"Regular enough you're on a first name basis with the bartender?" Fin asks, but if only he knew the full scope of my relationship with the people here.

I'm intrigued by the griffin. I think it's cool that Atticus has some mythicals here—even if he denies having more than the griffins, I know he does since I've brought a lot in for him—and it's quite interesting that Nora has mated one.

I mean no disrespect because my mate truly is the best, but she's not exactly exotic. She's a wolf, and they're highly common, so for her to be matched with a griffin, it's intriguing to say the least.

"Thanks, mate," I say, taking the drinks from Johnny, and I lead Fin over to my booth.

It's kept empty, mostly because some people may have

experienced some injuries when sitting in it. Although, this place is filled with the degenerates, the ones in the pack who aren't the traditional white picket fences people who work nine to five jobs. No, we're the people that go on recon missions, who deal with hunters, who help defend the pack from all the issues they don't even know about.

"Nice place," Fin remarks, judgement lacing his tone.

I ignore him. He's here as back-up because whilst human me can very easily disarm and maim most of the people here, as soon as we shift, I'm at a disadvantage. Foxes are predators, but compared to tigers, lynxes, and even the rare African elephant that resides here, I don't stand a chance in my shifted form.

A griffin, though, well, you'd be pretty stupid to take on a griffin. So, Fin makes me even more untouchable. Disappointing since I'll not be able to get into any fights, but handy when we're checking out a literal snake.

"So, Nora," Fin starts, and I kick his shin. "What?"

"Don't mention her fucking name around these people."

He rolls his eyes, an action Micah was right to point out. All this man does is roll his eyes. Maybe griffins have bad eyesight. It's not something I know about them, but I'll find out.

"Fine. What's the plan?"

"Oh, my fucking god," I groan, throwing my head back against the wall, cringing at the pain. Sadly, it reminds me this isn't a fucking nightmare. Nope. I'm actually stuck with the annoying as fuck chatterbox.

"What?"

"Go play darts," I command, making a shooing motion so he can get out of my booth. I want him gone. He sighs and takes his drink—the one that is going to be added to my tab, so he best fucking drink it all—walking over to where a group of oxen are at the dart board. He can figure his own shit out.

I drink, and I watch. Where the fuck is the snake? It's frustrating, especially since I'm wasting precious Nora time waiting for him to show up. It's not cool.

Speaking of this being a place for degenerates... why does he come here? Why does a picket fence, nine to five, slimy snake come to a bar for shifters to hire? Hm. That's going to be a question I need answers to. I head back to the bar, sitting at the end next to The Spider. He's not an actual spider, despite claiming to be—*there's no such thing as spider shifters*—but his shifted shape is something I still don't know.

"Fox."

"Spider."

He cocks a leery brow at me, and his real eye darts over to where Griffin is having a laugh with the oxen. "New company?"

"Meh," I reply with a shrug. "He was meant to be here for his power, but he's a bit pathetic, so I'm using him as a bargaining chip."

The Spider laughs. "Smart lad."

"I'm here for information."

"What are you offering?" I hum, making a buzzing noise, but don't comment. "I see. Information on who? You know I'll give you a fair price."

"Seb. Snake shifter. Works at Legal Pride."

"Sebastian Viper. Real surname unknown, despite his claims that it's the truth," The Spider says, and I raise a brow.

"That's the one."

"Hm. I know he's messed up in some shady shit," he

says, shaking his head. "Buy me a drink, and I'll tell you all about it."

"That's your cost? A drink?"

He nods, and I beckon Johnny over. I fork over a couple grand that I got from Atticus, and cover The Spider's tab for the entire night. Only once his drink is in front of him does he start to speak.

"Seb made a deal a while back, one that he's desperately trying to get out of," The Spider says. "He's a fool, but he's not the man you're after."

"He's not?"

He shakes his head. "No. You've got a snake in your midst—not a literal one—and only then will you find the truths you want."

"Fuck." He said the snake is in *my* midst, meaning it's a contact I've dealt with, and not one of Atticus's people. Fucking great. "Are you going to share the name?"

"Zachary."

I close my eyes, an annoyance filtering through me. Zach is my contact for imports, and the fact that he's betraying us makes me very, very angry.

At the end of the day, we all work for Atticus in some way, shape, or form. He might not be our only client, our only boss, but he's the one who houses us, who keeps us safe, who gave us a chance when nobody else would.

He gave *me* a chance, and I refuse to let him be taken for a fool.

I hang around for another minute or two, but The Spider has nothing more to say. With a sigh, I leave and make my way over to the booth where Fin's sitting, waiting for me. He's like an eager little puppy, but this time, I don't need his back-up.

Not that I really needed it the first time, since he's done absolutely fuck all.

"Go home," I say, and Griffin gapes at me in shock. His drink—the one I bought for him—is only half drunk, but I can get revenge for that later. "I've got a late night ahead of me."

"But..."

"You fulfilled your purpose, pretty boy. Go home."

He glares at me, letting out a little huff. "I can help you."

"And you did," I reply, patting him on the back. "Foxes work alone, little birdie, and I've got somewhere else to be."

"I don't—"

I tried being nice, but I'm fed up with it now. I rise from the table, and smirk at him. "Feel free to stay. They're already selling off your organs. I've got dibs on your heart, but the rest will go for a pretty penny."

"Why are you being like this?"

"Because I need to go so that I can end this threat to our mate," I say, and his eyes flash red before he nods.

"Great. I'll fly back," he says as the two of us leave the bar. I give Johnny a wave, knowing he'll reach out if Seb does show his face, but I'm not as worried about him right now.

The Spider doesn't lie, and I've got a panther shifter to beat some answers out of.

We're making progress, little mouse, and I'll cut off the head of the snake so that you're safe.

It's just not a literal snake like I first thought.

27

NORA

"*N*ora, hi," Dr Abbott says, smiling at me softly from the other end of the video call. His room is brighter today as if he's got the main light on instead of all the lamps. Today's outfit is a maroon sweater vest with a yellow shirt underneath. I can't see his trousers, but if I'm being honest, based on the top-half, I don't want to.

"Hi," I reply, looking down at my hands so that I don't need to focus on him. He's scheduled a call despite us having agreed upon Wednesday instead, so I'm a tad bit nervous about talking with him.

Because we all know what he's done it for.

Griffin Abbott. His only child. My newest mate.

I set boundaries yesterday, declaring that we'd not be discussing my sex life until at least our third call, but I'd like to now change that to *never*.

Because sex with your therapist could be hot—*I know you kinky bitches think so, too*—but discussing it when the person you're having sex with is your therapist's son? Yeah, no.

"I know we agreed to have another call on Wednesday,

but I wanted to touch base after hearing about your newest mate bond," he says, voicing what I already knew.

"To Fin." I raise my eyes, looking at him underneath my lashes, and a shy expression crosses my face in the tiny little box where I sit on the screen. He's got a blank face, so I can't tell what he's thinking. I suppose it's something he's mastered over the years. "I mated with your son."

He nods, a bashful look appearing on his face, one I've seen on Fin before. Oh, this is freaky. "I wanted to talk to you about your options going forward."

"Options?" I echo, panic filling me.

"Do you want me to send your files over to a different therapist? We've got another two in the pack I think would work really well with you. We obviously have more, but those two focus on the kinds of help you need."

I freeze, not sure if he's asking because it's going to be too awkward to talk to him or, worse, if he doesn't want to handle me anymore.

Is this because of Griffin? Did Fin ask him to not talk to me anymore?

Why am I trying to doubt my new mate?

"Psychiatrists really shouldn't treat those they have multiple concurrent relationships with," George says, and I nod slowly because that makes sense. But we've just started talking. We've made a little bit of progress—I'm not trapped in bed anymore, so clearly we've moved forward a tad.

"You're my daughter by mating now, even if the bond is not fully complete, which now adds in a social bond that we'd not have had otherwise. That means that my advice could be altered—purposefully or not—and you may not get the best help you need from me."

I frown, messing with the sleeve of my top instead of

looking at him again. I don't want to see his face as he breaks up with me.

What is it about me that causes men to discard me like I'm nothing?

What have I done to cause this kind of treatment?

He keeps talking, though, used to the distance from me. "My goals will always be to help you, and to get you to a stable place. But then we *will* have a relationship outside of these sessions that may alter our relationship within the sessions. You'll have dinner at my house, I'll likely have dinner at yours. Your children, if you ever have them, will be my grandchildren. Your troubles become mine in a way."

"I get it," I say, looking at him properly now with determination in my tone and body language. He's offering me a choice, he's not outwardly rejecting me just yet. "You're worried that you'll help me in a selfish way. That you'll maybe give advice that will benefit my relationship with Fin, more than what would be good for me." He frowns, and I shake my head. "That sounded weird. Here's a scenario. I decide that I want to reject my mates." He gasps, pure horror filling his face, but I plow through with my meaning anyway. "Yeah. You're not going to work through that with me and help me do that when the person I'd be rejecting and condemning to the life I've lived would be your son."

"I'd never support that no matter who the people were," George says, but he nods. "But I understand your extreme point because I know you'd never do that. You're right. It may be hard for me to separate you as Nora, my patient, and Nora, my son's mate, in certain situations, and then in those situations the advice I give you might not be the advice you would get from an impartial person."

"Will that be something you're willing to handle?" I ask, wringing my hands together nervously. I make sure they're out of frame so that he can't sense how uneasy I am whilst I wait for his answers. "Even just for a little bit whilst I try and get out of this depressive episode?" He nods, and I sigh in relief. "I don't want to have to do this again with a new therapist."

"No?" he asks, and I shake my head. "Okay. Well, another issue is that *you* may hold things back. That there might be things you don't want to share with me, but that you'll need help processing. I don't want you keeping things to yourself that could harm you."

"You'd not break patient confidentiality, would you?" I ask, a slight trepidation to my tone. He immediately shakes his head, and I sigh in relief. "I trust you. I think that's something we'll have to come to when the time arises."

"I agree," he says, and I nod. Some tension fades out his shoulders, too, tension I didn't realise he was carrying. It's kind of nice to know that he was affected by this, too. "Now, is there anything you want to say on the topic?"

"No."

He nods. "Great. So, a lot happened after our call yesterday, and I'd really like to get into it. Did you take the sleeping pill last night?"

"No." But before he can lecture me, I rush to add, "But I slept for like three hours"—not in a row, but in total, but I keep that to myself—"so I've slept a decent amount even without the artificial aid."

He cocks a brow, and I sigh. Yeah, okay, that defence sounded better in my mind, especially since I kept the worst parts from him.

"What stopped you from taking it?" he asks.

"Fear." Just like I told him.

He nods, writing it down on his stupid notepad. "Fear of

what?" I don't answer, and so he wisely moves on. "What kept you up last night then? Why couldn't you sleep?"

"Fin and Voss went out to investigate Seb, one of the paralegals on my floor..." I trail off, not sure how to finish without breaking the unspoken NDA I've signed by being Atticus's mate.

I only know certain information because of my connection to him, and whilst this is my therapy session, I still feel uneasy about sharing it without his permission.

Maybe I should ask him if he'd mind.

But then what if he only says no so that I'm not worried, but then he's got to deal with the repercussions?

"Is this to do with the hunter threat?" George asks, and my eyebrows raise. I gasp, and nod. "I know all about the current threat we're facing, Nora, and your role in it. Atticus and I talked in depth before our session, but it was a warning for me and my family, not for you. I'm not sure if Fin has shared, but my family and I are rare shifters."

"I know," I say, and he smiles. "You're mythicals— griffins."

"Exactly. Which means when hunters come poking around, we need to be on extra alert so that we don't find ourselves stuck in their trap. We go for a good price on the black market," he says, and despite the joking tone, I know he's serious about it. Fin alluded to as much. "But he also shared that they've been targeting you, and that it might be something you bring up in our sessions together."

"Ah."

"So, Fin and Devoss went out."

I nod. "Yeah, and Fin came back, but Voss hasn't. He's gone to sort out the hunter issue, to get some information or something, I don't really know."

"I see," he replies, still making notes. "And that played

on your mind all night? You were trying to work out what he's doing?"

"No. I'm worried about him, of course I am, but I don't want to know what he's doing. As long as he's okay, that's all I really need to know." I rub at my cheeks, embarrassed about being so weak—so *selfish*. "It was just... it made me realise something. I'm useless."

He frowns. "Useless?"

"Yes. I have nothing to offer my mates, not like they do me."

"Let's talk about that," he says. "What do they offer you?"

"Atticus offers me safety. Strength. Support," I say, closing my eyes and thinking of the lion in my mind, but more importantly, I think of the feelings he ignites within me. "He's strong, and can protect me from anything."

"Mhm. What about Orson?" he asks, sounding a little distracted.

Next, a black bear appears in my mind, and a ghost of a smile appears on my lips. "He's caring. He's the one I can fall back on and trust to take over everything that I could ever need. He makes me feel loved, and taken care of, all while never judging me for not being able to do things for myself."

"Surprising for a bear." I don't like his tone there, but he moves on before I can comment on it. "What about Devoss or Malachi? What's their purpose?"

"Mal pushes me to be real. He doesn't realise it, I don't think, but he pushes me to open up, to be myself, to let people in. He's there to stop me hiding, to stop apologising just for existing," I whisper, my throat choking up as I think about my golden tiger.

"And Devoss?"

"He's cheeky," I say, my voice trembling now as tears fall down my cheeks. "He's got a past that is horrific, but it

346

seems to have only made him more protective over the people he cares about. There's so much mystery and intrigue about him, but I know exactly who he is on the inside."

"And what does he do *for* you?" George asks.

"He teaches me that there is no right or wrong, there's no black or white checklist like I seem to want. He's helping me understand the world in a way I never knew was possible. He's like my own personal gun, and I know if I ever asked, he'd point it at whoever I asked."

Except myself.

"Micah?"

"Micah's innocent. He's shy and bashful and is introverted in a different way to me. He helps me relax, and get out of my head. He teaches me new things, but different to the things that Voss shares. He enlightens me to a world of fun—movies, books, anything—and gives me a reason to live that isn't just surviving."

"And Griffin?"

"I don't know him as well," I say, this time opening my eyes so I can gauge George's reaction. There isn't one, though, which reassures me that this is okay. That for now we can handle intermingling our therapy relationship and our personal one. "But so far, he seems to offer me stability. He gets me in a way that the others don't, and I need that. I need the emotional connection, the emotional *validation* that he offers."

George nods. "So, what you've said so far is that your men each access a different part of you, and nurture their connections to you in a different way." I nod slowly. "So why wouldn't you do that for them? How don't you do that for them?"

"For the first three weeks, I denied everything. I've

denied being a wolf, I've denied knowing the shifter world, hell, I denied my mate bonds before I knew what they were."

"All valid due to the trauma you've suffered as part of the shifter world. How have things been since you have acknowledged the bonds that you share?"

"Well, I'm in therapy with you so..."

He smiles wryly. "You're a funny girl, Nora, but you're using your humour to deflect from the real topic," he says, and I sigh. "I guarantee if I asked each of your mates what you offered them, the first thing they'd say would be happiness."

I laugh, a dry, horrible sound, as tears well up in my eyes. So he's going there is he? He's picking on the one thing I've ever wanted, the one thing I truly crave.

Happiness is something I've yet to achieve, and he knows it.

"Have you never felt happy?" he asks.

"Not in a long time," I say, blinking back the tears. Or at least I try to. Instead they drip down my cheeks, unable to stay where they belong, and the salty bitterness coats my lips. "Not properly, anyway."

Because it feels mean to say that I've never been genuinely happy when these last few weeks have been some of my happiest.

They've also been some of my worst, but that talk is scheduled for a different section of this therapy session.

"I see. Why did you laugh when I said that they'd say you offered them happiness?"

"Because why don't I get happiness?" I snap, glaring at him like he's the one who personally stole it from me. "Why wasn't that my answer when you asked what they offered me? Why did I go on and on about selfish desires, about all the things they give me, when all I've ever wanted is to be happy?"

I wring my hands together as I break down. He's so sweet, just silently letting me get this out. "All I've wanted is to be happy."

"I know," he says softly. "And that will come."

"So you say." Because fate has given me second chance mates, something rare and beautiful, and still my first answer wasn't happiness.

Why aren't they enough?

"Right now your mind is struggling, but it won't forever." So he says. "How long have you been struggling this bad? Because from everything you've said, it seems like you knew your mental health was deteriorating, rather than it just coming out of the blue when your wolf emerged." I nod slowly, not sure I like where he's going with this. "You had a therapist back in Callent."

"Yes."

"So why didn't you reach out to her once you realised how badly you were struggling?"

Could he sound any more accusatory here?

"It became more apparent when I was here," I say, which is true, even if it's not the full truth.

"And yet, you did a lot of calls over video chat according to her," he says, and I blink back the tears of shame. How easily he reads me with those judgemental beady eyes. "So, let me ask again, why didn't you reach out for help once you realised how badly you were struggling?"

"I think I want to end our session here for the day," I say, and he nods without complaint. He places his notebook down, and smiles at me.

"We've had a very good session, Nora. We're making very good progress," he says. I don't reply because I can't really tell if I agree or not. Not when I feel this raw. "I've got time for a call tomorrow, either at 10 am or I can do one later in the evening. It's my anniversary with my mate, so we're going out for lunch. Which would you prefer?"

"Um..." Neither to be honest. I don't really want to ruin his anniversary by talking about the doom and gloom that is me.

"I'm hoping you take your sleeping pill tonight," he says, giving me a smile. "So, we'll do the evening chat. I don't want to risk you needing to set alarms and worrying over making the appointment, and that being the reason you don't take it."

I nod slowly. I'd like to say that I'm not sure if I'm going to take the sleeping pill, but I already know that I won't. But if he wants to live in a delusion where he thinks I might, that's his prerogative.

"Is there anything else you want to discuss before I go?" he asks, and I shake my head. He nods and ends the call after saying goodbye, and I burst into tears.

The messy, gut-wrenching, soul-destroying kind.

I hate therapy. I hate George. I hate my mates. I hate being this fucking miserable.

But most of all, I hate myself for not being enough.

I pull the blankets up over my head, cringing when the laptop falls to the floor, and fully break down.

I don't want to fight.

I *can't* fight anymore.

I just want to die.

28

NORA

A warm body gets into bed with me and tugs me from the centre of the bed and up into his firm chest. My nose is blocked from the crying session, so I didn't scent who it was when the door opened, but as soon as I'm in his arms, it's abundantly clear.

Only one man can hold me as gentle as this whilst being as massive as he is.

"I've got you, little cub," he murmurs, pressing a soft kiss to my hair. "I've got you."

And that sparks off another round of tears. Orson doesn't let me go, though, instead, holding on as tight as he can without hurting me. It's a good balance, the safety of a weight on my chest helps loosen the panic within a little, but it's not so overbearing that I feel trapped.

"What happened?" he asks when my sobs quieten a little. "Was this... did something happen during therapy?"

I shake my head, not able to answer him. Any of the others, and I'd not really hesitate to open up, but Orson? After what he shared with me about his sister? I can't.

"That's not fair," Orson says, and I hear the hurt in his

voice, even if I don't smell it. "I shared my past with you so that you knew I'd do whatever it took to make sure you knew where I stood. I want you to share everything with me, Nora, the good, the bad, and the ugly."

Maybe he does.

But I think he wants to hear everything except the truth.

"Things are just hard," I say quietly. That's not a lie, but it's not sharing the full weight of my truth, either. "There's a lot that I need to do, and there's just no point doing it."

And by it, I mean living.

I don't want to be alive right now. I just want to be that blob of nothing.

"Anything worth doing is worth doing poorly," Orson says, and I frown at his chest. That makes very little sense to me.

"What's that supposed to mean?" I ask when he doesn't elaborate any further.

"Doing something, even poorly, is better than not doing it at all," he says. "You expect perfection of yourself, no matter the situation, but sometimes putting in twenty percent of the effort is better than putting in zero."

"But why put in effort doing something when you'll need to redo it?"

"Because even the little efforts can be helpful," he says, softly rubbing my back. "Brushing your teeth for ten seconds is better than not doing it at all."

"Maybe, but it's not going to fix my teeth."

"What's wrong with your teeth?"

"I'm positive I've got about 87 cavities, and need a good seven fillings," I say with a shrug. "They're more yellow than I'd like, the enamel pretty much worn away from years of neglect."

Depression is so bad that people die.

Why am I ashamed that it's caused me to not brush my teeth?

He kisses my head. "Then we'll visit a dentist once you're feeling a bit better."

I roll my eyes, but don't fight to be let go. He's not going to let that happen.

"At the end of the day, little cub, doing something poorly is better than not doing it," he says. "Especially when it comes to self-care. Because even with the bare minimum, you're better off than you were before."

I nod slowly, seeing a little bit of logic to his words.

"Do you want some help to get out of bed, or are we chilling in here today?" he asks. There's no judgement in his words, his voice as gravelly as normal, with no inflictions or hidden messages.

He's being genuine, and offering the care he's so good at providing.

"I need a wee," I say, and he nods.

"When did you last poop?"

"What?"

"When did you last poop?" he repeats, and I push away from his chest to gape at him. He's got a serious expression on his face, if you ignore the crinkles at his eyes that show he's testing. He doesn't let me leave his embrace fully, but grants me that little bit of space. "What? I'm concerned. You've not been eating properly, and—"

"No," I say, shaking my head. "No. You don't get to talk about my bowels. Not even a little bit."

Mirth flashes through his eyes as he gives me a small grin. "I need to know if I'm going to have to wipe poop off your booty, or—"

I shriek and jump out of bed, racing into the bathroom. I know he's not going to follow, since he willingly let me go, but the teasing nature of his words has forced me to get up and go to the bathroom.

I owe him for that.

I do my business—*wiping my own ass*—before joining him back in the bedroom. He helps me change clothes, still just sticking with pyjamas, and then he brushes my hair.

He uses some water, brushes out all the tats, and then plaits it for me. It's a basic French plait, and he seems so proud of doing it.

Then we go downstairs where breakfast is ready. He's had it in the oven, keeping warm, and quickly plates it for us.

"Where is everyone else?" I ask, looking around as if they're just going to appear.

"Atticus is in his office on a conference call. Malachi is at work picking up some files, and I think Micah went with him," Orson says. "Griffin's at home getting a change of clothes, and Voss is..." He trails off

"Yeah," I say, laughing. "Even if you told me you knew where he was, I'd not believe you. I still don't even know his birthday."

"He's a mysterious guy," Orson replies as he sits down to eat with me.

The front door opens, and Griffin comes in with a rucksack over his back. He's wearing a tight-fitting pair of navy joggers, a black t-shirt with a blue jacket over the top, and a pair of trainers on his feet.

Do men just live in athletic wear?

I'm not sure, but I know most of my men do. It's a good thing they look so good in it.

"Oh, hey," he says, grinning at us with a cheeky smile. "What's going on?"

"Breakfast," Orson says, motioning to the plate in front of us. "Want some?"

"Sure," he replies. He drops his bag at the doorway, ignoring the dirty look Orson shoots it, and comes to sit in the seat next to me.

He kisses my cheek, and I smile up at him.

"How was therapy?" he asks, and I sigh. "That fun, huh?"

"Yeah," I mutter, spearing a piece of sausage with my fork.

"Well, my parents are off on a disgustingly romantic lunch date later, and I'm fucking starving after hearing about it, so thanks, mate," Fin says, taking a plate of food from Orson.

"Are you good to chill with Fin, little cub?" Orson asks, and I nod. "Amazing. Atticus needs me to run an errand for him."

"Doesn't he have a PA for that?" I ask.

"Yeah," Orson replies with a cheeky grin on his face. "You're looking at him."

He drops a kiss on the top of my head before kicking Fin's stool. "Shift that fucking bag out of my nice clean kitchen, or I'll kill you."

And then leaves.

Holy wow.

"What was that about?" Fin asks, gazing after him in astonishment.

"Orson's very particular about cleaning."

He laughs, and I push away my plate. It's still pretty full, but I can't eat anything else.

"Your dad is staying on as my therapist."

"Yeah?" Fin asks, and I nod. "Good. I hope he can help you."

"Me, too."

"So, I've heard from Micah that you've been watching *The Big Bang Theory,* and it's one of my favourite shows. Want to head through to the living room, and we can watch it?"

I nod, looking at his bag as we walk past, and he smirks at me.

"I'll move it soon. Maybe."

Well, at least I get to spend time with him before Orson kills him.

Griffin

"I wish I had a depressed friend," Nora says, and I look at her in surprise. We're sitting in the living room, our show running in the background, but her mind hasn't been focused on the TV for a while.

I've been content to sit here with her, though, hoping that if there's something she wants to share, then she will. But now that she has... I'm so confused.

"What?" I ask, sure I didn't hear her properly.

She sighs, turning to face me with a suspiciously blank look on her face. "Someone who is going through something similar, gets it. You're all amazing, don't get me wrong, but..."

"But we don't get it," I say quietly. She shakes her head, and smiles, even if it looks like she's about to burst into tears.

"That's a good thing," she reassures me. "But it means when I think certain things, I can't share it."

"Try me." I don't like the idea of her keeping secrets from me, especially if it's to do with her health.

"No."

I grab her by the waist and pull her into my lap, causing her to giggle, and start tickling her sides.

"Fin, stop, please," she says through her giggles.

"Talk to me then," I demand, leaning forward to press a kiss to her neck. She takes a deep breath, and I can smell her pain, the emotional twinges to it making my heart ache in a way I can't fathom.

"How am I meant to explain to your dad that the reason I didn't reach out for help the first time I felt things slipping... was because I wasn't sure I was going to be alive to fix it."

It's like someone's thrown a bucket of ice cold water over me, and my brain has completely frozen. "What?"

"He asked why I let it get this bad when I realised I was struggling much sooner, and then I ended the session so I didn't need to answer."

"Okay..."

"Which means he's going to bring it back up tonight, and I don't have a good answer. How do I rationally explain the reason when things started getting bad, and I realised, that I chose to do nothing instead of asking for help. In my head, why waste time trying to fix my mental health when I'm going to be dead in a week. How do you say that to someone who doesn't get it? How do you say that to someone and expect them to not want to lock you up or hide the dangerous objects?"

"But if you had a—"

"But if I had a depressed friend, they'd get that. They'd understand what I mean. I don't want to die, Fin, but my mind does—my wolf does. And I can't say this to you because I can smell your anger and your worry and your hurt. I can feel how tight you're holding me, like you're scared I'm going to disappear or do something to hurt myself. I can't share all the scary things that my mind says to me because then it becomes my job to make sure you're okay with what I share. It then becomes my job to make you feel better about the way I'm feeling."

"But—"

"But you don't mean to," she says, disentangling herself from my grip. She's got a soft smile on her face, but her eyes are sad. "And I know that, nobody ever does."

"I don't want—"

"But the thing about being ill, about your mind being the very thing working against you, is that sometimes suffering in silence is genuinely the easier path. You're alone, you're scared, you're exhausted, and you just want to be done... but at least you've only got to deal with your own chaotic mind. Sometimes staying silent seems like the only option for survival. When your mind wants you dead, you've got to work so much harder to wake up every morning. I don't want to be dead, I just want to be done living."

Sometimes staying silent seems like the only option for survival.

She's not okay. Nora's truly not okay. How much of what she's showing us... is actually the truth?

29

NORA

"*A*tticus," Voss says, coming into the room with a serious expression on his face. It doesn't suit my cheeky fox, but the tension in his body, the blood on his chest, the fucking mess of his hair, well I know I'm seeing the work version of my mate.

I get the love, the grins, the smile.

Everyone else gets to see this version.

It's jarring, but after hearing about his past, I'm kind of glad he has an outlet for his pain. He does good work, mostly.

You know, if you can ignore the blood involved.

And it really makes me appreciate the version of him I get so much more.

"What's going on?" Atticus demands, rising from his position on the sofa. Micah and I stop doing our jigsaw, our eyes darting between Atticus and Devoss with identical narrowed eyes.

"I've found out who the leader of the hunters is," Devoss says with a sigh. "And I've got news from Kennedy."

Kennedy?

I look at Micah in surprise, and he shrugs, not knowing what's happening there. Hm, I love spending time with Micah, out of all the guys, he's kind of like my best friend.

But, damn, do I wish he had more insight into the pride goings on, so that he could soothe my nerves.

"My office," Atticus demands, an iciness to his crisp tone. Voss nods and heads straight upstairs without a backward glance.

I wish he could tell me what was happening.

"Atty," I whisper, fear filling my tone.

"Don't worry about it," he murmurs, dropping a kiss on my head. "Finish your jigsaw before your therapy session."

"Finish," I gasp, looking at Micah in surprise. Micah, the traitor, just laughs and puts another piece in.

Atticus smirks as he crouches down next to me, his eyes raking over my face, likely reading more from me than I'm comfortable with sharing. He tucks a hair behind my ear, and presses a soft kiss to my temple.

"We've not really discussed things with Kennedy, since I was under the impression that you don't really want to know." He's not wrong. "But we can once you're up to it," he offers, and I nod slowly. "And the hunters? Well, that's something I'll only share if it's needed. I'll always take the burden of your anxieties, little queen."

"Atty—"

"No," he says, firmly. He presses another kiss to my temple and rises to his feet as he looks at the table with a wry look on his face. "Micah has just done a middle piece."

With that bomb dropped, I turn around to glare at my tiger mate. Atticus is amused as he leaves the room, and I sigh, shaking my head when I see that Atticus lied.

Little sneak.

"As if we're getting this finished today," I say, rolling my eyes. Micah laughs, and I start trying to put another piece together.

"It's going to take a very long time," Micah agrees, sounding as excited as I am about it. He waits a beat before placing his hand over mine. I slowly raise my eyes to look at his face, noting the slight frown. "Are you okay, pretty girl?"

"Nervous."

"That's understandable, but Atticus is the baddest motherfucker around, and he'll protect you until his last breath."

"That's what I'm worried about, Romeo."

"Romeo?"

I shrug, smirking at him with fake humour on my face. It's only fake because I can't bring myself to let it be real.

"Well, at least I was the first to get a nickname. Point to me," Micah says, and I smile just for a second before my lips go back to a frown. "Nora, sweetheart, look at me."

I didn't realise I wasn't anymore. I do as he says, and the fierceness in his face surprises me. With the way that his brows furrow together and his ebony eyes harden with determination, and the way his lips pinch as he fights not to get angry, he looks so much like Mal.

It's startling to see because whilst they always gave similar facial features, their personality's make them look so vastly different.

"You're going to be okay. Kennedy's a weasel, but he's not going to get to be involved in your life anymore," Micah says. "And the hunters will be dealt with. Please trust in us."

I nod, and we fall to silence for a moment.

"I can't find where this one goes," Micah says, handing over a side piece. "Check yours."

And we move on.

But the tension within me doesn't fade as I imagine the conversation that Atticus is having upstairs with Voss, and I think about all the ways that things are changing outside my little bubble.

How long can I continue to hide out at home and let the real world pass me by?

"Nora," Micah murmurs, and I raise my head hesitantly. "Are you done now?"

"No, of course not."

"You don't need to lie to me, pretty girl," he says, giving me a soft smile. I see the worry in his ebony eyes, though, the slight crinkle across his forehead. "If you're done, we can move on and do something else. Even if it's just cuddles."

"No," I reply, shaking my head. "This is helping keep my mind busy."

He nods, and I start hunting for the piece I need.

I'm not lying. This is a good activity to keep my mind busy. And, well, these worries aren't going anywhere, so it doesn't hurt to pause them for a little bit.

It means I've got plenty of content for my therapy session in a few hours.

Dr Abbott will love that.

Atticus

"So, what do you want to go over first?" Voss asks, not looking my way as I silently close the office door behind him. He's sitting on my arm chair, his shirt on the coffee table in front of him, with a first aid kit sprawled open on the arm of the chair.

He's got a deep cut on the right side of his ribs, and I'm very happy Nora's not seen that.

It'll heal, of course, but not immediately, and she doesn't need to worry about him. Especially not after I told her last night that Voss would be fine, that he's a capable man and can handle whatever he's gotten himself into.

"What happened?" I demand, gesturing to the wound as I move to sit on the sofa in the seat closest to him. I'd offer to help, but I've got no fucking experience with stitching the skin. "Voss?"

"A little accident with a cunt and his claws," Voss says, shaking his head. "But it doesn't matter. Not only did I rid you of a snake, I've found out more about the hunters."

"Seb panned out?"

"No," he replies. "Seb's still someone I want to talk to, but I don't think he's involved. No, I found another man— Zachary."

"He's—"

"He works down at the docks, and is in charge of a lot of imports. He's my contact, anyway, who I use to smuggle me some shit in." I raise an eyebrow, and he waves me off. "Trust me, you don't want to know."

I think I might, but it's not important right now.

"Well, he decided that he wanted to betray the pride and has since lost his life for it." My eyes flash in annoyance. "Don't worry, Mal is aware and will work it out."

I nod, my eye twitching.

"The good news is I know exactly who is in charge of the hunters."

"Who is it?" Adrenaline runs through me, a need to know, a need for answers. I'm sitting forward on the edge of my chair, holding onto the urge to shake the damn fox to get him to answer me faster.

"Are you sure you're ready to hear it?" he asks as he finishes sewing up his wound. He drops the needle into a baggy before meeting my eyes. "Are you sure?"

"Yes."

"Cevon." A loud, feral roar leaves me at hearing my brother's name. The fox doesn't flinch.

"How sure are you?" I ask.

"Very."

I snarl and slam my fist down on the chair, hating that it doesn't hurt. I need the pain to ground me. "Fuck!"

"Fuck, indeed," he says before shrugging. "Don't get me wrong, I fucking hate your brother, and I'm not happy he's letting his hunters target my mate."

"But?" I ask, raising an eyebrow. How is there a but here?

"I know what it's like to be in the kind of pain that he's in. As someone whose mother was murdered whilst pregnant with my younger brother, I get what it's like," he says, and I gasp, but he ignores it. "Obviously, it's not the same as my mate and unborn baby being murdered, but I get the murderous urges and the need to do something bloody to control the demons within."

I gape at him, pure shock filtering through me. I don't even know how to speak.

He smiles at me, and this one is a genuine kind of look on the fox. "I'm sorry," he says, softly.

I nod, but don't reply. I pack that away for later, for when I'm *alone* and can think about it properly.

"So, Kennedy," I say, and he nods. "Why are you bringing me this news instead of Mal?"

"He's on his way back, but he had another meeting," Voss says, and I nod with a small frown on my face. "Kennedy signed the papers. Here." He passes me over an envelope, and I smile. "It's an invitation for *you* to go to the ceremony."

"Fucking knob," I snarl, and Voss laughs. "But that's what I wanted. Thanks." I rub at the back of my neck, sure there's more I need to be asking, but my brain is whirring.

I can't focus.

"He's got some of her belongings that he's sent down with a pack member," Voss adds, somehow sensing my inability to talk properly. "I'm not sure what they are, but they'll be here in the next day or two."

I nod, and he sighs.

"I'm sorry for dropping this on you," he says.

"I'm the King," I reply, shaking my head ruefully. "There's nobody else who should shoulder this."

"Do you want me to get Nora?" he asks tentatively.

"No!" I snarl, glaring at him. "She's got enough going on without needing to worry about this."

He nods slowly. "I want more details. I want to know everything."

"Yes, sir."

He gets up from the sofa, shrugging on the blood-coated shirt, and puts the first aid box back together. He then walks over to the table at the right and fills a glass with some bourbon before placing it in front of me.

Voss sees himself out, and I sip at the bourbon that he's poured me before grabbing my phone from the desk.

I take a deep breath and call a number I've not used in fucking years.

"Hello, brother," Cevon's voice answers. Pain washes over me, and I hear him laugh. "It's been a while."

"It has," I say. "I think it's time for you to come home."

He laughs again, this one sounding manic and freaky. *Oh no.* "I don't have a home anymore, Nix."

"Phee, please," I beg. "Please, come back to the pride. I can help get you out of whatever situation you've got yourself into."

"The *situation* you refer to is one I've created myself," he says, sending tingles down my spine. "I've clawed my way up, and I'm the King here. Don't call me again."

He hangs up the phone, and I choke out a sob.

My brother, my baby brother, sounds so fucking different. He sounds pained like he's been living with the demons in his head alone for way too long.

I blink away the tears, not letting them fall, before sending one last message.

ATTICUS

> You don't need to fight the demons alone, Phee. I love you.

CEVON

> Love died the day my mate and son were taken from me.

> The day you chose to turn your back on me.

I flinch, not understanding what he means. I never once turned my back on him. He left, he chose to throw away our brotherhood, to throw away the pack.

I knew nothing of his mate dying, nothing of a fucking pregnancy.

My nephew, my sister-by-mating... my fucking brother.

I hesitantly key in the words and wait for a reply.

ATTICUS

> What do you mean by that?

But then the phone buzzes again, and I dart to grab it, only to see that the message has failed to send.

366

He's fucking blocked me.

Fuck! I roar, throwing the phone at the wall, watching it shatter to pieces.

I down the bourbon and pace the office, taking the time to calm myself down. I spot the gold envelope on the table, and know that it's time to share with Nora what I've done.

Let's hope she's in a position to handle it.

30

NORA

"Can we talk?" Atticus asks, and I blink at him slowly before nodding. He looks the exact same as he did before going upstairs—same pair of joggers, same socks with a hole in the big toe—except for his hair.

Now it's messy as if he's ran his hands through it multiple times, and I don't like it. Not even a little. He's nervous, and that in turn makes *me* nervous.

He leads me back upstairs and takes me down to his office. I've only been in here the once, and it's not exactly the most comfortable of rooms to have a heart to heart in. So that's nerve-wracking.

"I did something," Atticus says, holding his hand up as if that's going to stop the thoughts within me from racing away. "Something you might be happy about, or something you're going to be pissed about."

"What is it?" My tone shows I'm already preparing myself for disappointment, and it causes the usually steady man to falter.

He sighs and grabs an envelope from his pocket and

hands it to me. I read the name on the front, *Atticus Phoenix*, and frown.

Why is he giving me an invitation for him?

"Just open it," he says, and I nod slowly.

I open up the envelope, and see a delicate golden card with gorgeous handwritten calligraphy. It takes me a second to read the details properly, and that's when I realise Atticus has been invited to a mating ceremony.

A mating ceremony for my brother.

Tears well up in my eyes, and I flip open the card to see more, but a little piece of paper falls out instead, this one addressed to me.

With a shaky breath, I open the letter. I don't know if Atticus has read it or what, but I don't recognise the handwriting.

Nora,

I'm so glad to hear that you've found a new mate, that you've found a way to finally be happy after everything that happened here.

From what Kennedy has told Mum and Dad about him, he's a stellar guy. Well, from what I inferred that is.

I'm so grateful your mate fought to get you here, that you're getting a chance to heal from the situation. A selfish part of me is happy that I'll get to see you again, and that you'll get the chance to meet my mate properly.

I can only understand how hard this will be for you, but here's my number if you want to reach out and discuss anything. Whether that be the ceremony, the past, or nothing in particular. I'd like to reconnect with you, but only if you want to do the same.

I'm sorry I wasn't there for you. I may have been a child, but I understood what happened that night was wrong. I wish things were different.

It's been six years, but I still remember the way we used to play games together, and how you'd help me with my reading for school. How you'd sound out the words and help me learn how to look them up.

I know that sounds like pathetic memories to hold onto, but that's all I have. Well, unless you'd like me to outline the fart episode—I was saving that for... I'm saving that for another time.

I love you so much, and even if you don't come to the ceremony, I wish you endless happiness in your mating like I hope to have in mine.

Love always,
David

(The better sibling, since I didn't steal your discarded trash!)

I burst into tears and step away from Atticus, who reaches for me. I can't... I need some time alone.

"I need... I need a moment," I whisper, and he nods slowly, but I can smell his unhappiness over that. "I'm going for a walk."

A plan is starting to form in my head, and I need the time alone to either go ahead with it or to fight it.

"Let me come—"

"No," I say, cutting him off. It's mean, I know, but he's gone behind my back and orchestrated something that I'm not sure how to handle. Something he's dropped on me during the shit show that is my mental health. "I'll not go far, Atty, but I need out of here."

"Okay," he whispers, and if I were in my right mind, maybe the sorrow in his voice would cause me to stop.

But it doesn't. It only confirms things for me.

I run out the room and head down to my own. I pack a quick bag with what I need, and put on some shoes before leaving. Micah calls my name, stumbling to get up and follow, but Atticus handles it, and nobody comes out after me.

I don't leave the property, knowing that my best chance to get away alone for longer than five minutes is for them to not be as worried. I'm behind the gates here, and whilst very stupid since shifters can climb, they act as a sort of barrier as I walk as far as I can, collapsing under a tree a little far off.

I pull the letter out again, my eyes fixating on one line.

I'm so glad to hear that you've found a new mate, that you've found a way to finally be happy after everything that happened here.

I'm not happy. I'm not sure I'm ever going to be able to be happy.

I wish you endless happiness in your mating like I hope to have in mine.

I'm toxic, bringing down my men, and they're never going to be able to be happy with me in their lives.

I just don't understand how David thinks I'm happy. Did Kennedy spin this tale? Did Neve? *Atticus*?

Was it the dress? The smile? What portrayed something I don't really feel? What conned them into believing it?

I open the bag and look at what I brought out, thinking that now is the best time to do this.

Death is easy. Some would argue it's the coward's way out, but I'd argue that after six years of pain and darkness that death is actually just inevitable.

At least mine is.

I open the water before pulling the pills out of the bag. My hands are shaking, but there's no tears in my eyes.

It's time to finally do what I should've done six years ago.

It's time to finally give in.

I pop out the first pill from the packet, and I hear a howl in the distance. Or maybe in my close proximity. I can't really tell, but it's loud and full of pain.

I pop out the second pill, thinking it'll be easier if I can do them all together at the same time. Only one swallow then.

There's another howl, this one makes my chest burn, but I don't understand why. I don't care, either.

Whatever is happening isn't my problem. Not anymore.

A third pill is followed by a third howl. This time, my hands shift into claws, making it impossible to pop out another pill.

I look at them in surprise, dropping the pills onto the ground, as the midnight black paws look back at me.

There's a fourth howl, this one rattles my body

completely, and only now do I realise where it's coming from.

This howl comes from me, it comes from the wolf within.

The barricade in my mind has been broken down, and she's there, ready to take over.

The question is, is she here to help me kill myself, or is she here to make one of my men do it for me?

I try to fight her back, to put the block back up, but it's too late. The pain she's been under seems to have disappeared and left her with nothing but strength.

She's stronger than me now.

I scream when she forces the shift on me, overpowering me easier than I have ever thought possible. She pushes forward, shifting my arms, then my shoulders, then my body. My head is the last thing to change. It's happening in slow-motion to me, but I know it took less than a second for her to take control.

And then, I'm on four legs, looking at the world through amber eyes instead of my brown ones.

I'm a wolf.

She growls deep, and starts attacking my bag, shredding the contents, making it impossible for me to try again using the same supplies.

"What the fuck is she doing?" Orson roars, but my wolf doesn't look up from her attack, so I can't see what's happening. I take a deep inhale, the scents of cedar, patchouli, and mint, lavender, a citrusy mix of lemon and lime, a sickly cherry pie and cinnamon, assaulting my senses.

All of my men are here—the sickly cherry pie clearly belonging to Voss, despite his scent changing every day—and I'm not sure what their goal is. I've not killed myself, despite *my* goal, but maybe they're going to do it for me now that I've shifted.

That makes me sad. I never wanted them to have to deal with the dying part. Of course they'd see the body, but my hope was that I'd already be gone.

"She's feral," Micah says, and his voice is broken.

"No," Atticus says, his crisp tone causing my wolf to stop what she's doing and cock her head. There's power in that word, there's power in that man. "She's not."

"She's not?" Three identical shocked voices say—Malachi, Devoss, and Griffin.

"She's not," Atticus repeats, this time something like awe is strong in his voice. I feel the shift in the air, a brief disturbance in the wavelengths, before I scent a lion. It's strong, and delicious.

I turn to look at him, seeing the giant lion that I recognise now as my mate.

That we *both* recognise as our mate.

"She's beautiful," Micah whispers, and my wolf's tail wags ever so slightly at the compliment from our pretty tiger mate. "Aw, she likes the compliment." I watch him kick Voss, who glares at him in response. "Compliment her."

My wolf purrs. We like this male. He's a good addition to our pack.

"You're so big," Voss says, and I snarl, as does Micah.

How fucking rude.

"Shit compliment," Micah snaps before slowly taking a step towards us. Atticus roars, and Micah freezes. It seems the lion doesn't want to share my attention.

Her attention.

No... *my attention.*

My wolf nods, and I feel her energy working in sync with

mine. We've merged together. We've bonded again. When? How?

How did it happen?

I think about being human, and I immediately shift back, the instinct so easy, the motion so fluid.

"What the fuck?" Orson demands, looking at me in shock.

But I don't know how to answer that. I don't know how to explain what went down here. I look at the mess she's made, and get a flash of anger from her.

This is directed at me, though, at the choice I made for us both.

Clearly, she's over her grief, and she's ready to move on, and stupid me should just get with the program.

She nods in my head, pushing forward her agreement.

Fucking wolves.

"I tried to kill myself," I whisper, hearing gasps, and one loud roar, but I can't bring myself to look at them. I don't want to see their anger, or maybe their pity. I don't want to have to burden myself with their feelings, too. "I tried to kill myself, and she shifted to stop it."

"Of course she did, little warrior," Mal whispers, his voice as soft as mine. I raise my head, panic in my gaze as I meet his amber eyes. He gives me a small smile, and steps closer to me. He's wearing a pair of flannel pants, and a pale blue t-shirt. His feet are bare, showing off his horrible toes.

"She's not feral," Voss says, and I give him a grim sort of half-smile when I turn to look at him next. He's wearing the same clothes from earlier, the jeans and t-shirt, but he's showered since his conversation with Atticus. His curly red hair is much fluffier.

"She's a part of you, pretty girl, even if it's never felt like it," Micah says. The tears in my eyes fall, and he gives me his own sad smile. His heart-shaped lips are full, the pout on the bottom clear to see. It makes me want to sink my teeth into his orchid coloured lips, to draw blood and moans from him.

Shit, Nora, no.

The lion shifts, and my Alpha King is standing in front of me. At 6'5" he makes me feel tiny, especially with all the power running through him. But his head is bowed, ever so slightly, like it was when he gifted me his submission the other week. He's doing his best to make me feel comfortable because that's what he can offer.

"She shifted to save you, little queen," Atticus says. "She pushed aside her grief, her pain, to save you from yours."

"Just like you did for her all those years ago," Griffin adds, coming up to my left side. He's stocky, a firm presence at my back. He's got wide shoulders and hips, and I can slot right in with him. I didn't sense him move, not until his large hands rested on the small of my back. "Death is easy, baby girl."

"But survival, little cub?" Orson asks, stopping in front of me at Atticus's right. My giant teddy bear, the one who has made it his mission over the last few days to make me feel as loved and cared for as he could, gives me a smile. His hooded hazel eyes glint in the winter sun. "*Survival is Hard.*"

The End

If you'd like to read the Prologue of *Survival is Hard*… you can download it here!

Nora's story will continue in the second book, *Survival is Hard*.

ABOUT THE AUTHOR

Letty Frame is a romance author who writes in the reverse harem genre. #whychoose, right? Letty lives in ever-rainy England with her fiancé and newborn daughter. Between baby playdates and boring household tasks, Letty gives the voices in her head the freedom to tell their stories. Whether that's in the form of a wolf-shifter on a quest to defeat her stalker or a witch trying to find her place in the world, Letty loves every story they bring her!

ALSO BY LETTY FRAME

The Luna Series

Luna

Mated

Allies

Healer

Stalker

Destiny

The Primordial Queen

Secret Witch

Oracle Witch

Second Chances

Death is Easy

Survival is Hard

Happiness is Earned

The First Shift

Baby's First Howl

Mama's First Howl (pre-order)

SOCIAL MEDIA LINKS

If you want to join my ARC team, you can sign-up here!

ARC Team

Subscribe to her newsletter to receive monthly updates about new releases, and for exclusive teasers and POV scenes from the guys.

Newsletter: www.lettyframe.com/subscribe

Join her reader's group on Discord to hear about release information first!

Discord Group: https://discord.gg/gPthmJFZae

Feel free to follow her on any of the following platforms too (click on the icon for the relevant platforms):

Printed in Great Britain
by Amazon